SYGHT

BEN MURRELL

First published in Great Britain in 2021
This paperback edition published 2021

Copyright © Ben Murrell 2015

Cover by Nick Castle
Edited by Emily Yau

The right of Ben Murrell to be identified as the author of this work has been asserted by him in accordance with the Copyright, Designs and Patents Act 1988.

All rights reserved. No part of this publication may be reproduced, stored in a retrieval system, or transmitted in any form or by any means, electronic, mechanical, photocopying, recording or otherwise, without the prior permission of the copyright owner.

This is a work of fiction. All characters, names, places, incidents and dialogues are products of the author's imagination or are used fictitiously. Any resemblance to real persons, living or dead is purely coincidental.

A CIP catalogue record for this book is available from the British Library.

KDP ISBN: 9798496969321

For my Dad, who made me the sci-fi geek that I am.

To my Mum, who never got to read it.

ONE

There was a feeling. A rush of energy that ignited every nerve-ending in his body. It sparked instantly; a match had been struck. Although dangerous, it made you feel alive: a new lease of life as you held on, not out of fear but out of the need of control. 'I am at one with this beast', as many people said.

Although cliché, everyone thinks, from time to time, that they are super human and that feeling, that adrenaline, is often confused with complete stupidity.

But it didn't stop people pushing that machine, a 1968 Ford Mustang, to the limits. It would roar as you tightened your grip, and you too would roar back inside. It listened to you. It breathed, purred, even when stagnant. It needed someone to test it, for the beast itself to feel alive. It would whisper, 'I dare you', the only words one could hear echo out of the exhaust as it stood idle, with the keys in the ignition. It may have been built by humans—just a piece of machinery—but it had a heart.

And a V8 engine was a big heart, a powerful one at that. Sitting inside the vehicle, when it was left to its bare bones, it was though you were a fly strapped onto a rocket. A seat, steering wheel and pedals—it needed nothing more.

And when Gil slammed his foot down onto the pedal, it threw him back into the bucket seat.

Gil had little experience with driving, especially because anything with a combustion engine was now banned for almost forty years and any production lines had been ceased due to the Uniformed Act of 2045.

The car slid over the gravel wasteland as the rear tyres struggled to find grip, which panicked him immediately, the fear of crashing and the aftermath flooding his brain with unsavoury thoughts. He wasn't as confident as his best friend Rix in the passenger seat next to him, whose screams, unlike his, were out of joy rather than trepidation.

"PUT YOUR FOOT DOWN!" she cried over the firing pistons of the engine.

He changed gear. He had taught himself how to drive a stick vehicle, after learning what one was in the first place, when he found this antique hidden away, left in a disused garage lot. The new generation had no idea what cars like this were, no one drove nowadays. It was all automatic. You typed in your destination and the vehicle took you there. Tracks and sensors guided all cars. He knew it reduced accidents majorly as there was no longer room for human error. It made it a safer place for him to live in. He was savvy, though; he didn't need the reassurance that others needed. Computers controlled the roadways, but Gil wanted to know how to drive, to feel that rumble. Being chauffeured around was easier—not that Gil ever used the transport network. He wanted to have to fill up the tank with petrol, or enjoy deciding what freshener to hang from the rear-view mirror—alpine wood or summer blossom. His father and his father's father cared and so did Gil. The world, however, cared no more.

"Faster!!" Rix screamed again. The passenger window was missing, the sound of the scream blended with the revs from the engine.

Gil was surprised that this car was still working at all, after all these years. He was thankful that Rix knew mechanics and electronics—basically everything that he was naive in the details of. This had been their project, to restore this old relic and bring it back to life. Rix was right: driving was fun, even at 80kph. Why would anyone not want to be doing this?

He turned the wheel and drifted around the long bend, kicking up the surface dust. They had found the car in a lot of abandoned garages on the outskirts of the city. All of them had been broken into and the contents thieved. Thankfully, Rix and Gil had looted the car before anyone else had the chance to, when they'd found it hidden away in one of the locked, dilapidated concrete sheds. The car had been retired. It had served its duty. In their minds, it wasn't theft, but an honour to the old car: what use was a vehicle if it was left stagnant? And with no one owning a vehicle to store, the disused lot of garages had become their playground.

The Mustang roared once more as Gil double-pressed the accelerator, pumping the engine full of the thick brown liquor it needed. Siphoning the fuel it needed had become the trickiest part. After searching around the city for any old vehicles that still remained—of which there were none—it had come to 'Slick', a manmade alternative that represented the fuel of the old era. It was expensive to buy, as it was becoming harder to find the ingredients needed to make it. Slick had to be made correctly or any machinery that ran on it wouldn't work. Gil was never the haggler or the 'go to person' when you needed something of this nature. Rix had a way with sourcing the right connections She would often bargain for the slick on the backstreet markets in exchange for high tech electronics, red grade level. She had enough tech implanted in her body; she always had spares. The majority of people in the city could not afford such advanced technology, so it was not a challenging deal to make. If you knew the right people—and Rix did—one could get slick with ease.

He had completed the circuit around the lot and slammed on the brake for a flashy finale. The car skidded to a halt. The dust plume surrounded the

Mustang and the two listened to the ticking over of the engine.

As he removed his wet palms from the steering wheel, the leather began to peal. He wanted to keep his nerves hidden from Rix. He had been terrified of hurtling around the garage lot.

"Did you want to drive?" he asked. Rix was looking out of the window, gazing up at the high-rises of the city. The modern skyscrapers loomed over the streets below.

She turned and he caught a flash of the jagged electric-blue tattoo Rix had down the side of her face. It may have only been a micro-display panel to simulate what was referred to as a 'real tattoo', but it was something he knew he could not pull off; it would have never matched his 'style'. He often wondered how Rix could do anything and it always suited her. Maybe he had to make more daring decisions.

"Nah, I'm good. Passenger is way more fun. Plus, I get to see the expression on your face when you go around every tight corner. Classic."

He thought he had been successful in covering that up, but he guessed not.

"Look at it," she said as she looked back up to the city skyline. "I hate this city sometimes. Tech rules everything... If you're rich, then you get it all—anything you want: new comms, upgrades, any grade electronics that suit your needs. But the poor—or what is considered poor—barely survive. Any outdated tech just stops working and anything you do need for your health, you are always in constant debt with the company that loaned you it. I mean, yeah, not all of it is expensive—"

"Like Syngetical?" Gil interrupted.

"Yeah, well no. I didn't mean them—and that's me not being biased; you know how I feel about that," she said defensively.

He knew his question would wind her up. They had been friends long enough to know what annoyed the other. Not much annoyed Gil. He was from a poorer state of life, and so he had learned to be relaxed about most things. Unlike Rix. Most of all, she hated being referred to as a 'cashoid', someone who had wealth and drowned themselves in tech—so much so, she basically may as well be a cyborg.

Rix continued to ramble on about how the society had changed from the way it once was, her fist clenched, her thumb scratching at her index finger. He knew her agitation was building. This was a coping mechanism for her—focus on the pain from the infliction rather than let it show. The older the pair grew, the more Gil could see how her anger was becoming more uncontrollable. He had never seen her unleash it fully, nor could he see why it was becoming worse. When it came to life or survival, she had nothing to worry about.

Neither Rix nor Gil had been around when the new era began. Gil's grandparents had told him the stories. He enjoyed listening about the past and wanted to know what the older generation was like, before 2045, when there was more freedom, when there was a fairer divide between what you needed and what you wanted. Some, like Gil—and even Rix at times—wanted it to be like that again. They had been born surrounded by technology—they were part of this new generation—and even they disagreed with how it was controlled. There were others too.

Gil gazed at Rix—or a better way of putting it, *stared*—and wondered why someone like her, from the wealthier side of this world, would be friends with someone like him. Maybe because, in some sadistic way, she wanted to rip it all apart. To go back to the basics, like this Mustang. She may have been a child of this new generation, covered in tech, but she understood the ways of the old and appreciated them too, as he did. Every so often, you had to treat yourself to something special—in this case, it was an empty garage lot and a full tank of slick.

The purr from the car was melodic, soothing, as if it was out of breath, regaining its strength to go again.

"I get it," he said finally. "Some have this greed. Like you…"

Rix gave him a sharp look.

"Don't you dare compare me to that species."

"I wasn't!" he said. "I was saying you aren't like them and that's a good thing. The rich have already become the richer, so what else is there left to buy?"

"Human life!" she said angrily.

"It was a rhetorical question. What I wanted to say was, there are people like you and me, who look out for the ones that struggle. We support each other. Now the poor have already died out, it's everyone else—those who are somewhere in-between—who are now clinging on. And I like that we have that community, that secrecy, so far away from the rich. They have no idea of what we do. We live, and for now, that's all that matters."

He could see that Rix was brewing up a storm inside. He had to change the atmosphere in the car. He pressed his foot down hard on the accelerator and the engine revved. She slowly smiled. The roar of that engine, which they had put back together, was their victory song.

The road was straight ahead of them, lying baron in wait. Garages lined either side. He revved the engine again. A cloud of dried powder kicked up out the back of the exhaust. The car screamed in the overture of its pistons: 'let me tear this road up'.

Gil felt that energy, that surge of wanting to go as fast as you could and the Mustang forcing you to hit that red line on the dial.

"Do it, Gil!" Rix leaned forward in her seat. "Let's see what this beast can really do."

He kept the revs high. He wanted to launch down the strip in front of him as fast as he could. He placed his hand firmly on the handbrake. The vibration feeding through the steering wheel was violent. He knew that, as soon as he released that button, he would have to have two hands on the wheel.

He was in control. To live, just once, even for a moment, on the edge of 'what if'. It was his time not to be careful.

There was a track they had roughly mapped out. There were a fair few sharp turns and it ended with them crossing the disused rail tracks that ran along the far end of the garage lot.

He tapped his thumb, lightly releasing on the handbrake, waiting for that right moment, that particular roar the engine had, at its peak, when it sounded like it was ready to blow.

The tyres were eating into the wasteland, the car clawing, wanting to be set free.

Rix grabbed his hand and pushed the button in.

"NOW!" Together, they slammed the handbrake to the floor.

The wheels spun, flicking debris and gravel up into the air. The smell of burning rubber filled the cabin as the tyres attempted to find grip. The rear end of the car swung from left to right. Gil threw both his hands onto the wheel, struggling to keep it in line with the road ahead.

The Mustang wasn't fighting back; it was toying with its passengers. It wanted to play as much as they did.

The grip on the tyres locked onto the road and the car hurtled forward, throwing both Rix and Gil hard into their seats.

"YEAH!" Rix screamed. Gil looked over and laughed, keeping his foot down on the pedal.

Straight into third, then fourth. There was something satisfying when a gear change was smooth, as though the car was applauding you, giving you a boost of power.

The needle on the dial climbed quickly as the car plummeted down the stretch, towards the garages at the other end.

"Do the course we set out!" Rix screamed.

"Sure? Do we have to?" he shouted.

She only grinned and bounced in her seat.

He could see nothing in his rear-view mirror other than the yellowish cloud of dust that the tires were kicking up.

The line of garages ahead approached quickly and he had to turn the wheel hard to the left. The last garage had its side wall missing, so he knew he would be able to cut the corner slightly, giving him room to drift.

As expected, the rear end swung out as he took the corner and he countered it by turning into the drift. The back of the car clipped the wall and scraped along the queue of garages.

"Hey, mind the paint job," Rix shot out.

Gil thought he had control of the car, but that manoeuvre was a lot closer than he wanted it to be. A tiny bead of sweat formed on the top of his forehead as he quickly glanced into the rear-view mirror to see the scratch along the rusty metal garage doors. No one could tame her—not this Mustang.

Back down to third, and he hit the floor again with the accelerator.

The speed rose as they continued down the straight. A long, wide bend up ahead would take them back behind the set of garages they had almost ploughed into.

Nearly 100kph. He pushed down on the brake pedal and swung the wheel to the right. The Mustang skidded sideways on. He dropped the gear down to second and kept the revs high.

The car slid along the bend gracefully. Out of the corner of his eye, he caught a glimpse of Rix laughing.

The motion. The car. The power it had, breathing life into its pipes. All things the world had forgotten. Banned.

The car smashed right through a wooden hut as the drift over shot. Wooden panels flew, exploding in all directions. Rix continued to laugh as if she were somehow enjoying this.

He had to hold it together. He had tried to show off and had only put even more fright into himself. He was not one for the schematics of danger. He would have never taken such risks if it weren't for Rix.

Fighting against the wheel, the rear end of the car shifted from left to right. His foot accidentally pushed down onto the accelerator, and because he had dropped a gear, the surge of power fired them down the straight.

This car had too much power, more than he could handle. Even though he was the driver, telling this machine what to do, it was the Mustang that wanted to see both of them squirm.

In front of them, and approaching at a fair pace, was the end of the lot. A tall rusty metal fence, with circular barbed wire along the top, divided the land, separating the lot from the disused train track on the other side.

"Take a left and we'll spin her back round to the start," Rix shouted as she leaned out the window, the words muffled by the mouthful of air rushing into her lungs.

He nodded. He knew if he had voiced anything, it would have come out high-pitched and squealed, showing his true internal fear. But a nod oozed, 'I got this'.

The Mustang rocketed along the straight as he climbed the gears once more. He checked the speedometer, but the pin wasn't moving from zero. One of the minor knocks they had had must have broken it.

He tightened his grip in prep for the left turn ahead. The gap looked too tight to be able to take it at this speed; he was going to hit either the fence or the last garage on the corner.

He nudged the car over to the right so he wouldn't be cutting the corner as he had done previously.

He hit the brakes.

The wheels locked and dust flew up in the air around them. He had to make the turn before the track ahead was invisible.

As he started to make the turn, easing over to the left, he blinked. Something switched, or at least felt as though it did. He felt fear, terror, guilt—an 'I knew I shouldn't have done it' feeling. He had to be imagining it. He felt as though he were outside the vehicle. In that split second, he had lost control of the car, and it continued to hurtle towards the garages. He told his brain to turn the wheel. 'MOVE!' he shouted at his hands. Nothing.

Then there was a beat. A hard beat from his heart that was choking him, as he looked down on this image from above. The car made impact. He saw faces smash into the windscreen, heads crack open the moment the wing mirror hit them. Rix was splattered with blood. The sound of cracking bones, multiple bones, and that final pop of a flattened skull.

He took a hard in-take of breath. He had to place himself back in the car, back with his own hands on the wheel. This image he was seeing—his mind was making it real, but it couldn't have been. He felt no pain, no injury. Why was he processing this horrific scene, mowing down innocent people, when it was a vision of something that was *about* to happen—or was currently?

He tried to catch his breath. A tightening of the chest. Panic. Short stabbing gasps as he, without thinking, swung the Mustang to the right—not left, where he had initially wanted to go. They ploughed through the fence, taking the majority of it with them. The car tangled in a metal-meshed carcass, the piercing twisting metal sound overpowering the screams from within.

The wheels rumbled over the train tracks. The steering wheel vibrated so hard it hurt his hands. He had to let go. He floated off the seat, smacked his head on the frame work of the interior.

The car skidded over the second rail and got caught. It threw Rix against the side of the car and Gil towards the stick. Then, the car lifted off the ground. It was going to flip. He closed his eyes tightly.

But it didn't get that far and the Mustang fell back onto four wheels. He and Rix both hit the roof of the car and then landed back into their seats.

A dying cackle came from the car as the pistons ticked over and faded to quiet. The engine cut out.

Gil breathed heavily. All he could do was replay the image in his mind, the bodies strewn all over the car. What had happened? The noise, the dying sound of innocents. It was as though he had hit a strike and they were bowling pins. He remembered it all, as if it was real.

"WOOOOOOOOO!" Rix hailed from the passenger seat.

He had to wonder—with the technology that flowed through her—whether Rix felt fear. That moment where you think you're going to die and everything skips a beat—did the tech suppress it all; did it control *her*?

She was covered in dirt. She had a few small cuts and abrasions, but nothing major.

The car had spun, now facing the direction he should have taken. That fatal left turn. He looked ahead, wide-eyed, through the windscreen, which—he was surprised to note—was blood free.

Where he would have turned was a group of

raiders—those from a society of people who make a business out of upgrading what they can find.

"How did you know not to take that left turn? We would have killed all of them, Gil. Ha! What a drive."

He had nothing to say.

"Wait!" Rix took off her seatbelt and faced him. Out of the corner of his eye, he could see that she was gleaming with joy and ecstasy, as if she had had a revelation.

She chuckled.

"Gil, do you have syght?"

TWO

The pit was on the outskirts of the city, far enough away that it did not blight the picturesque views from the high rises of the global conglomerates. They wanted pristine; they desired a view that no one was allowed to see, a view into the future that they controlled, not the government. Nearly all small businesses had been absorbed by the larger companies. The future was set within the clouds.

    Gil stood on the excavated ground of the pit and looked up at the dusk sky. It radiated violet as the black undertone of space crept through, sprinkling the vast landscape above with stars. Pollution levels had plummeted over the years and the air was cleaner, which meant the unexplored universes above were clearer than they had ever been. On certain nights, you could see the array of satellites that circled the globe and other planets without the use of a telescope. There were some advantages to this new generation. He couldn't imagine not being able to see the space above. His family often spoke of smog and how it used to cloud the cities in black soot, how if you blew your nose, it came out black on the tissue, like soft boulders of coal. The United party had cleaned that all up, mainly by shutting down everything that had created the smog in the first place.

Gil liked to work alone so no focus was lost on protecting someone else, if any situation were to arise. If Rix had joined him, he knew she would have thrown him constant questions about syght. He needed to process it first for himself, in his own head. He had no idea what had happened in the car.

He knew where all the cameras were—every salvager did. If you wanted to be able to search for what you needed, you had to do your research. In the beginning, his boss, Terry, had brought him down here to the pit so they could scope it out, to see what the workers did with the disposed rubbish. Anything that came from apartments were stacked at one end, already having been turned into cubes by the compactors that were installed in everyone's homes, ready for distribution to construction companies to use as building material. The other waste had to be dismantled and the pieces kept or vaporized. It was the cleaner way of disposing waste; vaporizing left no harmful or hazardous fumes—another great invention that was helping to save the planet. The machine, which was a huge black box, used great amounts of power. It was essentially a failed teleportation device. When scientists began experimenting with teleportation, they realised that it was actually impossible to break down and 'kill' one item to be able to send its DNA to an exact replica box for it to be rebuilt. It may not have worked on humans, but the scientists succeeded at disposing waste in a way that was friendly to the planet. Once it had gone into the black box, the deconstructed waste ended up as digital code within a network. It was code. And code could easily be deleted. Where one experiment failed, the outcome for another was established—and so came to be the vaporizer for unwanted materials.

Gil's task was to find the parts he needed before they got to the vaporizing stage. Despite the fact that he was never that adventurous, there was a small part of him that wanted to break in and search through the dismantled waste—Rix had clearly rubbed off on him. It would make his job much easier to complete if the components had already been removed.

His head wasn't in the game tonight.

"FWEET!"

A sharp whistle came from the other side of the pit.

He raised his hand. It was Midi.

Midi was the first other salvager Terry had introduced Gil to. He was a few years older and had showed Gil how to do what he did: where the entrances and exits were, what to do if the pit was raided by law enforcement and, of course, introduced him to the other salvagers. They were a close-knit family and always welcomed others, providing as much protection as they could whenever someone found themselves in a troubling situation. They looked out for each other.

Midi wasn't in charge—they all fought for themselves—but maybe, because he was older and always took home the goods to his boss—mainly wiring: copper if he could find it; silver wiring was rarer—the salvagers looked up to him.

Three or so years after that first meeting, Gil now knew what he was doing. He was part of the salvager group. You had to be young to be a salvager; as soon as you ran out of energy or you were caught, you knew your time was up. No boss wanted to employ a salvager who got caught.

Thankfully, security was low at the pit. No guards, just cameras. Most of the salvagers thought the cameras weren't switched on and were only a deterrent. Nobody was going to risk finding out.

Gil made his way over to where the sound of the whistle had come from, beyond the entrance behind one of the large sorting machines. The fence that surrounded the pit was electrified at night, but Midi, being the self-proclaimed master of coded electronics, had set up a bypass so, while its systems said it was online, it was actually switched off. To avoid suspicion, they had cut a door in the fence to allow one person through at a time. They had put a small hinge on it too, to make it easier for entry and escape, and to not keep bending the metal so its presence was obvious from the outside. From inside the yard, you would never see the makeshift entrance anyway as it was hidden behind a machine. You also had to cross a small river and climb the bank to get to it, so no one really checked.

Other than the moonlight, there were no additional lights. Every salvager had their own High Intensity Vision in Darkness Lens—or hi-vid for short. It was a small green lens, which you placed in front of your eye, that would allow you to see in darkness. It was adapted from old night vision goggles and the first-gen Spacial Lens. It was simple technology, with no requirement to be up-to-date or in any way hi-tech. It just had to function for the purpose intended. They were perfect for keeping you undetected.

Each salvager had accustomed their own strap to use the lens—some even had two lenses. But Gil only used one, fixed over his left eye on a pivot, so he could move it out the way if he wanted. He often thought he looked as if he had been in an accident that had resulted in a major head injury, the lens strap looking like a brace to keep his skull from moving.

He attached his head gear and made his way in to the yard. A green filter spread across the lens and immediately the darkness became visible.

He greeted Midi with a double hand slap.

"You're early tonight," Midi said.

"Yeah, Terry wants me to find a Goride chip—five of them. It monitors the power input and stops surges from happening or something."

Midi pushed a button on his double lens goggles

and the green filter disappeared. He was dressed in his traditional black attire and his frizzy hair was bunched up at the back.

"Terry got you working hard." He laughed.

"He likes to try. Seen anyone else here tonight?"

"Only Dana. I don't think she will be here long. She found a pile of old cracked holo screens, so she hit the jackpot."

"Easy night for her, then." He took a glance around the yard.

"Nah, not really, man. Boss was going to let her go. She hasn't found anything in weeks. She even tried Bulltwine's Edge and ain't no one want to be going up there."

"You ever been?" Midi asked.

"Not needed to yet. But brave of Dana to head up there. I'm not sure Terry would let me."

"You got a good boss, Gil. Keep him. Sooner or later, this place is bound to dry up. More salvagers, less items available to the likes of you and me. All we got to do is hope that the rich spend more and chuck out their old stuff here and not Bulltwine." He clicked his goggles back on and the green misted over. "You check in with me before you go, yeah? What does your chip look like?"

He pulled out the sample circuit board and showed Midi.

"I ain't never seen one of them. I'll keep an eye out. Handy, though, right? Through the hi-vid, you can see the chip has a 'T' on it. Might help you out."

"Does it?"

Gil flicked his lens around and saw what Midi was talking about. The letter 'T' illuminated under the green filter.

"I'll keep an eye out anyway for you. I got you."

"Thanks, Midi. I definitely need it tonight. Going to be here a while, I reckon. Wanted to head home early, which isn't happening. Terry has got me in in the morning for another one of his master classes in circuitry."

"Yeah, he has! He sees big things for you. You don't want to be stuck doing this forever. With what he knows, you'll be working for the big techs soon."

That was Gil's plan. He was determined to learn from Terry to aid his application to work at Syngetical. Work hard. Achieve what he wanted. That was an easy statement to make, however, very difficult to accomplish, especially when succeeding was against you, if you didn't have money.

"Then you get me a job and sort me out, so I can give up being here every night, right?"

Midi laughed and punched him playfully in the shoulder.

"Of course. Who else am I going to want to work with?"

"Rix?" Midi smiled and nodded slowly. Both understood what Midi was talking about. But Gil and Rix? That was a thought that was so void of truth. They were friends, only.

"What? No!" he said defensively, then changed the subject. "You still need copper, right?"

"Ha, yeah whatever, Gil. Nah, silver tonight with

gold coils—I'd take silver too." Midi walked off.

"I'll keep an eye out, then," he shouted after him.

Midi sent back a hand gesture as a response, an okay sign above his head.

The pit was quiet, although busy with salvagers. There was the odd clang of metal, but never any voices. No salvager wanted to alert anyone outside of their community that they were there.

Gil had been semi successful. He had found one Goride chip, though it could have been damaged. It had corroded slightly. Through the hi-vid lens, it was difficult to tell whether it was worth taking or not. Maybe Terry could fix the internal workings of a chip, but to Gil, it seemed unlikely.

He bumped into Dana, literally. Her overexcitement at finding a great haul manifested itself in an over-ambitious dance routine that could only naturally end in someone getting hit.

"Larana is going to be chilling for weeks after this." This was the only actual sentence Gil got out of her other than 'woops' and delighted sounds of happiness. After her celebrations she realised she could only carry so much in one sitting, Dana left, having hid the other screens in a hole she had dug near the exit to return for tomorrow.

It was just shy of midnight and Gil was bored. He wanted this job complete. The concept of syght was playing on his mind as he remembered Rix's words, how she'd tried to convince him of something that hadn't happened. They both knew it to be a myth., so why now the interest?

He yawned.

He reached the start of the shelf that held the cubes. There was no need to search these—no salvager ever did; there was no point. The compactor had done its job, and anything in them would have been broken anyway.

The pit's lights beamed on.

He ducked from plain view.

There was no movement, and Gil spotted nobody else; they had either ran or were hidden like he was. If the law spotted you, there was no way you would escape. They had all the means of catching you and they always made sure they did.

The exit was on the other side of the yard, a fair distance away. He stayed motionless. It wasn't always the best idea to run. You had a higher chance of getting caught and you risked exposing how salvagers entered the pit. His best tactic was to stay camouflaged until he could work out what was happening. His heart beat went into overdrive, as though he was back in the Mustang. This was too much for one day. This time though, he had no control over the situation. This is what they called, fucked.

There was no tannoy, no sirens, no flashing lights. Maybe they were trying to lure the salvagers out, or the lights switching on was just a malfunction in Midi's tech. To reassure himself, he forced himself to believe it was the latter.

It was weird that nobody had made themselves known, and he was vulnerable if he stayed where he was. Morning would come soon. Or they might already know where he was and wanted to toy with him first. He had now become the prey.

"Shit, shit, shit," he whispered to himself through panicked intakes of breath.

He had to get out of here. His only chance was to make a run for it.

He looked to the machine where the exit was, one-hundred metres or so away. If he were on the other side of the pit, he could have snuck along the fence behind the shelving unit of unwanted products.

He shot up and jumped into the yard, tripping over his own feet but managing to regain his balance without a fall.

As he began to run, he finally spotted someone at the other end, in front of the building that housed the vaporizing machine.

He sighed. Two steps he had taken into his run and someone had already caught him. Not only had he lost any haul he might have found for tonight, there was a lower chance of him getting a clean break. He paused to assess his options, and kept an eye on this figure.

The person was standing there in front of the doors to the warehouse, at the other end of the yard. Both he and the figure were equal distance to his exit. Gil thought he might have a slight advantage, being a few feet closer, but there can't have been much in it. The person was not dressed as law enforcement.

They were a lone figure, clothed in what looked like rags. They had a long stick with them. The only other detail that Gil could make out, due to the distance, was that they were bald.

It was a stand-off—but why? He took a few more steps forward in the direction of the exit, slowly inching his way towards his goal. The figure stayed still.

Fuck this, he thought. He wasn't waiting around to find out who or what they wanted. He double tapped the button on his techpack and it tightened around his chest and shoulders, then took a breath and ran.

The figure stayed still.

As Gil sprinted along the yard, he saw no one else—no salvager, no other person dressed in rags.

The figure moved their stick and pointed it to the ground, then began to sprint, towards him, running in a zig-zag pattern. They were quick, surprisingly so when they weren't running in a straight line. He might have been wrong on the distance between the figure and the exit. They were going to beat him there.

Gil had to make it to the fence before this person reached him. At the rate he was running, it was going to be close, if not too close. The figure was reducing the distance between the two of them quickly.

He tried with his might to increase his speed. His breathing became louder.

"Come on, come on..." he whispered to himself.

The figure then snapped direction and began to run in a straight line for him.

He was almost at the path that led to the exit behind the machine.

Gil still had a final burst of energy left, and went for it.

As he made it to the machine, the figure continued to run and was nearly upon him. He saw them raise their stick and swing it.

He squinted. This was going to hurt, bad.

He dropped to the ground and slid.

He legs buckled into the machine and immediately stopped his movement.

He collected himself and continued on, round to the exit, where he opened it and escaped.

The lights of the yard cut out. It was darkness once again.

He kept running, forcing himself not to look back at the pit. The fear of getting caught gave him the energy to run.

All he heard was the sound of his heavy breathing as he ran across the abandoned wasteland.

No thoughts. No what if.

He halted at a safe distance and glanced over towards the pit, that was now, once again, hidden in the shadows.

A bead of sweat trickled down the side of his head.

One breath after another.

He had avoided the pole. How? Syght? It couldn't have been. It was Gil being the evasive salvager that he was. What he had been taught and practised for moments like this. It was his decision to dodge the pole, anyone would have done the same thing. It was a natural instinct when someone was trying to attack you—avoid by any means necessary. A darker question began to pervade his thoughts: did he even know what was he was capable of?

THREE

Gil unlocked the door to his apartment. He still used a key, unlike most in the city who used either a fingerprint or an electronic seven-digit code. Gil was surprised that the scan still existed when it was easy enough to chop off a finger and be able to gain access to someone's place. Maybe it was only the elite who still had security like this. No one expected a key, though. And anyway, if someone could live with only a key lock protecting them, they had nothing to steal in the first place.

He threw the keychain into a small ceramic bowl near the door—one of his sentimental belongings, an heirloom he was given, a reminder of home. Handmade items were part of the "old" generation. He lived in *this* generation where imperfections and creative licence were lost. There was no hiding an artist's initials in whatever new creations anymore.

In the year 2082, technology was a dominant

force. If you didn't have it you didn't survive. That was it. His apartment was a blend of items that he had been given by his parents and what he could afford of technology.

He walked towards his media viewer, a square transparent piece of mounted glass that hung on his open, bricked wall. He double-tapped it. An image appeared—broken and fuzzy initially—but it gained focus after a few seconds. It was the news. Gil liked to keep up-to-date with what was going on, mainly the technology companies. He wanted to work for one of them one day and the best advice he had been given was to always know what they were up to. Good or bad.

He sat on his sofa, the day's events playing over, attempting to explain what had happened, the man in the pit. He was convinced that his escape was all his doing. The voice of Rix in his head played over as though someone was turning up the volume gradually, 'do you have syght?' It was another incident where syght may have played a part in his survival and this time, whoever it was had witnessed it too.

His reactions were natural to the situation. If someone threw a ball he would instinctively attempt to catch it. That was not syght. A large wooden pole swung towards him, he didn't need to know about syght to know to get out of its way. Rix had got into his head.

His attention diverted to the media viewer. It was about Syngetical. He was finely tuned in to the company's name.

'Syngetical CEO, Anders Hilgaard, announces his newest prototype for the Spacial Lens VX and says he is overwhelmed with the support for what this new lens will bring to the nation…'

If anything about Syngetical was on the news, he wanted to know. It was the one company he had always wanted to work for. Technology fascinated him. He always wanted to know more about what it could do and how fast it was advancing. He was home schooled, mainly in the old ways of agriculture, life lessons and practical manual labour, rather than about coding or synthetic AI infusion biometrics. This was what he wanted to learn about, although nobody knew about it. But he knew he was young and, if he could, it would take time to get to where he wanted. He had to learn how it all worked, how circuits spoke to one another, how they connected, what data flowed between its wires. He had to specialise in an area but had to know the basics first.

Syngetical was the ideal company. Not only were they one of the front runners in technology— providing sight to those that had lost it with 'The Spacial Lens'—Anders was helping the people of the world. He was trying to do good, in contrast to the government, that pack of hyenas who devoured anyone who couldn't afford to keep up. The company was helping the poorer classes to survive, giving them the chance to be able to see again. There had become a growing number of people over the years that had started to lose their sight. There was not much evidence as to why this was happening—a defective gene? The changing environment?—but Anders had provided a solution. Not that this helped the security firms with their use of retinal scanners. The rise in eye infections and disease had stopped the scanners from being able to read the iris, and the Spacial Lens made the retinal scanners even more unreliable. They were quickly removed from all buildings. However, the people supported Anders, despite the scrutiny from the firms.

Anders couldn't provide the lens for free, but had made it affordable for everyone. And the people were happy to pay. By doing this, more people could buy the lens which made Syngetical huge amounts of profits that Anders could feed back into research. Anders was one of the wealthy, yet he had not become corrupt by having money; he wanted to give back so society could grow again. People supported him, even worshipped him at times, for providing for families. As much as he could, he made survival achievable for those who struggled.

Gil idolised him. He was afraid to admit that to Rix. He never asked for her help either, for the opportunity to meet the man face-to-face, to be able to tell him, 'I want to be able to help people too'. It sounded cliché but nobody, especially Rix, wanted to have someone kissing their father's arse all the time. It happened enough in the media. Gil had to wait, choose his time: when he was trained in knowing how Anders' Spacial Lens worked.

A break in the news, the boring part he never

paid attention too. He made his way into the kitchenette to distract himself from the consumer bullshit of 'stuff' he didn't need or could afford, where there was a stack of old newspapers sitting on the counter. He sat on the stool and looked at the length of his apartment. From the stool, he could see through into his living area—if that's what you could call it—and into the one bedroom he had. He looked at the hand-me-down ornaments from his grandparents, the hand painted pictures that he was yet to hang on his wall. A scattered array of belongings for an apartment that hadn't quite transitioned into the new generation. A box of slightly-bent used nails he had found and the automatic hammer that still needed charging. 'Still need to do that', he muttered to himself.

He didn't have money, so any technology he had was the older versions, items he had scavenged and fixed up, or things Rix had given to him out of pity. Not being classed on the higher end of the social and wealth ladder, his dream of working for a huge tech company, or even been given the chance to interview for one, was impossible. His ticket in was Rix—not that he wanted to be seen to be using her for achieving his dreams. Her being his friend came first, but work was a very close second

He heard the news report continue on from the viewer and headed in to take a closer listen.

Staring at the Syngetical logo on his viewer, he was proud that this was who he wanted to work for—he would be providing people a life, rather than continuing to let the world be a playground full of the rich whilst everyone else clawed at the gate to get in.

The news report finished. He scratched his head and winced, forgetting that he had a cut from the crash in the Mustang. He had reopened it, the blood was wet again. He took a whiff of his armpit. He stank. His cloudiness over his own body odour was masked by the urgency of his near misses at death when he was driving the car. He had to wonder whether Rix had noticed his smell at the time, or Midi and Dana. Too many people had been forced to succumb to his odour.

He dabbed his cut with a used cloth that was covered in dried oil from some used gears he had be cleaning. It was time for a shower.

He started to undress and took off his trousers when he was distracted by the old stack of newspapers again on the counter, another relic from the old world. Not many knew what a newspaper was nowadays. He found it refreshing that, even though he was born in the new generation, he had family members who cared that he understood how and why the world had become the way it was.

There was a note underneath the first newspaper.

Here's when it all went to shit. Excuse my language but you are old enough and ugly enough now to use it yourself too. Just don't tell Grandma.

Also found this: the original decree of the 55 Act, sent to all of us when the new government took over.

You've heard all the stories from me and your parents. Now you can see it for yourself. Hope you like the collection.

Come visit soon, we miss you. But we understand why and know you are busy making your future...

Love Grandpa

Gil laughed. Grandpa was a hoarder and he knew he had sent the stack of papers so grandma didn't throw them out.

He picked up each one, glancing at the headlines as he did.

'PEOPLE SPEAK OUT: GIVE US A SAY'

'UNITED PARTY TAKES POLL'

'2040 ELECTIONS COULD SEE CHANGE'

The newspapers were full of information of how the new world-wide government had been established. Gil read snippets about how no country had individual parties or leaders anymore. This establishment wanted equality worldwide and the people agreed. The United party's slogan was 'Change for the Human Kind'. It was 'to improve the world', as one statement read. How did they think that this—the current world—was an improvement?

There were pages listing how the party 'listened' to the people, asked them what they wanted and it all came back to the same topic—advances in technology. People wanted better technology in daily life, technology to provide them medicines, healthcare, technology to improve the environment, to save the planet.

The more he read, the more he understood how the world had joined together as one, everyone wanting the same thing. They had a universal understanding that if life stayed unchanged, there wouldn't be a planet to live on anymore.

As he riffled through the newspapers, he noticed the dates in the top corner. The collection spanned over months and then years. Over time, he could see how the United party had grown. People wanted change and the party said they could deliver on their promise.

The last paper in the stack was one that was about a month after the elections had taken place. The headline read:

'THE GENO-LIE OF THE WORLD'

The United party had won the elections within

each country and internationally took control of every governing body. They then released the 'Uniformed Act' in 2045, which Gil's grandpa had included as a separate document.

The papers nicknamed it the '55 Act' as it was the fifty-five wealthiest people and/or companies that now controlled the world. In collaboration with the United party, they controlled the wealth of the world and, therefore, how it was run.

He picked up the 'Uniformed Act' and read the official new policies, recognising each one:

- **The use of all combustion engines on sea, land or sky will be banned.**

- **The use of any unrecyclable plastic will be banned. Any plastic manufacturing companies must now apply for a licence.**

- **All healthcare will need to be paid for.**

- **All taxes will be raised to aid the repair of the planet.**

- **One company per field of sale: i.e., one telecoms company, one vehicle manufacturer.**

- **All prisons will be shut down and scrapped.**

- Any minor crime (see additional list of definition of serious crime) will be sanctioned with heavy fines, restricted access to technology and removal of assets. **NOTE:** It is not a crime if it does not directly affect another human.

- Any serious crime (see additional list of definition of serious crime) will be sanctioned with the death penalty.

- The installation of cameras to all general public areas to aid the government and police.

- Killing of all animals for consumption will be limited...

There were so many policies. Gil hadn't realised how different it had been before. His grandparents told him the stories of how the new government supported the rich that had invested in this new regime. It was them who would change the world, prolong its survival. Smaller companies went under and the larger, more successful ones fought it out until there was only one company left within their designated field—or they let one of the '55' buy them out.

All of this had happened before Gil was even born, and his family had so many stories about it.

He had a memory of his mother, one night when

he was about twelve years old, after Grandma had given out a Christmas cracker to everyone, which had naturally become banned after the 55 Act was introduced. It was the catalyst to his mother's rage that particular evening. He remembered how she had ranted. He could hear her voice as though she was next to him.

"But at what cost?" she started. Gil picturing his mother's face, her mouth contorting to one side when she was angry as she spilled on. "The people got what they wanted. They spoke out and had their say, but did they think of the consequences? Of course they fucking didn't. And who will listen to them now? No one! The act has been written and with the rich becoming richer they could have done a nice thing and help the poor but they won't, will they?"

Time was short to carry on reading all the articles as he still had to eat, shower and then head over to Terry's. From what he had read, added to what he already knew, his reasons for wanting to work at Syngetical were cemented even more. There was at least one person trying to help the people who lived on the brink of collapse, anyone who wasn't one of the fifty-five 'saviours', as one newspaper described them as.

He threw a square vacuum-packed sachet inside the Volumizer. He pressed a button and a heard the hum as his food was cooked, ultra-fast.

He opened the door and a ball of steam followed. The packet was hot and had expanded five times the size. He opened it up and poured the contents onto a plate.

He shovelled the noodle and vegetable concoction into his mouth, the rusty metal fork clinking on the plate as he did so. Gil ate for energy, not to enjoy, and the artificial meat alternative for protein was certainly not enjoyable. The packets he could get were cheap, but they did what they were meant to do.

'BUZZ, BUZZ'

The door entry sounded and the viewer in the living space quieted as it changed from the news to a view of who was outside.

"Oi, it's me. Open up! You stopped shaking from yesterday yet?" There was a cackle.

He recognised the laughter straight away. The events of last night rushed back to his mind. It was a ridiculous notion to think that he had syght. Why would he have it, suddenly out of nowhere? But he couldn't deny that an incidence had happened, one he was unable to explain, one was skilful avoidance. He had to know more about syght first.

"Ha! I know you're in there. You got no other place to be! Come on…"

On the monitor, he could see Rix standing in front of the camera with a raised middle finger and a tongue out. He knew she was being ironic. She meant no harm. The raised middle finger was classed as a minor crime if caught, and Rix hated anyone who thought they were a rebel by doing it.

"…also put some trousers on."

He covered his lower region and his face turned red, bleaching out the few freckles he had.

"Got ya, didn't I?" She laughed.

He breathed a sigh of relief and removed his hand from his crotch. He hadn't installed a two-way camera. She couldn't see him. Whenever he was in her presence, he always got nervous sometimes and for no real reason.

He pressed the glass screen, which allowed Rix to enter. He ran to the bedroom and quickly put on some trousers and his torn navy work top, which had some sporting emblem on the front. He never had any idea to which team it was or even what sport they played, not that there were many sports you could get access to—the government had culled most of them—but the t-shirt was dark and comfortable so it served its purpose.

"I told you to keep this locked," Rix uttered as she came in.

"Sorry, I forgot."

"Right, I'm bored and I'm coming to Terry's with you. You can keep me entertained," she said as she grabbed a piece of fruit that was sat on the table.

"Hey! I spent good money to get that. Was saving it."

"For what? It would only go off by the time you got round to eating it. I'll get you something later to replace it. Chill."

"Every time you come to work with me, I never get anything done. I don't earn as much as when I'm on my own," he said as he picked up his techpack.

He fed his arms through the straps, pressed a button and it secured itself over his shoulders and around his back.

"I'll help! Pluuuuuus," she said, elongating the word as if she were an excited child, "we have to talk about this syght. We have to know if you got it. Can you imagine if you do? I couldn't stop thinking about it, hence why I had to come over. Tabs, come on! What if you do?"

It was the perfect opportunity to tell her about last night, but he chose not to. He knew how she would react. It would confirm her suspicions and push her to explore more. He didn't want that gloating from her, especially when he was uncertain.

"Please don't call me Tabs."

Gil's last name was Taberthorn and it was a nickname he had been given from before he moved to the country. Many in his school were given their nickname because they were popular; they got to choose it. Gil's, however, was not. There was always someone who bullied another kid, and Gil wasn't built to be the bully.

"And I don't think I do have syght…" He responded as though he was on autopilot. "I think I must have seen them before I turned the wheel."

But Gil had thought about this moment a lot, the vision he saw before what could have happened. He had never experienced anything like this before. How was it possible to see something happen before it did? It should have played out as he had seen it, what he had thought was real in that moment. Instead, he changed his mind. A simple turn of the wheel in the opposite direction. The 50/50 answer—you do or you don't, yes or no, left or right. There were only two outcomes: he killed all those people or he avoided it. That was the plain straightforward fact of that equation. On the walk over to the pit, he must have asked himself several times whether he had syght and 'Of course not' was always his answer—another black and white certainty. Syght was a myth to him, grapevine whispers, passed on from one self-entitled gossiper to another, each with some intervention in-between to make it sound more interesting to the listener. He couldn't remember where he and Rix had initially heard about it. School? Work colleagues? Neither himself nor she had heard about anyone who had the ability, so what made them so sure that he would? It was not a plausible thought to have.

"We need to test this out. We need to find a— Ah, what are they called?" she said, snapping her fingers as she tried to find the word.

Instead of responding, he thought more into what he had heard about syght, which was little. All he knew, or thought he knew, was that it was about decision making, making that right choice at the right time—nothing about seeing the future or witnessing a horrific outcome. That was just a trick of the brain, somehow showing himself that he was doing something dangerous and that he should stop. It had nothing to do with syght. Gil was certain, almost.

"GIL?!?"

Gil snapped out of his head and rejoined the conversation.

"You mean a Sense Shifter?"

"Yeah! One of them. Can't they test you or something?"

"Well, not really. I don't think so. No one really knows much about them. I don't think they are going to help. Most of what we know is myth, right? Aren't they blind? Totally blind. The very few that are in the world."

"Yeah, that's the point. They have mastered their other senses in this reality. Opens up their mind or something. Come on, we'll ask around, see if anyone knows of one in this city."

She headed out the door and dragged him along too.

He reached out and grabbed his keys in passing, knocking the ceramic bowl to the floor. He heard it break before he closed the door.

He sighed. The world of the old era had lost yet another artefact.

FOUR

Finding a Sense Shifter in the city was as rare as finding loose change on the floor, which was incredibly rare as money was digital, just numbers on a screen. Having credits was not the same as having money. Money was what you had in your pocket. The act of passing it over in your hand was now seen as a pastime. There were those that viewed themselves as collectors—mainly the elite and the wealthy, who would pay a high sum of credits to complete their collections—to be able to say they had the only mint collection of coins and notes.

Gil had not seen or met a Sense Shifter; he knew they kept themselves invisible to society. They were somewhat of an anomaly to humankind. Thanks to Syngetical, it was common knowledge that, if one had lost their sight, they could simply regain it with the Spacial Lens, a simple attachment to the retina that acted as their iris. However, there were a few who had lost sight in both their eyes, and if that happened, it was irreversible. The Spacial Lens was then void.

Gil had found out about the Sense Shifters through investigations with Rix as a hobby, years ago. His work colleagues and their mates passed on the information from what they had heard, and Gil kept a journal, notes on what he found. He found it intriguing, even if it was fantasy. They told him there were rumours that those who had lost vision in one eye had decided to blind themselves in the other. Some of these people became the Sense Shifters, those who heightened their other senses and had become masters of it—to feel the earth and their surroundings, to be at one with nature and what was left of it. Most of this sounded a bit unbelievable to Gil; it was just pure folklore to scare people away from a life of darkness. If the rumours were true, no one was going to take the risk and blind themselves fully without a guarantee in place that they would become a Sense Shifter. Gil couldn't think of a more ridiculous idea than purposefully blinding yourself to gain a skill that no one even knew was obtainable. He did believe that there were people who had tried it, to see if the stories were true or not. People had become desperate, living in this new generation, so if there was a chance to get one step ahead, they would try, even if it did mean living the rest of their life in the unknown. Though, with the introduction of Syngetical's Spacial Lens, hope was given and the rumours diminished. The world's new motto seemed to be, 'Live a life where Syngetical can help'. Gil would, and so would everyone in the street who needed it.

Gil and Rix made their way along Salvages Bazaar, a mile-long backstreet full of market stalls where you could acquire any thrown-out or damaged technology. If you needed spares or parts or even an upgrade and couldn't afford the newest model, this was the place to start. It was the high-end of rough. People ran their market stands to make the few credits they needed to survive. There were always cogs, nuts, bolts and wiring loose on the floor, which was the closest thing to getting something for free, but if it was lying in the street then it was less than worthless. Your technology was too old if it needed any of that. You could bargain with most of the businesses on this level, and there was also a goods for goods policy where you could make exchanges—something that Gil found incredibly valuable.

"You say we should go and find one, so where do we start looking? There isn't a place where they all hang out and you can go enquire," Gil said.

The backstreet was filthy. A constant glisten of oil settled in the gutter, resistant against any rain water that tried to clear it. The oil provided the only morsel of colour to the darkened street—a swirling dull rainbow trapped in liquid form. The awnings from each vendor were mucky and the name of every business was unrecognisable, but every regular knew what each stall specialised in. If you were a tourist, then the vendors were wary of you anyway.

"We need to ask the right people," Rix answered as she peered in to each stall they passed.

"Who are the 'right' people? You make out we are in one of those old generation movies and if we say the right words, then someone will overhear us and a magic door will open. It doesn't work like that."

"But chatter does spread." She turned to him and smiled.

He shook his head.

"Have you noticed it before? The 'syght'? Any other time or just when we did that drive?"

Rix was not going to let this go. She was convinced he had it. Gil less so. He was hiding the other time it might have happened, but again, Gil was unsure. He was starting to feel curious about it all. He couldn't base one strange encounter on something that they both knew was hearsay, but now there were potentially two. Every time Rix had asked, he had shut her down, but what if there was a slight chance that something like syght was possible? Why would he have it? And how? His thoughts were getting him frustrated. He was unsure. He had no definitive answer. He told himself it couldn't be true because it was the easier more logical answer.

"I don't know," he snapped back. "I'm not sure anything happened. I think it's all a myth. It doesn't actually exist."

"IT DOES!" Rix said.

"And how do you know?"

He wanted to her to explain, for her to tell him

something that made sense, to state why he would have it—not all this speculation. It was starting to drive him mad.

"My dad told me. That's why he helps all those in psychiatric mental hospitals or whatever they are called. People who lost their sight in one eye, it sent them all crazy. I've seen it!"

"I think your dad provided a troubled childhood for you," he joked, to which she punched him in the arm.

"I'm being serious. I stay clear of what he does because it bores me. But I still listen to the stories and theories; hard not to when he talks at you."

Gil hoped one day that her dad, Anders, would bore him with what he did. Whatever Anders said would be fascinating to Gil. He would absorb everything and put it into his own work, when he got that position in Syngetical, whenever that might be, if it ever happened. He almost didn't care which department at first. Maybe they could talk to Anders about what happened. Maybe he would have an answer. There was no right time to ask Rix about getting that chance to meet her father.

"Why don't you listen to him? I would! I'd love to hear about it!" He cringed at his words. He was acting too much like an excited child.

"Alright, why are you so eager to listen? In love with my dad, are you?"

"No! Of course not. Don't you want to know what he does, though, with his technology? He has changed the world in what he is doing. That's a huge deal. It's saving people's lives!"

Gil sounded like a spokesperson for Syngetical. It was hard for him not to sound proud about it when it was his dream to work there.

"That's his job! Not mine. I sort my own tech out, okay? I'm fed up with hearing about it, Gil."

He had touched a nerve. He hadn't seen Rix react like this before whenever he spoke about her father. He retraced his words to see if he had offended her somehow.

Even if he had syght, he definitely hadn't seen that coming.

He thought it best not to ask any more questions, especially about a job. He would wait on this occasion.

Rix waived to one of the stall merchants. A welcomed interruption.

"That Jacks?" Gil asked.

"Yeah, he is descrambling something for me. I was given the new portable Holo Palm chip and I want to hack into it so I can make it more powerful. Jacks thinks it's possible."

"You have one of those?" he asked in disbelief. Knowing Rix as long as he had, and even with her connections and sources, it always surprised him when she managed to obtain the latest of anything.

"Anyway, back to you, Gil, and syght. Dad said that everyone in this place all lost half of their sight and it sent them mad—within days. The reason why is apparently to do with choice. Having both eyes means you can decide between two choices: right and wrong, left and right, powdered chicken or powdered fish, whatever. Soon as you take away one eye, you are left without choice, so your life is already then predetermined."

"What? How does that make sense? What have your eyes got to do with making a choice?"

All he had seen on that drive was killing a bunch of people and, luckily, that was in his head. He would never choose to do something like that. And at the pit, all he'd done was dive under the pole being swung at him. Anyone would have done the same thing. If that was syght, then almost everyone would have it.

"I'm not explaining it right. I may have drifted off when dad was speaking—I was young when he told me. The point being is, you have your sight, Gil, so you have choice and the ability to make a choice. When we were in the car the other day, you were going to take a left, no?"

Rix was correct; he was going to steer to the left. At that last minute, he chose not to. He had made that choice, but out of panic. It was a snap decision. He did have a strange feeling, though, a beat where he had the option to change his mind.

"But you decided to turn right instead, and not left. You avoided flattening all those grubby raiders—which all I'm saying, wouldn't have been a totally bad thing to do. A Sense Shifter would explain it better than me."

"And if we don't find one, and I can't see us happening to bump into one out of nowhere, then

I'm never going to know if I have syght." This was the first time he had contemplated the thought. "Syght makes no sense. All I know is your half-listened to story from your dad and what I know through the rumours. I know who would know, better than anyone you think would."

"Oooooh, touchy, aren't we, syght boy?"

"Well, we are walking around achieving nothing because you won't ask your dad, and does anyone you know actually have any information about Sense Shifters? Other than what we already know?"

"Maybe?"

"Maybe doesn't help us. If you are so keen to know if I have it, there is only one person we can ask, and that's Terry."

Gil worked for 'Terry's Chips and Circuits', a name back from a time when the Bazaar first started when it was still a thing to put your name on the shop front.

Terry was the only original owner of his stall left in the Bazaar. The business did well, when Gil could salvage a decent number of circuit boards. His was a stall that was in high demand as Terry could upgrade anything. He was old—seventy-two to be precise—and with that came knowledge. Gil felt embarrassed about that at times. For someone who wanted to work for a high-end tech firm, he should know more than Terry. He was a great boss to him, though. He often gave him tutorials in how to work with various circuit boards and AI chips, training him up so he could be more than a salvager.

"Afternoon, Mr Florence," he called out as he entered the shop.

Terry was at a workbench along the left wall. His goggles were over his face, his head buried into a magnifying glass. The smell of melting aluminium filled the air.

Gil took off his techpack and threw it onto an old wooden chair next to the bench.

"Careful, will you? One slip and that board is ruined," Terry said, lifting up his goggles onto his forehead and giving him a stern look. "And you brought your girlfriend to work. Hello Rix."

"Very funny," she said dryly and stuck her middle finger up at him.

Terry laughed.

Rix nudged Gil in his side.

'Go on', she mouthed to him.

He felt embarrassed to ask Terry. If it was all myth then it was silly asking someone about a fairytale.

"I—"

Terry spoke before he had the chance to ask anything.

"Gil, did you manage to find any of the Goride chips? I could do with a few of them."

He was going to disappoint Terry, which he hated to do. He had always been good to Gil and looked after him.

He pulled out the one chip he had managed to salvage and handed it over.

"Only one?"

He nodded.

"Well, one is better than zero. I can work with one," he said without any hint that Gil had failed.

"Mr Florence, I have a question," he asked. "What do you know about Sense Shifters?"

"Hmmm," Terry moaned as he pondered at the board.

His question wasn't shunned. There was hope that the man did know something.

"Better keep this stored for safe keeping, especially with the likes of you around."

He turned to Rix and smiled through his thick white moustache, before returning to the bench, opening up a few small draws on the old medicine cabinet he stored his products in.

Terry had ignored the question. Gil was in slight shock that Terry hadn't answered him. He had not done that before.

Rix looked to Gil and shared a 'what the hell?' expression.

"Ah ha. Knew it was here somewhere."

Terry pulled out a small brush and gently stroked the bristles over the circuit board to clean it.

"Not in bad condition either. Take a look."

Terry passed it over and Gil held it. He guessed this had nothing to do with Sense Shifters. If it had, then Gil was lost.

"These were, strangely enough, installed on a lot of consumer products with heating elements after 2025. It was meant to be a revolutionary design to not only heat whatever you needed quicker but also reduce power outage at the same time. This little Goride chip was meant to mediate the power surge and stop it spiking. Unfortunately, the chip failed and cut the appliance off. It may have not been able to boil your water in a kettle, but for me, it works brilliantly for drawing more power to weakened Spacial Lenses."

Terry smiled. He always gave a speech as to where and how the circuit board came about.

"What's a kettle?" Gil asked.

Terry's face dropped.

"It's not important."

He turned back to the medicine cabinet. He had still ignored what Gil had asked. Why the avoidance unless Terry knew something?

"Ask the old timer if he's heard of syght," Rix whispered.

"What? Why? That's weird, me randomly asking him," he responded quietly.

"Fine, I will…"

She pushed past him, making him stumble over a stack of metal drawers.

"Terry, I got a question for you, if you don't mind me asking—"

A spark from the circuit board hit the magnifying glass.

"I'm not sure I have a choice in the matter now, do I?" Terry turned towards her with his goggles over his eyes. They were magnified.

"That's the thing I wanted to talk to you about:

choice. Have you heard of syght, Terry?" She sat down on a high stool opposite the workbench.

Terry wiped his hands on his apron.

"And what do you want to know about syght?" Terry asked.

His tone changed. He knew what they were talking about.

FIVE

"Not heard anyone talk about that for decades. I'm surprised there is still talk of it," Terry said. Then, as though realising how his reaction looked, he seemed to snap back to his light-hearted manner.

Gil stayed quiet. He had known Terry for a long time now and his complete disregard to his earlier question, yet answering to Rix's was strange. Rix often had a way of getting straight to the point, and it would have been difficult for Terry to avoid anything that Rix asked, but he still couldn't help but think Terry was hiding something, possibly.

"I thought everyone knew about it? We do…" Rix paused. "…sort of."

"You'll be too young to remember the announcements and coverage it had."

Gil was now fully intrigued. It was on the media. How had he missed this? In all the old papers his grandpa sent over, there was not one mention of it.

Syght was real: it existed. So, Gil must have it. But still, the thought would not register with him. He was getting ahead of himself.

Terry pulled up his stool to the workbench and perched on it.

"It spread soon as people started to believe this was true. With the deaths of many due to the changes in society, the growing divide between the rich and the poor, and with disease itself on the rise, it was understandable that people wanted to know how long they had left to live. They wanted to know how to make the right choices to survive or protect others. The idea of syght gave people hope. It all changed very quickly. I believe it was a small group of anarchists... not that they were violent... if anything they were more hippies..."

Rix and Gil looked blankly at him.

"...oh, sorry. You won't know what a 'hippy' is. They aren't around as such anymore—maybe out in the country..."

"Your family are hippies, ha!" Rix said to Gil.

"Shut up!" he replied, though he didn't really know if it was an insult or not.

"Basically, they wanted to go against the change for the new generation. They saw how this new government would affect people. I guess they were right, now actually, looking back on it. They wanted to save society. Anyway, they had coined the term syght, which showed you how long you had left to live."

"What's that got to do with seeing things before

they happened? That's what we heard," Rix said. "I don't get how it's about how long you had left to live."

Gil nodded in agreement.

"It's to do with choice and making the right one, no?" Rix asked.

"I suppose, in some ways, it meant the choice about whether you lived or died—not that you had a say in it. There is no way of stopping yourself from dying. Although I'm sure we aren't far off that, what with the rate technology is advancing."

"What did you have to do to use syght? How could they tell?" Gil stepped forward, now engrossed in Terry's explanation, wanting that confirmation that he had it or not. He wanted to prove Rix wrong.

"Let me show you."

Terry pushed himself up from the stool and stretched out his arms in front of him, his palms facing towards the pair.

"Hold your hands like so in front of you and close one eye and then the other."

"You are shitting us, aren't you, Terry?" There was no fooling Rix. Gil had tried many times and failed.

"I lie to you not," he said, still with his arms outstretched. "What this group had supposedly unravelled was this: if you close, let's say, your right eye, what you see is your hands in one place. The neutral position. But then you slowly switch to close your left eye. As the right opens, the image of your hands switches to a new position. This is what they called the lifeline position. The distance the image travels between your neutral and your lifeline position is—apparently—how long you have left to live. The bigger the gap the less you have to worry."

Gil and Rix looked at each other. Terry chuckled.

"Go on, give it a go. As ridiculous as it sounds, this is what they say is having the syght."

Rix stood and threw her arms out in front of her, then began to wink between her two eyes quickly.

"Okay, not a huge distance. Enough to say I ain't dying any time soon. Go on, Gil. When are you saying bye bye to life?"

"Not sure I want to know. Do you want to know when you're going to die?" Gil was reluctant to try. Once again, Rix was always the eager one to try something out. Gil had reservations, understandably too if it was going to say how long you had left to live.

"You are always too safe, aren't you? Let this be the most daring thing you do today. You would be such a rebel." She rolled her eyes.

"Fine."

Gil knew he would always give in to Rix. It wasn't worth the ridicule if he argued against it or, plain and simple, chose not to do something. He had become accustomed to this, to agree and go along with it.

He put his arms out in front of him and closed one eye.

"Remember, slowly switch—not what Rix just demonstrated." Terry looked over with a raised eyebrow.

Gil focused on his hands and begun to slowly switch his wink. The image he saw shifted, vibrated, as though he had a ghost hand of his own, a double image. There was a flash between one eye closing and the other opening where he saw himself as he was in Terry's stall, but also, at the same time, someplace else—a split image. It looked the exact same, but there was something different to it: a misplaced storage unit maybe, or the lighting from the sun; something was wrong. It was only a glance, a snapshot image, and then Gil saw his hand shift over to the left.

"Urggghhh," he let out and shook his hands as if something had landed on them. He studied his hands, turning them over repeatedly, checking they were whole, opaque, in the stall he knew he was in.

"What? How long you have left?" Rix smiled.

"Sometime yet, yeah. Long. Nothing to worry about," Gil said slowly.

"Well, thankfully, both of you have no need to worry about anything as the government shut down this wild story about what syght was. There was no truth to it. They carried out case studies and experimental trials, but there was no link to syght and how long people had left to live. So, everyone forgot about it and never spoke of it again." Terry readjusted his magnifying glass and took a look through it to the circuit board.

Gil noticed it again. Terry avoiding further questions by shutting the conversation down. That was it, now move on. Maybe Gil was reading too much into it. He again saw something that didn't add up: a change, a switch. He knew Rix was adamant too that it was about choice, making that right decision to better yourself or, in his case, avoid a tragic accident. Gil had experienced that, if that was what syght was. What Terry was talking about was different—not even close to the same thing. But he said it was all over the news—unless he was lying. Every bit of information they had obtained on their earlier quest, years ago, all related back to choice—nothing about how long you had left to live.

"Not so bad for an old timer like me, is it, Rix? Still know what happened in the past—not quite lost it yet," he said, looking over his shoulder at her.

"Your hearing is still in good form then," she replied sarcastically.

"So, how did you come to hear about syght?" Terry asked, ignoring her barb.

"My dad spoke about it a few times. I pay little attention when he speaks, most of the time. I must have heard wrong, as what you said was different."

Gil needed to confirm. He had the papers at home to check. If they searched harder, then maybe he and Rix could find someone that knew more than they had already dug up. He knew Terry wouldn't lie to him—he had given Gil a job, a home, a way of education that would help towards his career—unless it was an elaborate set up to just use Gil for his syght. Gil was thinking the absurd. Maybe Terry didn't know anything more than what he told Gil and Rix.

Passing on the story that many of his age knew. Terry was no liar.

He needed a change of scenery, and he still had work to do.

"Right, are you coming or not?" he said to Rix. "I want to finish my shift before tomorrow starts. I'll go look for more Goride chips, Terry."

"And what about Sense Shifters, Terry? You heard of them?" Rix blurted out.

It was the question he had avoided or chose not to listen to when Gil first asked—unless he hadn't heard. While Gil wanted to know if he knew something, he also wanted to leave and regroup. His mind was working overtime as it was and now he had no idea what to think—about syght, about Terry, about himself...

Terry stopped what he was doing and put down his solder iron.

"Come on, Rix. Stop harassing Mr Florence; he has work to do." The politest way he could think of saying it, without being rude to her.

"Some interesting questions you've asked tonight, Rix. You researching for something?"

"I wanted to see if Gil had syght."

"I don't," Gil confirmed.

"He nearly ran a bunch of people over and then he stopped himself," she added.

"Shut the hell up, Rix!"

He was stunned that Rix had blurted this out. He kept some information from Terry, killing pedestrians being one of them. Terry did not need to know every detail about Gil's life, especially if it involved a dangerous act, death and an ability that he was none the wiser to knowing what its true meaning was. Rix was stubborn, would never shy away from anything, but sometimes Gil wished she would think before she spoke.

"Have you been driving, Gil? You know what your parents would say about that."

"Yes, I know, Mr Florence. Just Rix being a total dickhead," he said.

"Language, Mr Taberthorn. There are elderly in the room." Rix smirked at Terry.

He usually tried not to swear in front of Terry—he felt guilty when he did—but it was Rix's fault. Terry watched out for him wherever he could. Gil's family, who were too far away to protect him, felt reassured to know that someone had his back in the city. Not that Gil saw himself as a kid anymore and needed protection—though his family would disagree.

"Well, I would be impressed if Gil had an ability like that, being able to tell when he was going to snuff it. He can barely solder a wire to a power chip," Terry said.

"I can—now you've shown me, anyway," he said, defending himself.

"And the fact is: syght was all a lie. The government proved that to everyone. No truth in it at all," Terry continued as he tidied his workbench. "Sense Shifters? If you mean the jokers down on Lower Mile that hustle you out of credits, claiming they can heal ailments without medicine, then yes, I have heard of them. But that's not what I would call them."

"What would you call them, Mr Florence?" Gil said as he put his techpack back on, pressing the button and feeling the straps pull taut.

"Idiots," he said bluntly.

"Happy now?" Gil turned to Rix.

She shrugged. He knew she hated it when she was proven wrong. Failure was not a quality she could relate to.

"Five of those chips you needed, right?" Gil shouted over to the workbench where Terry had gone back to work on the circuit board.

"Yes, five of them, Gil," Rix answered for him.

They walked out.

"Can you drop this syght thing now you know the truth to what it is?" he said. "We were wrong about it." Hoping Rix would drop the idea that he had syght. "It was a good story about what happened. I bet it's somewhere in one of my grandpa's newspapers."

They had their first lead and it was worth an investigation. Lower Mile wasn't a place they ever went to; they had no need. Now they did. He had to know what syght was—confirm the details, and whether what had happened to him was the very thing Rix was talking about. Was it syght or just him becoming ill? He had a feeling that there was something off with Terry. The man loved to talk and yet he was hesitant to answer Rix's questions, and had ignored his completely.

"Want to go see the Sense Shifter's in action?" Rix let out a laugh.

"Why? You feeling ill?" he responded. At least Rix was on the same page as him. Curiosity had taken both of them by the reigns.

"I could pretend."

As the sun dropped, Terry switched on the lamp that hung above him. It sizzled as the power surged into the bulb.

"Go on, girl. Still life in you yet," he whispered aloud.

He attached the last chip he needed for the Spacial Lens upgrade. But he would have to wait until tomorrow to see if his craftsmanship had worked. There was no way of testing a microchip for a Spacial Lens without the device and the customer present to test it with. Every board was unique and needed altering differently depending on the person.

He pulled the criss-cross metal gate across the front of his stall. He was old-fashioned in the fact that he used a numbered analogue padlock to secure it to the brick wall. An electronic coded padlock could be hacked.

He made his way to the backend of the shop into the small loading bay area where a door led onto an alley.

Before he left, he looked at the old intercom system that was attached to the wall. It was a small bronzed square metal box with punched holes through it on the front. It was a speaker as well as a microphone.

He pressed the worn black button on top of it.

There was a soft crackle sound.

"Gil, he's a confirmed."

Terry released the button.

Silence.

SIX

He mulled over the events of the day in his mind as they walked towards Lower Mile. There had to be something wrong with him. In some ways it made sense, that it could be syght. However, he had to be realistic. Was this all a coincidence, believing in something that wasn't true? Everyone has moments they can't explain, and he was human; not everything had to be explained. He didn't need to know why the body did certain things. A twinge of pain out of nowhere didn't mean his leg was going to fall off.

He held out his hands in front of him and repeated the test Terry had taught them. He winked between each eye and the image moved. But like last time, there was no alternative image or setting.

"See? Nothing happened," he said.

"Terry's stupid test isn't going to show you if you have syght or not, Gil. We need to find people that know about it. Sense Shifters. You can't tell me you aren't intrigued."

Rix was right. He was—more to what syght was, rather than whether he had it or not. What was the truth about the story? About history? He hadn't contemplated, really, if syght was a blessing to have. If he had no facts about what it actually did, then there was no reason why he would want to have it.

He was unsure if taking Rix to find a Sense Shifter was the right choice, but he needed someone with him. She would gloat; that would be the downside. Terry could wait for his microchips. Trusting him was out the window at the moment. There was something about him that was out of line and Gil had picked up on it. This was his chance to see what was true. Whether Sense Shifters were untrained self-proclaimed medical professionals or masters of syght, the answers were on Lower Mile. But he knew that if they continued on this journey to find out more, it might be a decision he would later regret. Should he feel nervous or worried? Again, his overthinking crept back in. This was why he needed Rix, to ground him.

It started to rain. Rix turned on her Forcella—a digital umbrella, a weak force field—which suspended above their heads.

Gil had to tell Rix what had happened at the pit. It was pointless keeping this hidden; she would find out sooner or later. He began to tell her: the fear of someone after him, chasing him and how he had no reason why. A Prank? Or something far worse?

"Oh, shit!" Rix responded with a suppressed

laugh.

"It's not funny. It really wasn't. They weren't police. I don't know who they were."

"Someone after you?"

"I don't know! They attacked me, so I guess so, but why. I don't think they were law enforcement. I thankfully avoided getting hit too, they would have caught me if they had."

"SYGHT!" Rix shouted.

He had tried the softer approach but as expected, Rix jumped immediately to one conclusion.

"No it wasn't! All me being a good salvager by not getting caught. But things keep happening, so I want to know if it's me or well, whatever the truth is."

"I told you," Rix said smugly.

"It's not. I don't think anyway… I'm only believing it because you keep telling me. So that doesn't make it true. But we need to find a Sense Shifter, today, now! Yesterday even—not knowing is now worrying me more."

"Let the adventure begin!"

"Can we not joke about it? It's not a story. This is my life. It's driving me mad thinking about it."

"Alright. Relax. I'll tuck you in and keep you warm and cosy if you're scared."

There it was, the full stop on his overthinking. Rix was now simply ridiculing him. It worked.

Lower Mile was a short walk from Salvagers Bazaar. The 'mile' was a winding inclined road. Most of the original shops and vendors had closed down and now the majority of the business took place outside on the road or in the porchway of the larger buildings.

"Oh, wow!" Rix mouthed when they reached the bottom and she took in the sight of hundreds of people queuing to see the healers in action. It made Salvagers Bazaar look like a ghost town.

They walked through the crowds. The cacophony of crying babies, healers speaking in tongues, crowds applauding—every person here truly believed they were going to be cured.

For every closed business, there was a thriving one in front of it. Signs read 'Let Kline take away the bad Toxins in your blood TODAY!', 'Need a helping hand? Let Tax fix your back', 'Rid your body of demons with Mystic Healing.'

"Maybe they can actually heal people," Gil said as he watched a 'sense shifter' massaging the head of an individual. The sign read 'Remove your inner voices with the power of telekinetic magnets.' Gil had no idea what the shifter was actually administrating but the person sat in the chair was crying, he hoped, in relief. The way Gil was feeling, it wouldn't be the worst idea if he signed up for the same treatment.

"AARRGHHHHHHH!" a scream came from up ahead.

They both turned to one another with a look of excitement and ran up the road to find out.

"Roll up, Roll up! For the only real sense shifter in town. Need that scan you can't afford? Or a medicine that is just too hard to swallow in credits? Let Shensi Hoo help you!" A recording on loop played from an old battered speaker that was perched on a large wooden medicine cabinet.

It appeared that Shensi Hoo had just put the shoulder back into the socket of her patient.

"As if we missed that," Rix said, disappointed.

"But look at the line. That guy can't walk properly. I bet he has a dislodged knee cap." He pointed at the fourth person in the queue.

He looked around and saw people ambling about in a worse situation than he was. This was all a distraction; nothing here was suggesting that any of these 'sense shifters' were the ones he and Rix needed. These people the ones Terry told them about. Maybe Terry had been right in the first place. He felt a hint of disappointment. He hoped—and at the same time, was also slightly relieved—that this was all a hoax.

Near the top of Lower Mile, where the road became steeper and the buildings were more decrepit, the sense shifters became more spaced out. It seemed the more successful sense shifters were lower down. If you had to come this far up Lower Mile then you must be struggling more than the believers and hopers who queued, wishing for their miracles.

"Can't be hard to be a sense shifter, right? We could do that. Tell them a load of nonsense, give them some herbs and send them on their way."

"She did actually fix that guy's shoulder," Gil

pointed out.

"It was dislocated, not broke. He could have done that himself. He's just dumb! Look, I'll show you how to be a sense shifter."

She rubbed her hands together and hovered them around Gil's head.

"Close your eyes, young Gil. I am sense shifter Ray and I'm going to remove all the bad thoughts and memories from your mind and throw them back into the atmosphere. Open your little tiny brain and let me scoop them out."

She threw her hands up in the air, and animatedly pretended to pull parts of his brain apart, throwing what was in there up towards the sky.

"Feel better now?"

"Yeah, I do actually. How much do I owe you?"

"One million credits, kind sir."

Gil laughed.

"See, I told you it was easy being a sense shifter."

"Oh, you think so?" A voice came from an alleyway between two buildings across from them. "You mastered it so quickly too. I am impressed."

A figure emerged, dressed in rags. The person was bald, with a long wooden pole and sunken skin patches to where their eyes would normally be.

Gil felt the cold sweat creep back into his body. The figure stood on the edge of the shadows. It was the same person he had seen the other night, he was sure of it. Even though the figure had been too far away for him to notice the disconcerting lack of eye balls, the bald head was unmistakable. Someone was after him and they had found him again.

"This one knows how to take a joke," Rix said, not noticing how he had suddenly stiffened, his eyes locked on the figure.

"We need to go, now, Rix. Go!" he whispered.

"What? Why?"

"That's the person from the pit the other night, the one that nearly caught me."

"Oh, shit!"

This was what he was afraid of: being followed, being hunted.

She grabbed him and pulled him away. He snapped out of his daze and followed her down Lower Mile.

They turned off the Forcella to make it less noticeable where they were. The rain was still coming down hard, and running on the wet cobbled road was a challenge in itself.

"Hood!" Rix shouted and both flicked their hoods up over their heads. They needed to blend in to the crowd. As they made their way back down, he could see that more people had gathered. They pushed and shoved past everyone. The further they made it back to the start of Lower Mile, the harder it was to get through the masses. It was as though they were running in treacle.

"MOVE!" Rix yelled at anyone who got in her way. Gil was a little more apologetic.

She let go of him once they were amongst the crowds. He tried to keep an eye out for her path but lost her.

"Rix!" he shouted over the noise. No response.

He ducked down low. His heart was pounding—or was it his head from the lack of oxygen? He hated to admit it, but for the past two days, he had held a fear of failure, always seeing that image in his mind, that person chasing towards him and for no reason that he knew. The adrenaline rushing around his body was unlike in the Mustang. This was not enjoyable. The panic was causing him to take short sharp breaths and all he could think was the question: 'what do they want with me?'

He thought he could sneak his way through; that would make it less obvious where he was. He had lost his location on Lower Mile and with Rix vanished too. He had to manage this on his own.

He came out between two 'sense shifters' to get a clearer look to where he was. He kept close to the building to get a wider view of the crowd yet keep the protection of the wall behind him. There was no sign of Rix, but also none of his predator. If he had a skill and ability, now would be the time he needed it to show itself again. He pushed past his denial and winked between each eye frantically. Nothing happened—as rightly so, because he still had doubt he could even do it; what he had witnessed was questionable.

He looked to his side and saw that the one 'sense shifter' hadn't noticed, and was busy sprinkling a powder over a lady who was sobbing into her hands, which were wrapped in multicoloured beads.

"Ah, you looking for softness in your heart?" the

other asked. Confused by the question, he just made a dramatic sigh in her general direction.

A hand grabbed him by the shoulder and pulled him backwards. He wriggled as violently as he could. He wasn't going to let himself get caught, not in daylight. No salvager ever got caught when the sun was up; he would be never be respected as one again if he was.

"GET OFF ME!" he shouted.

He was dragged backwards, knocking over part of the sense shifter's stall and into a building through an open door. He tripped on the step. He was chucked into a dark empty room.

He prepped his fists. He wasn't very skilled in the art of fighting and assumed that raised fists were the first steps that you should take when about to engage in combat. If he had already been caught, then he would need to try something more physical.

"What are you going to do with them? Put them away," Rix said as she closed the rickety wooden door.

Gil relaxed. It was Rix. He took a long exhale. He leant over, his hands on his knees, and caught his breath back. There had not been a time when he was so glad to see her.

"This door was open. I thought it'd be better we got off the road and found another way out of here. Are you sure that's who you saw the other night?"

"Definitely," he said between breaths.

"Come on. There must be a way out through the back."

"Wait a minute. I need to tell you something."

He had to be honest with her. If he had put them both in danger or at risk then she should know the full story.

"There isn't time for love stories. We aren't going to die, Gil."

He blushed slightly, but thankfully this was masked by the red cheeks he already had from running.

"No, it's to do with that person, thing, whoever they are."

"I saw, Gil. They had no damn eyes. Why are we even running? How the fuck are they going to find us when they can't see anything? Huh?"

"Well, they know one way or another; they found me again. Listen, Rix. At the pit, there was something I didn't tell you. The figure ran at me—"

"I KNOW GIL! You told me!" She was on edge as much as he was.

"…but if they had no eyes, how did they know where I was? That's not the point. That pole they were holding—they went for me with it. It attacked me!"

"And?" Rix was frantically looking about for another exit. Light on her toes, fidgety. Gil had not seen her like this before. She was becoming impatient, but Gil needed a moment to compose himself before the next stretch of running. He, of course, had questions. This thing had no eyes yet knew where he was. All Rix was focused on was escaping but she wasn't seeing what he was trying to explain.

"It swung for me and I dodged it. It missed me."

"So? They had a bad aim. They have no eyes. I would miss you if I couldn't fucking see anything," she said as she continued to scout around for another exit.

"Rix! They knew where I was. The pole was going to hit me square on and I had two choices—either get hit or miss it—and guess what? I survived. My point is: maybe you were right; maybe I do have syght and that is who we are—"

She turned back to him with a look of horror on her face. The collected person he knew was gone for the moment. Her short jet-black hair was all over the place. Why was she so panicked? They were off the street; nobody saw them come in here.

He looked past her and spotted the figure walking around the corner following her.

"GO! RUN! FUCKING MOVE, GIL!" she shouted and pointed to a staircase next to the door they had come through.

There was no hesitation this time. He bolted up the winding metal staircase, leaping two steps at a time.

"Gil, run faster!"

He was running. He knew how to do that well. Why was this person after him? Had he done something wrong? Was it the owner of the pit? If it was, he had put everyone else's salvaging job on the line now. Or, much worse, did this person know he had syght? Was this why? He had only told Rix about it and she was in as much a hurry to escape as he was. Unless it was Terry…

'Stop, Gil! Enough!' He tried to silence his thoughts, which were asking the most ridiculous questions. Letting his brain wander was not something he should allow to happen. But there was a chance he could be right.

With Rix climbing behind him, they ascended the staircase. Each level they passed had chains on all the doors. The staircase spiralled its way to the top floor, which had one door at the end. Above the door was a half broken illuminated sign that read 'exit'.

Gil pushed on the bar and it swung open to a rooftop.

"No, wait!" But he was too late. Rix had closed the door behind her. There was no handle to get back in.

"How are we going to get back through?"

"Would you want to go back in there when you know what is waiting for you? We'll find another way, Gil."

She was right. Regardless, if they were trapped or not, it was safer keeping the door closed and the person after them at bay.

Rix searched the rooftop and came to one conclusion: the next building along was an easy jump.

"You want me to jump from a building?"

"To another one. Not to the road."

She checked the distance then took a run up and leapt. She made it with ease.

Gil checked the gap and received the confirmation he didn't want: how high the building was from the ground. Salvagers did this sort of thing all the time, although not from such a height—not six floors up. If Rix could do it then it would be no problem for Gil. He had no time to worry about consequences. Either jump or get caught. He needed some of Rix's attitude towards life at times. Don't think just do.

He took a run up and leapt over the gap. His knee buckled as he landed. He had put too much energy into the jump...

The buildings took a similar pattern as Lower Mile did, snaking around the mile-long stretch. The healers, the victims, the poor, all below and oblivious to the happenings on the rooftop. If they wanted to scream for help, no one would have heard them.

They cleared five buildings, each with the same sized gap between them. It was more draining than Gil thought, even though the gaps were small. The trepidation of each jump was using up his stamina and energy.

"Can we stop for a second?" he asked, out of breath.

"Why? You want to get out of here, right?"

"No one is following us."

Rix checked the next building over.

"Fuck!" she yelled. The gap was too large to guarantee they would make it safely. "We'll have to take the fire escape down. We'll stop once we are off Lower Mile and back to the streets we know. They'll never find us."

She led the way down a rusty ladder on the side of the building that led onto a variety of descending platforms that connected to the windows. This was more what Gil was used to—not that he was taking his time, but at least this structure was connected to the building rather than him freefalling in mid-air. They made their way down the fire escape in silence. With all the technology there was, especially with what Rix had access to, it still came down to just using your legs—unless you were tied up, but even then, Rix probably had a solution for that.

A few levels down they came across a padlock on the grated floor. They couldn't access the next level down without abseiling over the railings, something Gil was not even going to attempt without a rope. But Rix pulled out her laser knife and cut through the lock with ease.

'CLINK'

The padlock broke open. She pocketed the knife and lifted up the panel of the floor so they could continue to climb down.

"If Jacks had modified my Holo Palm Chip by now, I could have brought up the schematics of all these buildings; then, we would know where all the exits were. Not only that, I could hack into the cameras and we could have monitored where our stalker was. But no." She looked over the edge. "It's clear."

On the last platform the ladder was stuck. Rix used her laser knife again and cut right through the railing. As soon as she was finished, the ladder slipped through the grips and broke off.

"Looks like we're jumping."

Rix went first to show Gil how it was done, lowering herself down whilst hanging onto the platform so she was dangling above the floor. She let go and broke her fall with a roll.

"Like that. Got it?" She looked up to him.

He copied, jumping down and breaking his fall the other way, rolling straight into a puddle. The wet wasn't what bothered him, though—he was wet anyway; it made no difference—it was more his techpack stabbing him in the back that was the issue.

"Thanks," he said, sitting up from where he still lay on the floor, trying to breathe through the pain.

"For what?"

"Helping me."

"Well, someone had to." She smiled.

She shook her body, trying to remove the excess rainwater from her clothes. She wiped her arms and ran her hand through her hair, slicking it back. Then she held out her hand to help him.

Gil obliged and let Rix haul him up, a little mightier than he thought it would be. He ended up face-to-face with Rix.

The droplets of rain had just enough room to pass between the two of them, landing on their skin and trickling over their lips.

Gil could feel the warmth coming back to his face. Their hands stayed gripped together.

"Now, are you ready for a little talk?"

The figure was back. Gil could see them in his peripherals, blocking the exit from the alley they were in.

The chase was over.

SEVEN

"I have an advanced space mechanics and quantum entanglement qualification," Cyra Wolverton muttered to herself, "and here I am sifting through data, looking for something so unbelievably hidden, it would be as though I'm splitting a quark and trying to find a preon—which is easy compared to this."

Cyra was a young scientist who had struggled to be considered as a leading professional in her field. She had decided to keep her financial history and wealth unknown, a choice that she had undertaken which had yet to prove fruitful. She had excelled through her studies and graduated with the highest marks of any prior student across the country, and to the best of her knowledge, the world also. Yet even in this new era of technology, money was still the currency used to pursue where you wanted to be. Cyra had to take the hard route, as many did, and worked her way up the ranks.

She had started by taking on a few mechanical jobs as a glorified factory worker, where she would assemble parts for the latest Proton series of vehicles, which was too basic for her intelligence. There was a slight advancement, when she moved to ATT Systems to work in the signalling department, where she aided other scientists in improvements to the network. Their attempts were to establish communications beyond the localisation of Earth. But this still was only formulas and basic calculations. The interesting stuff was left to 'the professionals', as she had been told numerous times by the leading scientists who had shunned her and her degree.

She finally ended up working for Syngetical—as everyone wanted to. The interest for Cyra was their development and exploration of what was beyond. That was the tagline on the job ad and with her background and love of most things unworldly, this was the dream role.

She smudged out a fingerprint mark someone had made on one of her six glass monitors, and sighed audibly.

"I told you not to touch the screens, Myles. That's why we have the AI gloves. You don't need to touch the screens, especially mine. You have your own."

"Again, why would I need to touch your screen?" her assistant and intern replied. "I don't even get close to it when I walk in or out of the room."

Cyra liked Myles as an employee as he did what

was required, no questions asked. She would have engaged in a little more interaction from time-to-time, and adopted a less abrupt demeanour, had he not had such a strange sense of humour, which she found difficult to work out, let alone connect with.

"Why are we doing this anyway?" she asked rhetorically.

"Because the orders come through from the hatch over there, as they have done for the past two years, and we carry them out," Myles explained in his monotone voice.

"Yes, I know why we have to. Are you being sarcastic? Obviously, I know. It wasn't a question. I was talking to myself aloud," she huffed. Myles smirked. "But if you want to talk about it—"

"I don't really," Myles interjected, more to wind her up than the lack of care and she knew it.

"Well, I'm going to anyway and you will listen. You do realise the nature of what we are doing, right?"

"I'm quite aware what we get paid to do, yes," he responded dryly.

There was not much variety in their day-to-day work. They filed through the data of every human on the planet, looking at details about when they were born, how they were born and their genetic code. In the data that was stored, they looked for patterns or strains within the DNA helix, particularly at nucleotides to see if anyone matched the Deja Vu nucleobase, a rare and improbable gene to find.

She reiterated to him what they were meant to be

doing, she often believed Myles had no clue.

"Thank you for describing my job to me. I had no idea what I had got myself into." Myles was scrolling through a list of pages on his glass monitor and swiped them off to the right. It automatically stored them back in their folder icon on his furthest screen, the memory bank to his hive of information.

"We are looking for something that doesn't exist, Myles. It's a waste of our time, is what I am saying."

She pressed the projected icons on the screen with force. Myles kept quiet.

Cyra had become more frustrated as each day passed. Her skills and—to her belief—her knowledge, were being underrated. She was capable of more and this mind-numbingly boring data analysis was below her. She did not work this hard to get to this stage. She wanted to be working in the Spacial Lens department, where she felt the real scientists work, where the real work was done. The employees there had the chance to be doing some good for the world, the opportunity to make a difference. She knew she had the ability to make great strides at Syngetical but needed to be in the right department to do so. There were not many people who wanted to aid civilisation, and Cyra was one of the ones who did. According to what she had read in the history books, attempts from those that truly wanted to "save the planet", as it was mockingly stated, backfired, causing the mass extinction of companies and a cull of the human race.

She took a few deep breaths to calm herself. She

was agitated. All she wanted to do was work on something she believed in, or at least something she could see a purpose in.

"We can't change the past but we can shape our future," Myles said, acting as ever the model employee.

"Don't quote the government's ethos at me. That's not going to help. But do you see my point? We have been told what the signs are to look out for and how the strand may or may not look. There are a lot of people to sort through and we still haven't found a glimpse or even a hope of one person having it. And if we do, then what? What's it for? Do you know?"

Myles was quiet for a moment and then responded with, "You are paid, right?"

"Well of course, in the normal credits we are issued, yes," she said, taken aback by the question.

"If you're paid then you are better off than seventy percent of the people down on the street level. We are on the thirty-seventh floor; we do alright."

Myles's point was fair. They were far from the highest level, but they had to be thankful they had a regular income and their work was safe. There were plenty below them without that privilege.

"But don't you want to know why? What this is achieving?" She saw him shrug.

The eternal list of people and their data. They had everything they needed on this database. It had taken the government seven years to compile it with the people who were currently living on earth, always updating it with every newborn. Cyra had mixed feelings over the technology. Yes, it helped them do their job and it was perfect for doctors or law enforcement so they knew who people were, but in some ways, it stripped you of being a human. Humans were a thumbnail, a few kilobytes of memory, existing as a file on a computer. If the government sanctioned the new law where every individual would have to have the Artificial Recording Memory Chip—otherwise coined as 'ARM'—everything would be monitored: what that human was thinking, doing and saying. Humans would become stripped of what being human was all about, individuality.

But this was no time to think about humans becoming less human. This was her job, for now—and only for now. She knew something better was to come and she had to make that happen. She was already working at the company where she wanted to be, so the hard part was done. Now, she had to prove her worth, even if that meant finding a person with a myth gene. She would be that person to succeed.

"Maybe when you find that person, you unlock the passage between space time travel and explore the wonders of the universe in a nanosecond of the time and you'll be hailed as the saviour of planet earth," Myles said as dryly as he could.

She smiled. "But then who would keep you company here when I was rocketing into the unknown?"

"Well, I wouldn't be here, would I? There wouldn't be a job. We would have found that one person. Contract terminated," he said bluntly.

"Oh, I didn't think of that. That's quite true. I guess I could bring you along as my assistant."

"You mean captain."

Cyra had made her reply as a courtesy, not wanting to insult Myles. She would never take him onto her next venture. This was about her. She had no time to help someone else's career too. Although, she had to question herself as to whether that was going against her own moral justice—wanting to help others in the world—the fact she would leave Myles behind. He was not captain quality, not with the amount of responsibility that would be needed. She gathered he was making a joke, or at least he should have been.

"One can hope."

A red light flicked on and a sharp alarm burst echoed in the room. Neither Cyra or Myles flinched. The regular alert had become almost background noise, an exaggerated way of saying, 'you have mail'.

"I'll go," Myles said as he removed his gloves.

He walked toward the far wall, which was covered in a frosted glass, behind which was a room that neither Myles or Cyra had entered, or even seen the other side of. They saw shadows mainly, of people busying themselves, walking around holding clipboards. Every so often, a task card would drop through the hatch, providing instructions for them to carry out.

He picked up the latest, a thin metallic sheet.

As all of them had, there was a blue pulsing button in the centre of it. Myles pressed it and a projected holographic screen opened up, two-inches above where he held the sheet.

"Here we go!" he shouted over to her.

The Syngetical crest appeared first and underneath, the phrase, 'This information is protected and not to be shared with anyone outside of the Syngetical Corporation or SeeTech Tower, with specific reference to floor thirty-seven.'

Cyra knew not to pay attention to anything Myles pressed until he read the note aloud. It had been the same corporate drivel for the past two years.

The text continued on, 'Update to brief, Research Order - 3765DVG.'

"It says to narrow our field of search to the age bracket 13 - 24-year-olds, no specifics to gender or race or location," he said as he walked back to his chair.

"Are they saying that someone outside of that age range can't have the gene?"

"Doesn't say. There's more," he said and began to read out the instructions. "For specimens already disregarded, please remove them from the 'Not Applicable Folder' and reinstate them into the 'Active' folder immediately."

"WHAT?" she exclaimed.

'Please place your fingerprint onto the centre blue button to confirm, agree and disconnect this message.'

Myles obliged.

The hologram vanished and the blue button pixelated into nothing, leaving them with a blank metallic sheet. He discarded it onto a pile of others that matched. It clinked as it hit the pile.

"This list will be endless if they keep resubmitting people we have already looked at," she said, with an angry tone to her voice.

"You carry on searching. I'll find all the cases that match the brief from the folder and throw them back into the mix," Myles said. She could tell he was suppressing the urge to make a sarcastic joke. She had spent enough time with him to know when he wanted to. She was thankful he kept quiet.

"Thank you," she replied bluntly, and then softened her voice. "Sorry, it's not your fault."

"I know it's not. I just read the message to you." She shot him a look. "If you disagree with it, go and talk to them. You're the one in charge here, not me."

He pointed over to the frosted glass wall, where there was a shadow of someone standing in the centre of it. She could tell from the outline that they were folding their arms, but she was unsure of which way they were facing.

Cyra had no problem with completing orders or being told what to do. The issue she had was when those tasks were pointless. Her specialities were redundant here. They were being wasted, especially when what they were searching for was as close to hypothetical as one could get. She had made notes and done her own research to work out why this Deja Vu gene was so important, or how it would exist in human DNA—to no result. There was no meaning to it. It was a made-up word. A gene that made you think you were seeing something that had already happened made no sense to her, if that was even the correct definition of it. This was her frustration. She couldn't help but think it was bullshit. Tell a person to build a house and they will; tell a scientist that something exists and they'll spend a lifetime trying to work out the equation of how to find it.

"SHIT!" she yelled across the room. Angry at herself for accepting this dull, unfulfilling position. Her frustrations now vocal, to release the tension she held over not wanting to do this exact job.

Cyra rarely swore, especially in front of colleagues. She saw it as a sign of weakness or one's lack of control, but now, she had had too much, too much of the same daily routine and the secrecy of what they were doing. She was a scientist after all. Anything was solvable when given the correct information to work with.

She shoved the chair out from underneath her and walked over to the other door near the hatch, the only door she had never been through before.

She typed in the nine-digit code and the light flashed red. She typed it again. Same response.

She paused for a second. Still. Her stretched-out finger shaking at the realisation of what she was doing. What she had wanted to do before but had never had that overpowering drive to want to scream at the very people prodding her to 'do this' and 'do that' constantly, each time to no result. This door, although she had not seen where it opened out on too or to whom, could only lead to the people behind the glass. For her particular role, this was the epicentre of the company.

She raised her arm slowly to the central button, which had a circle with an 'X' in the middle of it. She pressed it and entered '100586'.

Cyra and Myles' screens froze and went to complete black. The light on the coded pad turned green and the door unlocked.

Cyra took a breath. Now was her chance to make that change, not for civilisation but for her. She held the cold metal handle of the door, contemplating the endless and unanswerable question of 'what if'.

The figure's shadow through the frosted glass directed its attention towards the door.

Cyra was that scientist. She had already solved the equation to this one.

She opened the door and stormed through.

She had entered the emergency code.

EIGHT

The four drone cameras emitted a hum as they hovered in front of the tall cream leather chair. The shutter over each lens was closed. Filming had not yet commenced. The room was small. Camera crews and 'behind the scenes' people were not needed anymore. A drone camera did everything you needed it to as long as it had a pilot, who would be sitting in a similar-sized room over in the news channel building, across the other side of the city.

Most referred to the room by its nickname, the 'mad' room, rather than its official title of the 'Live Broadcast' room. It was painted in a colour of 'White Dove', which was meant to have a serene and welcoming feeling of warmth. If you were about to go live across a number of news channels, then it was crucial you felt relaxed. However, instead, it came across as bleak, giving out a surgical vibe that was more akin to that of an isolation cell. Being this particular shade of white also helped the editors to superimpose any graphics required and also allowed holographic/3D filming. For anyone who owned a Holo Vortex display screen, it could display a 3D holographic image of the person being filmed. It allowed the public to feel more connected to whom they were listening. The idea was stolen from the cult film Star Wars when a fan of the franchise was designing the system.

The overhead spotlights were switched off and three light panels faded on. The drones activated, the lens caps on all of them flicking open simultaneously and reversing away from the chair.

Anders Hilgaard, a tall unkempt man with shaggy mousy blond hair, entered the room. Dressed more casually than one would expect when appearing in front of the world, he was muttering to himself and holding a handful of papers.

He approached the table behind the cameras, which held a water dispenser and a set of round white circular disks the same colour as the walls. He picked one up and secured it to his temple. He never liked to use two; he liked to still 'be' in the room when he went live.

'BING'

A noise from the drone cameras sounded.

"Yes, all clear. I can hear you," he responded.

He went through his notes once again and then put them down on the table. He took a glance at his watch. No matter how many times he had to do this, before he spoke those first words to camera, there was always that feeling of nervousness, especially when all you were looking at was four eyeballs—the cameras on the drones.

He perched on the edge of the leather chair, with his feet on the rest about a foot off the ground.

He took a deep breath.

Then a smile slowly emerged on his face. He knew how to portray himself as friendly, trustworthy. It was all in the eyes.

"And we are welcoming a very special guest today. We are pleased to be joined by Syngetical CEO, Anders Hilgaard, to talk to us about the new Spacial Lens VX. Morning Mr Hilgaard."

The voice resonated in his head and ears.

"Morning to you all and thank you for having me on. It's an absolute pleasure. But please, call me Anders," he said. Within the room, by himself, this conversation was to be heard by millions world-wide. Despite the advances in technology, and the fact that Anders did not have to leave his building and waste time travelling, he always found it intimidating addressing an audience he couldn't see. He was alone, yet felt vulnerable—a feeling he was never able to shift, no matter how many times he spoke to the media.

"Let's start off with you telling us about what's going to be new with the VX."

He chuckled slightly and began his rehearsed words.

"As with any new product, the early stages are key: trial and testing, failing and then starting again.

We are still learning what is going to be possible through the prototype stages, as we all feel here at Syngetical that we can improve on the previous Spacial Lenses already out there. That's not saying that our current lenses are out of date or do not work. If anything, we are learning and developing our products from the feedback we get from our customers. We will still be updating the current lenses and you will only really need to fully upgrade if anything is damaged or deteriorates. What we hope will be new with the VX is a faster shutter system on the iris, a quicker response time when the pupils dilate between light and dark, as well as with short and long distances. A recording facility, which would be voice activated to be able to record memories and events, or even used for witnessing tragic accidents or crime. We wanted a way for people to be able to see their lives and for others to accurately share it, without missing any details."

"Would you not be worried about the public's reaction concerning an invasion of privacy? For others to access what people are seeing?"

"Well, this was actually something that came from our customers. Numerous pieces of feedback prompted us to start thinking about this process and how this could be done safely and securely. It would be down to the individual on what they wanted to record and share. Each lens would have its own unique ID and would only be accessible through a three-stage process, which we are still working out."

"Will there be any other surprises in the lens we

can look out for?"

No matter what Anders gave the media, they always wanted more—to siphon every drop of information, to use it to improve their ratings, to be the first to receive the news. Anders was wise to this and had learnt over the years not to divulge too much, whether it was the name change from his food store business, providing lower cost food for everyone, or the details of the water supply company they bought out so that people had fresh clean water for free. In that instance, he had learnt the hard way, saying too much: he had explained how the government had owned it before and raised the water prices so high that it would cost as much as oil did for the same measure. It was something he had told the media as an off-the-cuff comment, but he later received backlash from the government, which tried to class it as treason.

But Anders was clever; there was no reason for him to share anything he didn't need to. He did feel that small sense of guilt for not doing so, though. It sometimes felt like he was lying to his audience by not sharing everything, the very people he was trying to support.

"Ah, now that would be telling. Can't be divulging all our development processes. Broken promises are harder to mend than any of our products. Am I right?"

The news reporter smiled and nodded. "We have trialled the new VX lens prototype and have been overjoyed with the results and what it means for the nation. For those who wish to be able to see again and those working in psychiatric hospitals with patients who have lost their sight, this new lens is for you. This will allow a better way of living and seeing the future with the rest of us."

Anders smiled down the camera. He hoped his heartfelt speech did what was required, not for the public but for the media. He had already gained the trust of the public. It was the media, controlled by the 55, he wanted to avoid getting in trouble with. 'Kill them with kindness' was a phrase he had come to live by when it came to media conferences.

"As we all do, Anders. One final question before we let you go. I am sure you have plenty to be getting on with in your day…"

Anders nodded.

"What are your thoughts about the government's new A-R-M chip? Are they taking away from what you are trying to achieve with the VX lens and is it a breach into what people want to keep private?"

He took a beat to respond. He had to be careful what he said here. A younger Anders would have rushed in with an answer. That had not boded well in the past. The government was powerful. The less they knew and the less controversy he had with them, an easier life he would lead.

"I think we are working on very different concepts," he said calmly. "Syngetical's is to help to provide a better value of life for those who have lost something from their own lives. Meanwhile, the government hasn't fully finalised what they want to do with their chip. I imagine it would be adding to the current database that is already established."

"Very diplomatic answer there, Mr Hilgaard."

"Just an honest one. I cannot speculate too much into their design when I've not been privileged with any of the details. You would have to ask Ms Xing."

Anders was pleased with himself of how he avoided giving his honest opinion. It was the perfect transition for the news reader.

"And for all our viewers, the High Chancellor Vivalda Xing will be joining us next week in a live forum to discuss whether their chip is an invasion of privacy or a benefit. Now, I know you're a very busy individual, Mr Hilgaard, so is there anything else you can enlighten us with before you leave us today?"

Anders pushed his nail into his leg, a release of the frustration that had been slowly starting to build.

A slight exhale with a smile. Anders had to give it to the media. They knew there was something he was holding back. But what good is a wrapped birthday present if you already know what was inside?

"Nothing to add, though there is a launch date in sight. We are hoping within the next half year or so for the VX."

"Something we will all look forward to hearing more about. Thank you for joining us today and good luck with the prototype. Anders Hilgaard there, speaking live from SeeTech Tower. Coming up next in our news brief hour…"

The newsreader's voice faded from Anders' ears and an automated response announced, "Session terminated."

He exhaled and placed his palms onto his thighs.

'BING'

The drones' shutters closed and reset to their neutral position.

He removed the white disk from his temple and positioned it on the table next to the other one, then collected his papers and left the room.

Anders walked with haste into the noisy laboratory.

"Sir, I found something of interest that you might want to take a look at," said Felcion Trux, Anders' head researcher and one of his core scientists working on the Spacial Lens concept.

"Is it the answer?" he replied bluntly.

"Not exactly, however—"

"Then do I need to know?" he interrupted.

There was a pause.

The other two researchers in the room sat quietly, focusing on their screens as they clicked and swiped.

"We have made ground. We found a pattern," Felcion said awkwardly, not knowing whether he was allowed to speak or not.

Anders turned away from the scientist, and extended out an open hand behind him.

"Give it me."

He walked over and handed him a screen.

"Glove!" he barked.

Felcion panicked, ran over to the main console and frantically looked for a spare glove. Each researcher was assigned their own so it would always be known who was accessing what data, where in the building and when. Anders couldn't allow just anyone to be able to see and use this information—it was every human's identity stored on the network, and someone might want to get their hands on it. It also gave information on how hard his researchers were working and who he needed to replace. The screen also wouldn't work with human flesh, the glove was essential—another security feature of the system.

"Give me that," Felcion whispered to the other researcher, who then removed his glove and handed it to him.

"There you go sir," he said, handing the glove over and taking the screen back from him. Although the glove was not assigned to Anders it would still work on the information he was accessing.

"Expand it," he said.

Felcion slid his finger over the top edge of the screen and hit the purple spot that appeared in the top right corner. The data projected out in front of them.

Anders moved and stood in the centre of the room, where he was able to sift through what was being shown to him.

"As you can see, sir, the pattern occurs numerous times within these fields, so we have deployed the teams to pinpoint their searches around these parameters. It's not much to go on, but it's a huge step from what we had, especially if it works out to be correct."

"And if it doesn't?"

"Then, we still would have eliminated people as we would have done, in this particular bracket."

"Is that not a waste of time when we could be searching all fields and potentially finding what we want faster?"

"Sir, we have found no clues or any signs in months. This may be a very small incline and a push, we feel, in the right direction."

"My time is limited, Felcion. I need this for the new VX—"

Anders stopped himself.

"I'm sorry, sir, what did you say?"

"Nothing that concerns you!"

Anders knew he wouldn't question him. He was the boss and could tell Felcion liked working at Syngetical. He wanted to keep his job. Anders gave the scientist a look, enough to suggest, 'not today'.

"Focus on the ribosomal ribonucleic acid linear molecules," he said. "You can see in these specimens that they have abnormalities in their lengths, so that might link to the messenger RNA too. We have to be precise. If there is a fault between the messages sent from DNA into making proteins that might be our link."

"We didn't see that," Felcion said. "Our pattern was that these people all became sick around the same time in their lives and of the same diseases."

"You have to look deeper—not at what the outcome is, but where it starts from. If its RNA disease or Toxic RNA, it may be the thing we are looking for rather than the messages sent from DNA by RNA. If our specimen has that, it may be the mutation we need. Their abnormality might unlock the key to how De—"

He was cut short by an alarm.

The screens in the room froze and switched to black.

A door next to the one Anders had entered through swung open with gust as a woman, determination printed all over her face, stormed in.

Cyra had not planned what she was going to say. Someone, whoever it was, was going to experience as much wrath and frustration as she could muster without losing her job in the process. She still wanted to work at Syngetical, but in a job doing something more worthwhile that utilised her talents. She knew she was capable of more.

"My name is Cyra Wolverton and I have been working in that room for two years now, looking for something that we may as well class as invisible. I am a scientist and a fucking good one too. I spent my life educating myself in the mysteries of space mechanics and understand enough that I should not be scrolling through people's names for a living. And to add—"

She looked up and realised who she was speaking to. Horror filled her lungs, brain and heart. Every other organ that had blood flowing through it froze when she saw Anders standing in front of her, that voice in the back of her head whispering, 'what have you done?'.

"Shit, Anders Hilgaard. I...I'm so sorry...I, I thought...I wouldn't have. I'm going to leave."

She flustered, her feet planted firmly to the tiled floor, her legs too scared to move, yet her brain was screaming to get out.

"No stay. See, Felcion? This is what I mean. We have to look deeper. Where does it all start from? Cyra Wolverton here is frustrated that she is doing unmeaningful work, but we only saw the outcome: the rage, the built-up anxiety of knowing she is better than this, that her skills are not being tested enough."

She calmed slightly. He understood. The CEO, her boss, could relate to how she was feeling. If only she could have explained it how he did in that moment. He put it so well, so eloquently, as if he had been there himself. Why didn't she think of saying it like that?

"Please don't fire me, sir. I was— I wanted to ask what this is all for." She was here now so she may as well ask the question she had been asking herself for months. Not many had been in this predicament and she needed to take her chance. This was the person who could finally give her the answers she needed. "Does what we are looking for even exist?" she said, cowering.

"Does anything exist before it is first discovered? Anything seems an impossible feat until you work out how to do it. Space was a phenomenon five-hundred years ago. Look at all we know about it now."

She thought how about five minutes ago, Anders didn't know who she was and she regretted introducing herself the way she had. Her heart was still racing. She hated the unknown, the long drawn-out anticipation as the predator toyed with its prey before it struck. If this was his way of firing someone, then she had to hand it to him. It was her mistake that had brought this situation about.

"I like your energy, Cyra Wolverton. Let's see what you are capable of. Take a look at this screen. What do you see?"

Anders directed her to the projection that was illuminated in the room. She took a few steps forward. What was she looking at? This data was new to her. Algorithms, DNA molecule streams and the dissection of the molecules within each human, put back into simulations. This was the data she should be working with, not what she was sorting with Myles.

"We have made some progress in this matter, further to the orders that you just received. As you mentioned, microbiology is not your field of expertise..."

She heard Anders, but ignored him for a moment, allowing herself the time to let her brain to absorb what she was looking at, to process it—that enjoyment of seeing data she had studied, that feeling growing inside where, finally, she felt at home with something in the workplace.

"Cyra?" Anders called over to her.

"There's a pattern in the RNA molecules. I'm not quite sure what it is yet, not without further investigation, of course. Is this to do with the Deja Vu gene?" She diverted her attention from one specimen to the other, attempting to decipher what the exact pattern was. This complex structure would not be easily solved in a few minutes.

"And look at what you now know about the Deja Vu gene that you were unaware of before you walked into this room. I would like to show you something, Ms Wolverton. An opinion of yours would be beneficial if you are as fucking good as you say you are."

Still embarrassed that she had used the 'f' word in front of him, she now felt a great sense of relief that he had said it too. He was not angry about her outburst. If anything, he was almost encouraging more. But best to not be doing this every day in the near future. She had to prove her worth now.

"Oh, I would love to," she said, both delighted and overwhelmed with the offer, yet no hesitation to what she was signing up for. It had to be more fulfilling than what she'd been doing that morning or for the past two years. "I mean, if I can, of course. What is it? Something you are working on?"

"Felcion, carry on your work here and report back to me when you find something. Cyra, if you would, follow me."

She had a momentary thought, a blip, about Myles. He could be his own captain now.

"I assume you are aware of the Spacial Lens, Cyra?"

"Yes of course," she said immediately.

"Well, we are in developments of taking our Spacial Lens to the next level, yet we keep hitting the same hurdles and can't quite work out what the main issue is. I wonder if you might be able to work that out for us."

There was an urge building inside her. She wanted to scream with joy. The Spacial Lens, the very department she wanted to work on, was being offered to her. Trying to look as if she didn't understand that this was a job offer, and not wanting to ask, she replied, "I would be delighted to take a look."

"Good. The new ID Lens is something that will change our future…"

She was listening to Anders, but not fully present. She was being escorted by the CEO to—what she could only take from the conversation to be—her new position. There was plenty of time to learn. Now, she just wanted to enjoy this rare moment. This was the start of her career, this very moment in time. It may have not been glamorous, but she did it with gusto.

'You've got this,' she told herself. Nothing was going to stop her from getting this lens to work. She would not let Anders down.

NINE

"Through there." The figure pointed using their pole.

"Fuck you!" Rix replied without hesitation.

She looked around. Gil guessed she had the same idea as he did, trying to find a means for a possible escape. The figure held their pole aloft, acting as a barrier to the only exit back to the road.

"All we want to do is talk. It would greatly benefit you if you listened, Gil."

Another person arrived in front of them. This one had lost only one eye. The scar over the patch of skin looked fresh, messy, as though the cover-up work was rushed, like a kid with a crayon. On their remaining eye there was a device similar to the ones the salvagers wore at night in the pit. It had shutters on and seemed to move and refocus with every movement of the head.

"What do you want with Gil?" Rix was defensive.

The figure used their pole to indicate to something behind them. A steel door swung open to reveal someone else stood in the doorway. He was big, broad chested, somebody that neither he nor Rix could stand up against.

"Fine, yes. I was down at the pit and I shouldn't have been there. My father is really ill and I needed to find a particular circuit board for his heart replicator. Without it, it can't keep him alive. I thought the best place was to check the pit where all the rubbish goes. I'm sorry." Gil dropped his head solemnly.

There were very few rules salvagers stuck by, but one key one was that if you got caught, you deny everything; you lie convincingly enough to make it sound like the truth. Use a family member, play on the strings of pity. So, Gil did. Hopefully it was his saving grace.

"We know you were looking for Goride chips for Terry Florence…"

Rumbled at the first stage. Gil had not been caught before, so he had no previous experience on rely on. He had no back up. Now he was worried.

"…we were not there to punish you for being in the pit. We were there to test you."

"Test him for what?" Rix blurted out. Gil tried to softened her rage by holding up his arm across her chest, as if to hold back the riled-up rottweiler ready for attack.

The figure pointed with their pole again.

"Through the door, right?" Gil asked, to which the figure nodded.

Gil began to step towards it and encouraged Rix to follow.

"You can't be serious? What are you doing?" she whispered.

The door led into a dark hallway where they were met by yet another figure dressed in rags who indicated to follow them. They were more than outnumbered, but Gil didn't feel threatened by them. They were calm, yet very to the point.

"If they wanted to hurt us, they could have easily done it by now," he whispered. "And they aren't law enforcement. We both have our laser knifes on us just in case. Other than the big guy we just met, what else they going to hurt us with? Most of them have no eyes and this one here has a wooden pole, that's it."

"My thumb is already placed hard on the button of my laser knife ready to use."

"Relax, Rix. I don't think they want any trouble."

They were led into a large windowless room. Concrete pillars were dotted all over and the centre of the room held what looked like a training area. Makeshift portable lighting, soft padded mats and old wooden chairs were scattered about the floor. There was no technology here—back to basics. It wasn't too dissimilar to being at home with his parents in the country.

They were led into the centre and the figures surrounded them in a circle.

"Leave us. They are not a threat," the first figure that Gil had encountered said.

The others retreated into the darkness of the room, followed by the sound of doors opening and closing echoing around the pillars.

"That's your mistake." Rix smiled as she pulled out her laser knife and held it towards them.

"RIX!"

"Who are you and what do you want with Gil?" she said, forcefully throwing her voice at the figure.

They were unresponsive.

"Come on! You've chased us enough today and I want to know who you are."

The figure simply tilted their head.

She raised her laser knife and launched towards them. The person stayed motionless until she was almost upon them, then they used their wooden pole to knock the laser knife out of her hand. They then spun the pole and hit her in the back, taking her down onto the floor where they held her there, pinned to the mat. This was executed in one movement. It was almost as though it had been choreographed, it had been performed so quickly.

"GET OFF ME!" Rix screamed in anger.

"How? How did you do that? You can't see her."

The figure released Rix.

"Because he guessed," Rix rolled away from them and shot straight back up, ready to go again.

"Not that it particularly matters what my gender is, but if we have to be specific, then I'm the same as you." The figure looked towards Rix. "Looks can cause assumptions on what one should be. Just because I have no hair it does not mean I am male.

Just because I have no eyes it does not mean I cannot see."

She twirled her pole and it stopped a hair's width away from Rix's face.

"You missed," Rix said sarcastically.

She turned and swept the pole against the back of Rix's knee's, taking her down to the ground once more.

Rix fell with a scream into the matting.

"Who are you?" Gil took a step back, still in shock of this woman's ability to defend and attack without being able to see. He was impressed. He would not want to stand up against her. It seemed that having eyes was a hindrance in combat.

"I am Freer. But your question should be what am I, not who."

Rix scurried back up and swung a roundhouse kick towards the woman, but she dodged it completely. A simple step to the right and Rix was left off balance again.

"You are a Sense Shifter, a proper one." Gil was in disbelief. They did exist. Astonished that the rumours they had heard were true and that Terry was either wrong or lying—he hadn't decided yet—he ignored what Rix was attempting to do.

"You are correct," Freer said, and then directed her next words at Rix. "Please, for your sake, stop trying to hit me. I am not here to hurt either of you."

Gil grabbed her and pulled her away. Knowing that Rix could fight, it was odd to see her not be able to make contact with her opponent.

"I must explain a few things before I tell you why you are here. Have you heard of syght?"

"Yeah. Well, we were told something different about it, that it was all a myth, a conspiracy that the government shut down…"

"Well, that did happen. Terry Florence was right to tell you that story."

"Gil never said Terry told him that story," Rix jutted in.

"You are correct. Gil never uttered those words. Terry told us. Terry was part of the original group that wanted to state to the world that syght predicted how long you had left to live."

Terry was right and wrong at the same time. Gil was confused on what was true now. Either way, he wasn't a traitor nor a spy trying to set him up.

"Who'd have thought that old timer Tez was a sense shifter, ha!" Rix said.

"He's not," Freer continued. "After the government shut down the rumour, the small group of anarchists realised they had been interpreting it wrong. Syght instead depicts which choice to take during in-the-moment scenarios."

"So, it has nothing to do with dying?" Gil asked.

"No, nothing. It's about choice. Let me show you."

Freer placed two arms out in front of her. Gil had seen this test before. It was the one that Terry had showed them in his workshop.

"We've done this before," Rix said monotonously.

"I know. But Terry explained it incorrectly. You can do the same test and I'll show you what it is meant to show you. Place your arms out in front of you and look at me as you do it."

Gil copied, as did Rix.

Freer threw the wooden pole towards him. He cowered away and it hit him before falling to the floor.

"What was the point of that?" Rix had become defensive again.

"To show you that Gil wouldn't catch the pole. Now, this time, as I throw the pole, I want you to blink one eye at a time as quickly as possible and switch between them, okay?"

Gil was unconfident that whatever Freer was trying to prove was going to work. He had become a punching bag, standing there whilst someone he had only met a few moments ago threw objects at him. He was lost on what point she was trying to make.

"Could you pass me the pole?" Freer asked.

Gil and Rix looked at each other. For someone who was more aware of their surroundings than anyone Gil had met, couldn't she pick up the pole herself? Why did he have to pass it back? She had read every movement of Rix's attack, but she needed a simple pole to be passed back to her.

"I know what you are thinking. I will explain in a moment. For now, this is how syght works."

Gil picked up the pole and handed it to her, and then put out his arms in front of him and started to wink with each eye.

Freer threw the pole and Gil attempted to wink faster. As the spear hurtled towards him, he could now see what she meant. He did have two choices. With one eye, he could see his hand missing the pole in his attempts to grab it, his hands passing through it every time. Through the other eye, he could see himself catching the pole and at which point on the pole itself he would grasp it.

And then it was all over. Barely a second had passed and Gil was standing there with one eye closed, an outstretched hand and a pole in his clenched fist.

Rix's gaze was focused on him.

"I knew you had syght," she said, not moving a muscle.

"When we see through both of our eyes, we see an amalgamation of two separate realities that are almost identical. This is how we perceive life. When we close one eye and then the other, as you have just done, we see two different worlds revealing themselves to us. Therefore, there are always two outcomes to anything. You catch the stick or you drop it, this is our ability to control choice in life, yet it is oblivious to most. Most are unaware of the split because they aren't looking for it. The majority subconsciously choose an outcome, depending on whatever eye is more dominant or how they blink at the time the situation is playing out. People are led to believe that everything is either predetermined—no matter what you do, the outcome is the same; we call these people pessimistics—and then there are people who think you are in control of what you do, who are optimistics. It's how we categorise human beings: by the attitude someone takes in life, positive or negative—again, two outcomes. You are either one or the other, but that does not mean you have syght. It's not how you look at the world and your viewpoint that depicts if you have it."

"So, how does this link to syght then?" Gil asked.

"It's the people that can master this ability to choose between the two realities, split them apart and see the two clear outcomes to a situation; these are the people known as having 'the syght'. They are in control of what outcome they get, rather than just accepting what happened in a given situation, unknowing the outcome of both choices.'"

Gil had not looked at life through that perceptive before. It was fascinating that this was possible, the ability to see either choice before making it. It was a mind-blowing thought for him to comprehend.

"Gil does have the syght, then. I knew it. I told you in the car!" Rix exclaimed.

"We aren't entirely sure yet. But Gil does fit the criteria."

"What criteria is that?" he asked, perturbed about what that really meant. Was he abnormal in some way? Was it good to fit the criteria needed to have syght? Was he in danger? If it was a fighting ability like Freer clearly had, then he was in. Sign him up and get training. However, there must be risks to it. There was a reason this colony of people were a myth, kept secret and lived through smoke and mirrors. There had to be consequences that Freer hadn't mentioned. Those are what Gil was worried about.

"If you have it then it starts in your mid-teens up until about the age of twenty-two or twenty-three. If you stay oblivious in that time, then you lose it and you never get the chance to learn how to control it. The body rejects your understanding of syght, as such. We aren't entirely sure the reason why; we just know there is a limited time span."

Gil was in his prime to learn syght. The few instances he had witnessed, it was his body, his mind telling him he was ready, prepping him for what was to come. He had been gifted this—it was a big decision whether to keep it or not. There was no going back if he chose not to.

"Are Sense Shifters people who have syght too? Do you have it?"

"As you can tell, I have no eyes so I don't have the ability to see or choose between the two realities. Instead, as our title suggests, unlike the false prophets on Lower Mile, we shift between our senses to create the world we live in. We do have choice, but it's much harder to master. It takes years. But we use smell, vibrations and touch to map out what's in front of us. We feel our choice rather being able to see it clearly in front of us. We are not bound to one individual reality and can adapt the skill to be able to move between the two. We just can't see when we have. As such, we have chosen to live free from reality. There aren't many of us who can do it. But we always encourage anyone who has lost their eyesight to join us and we train them, support them, give them the chance to become a part of something much grander. There are many more Sense Shifters than there are people who have syght. To have syght in its true form is very rare."

He wasn't sure whether he should feel honoured that he might be one of the very rare. Though, finally, he might have one up on Rix.

"Is it true, then, about those who lose one eye? That it sends them all crazy?" Rix asked.

"Having one eye restricts your options of choice. They are taken away from you so you can only live on one linear path. This indeed did start to send people mad. Thus, why the Spacial Lens was invented by Syngetical. You, of course, know all about that," she said, turning to face Rix.

Gil may have not known much about Sense Shifters, but they sure knew a lot about them.

"We have a few here with us—those who have one eye and one lens—trying to learn how to master our way of living, to see if it is possible to have a mixture of both abilities."

Gil nodded, smiling. He was proud that Syngetical was helping the world. One day, he would be part of that too.

"There are a lot of components that create the blueprint to syght and how it works. It takes time to learn. There would be no use for me or you if I tried to explain everything to you now. It doesn't work like that. You need to experience it, see it for yourself."

"So, the pole? Explain why Gil had to give it to you," Rix said confrontationally.

"For me to be able to sense where something or someone is, it has to be moving through the air. If it is a stagnant object, it makes no sound. There is no movement, so there won't be vibrations in the air for me to detect where it is. If an object or, let's say, your foot has energy behind it, it pushes the particles in its path, therefore creating sound, tiny vibrations of movement so I can locate it. Hence, why in a fight, I would always beat you." She smiled at Rix.

"And buildings? How do you know your way around?" Gil asked, more politely than Rix had.

"I've been here for a very long time. We learn how to move around, we map how many steps there are between each point and build a construct that we can see and feel comfortable in. That's not saying that from time to time I don't make mistakes."

"Let me understand this correctly. You are a Sense Shifter, part of a group to train others who are blind in the ability of syght so they can live a normal life. So, why am I here? Are you going to train me?"

"Not to train, no—to protect."

That was the consequences Gil was afraid of hearing. He was a nobody. Barely anyone knew him. Why would he need protection?

"From who exactly? Have you seen Gil? He's hardly a rich, power-hungry leech, wanting to take over the world, is he?"

He was unsure whether that was meant to be an

insult—Rix's words were often some kind of a slur towards him—but this time, it was actually the truth. He knew he was none of those things and wanted to avoid being a rich power-hungry leech at all cost.

"There are certain people in the world who want to master syght. They want to be able to conquer it for their own good. Anyone who knows how beneficial someone with syght could be is too old now to learn it themselves. They need someone young. They need people like you—if you do in fact have it, that is. They could use you to conquer anything they wish. You aren't magical, but the power of choice and being able to decide the outcome is one of the most influential tools you can have. It could tip the balance of the 55. They all want something greater. At the moment, they are of equal worth. If one of them had someone who could control syght, then I would hate to imagine what might happen."

"I would deny I had it. There is no proof. I wouldn't say."

"Hang on, what if I have it too?" Rix said.

"You are a child of the future generation. With the amount of technology you have implanted in your body—as useful as it is—the AI biometric circuitry and microchips naturally slow down your reflexes and the time it takes to process your reactions. You would never be able to quicken your blink to anything beyond a microsecond, which is far too slow for syght. You have sacrificed one potential ability for the sake of living in the modern world."

"What???" Rix was frustrated again. She kicked at the mat. She only had the technology because of who her father was. For the first time, though, Gil could see how she was restricted by her privilege. Her reaction was an odd one, though. She had everything already. Why would she want syght too? Gil had nothing compared to Rix. If there was the chance that he might have something, then surely, he should explore it. He had not asked Rix once if she wanted to have syght, but her reaction answered that very question.

"Gil, the 55 are very persuasive. At first, they play nice and offer whatever you desire: unlimited credits, an unimaginable way of life that is all laid out for you to take. That's tempting enough, but it turns dirty very quickly. They take unkindly to being told no. They use torture. Not only on you, but your family, your friends." She looked at Rix. "They have the means to track them down and they will. They will kill without hesitation and all in secret. They can erase you and everyone you know. If you learn how to control it you can be better at masking it. You would then need training so if you are caught you know how to escape, fight, evade capture, as you did in the pit with me. It may have felt simple at the time and you were in the dark about it then. Imagine what you could do if you understood it."

Gil was undecided. Syght seemed a greater curse than it did a gift. He'd rather remain as the quiet, unknown kid from the country than become someone who was always looking over their shoulder

"I'm only two years away from losing it, so I could just hide? They wouldn't find me. They don't know who I am."

Hiding would be easy for Gil. He could stay in his little rundown apartment, out of sight of anyone, with only Terry and Rix aware of where he was. He would be bored. Two years of looking at the walls, having the same routine every day, not being able to change it in case he was caught. That did sound gruelling, counting down the days until he could step outside his front door again and feel relatively safe. But if he had training to hone in on a skill he potentially might have, he wouldn't have to hide. Having watched Freer's displays towards Rix, he was impressed. If that was the standard he could get to, no one would ever challenge him. He was a rare specimen. It would be a shame he if didn't explore the possibilities. His curiosity was beginning to outweigh his fear.

"It's too late for that. You already know you have it, so it will only grow. It will get stronger and you'll start seeing it more. And if we know you have it, then others will too."

She made a valid point.

The importance of syght still hadn't fully sunk in. If there were people who knew how valuable he could be, then it was better to know how to use syght than to leave it.

"Gil is big-time important now. I'm going to start getting jealous if everyone starts coming after you," Rix said, shoving him playfully.

"I'm not sure if using me to destroy the world and potentially killing me is a good thing to be jealous over."

"This is your choice though, Gil. We can only advise you and tell you how it might play out. We as Sense Shifters would like to train you in the ability of syght, to teach you how to control it and be able to use it—not for your own benefit, but to prevent others who may want to use it for harm. I would be your trainer and I will teach you all I know."

"Do I have to decide now?"

The offer was tempting—private tuition on something only a few hours ago he thought was a fairytale. It was a big decision to make, to give up everything to start working on it—not that he had much going on in his life other than learning from Terry. He was young. He could do both. Late nights and early mornings were no different to working at the pit. On the other hand, he was not that brave. He would prefer to stay out of trouble. This dangerous flair only came from being with Rix and he assumed this was something she could not be witness to.

"You can think on it. But remember, the longer you leave it, the more time you give others to learn of your skills. I have to state, though: this has to be done in secret. Your friend here will not be able to accompany you through your training."

"Gil, I'm going. Are you coming?" Rix was in a mood.

He knew it was easier to go along with her until she had calmed down. Gil knew that Freer's statement telling Rix she couldn't do something wouldn't land well with her. She had to be able to do anything.

He had heard everything he needed to know for now, and at least he could now relax somewhat, knowing that the people after him were Sense Shifters and nothing more. But now he knew there was a greater danger on the horizon.

"Any other questions, you can keep until the next time we meet—if we do meet again, that is."

"How do we get the fuck out of here?" Rix looked around the room.

"The same way as you entered. Head towards the hallway and Soro will meet you there. She pointed in the direction they had come.

"Fine." Rix stormed off, leaving Gil behind.

"Will it work on me?" Gil asked.

"What? Syght?" Freer answered.

"Yeah."

Syght was going to be a challenge to control. His fear was not grasping the concept of it and having the focus to be able to split these realities and control his choices. It was hard enough choosing chicken or spicy pork flavour for his noodles, let alone the complexities of syght. If it didn't work, then his life could be in danger. It was a lot to digest, especially when this information had been thrown at him so quickly.

Of course, he had to wonder if he, Gil Taberthorn, was capable of mastering syght, when he himself was no one he classed as special or outstanding.

"It's something only you know, something only you can feel, and if you allow yourself to accept it. Time will tell."

"GIL!" Rix shouted from the other side of the room.

"Think about what I said. For now, I know you must have questions, but save them for next time."

Gil nodded.

He followed Rix into the darkness of the room, a whole new world of thoughts bundling around in his mind.

TEN

A new dawn had risen in the city...

The High Chancellor of Axeon City was Vivalda Xing. A ruthless woman within the United faculty, she was stern, military in her methods and not one to cross. She had been known to take matters into her own hands on more than one occasion and the outcomes had not been pleasant. She set an example, no matter how extreme that might be. She'd once publicly slit the throat of one of her own aids for taking a piece of fruit from a vendor without paying and stating, 'it's for the High Chancellor'. Vivalda detested any sort of criminal activity, and as the people had crowded around Sal Rector's body as it lay in a pool of dirty rain water, she hoped it sent the right message, setting a precedent for what happened when you committed crime. You were caught. You were executed.

Vivalda did have alterative motives: she wanted

the top spot within the government, to be part of the board that governed all of the High Chancellors within the Supreme House of the Uniformed World. The board consisted of five members, all who had helped the United party become victorious in the 2040 elections and all still held their position. Vivalda disagreed with some of them. There needed to be an injection of a younger generation on the board, someone that understood what this era needed. She believed that was her. She wanted to prove that she deserved a place on this council when a place became available, whether that be due to natural causes or some divine intervention—not that she would break her own philosophies on crime and order. She knew how to push forward if she wanted her opinion heard, even if it took years, decades even.

Vivalda walked along a corridor within the United's complex building, flanked by the two aids that always accompanied her—security, note takers, handlers, whatever she wanted them to be. They always walked behind her and never within one metre of her personal space. She was on her way to the inter-global reality conference room, a place that allowed a secure virtual gathering of all the High Chancellors without them having to travel anywhere. The United government parties from around the world met quarterly to discuss matters and which steps they would take towards further progression. It was this board that had sanctioned the new act and supported all of the selected 55 to help enforce their plan within the world.

Every city had its own United party leader, known as the High Chancellor. Their job was to control the city under the new laws and support any of the 55. They had the final say in any matter within their own city and the right to overrule any decision they felt unfit to service their region. No matter who you were, if the High Chancellor disagreed, you would lose.

She marched through corridor after corridor. She stopped for no one, not that anyone would want to approach her. Every employee in the building shuddered when she passed their offices and she knew it. She could feel their fear. A dirty smile broke across her intense expression. From her flawless complexion to the straight slick alignment of every strand of hair, to the fine tailored corseted waistcoat, Vivalda was perfection. Her attitude was intimidating enough, but there wasn't a blemish on her… that you could see.

She stopped outside the surveillance room.

The room monitored every camera in the city, the only room in the building that always had personnel 24/7. Only the teams that were on rotation to work in the room were allowed in—and the High Chancellor, of course. Everything was recorded and kept. Nowhere within the city was unmonitored. With the sacrifice of privacy, crime had dropped dramatically. The street cameras, CCTV and drones were everywhere—even the vehicle roadside cameras monitored the dilation of the general public—capturing everyone's movements as they filed to work, or to the slaughter, as some would put it.

Vivalda always found a sense of peace when she was in this room. She loved that she had the ability to watch every person in the city with them having no idea that she was watching.

Through the glass soundproof wall, she noticed an odd image on one of the smaller monitors in the top far corner.

She positioned her eye in line with the retina scanner and placed her ring finger on the pad. The door buzzed and unlocked.

Each wall was covered with either a multitude of glass monitors or a series of mini projections of what each camera was focused on in the city. There were four sectors of Axeon City and the drone cameras could manoeuvre to any part they wished. There was a team of around twenty-five people who monitored different districts and a smaller sub-team that covered any footage taken though individual telecom cameras and holographic devices. It was impossible to monitor every device in the city—footage would only be flagged if triggered by certain words or images—but Vivalda had plans of expansion to make it possible.

She took a walk around the room. Every employee sunk into their chair as she passed, afraid of making a mistake. The noise of each footstep from her boots sounded like a metronome keeping the beat for the workers. Click, slide, scroll, zoom—the monotone actions of a terrified employee.

"Oh my, High Chancellor Xing. We welcome

you with great—"

"Enough!" She stopped the traditional welcome that most felt obliged to give every time she entered the room. There were days she wanted the flattery, but she could not be bothered to hear the dribble today.

"Would you like to know the—"

"No." She stopped the manager once again. "What is happening on this screen?" She pointed up to where she could see the anomaly.

"It's the pit," one employee said flippantly. Vivalda was not impressed.

"I can see that." She turned to the manager. "Get him out of here, now!"

The manager froze. Vivalda held her fierce stare until they had completed the task.

"What did I say?" The employee was ushered out of the door by the manager—shoved rather than of his own accord.

"Now, tell me why this image looks wrong to you," she said, waiting for an answer. It had to be the correct one.

"It's the pit. We don't monitor it fully as it's on the outskirts. Nobody goes out there. It's only the workers—"

The manager was flapping.

"My concern isn't what we are meant to be doing or not doing. We do monitor every camera in this city. That is your job to do so. My problem is why is it displaying a night-time image when it's ten o'clock in the morning? Where are the damn workers and why can I not see them?! Look at every other image; there is sunlight!"

The manager slowly looked up at the monitor.

She had an eye, which allowed her to catch the smallest of details and this was one of them.

The manager scurried over to a workstation, which she knew was the main control hub to all the monitors. He pressed a few buttons and brought up the image on a projection.

The pit was still in darkness. Still. Quiet. Lying in the shadows of the city.

"It looks as though it is caught on a loop," they said hesitantly.

"So? Fix it! We should not be having problems like this."

All she needed was for her plan to go ahead, what she had been working on so she wouldn't have to rely on imbeciles like this.

The manager said no other words and turned back to the hub. The screen cut off and returned with a brighter, busier scene on it: the pit in daylight, alive with workers.

"Find out what the problem was and do not let me see this again!"

She exited the room in a worse mood than when she had entered and continued on along the corridor to her meeting.

When she entered the inter-global reality conference room, both of her aids stood outside and guarded the door. Not a single word was exchanged between any one of them. It was understood what was going to happen.

Inside, the room was set out as a chamber of commerce, with three walls of banked seating and a higher platform with a table against the fourth. Every part of the room was a shade of navy blue to help the projections display the template of the other members who were joining.

Vivalda took a seat and removed a black rectangular box from her pocket. She lifted the lid and took out Syngetical's Displacement Lens, an upgrade to the virtual reality goggles. She put them on as one would normal glasses and tightened the arms.

She then took the four circular disks from the box and placed one on each foot and each hand. They were secured by a magnetic charge from the disk and the four nanodarts that lived under her skin. Nanodarts had been invented to help clean the blood and kill any viruses that the white blood cells struggled to defend against. You had to have all four nanodarts and they were expensive, as were all healthcare fees—these especially. Government officials were given them automatically, free of charge—it would set a bad image if the people running the planet became sick and died; society needed leaders to help it progress. The nanodarts could also operate with the projectors and imagery scanners to portray a more realistic digital image of a person, which came in useful in these meetings. Using this technology, you could feel pain, variations in temperature and interact fully with others, whether that be a handshake, a punch and if one was daring to try, sexual interactions.

She double tapped the disk on her right hand, joining the conference. The projectors illuminated and transformed the plain royal blue setting into a busy commerce room full of all the High Chancellors from around the world. She cared not for the other High Chancellors, so she sat in the top tier seating. She liked to take in her surroundings, be above them all, just as she thought she was. She noticed that most of them were creatures of habit and sat in the same place every meeting. The closer they thought they were to the front, the higher chance that they'd have a say or their questions answered. They were wrong. The Supreme House rarely ran a Q and A section of the meeting. They spoke; you listened. As a generic High Chancellor, you had no say in this room. It would only go against you if you tried. As such, Vivalda knew her attack had to be from a different angle, a one-on-on conversation, an 'I'll do a favour for you if you do one for me' scenario. It was not a crime—depending on what the favour was.

"Order!" Giles Faverton III shouted. He was one of the five original board members, one that Vivalda wanted to see gone so she could take his place. He frustrated her: he served no real purpose other than speaker to the floor and he was taking up a seat—her seat. She had plans, ideas to accelerate this Supreme House forward.

"High Chancellor meeting now in session, with the full board of the Supreme House of the

Uniformed World…"

Vivalda felt accustomed to the way the Supreme House worked. The five board members were all equal in ranking. No one made the final decision; it was a collective vote. The old generation deliberated for too long. This way was much better: it either passed or about the matter was passed. She knew that if she had had power then, more would have been achieved. If it was wrong, then you can revalue it, make another decision on it—not that she would need four other members; she could run this world herself. A thought that brought a small smirk to her face—she could dream.

"…for all those in session please state 'I'."

A resounding 'I' was said aloud by all the attending High Chancellors. A counter above the Supreme House table rallied through the numbers until it hit 437. Three High Chancellors were absent.

The table deliberated for a moment and then readdressed the room.

"We have a slightly different order of proceedings for out meeting today. We will not be updating you with the improvement statistics for crime, air quality, ozone layer or revenue, or any amendments to the Uniformed Act, which there are a few," Giles Faverton III said.

Vivalda's ears pricked up. This was against the usual standings. Axeon City always rated highly under her reign and she wanted all to know about that.

The most senior of them all, Lady Evelyn Dodd, continued, speaking in a frail voice. "The first point we must mention is an update from Anders Hilgaard about syght. We have been told that Anders and his team at Syngetical have made a breakthrough in finding a cure, having narrowed down the age bracket for those in which this fatal disease can occur and found the abnormalities within the DNA that cause it."

Vivalda sighed at the name. This was not a conversation she wanted to listen to. She did not care what Anders was doing, locked up in his laboratory. She avoided him enough as it was, and they both lived in the same city. He already had all the attention on him. Why did the Supreme House need to waste more breath talking about him? She wasn't jealous of his successes. She had her own. She already had more power than he did and influence. She wasn't liked by many, but she preferred it that way. She didn't seek fame—some fortune, yes, but not to the level Anders had risen to. She wanted respect from him that she didn't have, for him to understand that it was her city and her rules, that he needed to know his actions have consequences that affected her work, her successes, her wellbeing.

A bearded man who went by the name of Sawyer J Linefold then spoke. "To add, he would also like to thank us for allowing him exclusive access to the government's database to help him with his research. Not everyone here may think he is with the United party, and some may even think he is against our Uniformed Act, but in this case, he is finding a cure for a disease that may affect us in one way or another. His actions in other sectors will be under scrutiny at a later date."

A cheer came from the room. Vivalda clapped sarcastically. She knew Anders was untouchable, however much she wanted to see his work and business under scrutiny. The government was weak in taking action upon those who were self-sufficient, especially when the public favoured them. The government wanted the control; they wanted the power. They had shut down the 'syght' myth decades ago as they didn't want people thinking they could control when they died. Of course, the government couldn't control this either, but they wanted to make sure they could control how a person led their life before their eventual death. Anders was committing no crimes. All he was doing was helping the nation. He was an outsider to the 55, so he lacked government support or backing. But the government's problem with him, with Syngetical, was that he didn't need the government. Everything he had created or set up was off his own back. The government had targets they wanted to achieve by the year 2105 and Anders was preventing that, one of which was to manage the population so they were able to maintain the planet they lived on. The population had dropped significantly since 2045 already, but the government had targets to cull human life further. But with Anders' technology and his affordable food store chain, which had squashed out any competition, he had plateaued the numbers, not to mention the water supply he controlled, managed and kept free for every city in the world.

There was no crime for helping the poorer classes, yet.

Professor Polyanna Raymond-Hall, the youngest of the aging line up, coughed before she spoke.

"We must move on to our next topic as it is rather an urgent matter and one that requires discretion amongst the High Chancellors."

The room fell silent, a rare occurrence in the inter-global reality conference.

"It has come to our attention that the beloved 55 that we have made partnership with for all these years, who have helped shape earth into what it is today, are pulling away from us. We have given them this opportunity to excel in areas that most of them would never had had a hand in otherwise, to savour their businesses and invest in the technology field that we as a society wanted and needed to progress in."

This was common knowledge to Vivalda. She was wise to how the 55 worked and had seen this coming a long time ago. If she was in charge, she wouldn't have allowed it and would currently be controlling the issue within Axeon City. That is how she saw herself being a leader: control those who think they are above you, even when they have no power at all. She would not allow corruption to be above the rules.

The central figure at the table, a white-haired man who was known only by Aydar, stood gingerly and picked up where the professor left off.

"Over the last few years especially, we have seen a surge in the 55's revenue. We all knew they were selfish, out for their own and focused only on themselves and their close ones around them. Their greed has always been great. This is why we partnered with them. We needed their money to help our vision progress. We gave them the opportunity they wanted. But what happens when the 55 have everything they could possibly require or obtain? They go for more."

Vivalda had two of the 55 in her city and she knew what they were like. They did their own business. It was almost as if they had their own law. It infuriated her that they classed themselves as above her. If she tried to impose anything directly towards them, she knew there would be consequences. She had to play the game cleverly.

"The annual 55 gala is coming up in a couple of weeks. As you know, normally, United party officials are not invited. No government body is not allowed to attend. There is speculation of an auction, and if rumours are to be believed, this year it is going to be the most gifted prize of them all. We want to know what that auction is."

"Oh, please. We all know it's a lavish over-the-top event to show off who has the biggest ego," said one of the High Chancellors, a well-spoken, distinguished fellow named Hirst. "And we all know that each is as small as the other." He made a gesture with his little finger. There was a murmured laugh.

"High Chancellor Renolt of Eastern America,

Washington City here." Another piped up, a man named Renolt, who had a thick American accent. "How do you propose we do this without getting caught?"

"They probably started the rumours themselves to get all the 55 to attend," another High Chancellor said.

Vivalda was surprised at the Supreme House for not ceasing the conversation from the floor. They must be rattled.

"If you poke a stick at the wasp's nest, then you are going to get stung." High Chancellor Jarhab King spoke out from the first row.

"We united everyone together so that situations like this would not occur anymore," the professor responded, silencing the room once more. "The world had to be on the same page. If it refused to, then humanity would have corrupted itself. There had to be order, control and also improvements, which we have held together for the past forty-two years. If we allow such auctions like this to happen behind closed doors, then what's stopping the 55 revolting against the Uniformed Act and resorting back to the old generation's way of life? We know, we saw, we lived that life and it failed to work properly: too many opinions and not enough decision making and it affected everyone."

"Are you proposing we send one of our own into the lion's den?" High Chancellor Otawengu asked. The image of her flickered as she spoke.

"This year's gala is taking place in Axeon City,

but I'm afraid High Chancellor Vivalda Xing is out of the question…"

Vivalda held her composure. Before even given the opportunity to do something, it was snatched away—not that she wanted to be the Supreme House's dogsbody, snitching on the 55 and end up having to deal with it. It was the straight dismissal of her abilities to do her job that annoyed her. But confronting them was not worth her energy. She had her connections with the 55, a secret to the government. If she needed to, she would get into that room.

"…we propose two High Chancellors from cities that have no residence of any of the 55. The smaller and lesser-known cities would be more ideal, as the members would not recognise them. Please raise your hand if you are one of those cities."

Giles' question caused most of the room to raise their hand. After all, there were 440 cities and only 55 of them.

She was not even asked if this would be acceptable. Axeon was her city. To have another two High Chancellors come in and do the bidding of the government, under her reign, was outrageous. She clenched her jaw. She could not give in to the temptation of abusive language or aggressive behaviour towards fellow government officials. She wanted no red flags against her name. But whatever the outcome, those two High Chancellors were not stepping foot in her city.

"And of those who would like to take on this

task, please keep your hands raised. Not only will this go on your record as an outstanding contribution to the Supreme House, you will also be rewarded handsomely for your efforts."

Vivalda's fist tightened. Of everything she had done with Axeon City, it would be a spying mission that rewarded her with the credit she needed and wanted. With her hands crossed over her lap, she dug her nail into the back of her hand, trying to suppress her rage. The force punctured the skin and drew blood. A blob of red liquid rose to the surface and trickled along the back of her hand. She wiped it away with a concealed handkerchief she kept hidden in her corset. This was a task that would get her into hot water with the 55, but it was nothing she couldn't handle, though. She didn't want to take on the task anyway. It was below her, mere playground antics. She had no time to be spying on the 55. She already knew what her two were up to. At the same time, that offer would go on her record, the very thing she needed for her career to progress, to establish her name amongst the Supreme House. It was a difficult decision to make. It wouldn't be so much a career suicide move, but more a 'to be confirmed' risk.

"So, who would like to volunteer?" Giles asked.

Every hand in the room shot down. The High Chancellors knew how the 55 worked, especially the ones who had any of the 55 in their cities. They did their own thing as long as they lived by the rules—or were at least seen by the public to be abiding. The control had to lie with the High Chancellor or there would be uproar amongst the citizens. Being a spy would only start a war against them.

"This is corruption against our very own! Regardless of what we think they are doing, if we stepped one foot into that gala, it would create chaos amongst the most powerful people on this planet," Renolt said.

"He's right," Towei said. "They helped us create the new generation. They could quite easily take it all away. We control how the 55 work. Even if they think we have no say in the matter, we do. The Uniformed Act works because we have the funds to be able to make it work. We give one of the 55 another investment opportunity, we get the control of how our society is run and what we sanction. Without us at the helm, the 55 would end up playing a battle of last human standing. Yes, we control them, but we cannot do this. It would break the relationship we have already. We have to work in harmony even if, at times, there are things we don't agree with fully. This is one of those times."

"High Chancellor Towei is right," said Watersmead, who was a neighbouring High Chancellor to him, and as such, they always supported one another.

"Do we have to send one of our own? If it's being held in Axeon City, why not send Anders Hilgaard?" Hirst proposed.

"He's not one of the 55. He would be in the same situation as we would be." Aydar sat down in his chair.

Sending two High Chancellors to her city was an insult but suggesting Anders to be the mole was an utter disgrace. There was no chance that she would let Anders receive the praise or worm his way out of the punishments already coming to him. If she had to take care of this, she would. She wanted no involvement with Anders and that was a policy she stood by. There would be a time for redemption with him, but that was not now. She had to be the sacrificial lamb.

"High Chancellor Xing—" Lady Evelyn Dodd started, looking at Vivalda.

But Vivalda already knew what was coming.

"I will sort this myself."

How, she did not know—she had not come up with her plan yet—but asking Anders was a straw she was not willing to pull. She stood and removed her Displacement Lens, leaving the members of the Supreme House in bewilderment as to what she would do next. She had no plan as of yet, but either way, they did not need to know how she got her work done. She wanted that gold star against her name, and if she had to jump through hoops, then so be it.

She let out a scream in the empty inter-global reality conference room, a deep, piercing cry of rage, the type that made every muscle rigid, your vision blurry and gave you the urge to want to break something, destroy it of all its meaning and purpose. There were only a few things that triggered this response in her and this was one of them: doing the

Supreme House's dirty work and for something that felt like bribery. She would have her day; it may not be now, but she was seeding her future, which had already begun.

She threw the disks and the Displacement Lens across the room and stood in the middle of the chambers, taking heavy breaths, her fists clenched.

She exploded out of the doors, hitting both aids as she stormed through, the hurricane that was building up inside of her leaving a trail of destruction through the corridor as she made her way back to her office.

"Atalon Keel does not pay me enough for this," she muttered under her breath.

ELEVEN

It was an awkward walk from the room where Cyra had unknowingly accosted Anders Hilgaard. If she had thought about her actions before bursting in and unleashing all of her pent-up anger towards the owner of Syngetical, then she wouldn't have been making her way to an office so she could give him her opinion on something. At least the silver lining was that this finally established her as a scientist, someone who knew what they were talking about. Anders had trusted her because she had stood up for herself. It was an unorthodox move, but she was proud she had made it. It was more the embarrassment that it was her boss's boss's boss that she felt ashamed of.

"Can I say again, I'm so sorry for accusing you and your company that your work is not fulfilling enough." She cowered away as she said it.

"Everyone has feelings and you are entitled to

your opinion," Anders replied.

It was a nicer way of saying, 'you are wrong, don't you dare question me again.'

"But you are right, Ms Wolverton…" Cyra was stunned at his admission. As they ascended the lift that was sending them skywards, he brought up a virtual display with data about Cyra's previous work. "… as qualified as I can see you are, it is frustrating when you are doing work that you feel is below you, and we apologise for suppressing those skills. From your previous history of employers, I can see why they put you in at data analysis level."

"Well, it's difficult to get great jobs when you don't have the money behind you to do so."

"I managed it." The starts of a smile crept in on the left side of his mouth.

"Not to sound rude, but times were different then, Mr Hilgaard. Now is a bit more cut-throat."

Cyra had worked hard to get to where she had already got to with her career and life. She was still young, not in her thirties yet, and no company was going to take her seriously, despite how better qualified she was than most twice her age. She needed someone to give her a chance. Though, she had to be careful not to talk back too much. She was wary of coming across as not appreciative of the opportunity.

The lift continued up. She had never been to any of these levels in the building before.

"I'm taking you to my own personal workshop, which is next to my office. I'm working on something new, technology made for our future, which the majority of people, if not all, have never seen before, let alone tried to comprehend."

"I'm more a theoretical scientist rather than someone who works on actual hardware tech. You sure you need someone with my skill set?"

"You might be surprised," he said with a smile.

She noticed there was a tone to his voice, like a proud father, a reassurance that she could do this job. She felt honoured.

The lift arrived at level 186. The doors opened onto a view of Axeon City. It was breathtakingly high. Cyra was cautious of walking out of the lift. The glass panel floor-to-ceiling view was incredible. The city was relatively flat, so the view continued on past the city and into the surrounding forests.

The sun was on its descent on the horizon. Its warming glow only highlighted the feeling that she was walking on the clouds. Her legs were ready to buckle from underneath her.

"Too much to take in?" Anders asked.

She mouthed words that had no volume to them.

Anders went over to a small panel and pressed two buttons. The walls and ceiling instantly clouded over and returned back to the same office walls she was used to on the floor she worked on.

"More to your usual setting?"

She nodded. She was taken aback at how easy it was to transform the aesthetics of the entire floor.

"Most floors have this feature installed, but due to the nature of what we are working on, for security reasons, we can't allow every floor to have a view."

"I think I feel better for it," Cyra responded. The light-headedness now fading.

She followed him out of the lift and down to a 'T' junction where they turned right towards a room at the end of the short corridor. She thought about how few people must have been up here. Those who had walked along these corridors and been shown the secrets to Anders' enterprise she could count on one hand, no doubt. She was bursting with sheer excitement, as well as the relief that someone also now believed in her.

"This is my workshop and the other end is my office."

She looked over her shoulder and saw a replica door of the one they were heading to at the other end.

Lined up on the wall next to the door were four panels. The first was a retinal scan. A green light illuminated after Anders looked in its direction and opened his eye wide. The second panel opened up and a thin metal stick protruded with what looked like a piece of cloth on the end. Anders leaned forward and placed his mouth over it. There was a short whirring sound and then another green light.

"Mouth swab—the only one in the building." He answered the question Cyra had in her head.

The next one was for Anders' handprint. He placed his right hand on the panel. It scanned and a third green light shone.

'DING'

He opened up his hand where he had a Holo Palm chip installed. This was the first time Cyra had seen anyone with this new chip and she was quite impressed by it. On his palm, a six-figure number now displayed.

Anders entered the number into the keypad and the final green light switched on and the door unlocked.

"You have to do that every time you enter this room?"

"It is the most secure room in the building. If any of the stages are failed, I am alerted immediately and provided with the DNA record from the person who tried to access the room. No matter who it is in the world, I will know their name, age, blood type, employment history and if they work for the company or not. Then I have the option to allow them in or to lock down the floor. But, no is the answer to your original question—do I need to do that every time… Once the system knows I am on this floor, both my office and the workshop are unlocked and the lift is then shut down to anyone coming up. The number is simply removed from the lift panel. 186 is an invisible floor."

"You must be working on something quite important to require all that."

"Let me show you."

He pushed the white double door open.

It was as though she was walking into a museum of advanced technologies. There were shelves that covered every wall, displaying all the variations of lenses that Syngetical had ever produced. The lower shelves contained volumes of books that she could only assume contained details on circuitry, microbiology and experimental cases where technology was infused with humans.

They walked down a central concourse. On either side, Cyra was met with an array of desktops with tools and instruments she recognised, though there were some hardware components that were alien to her. She noticed a spherical ball that contained what looked like a thunderstorm hovering above a small chrome square. On another table there was what looked like a Holo Vortex device. The picture it was displaying was full colour and looked as though the person was real—a fully 3D image on a loop pattern. The difference was the figure was able to step off the device and pick up physical objects in the room and move them around. There was also a stand full of a variety of wires hanging from hooks. One wire looked as though its metabolic state was that of a ghost, with the electrical current visible. Sporadic darts of yellow static shot up and down within the ghost casing.

It was at the final table at the end where Anders stopped.

"This is what I wanted your opinion on."

Cyra had a thousand questions about the rest of the technology in the room. She knew that Syngetical was one of the leaders in advanced technology, but what she saw in this room surpassed all of that. This all looked as though it was from another planet. It was all too advanced for this generation, Anders' side projects to keep the world moving forward. And she was the one who would get to see them all before anyone else.

He pointed to a translucent stand in the middle of the table. Two lenses were side-by-side, orange in colour. Next to that was the skeleton frame, which the lenses would fit in to. It was a glasses frame, minus the lens, with four circular disks attached to the top and side. The discs were on pivots to cover the lens when they were in place.

"I'm not sure what I am looking at," she said as she stepped forward to inspect.

"It's an ID Lens. The prototype version. Over the last five years, I have personally been working on this project in my spare time—time, which I can assure you, is limited. I've been through many tests with it and I can't quite get it to perform to its full capabilities. There are glimpses of it working, as though it has a loose connection. Something is missing and I'm not sure what it is. I want to see if you might know what that missing link is."

"What's it meant to do?"

"I'm not sure I can tell you that."

"Then, how am I going to be able to fix it if I don't know what it's meant to do? It's the Deja Vu gene all over again, Mr Hilgaard. I can't keep working on different projects if there is information I'm not meant to know or if the outcome is an impossible one to find. I think it would be easier if I left."

She was annoyed that she had been lured in to

what felt like an opportunity, only to be misguided, again. It was the same thing on a different scale. She wanted to lift the veil to see the true nature underneath. Still, no one was going to give her that information.

She headed towards the double doors, her mind full of realizations on what she should be doing. It was time she left Syngetical. She had to stop hopping from one sector to another, only to realise that each time it was always the same pointless work.

"Can I trust you?" Anders called out.

She stopped.

"Can I trust you?" he said again.

Cyra couldn't quite believe that she had the guts to reply the way she did, but her answer was full of honesty.

"Me being able to do my work, what I have spent my life trying to achieve, has nothing to do with trust. How can you trust me with something when you hide from me what it is? And you don't give me any reasons as to why I shouldn't be telling anyone?" Anders' eyebrow rose. Cyra wanted to progress. She wanted her dedication to her work taken seriously. "I have worked here for two years with mountains of sensitive data and never spoken to anyone about it. Why would I start doing that now when a potential new opportunity is being dangled in front of me? You should give your colleagues more respect. I'm not a child promising to not eat the candy in front of her, only to steal it in plain sight when nobody is looking, so don't treat me as one."

There was a silence between the two. Cyra stood her ground. She wasn't going to be made inferior because of her beliefs.

"I think I should have hired you myself," Anders said. He looked taken aback by what Cyra had said, but impressed too, proud even, that she had the guts to do it. "Not many of my employees stand up to me like that. Trust me when I say this is a project that will change the way you know reality. I'll get you an NDWK set up."

"What's that?"

She favoured this new 'stand up for herself' attitude. It seemed to be getting her places, quickly. She was, however, used to a trial period and a review, but this was a straight offer for the job. She was curious to know what exactly this lens was capable of. If it was that advanced, what could it possibly do? Her answer would be yes obviously—she would be stupid to say no, especially after the last few years. She would be a hypocrite to herself.

"Something we issue to all employees who are exposed to highly sensitive information. It's a non-disclosure will-kill form. I don't think I need to explain what that means, but in case you don't understand it: if you disclose information outside of this building or even to someone inside, other than the people stated in your contract, you will be killed. Hopefully, it will show you how serious I am in using your skills and giving you what you need to know."

Wide-eyed, Cyra nodded in agreement.

She thought back over what he had said. 'You

will be killed.' Was that legal? The phrase continued to plague her, on loop in her head. The slightest mutter of anything she would be doing in this room and that was it. The end of her life. It was shocking to hear. It sounded more like a threat than a clause in her contract. Did she want to sign it if it could result in that? Regardless of how much she wanted to excel, was it worth it? She wondered how Anders would even know. What if she was set up and information was leaked that wasn't her fault? It had to be a bluff. No contract was allowed to actually use those words. Her degree was in science, not law, but what she did know—what most did—were the basics. This had to be for show only, to scare. It was not something they would actually administer.

"Here, take a look at the summary of an agreement."

Anders slid his finger over one of the glass screens and loaded a document.

The finer details of her contract stated: 'discussions with other employees about anything that appears in the 'workshop' is prohibited. Mr Anders Hilgaard is your point of call and will be the only recipient of any discoveries or information shared. No other employee, no matter whom it may be in the company, is to be spoken to about anything. Breach of contract will result in termination of employment and of life, effective immediately.'

Anders was serious. The terms were strict about who she was allowed to speak to and about what. When she read it, the termination of life stood out prominently. She had never read that in a contract before. What Cyra was working on was far more secretive than she had imagined, especially if death was the solution to breaking the rules.

She felt a rush of adrenaline that was shortly followed by fear. The responsibility of gaining an opportunity to work on a unique lens that could change the world, again, was a thrilling idea. Being able to say she had been part of the process would set her up for life, but with it came the underlying threat that if she slipped up, she would be killed. No questions asked, no trial, no trace of her existence. The saying 'the greater the risk, the greater the reward' was evidently true.

"Take a look at the prototype and get yourself used to the mechanics of it all. It will take you some time to understand the internal workings of how a Syngetical product works. I would probably estimate about a month, with homework, depending on your ability to learn and memorise large amounts of information. The books over there—" he pointed along the wall that had the shelving unit "—will give you a complete breakdown of the Spacial lens and its workings. This notebook here—" he picked up a brown leather journal from the desk "—contains my notes on the construction and testing of this ID Lens. Closer to us on the bottom shelf—" he pointed to the set of shelves next to his desk "—books on circuitry, wiring, soldering, chips, biometric chips, power sources... All the basics that you would need to know. That shouldn't take you long to read through—a week or so? Then the books behind me list all the new inventions laid out in this room: what they are, how they work and how they were put together. These volumes will probably be of no use to you as they are unrelated to this new ID lens, but you never know. This should be enough to get you started. Any questions—" he pulled out a small rectangular glass screen and swiped a few times "—note it down here."

A display opened up and hovered above the wall to Cyra's right.

"All you need to do is say the word 'note' and then say what you want to bullet point and it will type it up. Say 'end' when you want it to stop noting down what you say."

On the display, the device had recorded Anders saying, 'and then say what you want to bullet point…'

"If you sign the NDWK, then I'll set up the system so you can also enter this room without me present. Not my office—this room only."

He had thrown a lot of information at her: books, volumes, notes, tech, the criminal action of murdering someone… She felt flustered, but she needed to keep her composure. After acting so strongly, she could show no signs of weakness. She swallowed, and then, allowing her larynx to drop back to its normal position, so her response would be of normal pitch, she said, "Errr, thank you. Yes, it's plenty to get started with."

Thoughts were racing around her mind,

accompanied by the small and growing palpitations of the heart, the flutters of breath. Keep. Under. Control. Her inner voice kept projecting loudly in her head.

This is what she wanted, though. Maybe it was the extreme version of what she wanted, but she couldn't go back now, not with all these questions that would never be answered, even about what she could see in this room. She paused. What if it was too late to go back anyway? Anders mentioned this contract, but she would probably be forced to sign it either way. She had already seen this room, opened the door to the place that no one knew about. This wasn't an 'if' you sign the contract, it was a matter of when. She was too afraid of the potential consequences. There was no way she would reveal a single word. This never happened.

"I would advise reading the NDWK document thoroughly. It's not one you would want to gloss over. And if you decide not to continue with this, then you still have your job searching for the Deja Vu gene."

"Will anyone ever explain to me why we were searching for that?"

"In time," he said.

"Can I at least understand what this lens does and why I am appropriate for it?"

Anders sighed, an intent look in his eyes.

"The ID Lens stands for Inter-Dimensional lens. The function is that the user is able to travel through space without having to board a vessel to do so."

"But you will need propulsion of some sort to be able to travel through space." Cyra was voicing her thoughts aloud, rather than speaking to Anders directly.

"Unless you are thinking of time travel, which would allow you to travel through space if the geometries of spacetime or specific types of motion were suitable, but that would be millions of scenarios you would need to play out. Then you wouldn't be in the same era of time as you started… Or are you suggesting somehow a leap through space, keeping time as the linear constant where this world and wherever you end up are on the same time frame and have moved at an equal rate?"

"That's why you are here: to work that out. This is your expertise."

He looked down at his palm where a yellow light was pulsing.

"Excuse me," he said and pressed a button on his forearm display. "Yes?"

A hologram rose from his palm and said, "Sir, Vivalda Xing is here to see you…"

"What? Now? I have no appointment scheduled to see her."

"No sir you do not, but—"

"Tell her I am busy and will schedule one for a week from now."

"I would do, sir, however—"

"No 'however'. She can't show up and demand to see me whenever she feels like it."

Anders ended the call. His expression looked

annoyed.

"Excuse me for a moment; there is a matter I have to deal with. Take this time to get yourself settled with the equipment. I'll be back shortly."

Cyra stood awkwardly as he stormed out of the workshop, closing both doors behind him. A 'buzz' suggested that Cyra was now locked in.

She sat in the chair and looked at the ID Lens. She wanted to pick it up to try it on.

The ability to travel through space without having to go anywhere—the idea wasn't possible. With her degree, her learning, her years studying, she knew there was no way of doing this. If that was what this lens was meant to do, could she make it work? It was incomprehensible. She almost wanted to laugh. But Anders thought it was achievable. He had already spent years on it. The time, sweat, frustrations and failures he must have endured to get to this stage was impressive. She admired him for coming up with the concept and trying to put it into reality. Now it was her turn to continue what he had started. She felt the excitement of notion of achieving an impossibility.

She placed both individual lenses into the frame delicately. It was a high-tech pair of glasses with many additions. Wary of picking them up, she left them on the stand they were perched on. She didn't understand what she was messing with yet, but she would, with time.

From where she sat in the chair, she leant down and peered through them.

All she could see was the floor and part of the other desktop. There wasn't anything special about it. Why would there be, when Anders had mentioned that he was unable to make it function? Without all the details, she was clueless on what she was meant to be seeing.

She removed the frames from the stand and placed them on her face. They were lighter than she expected them to be. They were less fragile than they looked and quite sturdy. She looked all over the room and there was no difference to how the lenses made the world looked. She stood up and walked around.

The framework was thicker than a normal pair of glasses, restricting part of her peripheral vision. Because of this, she caught her toe on the leg of one of the desks and she stumbled forward. As she moved to catch herself, the circular lenses shifted in and out of view at a rapid rate, covering one eye and then the other from different angles. Her vision became blurry and the room began to vibrate, as though the natural vibrations from her body extended to the rest of the space. Her vision became split; there was now two of everything. She was dizzy.

Once she had stabilised herself, the view returned back to normal. She took off the frames. They had made her feel sick. The fuzziness of seeing double—her brain couldn't keep up. It was as though she had spun around countless times.

Before subjecting herself again to that, she had

to know and understand how these lenses worked and what this view they were trying to create was. If that was the feeling every time, then she was going to need a bucket. She had no assistant, so she was going to have to willingly volunteer as test subject, something she now was not so keen on being. She was used to theory rather than the practical. She was intrigued, though. This was the challenge she need.

"Note: ask Anders what the lenses are specifically meant to do. End."

She took the frames back to the stand and left them there.

She was feeling an excitement that she had not felt since her studies. This was an exploration into the unknown. If it did involve some explanation to space and everything that was suspended in it, then this was beyond any theory she had been taught and more advanced than any practical.

But, as Anders had said, 'it only doesn't exist until you find it.'

She went over to the shelves and picked up the first book in the Spacial Lens volumes. She cleared enough space on a desktop and opened up the pages.

'Spacial Lens mechanics and logistical ideas', the top of the page read.

She knew she wasn't going to want to leave any time soon.

TWELVE

Anders walked along the corridor between his workshop and his office, his head lowered. He scrolled through the calendar to see when the meeting with Vivalda had been scheduled for so he could cancel it, but was interrupted by a voice.

"I make meetings when I need them, Mr Hilgaard," said Vivalda from where she stood halfway down the corridor. "I'm the High Chancellor. I'll see you when I need to."

He stopped and looked up with a blank expression.

"Amused to see me as much I am you, I see," she added.

"Why are you here Vivalda?" he asked bluntly. The two stood in the corridor between his workshop and his office.

"I knew you would cancel my meeting so I thought I would do it in person. I want to discuss with you the security behind your new VX lens and how it could be of use to the government. I want to schedule a meeting for tomorrow."

"I'm not here at weekends and my technology is not for sale. Now, if you please, I am a busy man."

He carried on walking towards his office. As he passed her, he could smell the sweet vanilla perfume she wore, the one with the gold embossed lid.

"The Supreme House wants to bring down your company. They believe you are fighting against the Uniformed Act and taking the law into your own hands. People respect you more than their own government. I come here with a warning."

"And why would you do that?"

"I have a way of dealing with it. But I want something in return."

Anders was not one for negotiating with government officials. He was surprised Vivalda wanted to go this route. Off the book dealings often received backlash, and this was something he wanted to avoid.

"What is that exactly?" He looked up from his display.

"I have stated what I require, Mr Hilgaard. It would be wise you grant it to me."

"And why would I trust in what you say, again. It hasn't really proved beneficial to me before, has it?"

He knew she was out for herself—she always had been, and sometimes at the expense of others. She cared not about who she hurt—or that's the way it came across to him.

"As you know too well, if there is something I need, then I will find a way of obtaining it. In this case, a meeting with you tomorrow to discuss how your VX lens could benefit me is all I require. In exchange, I keep the Supreme House on your side."

Anders thought about the offer.

He was not going to take it, but he needed her gone. He had other matters to attend to. She would know that his words meant more than his actions, and knowing her as he did, he could play her at her own game. Revenge was weak. Sometimes, though, it was the last card in the deck to play.

"Fine. When?"

"Two o'clock. Here, your office, away from prying ears."

"I knew I should have limited your access to this floor."

"It was in the contract." Vivalda smiled.

An alert popped up on his forearm. Someone had pressed the back-up sequence to gain access to the same floor he, Vivalda and Cyra were on.

"I have to deal with something. You have to go."

"Of course, you do. Make sure you are here tomorrow."

He headed back towards the lift, with Vivalda strolling behind.

"Goodbye Mr Hilgaard. I'm looking forward to our meeting."

The lift arrived and the doors opened to reveal Rix.

Vivalda was taken back, physically. She took a

short inhale of breath and held it. Anders had no pity for how Vivalda would be feeling. He ushered Rix out of the lift and towards his office.

"Goodbye Vivalda," he said over his shoulder.

They turned the corner.

"You know not to bother me at work, Rix."

"It's Gil," she said, her face full of delight. "He has syght, Dad!"

Anders stopped, frozen to the spot.

"How certain are you?" he asked.

"I've seen him use it! We met the Sense Shifters, the masters of syght. They exist. They know he has it too."

Adrenaline began to fill his body, the sense of achievement. A new chapter was turning for him; a long-awaited hardship had fallen into his hands.

"Then, I think it's about time we offered Gil a job. I could do with another set of eyes on a particular creation I have been working on."

'DING'

The lift doors finally indicated they were closed.

THIRTEEN

Gil was lying down on the faded brown sofa in his living area, throwing a split tennis ball up into the air that he had fixed using old rubber bands he had found on salvaging trips.

It had been a couple of days since his encounter with the Sense Shifters and he was unsure what to think of it all. The questions remained in his head: why was it him that had this ability? Why would he want to have it? He had no plans or dreams to save the world, not on his own. This was to be a life of secrecy. He was a regular young lad, as normal as you could get compared to most others his age. His salvager friends were not too dissimilar to himself and then there was Rix—well, she was a totally different specimen. She had the wealth of her father behind her and all the tech implants one could physically house in their body, but hated having them. She acted like a rebel, in the loosest sense, and at times, when she wanted to 'let go' and be dangerous, she would go bat shit crazy. It should have been Rix who had this ability. It suited her more. She would have the drive to want to do something with it.

Gil trusted Rix—he knew her well—but if she had had this ability, he knew he would end up in dangerous scenarios more often—something that he was happy to keep to a minimum. He still had the scab on his head from the crash in the Mustang. He kept weighing up the pros and cons, the huge consequence of the fact that people, who he had never met or would never have heard of, were hunting him down. It sounded like he was the only one who had syght, which also worried him. He knew about the 55. If they didn't have something, they wanted it. That was a world he would rather stay away from, especially after what Freer had told him. But his mind kept drawing him back to the curiosity of syght. Part of him did want to explore what he could do with it, what it could show him. Not many could say they had seen what syght could do.

After he had left Freer, he had returned to Terry's workshop to apologise for accusing him of being a traitor. As he threw the ball into the air, he recalled what he had said about the Sense Shifters.

"Why didn't you tell me you were one of them?"

"I'm not and, anyway, I couldn't say anything with Rix around. You know what she is like. She would have thought I was making it up, like some old git that's past it, that I was confused and had no idea what I was talking about, making up stories again."

"But you were part of that anarchy group. You found out what syght was. You were one of the very first ones."

"We may have been. There might have been people before and they encountered the same trouble we did, trying to work out what it was. But yes, we were the first to make it known."

Terry was one of the first. This detail just added even more to his fascination of the past. Before, he had only relied on the newspapers from his grandpa but now he actually had someone he could openly talk to about this and find out more.

Gil picked at the tennis ball and continued to play the conversation back in his head.

"When we first learnt about it, there was nothing to go on. Who was going to teach us how to use it? Or confirm that it actually was what we thought it was? When we learnt its true meaning, it was too late for me. We could only try to find others, help them develop this ability and protect them from those who wanted to use it against them. We prepared for a time when the 55 would learn about it and what it could do. It would change the world again and we had to avoid that from happening."

"Do they know now?"

"Stories come out into the open. Rumours travel fast. Nothing is secret, especially from those that have the money. There are always people willing to sell what they know for the right price."

Gil had spoken to Terry for a while. He needed

someone who knew about syght to advise him. Terry had thought it wise to accept the help from the Sense Shifters, so he could learn how to control it. Terry seemed to trust them and Gil knew he could trust Terry. Despite the fact he wasn't one himself, he supported their cause and knew who they were. They weren't some radical group ready to take down the government or sell themselves to the highest bidder. They were providing a new way of life—giving those with insufficient funds to afford the Spacial Lens a chance for something more, a purpose, a family.

He thought it best not to talk to Rix about all of this. Terry was wary, so maybe Gil had to be too. He had witnessed her reaction to it all, how she felt about not being able to learn syght. She was his closest friend, but maybe some elements of this new ability were better left unsaid. He didn't want to push her away or for her to have all this jealousy when he was still not fixed on the idea of wanting to master it himself. He had to have someone there, someone who knew him, someone his age to rely on—a friend. But at the same time normality. How it used to be before learning about this myth. Rix did not need to know everything, he could still keep some information from her if it meant keeping her as a close friend. It meant that Gil would need to judge each situation and gage her mood and reactions. That was a job in itself.

He rose from the couch, dropping the tennis ball into an empty fruit bowl. He had to go and see Freer. If he spoke to her more about it, maybe tried a day's training, he might warm up to the idea.

He packed a change of clothes in his techpack and kept a few of his tools in there, just in case. Better to be prepped. It was as though he was starting school again. He added two small vacuumed sachets of food and closed it up.

He left, locked the door and headed towards Lower Mile.

He could feel a sense of loss. A part of him was missing. He wanted Rix there—not to hold his hand, although he would have taken that right now. He was unsure what he was heading in to and the support from her—a joke, a jibe—would have been a helpful to take the edge off his nerves. This was the sort of ordeal that was usually the result of something Rix initiated. This was far from his comfort zone.

His Holo Display sent out a chime. As if on cue, Rix was calling him.

"Yeah?" he said aloud.

"Must be your lucky day. Two opportunities in the same week," she said dryly.

"What are you talking about? I'm heading out the door. I haven't got time for games, Rix."

"Well, you might want to hear what I've got to say, dickhead."

There she was, typical Rix.

"My Dad wants to see you. Thinks you're ready for a proper job, instead of being a salvager. Thinks your skills from Terry could be put to good use."

Gil dropped his keys to the floor. He was stunned. This had come out of nowhere. How was this happening?

"I put a good word in for you. Means you don't need to keep whining at me now."

He attempted to form words, something other than a mumble. Did he hear Rix correctly? Anders wanted to offer him a job?

"Hello?" Rix prodded. "Thought you'd be happy? I can offer it to someone else, but as you love my dad so—"

"No, no, no!" He snapped out of his overwhelming shock, his heart and brain rebooting themselves. "But why, huh? I don't understand. Yes of course."

He was shaking. He couldn't' process what Rix had just told him. If this was a wind up, it was not funny.

"What, errm, what does he want me to do? Like now? When? What would I be doing?"

It was true: opportunities arrived all at once, not that he would necessarily call syght an opportunity; he was still processing that. But Syngetical wanted Gil. Anders had asked for him personally.

He was a basic circuit builder, though. He was going to be under qualified.

"I don't know," Rix replied. "Why would I know? I also don't care. Just head down to his office if you want the job."

"What? Now?"

"No. next year. Of course, now. You are hard work, Tabs!"

He would let her off this once for using the

nickname. She had done the very thing he was too shy to ask her for—no liberties taken, but still an offer. The Sense Shifters would have to wait.

He stood outside the windowed walls of SeeTech Tower, looking up and admiring the glittering spear that was Syngetical. He took a breath, a feat he thought impossible to achieve, he was so excited. He was proud. He didn't necessarily deserve a job—there had been no interview process, nor was Anders even hiring—but that aside, he still had a position. Rix had not made that vital detail clear.

Gil owned no smart clothes. There had never been an occasion where he needed to wear them and the number of credits he received from salvaging went on food only. He wore his smartest dark-blue long-sleeved top and a pair of black jeans that had the least amount of rips in. It was what he wore down to the pit. Dark colours were classed as smart, he thought, and great when trying to blend in. The building must be full of scientists and mechanics who were far beyond Gil's capabilities around a circuit board. He wanted to be normal and like anybody else in the building.

He entered the foyer. It was a busy area. Everyone was walking around swiftly, a clear destination in mind. There was no milling around or dawdling. Syngetical gave the impression that work happened rapidly and without delays. He noticed that his surroundings and the attire of the employees were very clinical—he was concerned that his chosen style would not do him any favours. It was hardly the blend he was going for.

He approached the holographic receptionist. She may not have been real but Gil thought she was attractive. She had a friendly face and shoulder-length auburn hair that had a wave at the bottom, and a centre parting. Her eyes were blue, clearer than any ocean—not that Gil had seen the ocean personally. He was taken aback by her.

"Hello, I'm here I think to—"

"GIL TABERTHORN, WELCOME!" the hologram said before he had the chance to introduce himself.

"Yes, that's me."

"YOU ARE HERE TO SEE ANDERS HILGAARD."

Although strikingly beautiful, which Gil found absurd to think of a computer hologram of a human, she was intimidating, mainly due to the way she was shouting every response back at him. He wanted to hide in the shadows and yet she was putting him in the spotlight.

"If you could say it a little quieter? I can still hear you."

"FOR VOLUME CONTROLS, PLEASE PRESS THE HIGHLIGHTED BUTTONS BELOW FOR THE PREFERRED SETTINGS."

He looked down and in front of him, embedded into the facade, under the ledge of the front desk were two illuminated buttons. He pressed the decrease volume button hurriedly.

"Where should I go, then?"

"Please make your way into lift number 3.5. Mr Anders Hilgaard will meet you on his floor. I have alerted him that you are on your way."

"Okay, thank you, Miss, errr..." He was unsure how to address the receptionist.

"You can call me Hailey."

"Thank you, Hailey." For some reason, he could sense his cheeks warm.

"It stands for Holographic Artificial Intelligent..." She continued to detail the abbreviation of her name. Suddenly, all sentiment had left their exchange. Reality hit with embarrassment.

Gil couldn't see where lift 3.5 was as the lifts all increased normally in whole digits. He wondered why there would be a .5 anyway. He was reluctant to return to Hailey and get caught up in another exchange of falling tongue over feet to a hologram, so he looked for it himself on the concourse.

There were two main elevator shafts that serviced the building, which ran from one to six, positioned behind Hailey. Essentially, they were moving platforms rather than a whole box moving from one floor to another—a vertical conveyor belt. They operated as many other lifts did in the city: each one as an up or down only, so there would be no accidents, such as crushed mangled employees if one platform was moving up as the other was hurtling downwards.

On the edge of the wall by lift six, there was a

small glass display that read '3.5' with an arrow pointing to the left. Gil peered around the corner and at the end of a short passageway he could see a white fronted set of lift doors. From afar, you could confuse it with a janitor's closet. It did not suggest that it could be a private lift to the CEO of a major conglomerate. Though, hidden in plain sight was sometimes the best disguise, he thought.

The doors opened automatically as he approached and he entered the lift. Without pressing a button, he was taken up to the 186th floor. When he reached the top, he was met with an open view of the city. The sun glistened off the glass floor in front of him. He noticed there was a lot of free space to fall through between the floors. He delicately perched one foot out of the lift, expecting to hear a crack or see it shatter underneath his feet. He applied more pressure until he was sure the floor could take his weight, then he stepped out of the lift and stood on what he imagined was the edge of the stratosphere.

"I like this view of the city. All of the other buildings hide it." Anders stood, watching Gil exit the lift. "Others would rather look at the idyllic view of what we as people have yet to destroy, a paradise to distract from our own destruction. A true view of the city shows its flaws as well as its successes."

"This is… Wow! How am I doing this?" Gil was overwhelmed. It was as though he had ingested some hallucinogenic and he was floating outside his own body.

"Illusion," Anders replied. He pressed a button on a wall panel and the view suddenly switched back to the clinical walls, a ceiling and not much else.

"So, it's virtual. It's not real," Gil stated.

"No, the view is real. That is what it currently looks like outside. It's two-way epidiascope glass. For security, though, I can't be showing the world what we get up to all the time."

"I can understand that."

They reached the office door and Anders unlocked it via a number of security measures, including facial recognition and a code he entered that had been sent to his palm chip.

"Gil, please sit." He indicated to a chair opposite his own.

Gil nervously sat. He was in awe of being in the building, even more so to be in Anders' private office.

"Now, Rix tells me you have a set of skills that I might be interested in."

"What? Syght? Is that what Rix has told you? I'm not entirely sure if I do or what—"

"No, Gil. I was talking about your knowledge in circuitry."

What had Gil blurted out? He had put his foot straight into his mouth by mentioning it. Anders had to know already. Rix must have told him.

"Oh," he replied.

"I thought I would give you an opportunity, a chance to learn and grow with our company."

"Errr, wow. I have always wanted to work for

you, Mr Hilgaard. I don't know what I would do, though. Terry, my boss, was teaching me about circuits and chips. I know a bit about how to put them together and…errr, I could…" Gil was stumbling. The more he spoke, the more nervous he became. He now felt like he was at an interview.

"Don't worry yourself about what you are good at or not. I can worry about that. After all, you are my daughter's best friend and you have been in her life a long time now. It's only fair I look after you, as you have done with each other."

Gil was not entirely sure how he had helped Rix over the years. It was more the other way round.

"Thank you so much, sir. It has always been a dream of mine to work here."

"Call me Anders." He smiled. "Now, this syght you speak of. What's that exactly?"

Rix had clearly not said anything to Anders. What was he going to say? He was Anders Hilgaard, his new boss. He had to trust him. It would look terrible if he was caught lying on his first day. Too many people knew about it and it was still so early. He was still unsure if he even had syght—curious, yes, to get his training going, but no certainty he could control it, or use it to its full capabilities.

Gil explained to him about what he and Rix had gone through in the last few days. He mentioned his concerns, but also the times he had experienced something: a feeling, a vision of what he could potentially achieve.

"And these Sense Shifters?" Anders asked.

"Yeah, they are a group that found me—well us, really. They said they would help me learn syght, so I could protect myself."

Anders went quiet in thought.

"I had decided I wanted to explore it further and was about to leave to start training when Rix called me about your offer."

Anders' face lit up instantly.

"Well, of course you should go. You should learn, see what it can do. If anything, it would be useful as a form of protection. I think you are right to explore it. Maybe you can do both: work here and also train with these Sense Shifters. I think we could arrange something that benefits you in both areas."

There was something odd talking about syght with Anders, the Sense Shifters, their secrecy, the protection against others, yet Gil felt strangely comfortable talking to him, as though he knew everything already, a father figure who wanted the best for him. Anders smiled at Gil, a calm, peaceful smile.

He was excited, but more important than that, he now felt a sense of safety. If the 55 were going to be after him or whoever else, he would be safe here. His dream, his one goal he had wanted so much to achieve, had presented itself. And it was all thanks to Rix. He owed her. He was unsure how he could repay her, but he would find a way.

"You're probably wondering what you are going to be doing and what skills you can provide for Syngetical."

"Not to sound like a bad investment, but yeah." He didn't want to waste Anders' time or credits if he was awful at his job.

"No investment is bad. It's what you do with it to help nurture it, aid its growth, and then you will see it flourish. In my experience, if you invest in something that is already doing well, it is more likely to fail than succeed further. You have nowhere you can take it. You, however, are the perfect seed. Follow me."

This was all happening quicker than he could have imagined. Anders had given him a life-changing position in his company. Doing what exactly, he was about to find out. But it was a job, one he had wanted and one where he could help others.

This was the starts of his future.

FOURTEEN

Gil walked with Anders out of his office and along a corridor to a door opposite. He still felt overwhelmed that this was still happening. With this job, his choices in life had grown. Syght could not have seen this coming. What Gil found most comforting was that Anders understood that this training with Freer was also important, that he had to do it and that this position had to be secondary to him developing his syght. Rix must have spoken to him on some level, or he was a better boss than Gil could have ever asked for.

"Before we go any further, I do need your signature on a few forms, as I do with all my employees. They consist mainly of you not discussing any projects you are working on with other employees, not sharing information outside of the Syngetical corporation. The consequences of you doing so will result in termination."

"I understand," Gil replied. "Every company has their secrecy and of course I wouldn't share anything that is classified." He felt a sense of excitement to say the word 'classified', as if he, your everyday salvager, was important enough to be allowed such information.

"In your case, I have amended the form to also state not to share any information about syght, Sense Shifters and your training with any other employee, no matter who you work with—other than myself. I can't provide protection if everyone knows about it."

Gil agreed.

Anders handed over a screen and swiped the display to the bottom.

"Sign here please, Gil. And here. And place your hand on the glass so we can verify you and have your fingerprints on record also."

A blink of white light flashed behind Gil's hand on the screen.

"All done for now. Let me introduce you to who you will be working with."

'BUZZ'

The room looked like a high-tech version of Terry's workshop, with instruments, devices and tools that Gil had not seen before.

"This is Cyra Wolverton," Anders said, gesturing towards a woman who was perched at the centre table at the back of the room, hunched over with a pair of glass lens goggles over her eyes. Her hair was unkempt, frazzled—she had clearly not prepared for company.

A spark flew up and a small flame ignited.

"SHIT!" she said loudly and pushed the contraption she was working on away.

She then noticed the two men and stood immediately.

"Oh, hello. Sorry for swearing… the lens—having a few troubles getting the calibration precise enough. Not to worry. Hopefully will be sorted."

"Cyra, this is Gil, your new assistant."

She frowned, unhappy to have Gil here, it seemed—a great start to a working partnership.

"What about Myles? What happened to Myles? Is he still here?" she replied frantically.

Gil could tell quite quickly that Cyra was in need of a day off. The harsh strip lighting and no windows—he too had experienced the cabin fever effect.

"Gil is better suited for this position. He has knowledge of microchips and circuits and knows how to solder. The advanced components and techniques he can learn through the books and you can share your findings with him. You are one team."

Looking at the level of technology lying around the workshop, he was unsure if the skills he had in circuitry were enough. He would be more a hindrance than an aid.

"And Myles?" Cyra reiterated.

"He is still in the same position as he was before," Anders reassured her.

She nodded and sat back down in her chair.

"Gil, Cyra here will fill you in on anything you

need to know about the new lens we are working on. You two can talk about the findings and the lens itself in this room only." He then whispered into Gil's ear subtly. "Remember what I told you about not mentioning anything about syght to anyone. Absolutely nobody."

He wagged his finger and tutted.

"I'll leave you to it. Cyra, I read your note on the calculations you worked out. Strong work. How did they play out practically?"

"Well, it does work. Occasionally, sort of. It varies. I have to keep adjusting the calculations and then adapting the lens to suit it. The blink shutter speed is also shy of where it needs to be. It's quick but until it's at optimum speed, the calculations will be off."

"Keep me updated."

Anders left the room.

'BUZZ'

Gil jumped at the noise.

"You'll get used to that," she said bluntly.

Cyra sat in her chair and looked out towards nothing in particular in the room, glazy-eyed and in her own thoughts.

Gil stood motionless in the middle of the workshop. He waited for some guidance, instruction, information on what lens she was trying to improve, but none came.

"So, is that the Spacial lens you are working on?" he asked after an awkward amount of time had passed. She had obviously forgotten that he was still in the room.

"Huh?" she replied.

"The lens in front of you. Is it a new version?"

"Oh, this? Yes. Well, no—no, not really. Something better. A lens that can help you explore space physically."

Gil was confused.

"That's a bad description. I need sleep. Wait, that's not describing what I do."

He didn't offer another word and Cyra continued to mutter to herself, though he was unsure whether he should attempt to listen and respond. Was she talking to him at a lower volume or was it a conversation he was not a part of?

"Shall I read up on how the lens is put together?" he asked, trying to keep what he said simple.

"YES!" she said with delight, her wide eyes highlighting the dark circles underneath. "Over there. The book about the Spacial lens and its components. Start on chapter eight, I think it is. And then those two volumes about circuit boards and chips etc etc." She waved her hand in a general direction towards where the books had been left. "Read about whatever you don't know how to do."

Gil took it upon himself not to ask where the particular books were and set about finding them.

This was sink or swim. There would be many aspects of the job he would not know how to do. His training from Terry was limited. It looked like there would be a lot of reading ahead and not much aiding

Cyra. He knew he was going to be an appalling assistant. At least by starting with reading, he could judge how prepared he was, whether what Terry had taught him over the years was enough. The newer technology he knew he would have no idea on as he had never encountered it before. He worked on old tech not so anything unreleased or unspoken-of technologies would be a mystery to him. But Anders' words had included 'assistant', so it wasn't as if he was expecting too much from him. Cyra would advise him on anything she wanted him to do.

"I'll give you this, which I've been keeping notes on… about this new lens that I, now we, are working on… when you are ready for it, but don't trouble yourself yet with it. No questions needed."

Gil replied with a confused nod. He had no questions yet. He knew nothing about this lens. The Spacial lens he did know of, though.

He found a worktop and cleared some space.

"Make yourself at home. Sorry, it's a mess. Forgot what day it was."

"It's fine. I hadn't planned to start today."

"If you don't know something then ask me—if I'm not busy, that is, which I am, but if I'm concentrating then don't ask. Don't say anything. Actually, don't make notes. Ask me. Tomorrow maybe. Are you here tomorrow?"

The words were falling out of her mouth as though she was being sick. No control, bringing up anything, not able to stop.

"I am here tomorrow," he replied.

"Good, that helps me. I might leave early today, rest and then come back…" At this point, she went into her thoughts again: more muttering to herself about what she was doing.

Gil had plenty of information to be absorbing and it would take a while before Cyra allowed or realised that Gil was now part of this team.

FIFTEEN

It was still late afternoon and Cyra had gone home early to rest. Gil followed soon after. The workshop was eerie on his own. He'd rather them both be in the room working together, even if Cyra did not acknowledge him.

Gil headed over to Lower Mile. His techpack was still filled with items he thought he might need. It was quiet. Many of the vendors were closed. As he looked around, he realised that, in this precise moment, he was no better than the queues of people that would soon be lining the road, each hoping they could be cured. His belief was in syght. The only difference was that he had already experienced it. He had seen a glimpse of the two realities.

He found the alleyway that they'd been caught in when they'd climbed down the fire escape. The ladder was still in the puddle they had left it in.

The door ahead was closed, with two large

dustbins on wheels blocking it from opening. The handle was hanging off, held in with two screws, and the rust was peeling around the corners as if it had been a long while since it was used. To look at, this was no entrance at all, rather an area that had been sealed shut for a reason. The illusion was hidden well.

He approached.

"You came back then."

The voice came from behind, startling him.

Freer was standing at the end of the alleyway, smiling.

"How did you know I was here? I didn't knock."

"No need to. We are Sense Shifters for a reason."

So, you're psychic too," he said, with a hint of sarcasm.

"We have many abilities. And sometimes even we have to have eyes in some places to protect our community."

She pointed up to two cameras above that monitored the alleyway and the door.

"We aren't complete technophobes."

At that, he realised what he had said sounded a bit stupid.

"They are operated on a closed circuit so only the screen it's connected to can see it. There is no benefit for us to be known by the government or the High Chancellor."

"I guess there is another entrance?"

"A few. We try to avoid activity in one isolated area."

"Do you not use this one anymore?"

"We do. We disguise them so they aren't so obvious. Follow me."

She walked off around the corner. Gil quickly followed.

She led him up Lower Mile to the next small turning from the main road. It was a slim alley, and they had to walk in single file. The damp from the stones above dripped down. Then the alley opened up to a forecourt, no larger than the size of Gil's living area. There were three boarded-up windows that he could only assume were shops of some nature.

"In here," Freer announced as she neared the far-right corner.

He was unsure where she meant. There was no door along the right side. Boarded-up windows were tricky to climb through when they were nailed shut.

Freer pulled out a door handle from her pocket and inserted it into a round hole on one of the wooden panels.

She levered it down and the door opened.

"You would be surprised how many people ignore doors without handles on them. Remove the handle: hide the door."

He had never thought of it like that before.

He followed her into the building and she closed the door behind them, using the same handle again. She hung it on a hook beside the door.

They walked along a slightly brighter passageway than the one they had entered through the last time he was here, passing open doors, which led into bedrooms, living spaces, kitchen facilities. This was more than the training area. He could now see that the Sense Shifters lived here also, a hidden community needing the outside world when they chose to. He wondered what they 'did'. Living in secret and training for something that would never come to pass seemed pointless. There was no end goal to all of it. They used their abilities to protect others and give people without sight a new purpose in life, to enjoy living again. They helped people, which was noble, but they lived non-existent in society. Maybe he didn't understand it fully. It made no sense to him.

"What do Sense Shifters do?" he blurted out.

Freer stopped.

"We protect those from others wanting to use their abilities for their own greater greed. We give an alternative life for those—"

Gil interrupted.

"No, I mean, once you have done all that. What do Sense Shifters do? Are you recruiting? You must be building an army or some kind of anarchist group to take down the government. What do you do with your life?"

It did intrigue him, how they filled the rest of their time. A secret society was always going to be mysterious. It must be more exciting than what Gil did—read old newspapers and throw a tennis ball around.

Freer smiled slightly. Gil missed the humour.

"Life is not necessarily having a plan and sticking to it, Gil: to grow up and work your way to the top. Some need help and support and we provide that. And depending on each person's circumstances, we are generally happy to grow and develop these people to train others. We train not to attack but to protect. I think you misunderstand how powerful syght and being a Sense Shifter is to those who want more. Our abilities make people like us—like you—more vulnerable. So, what do we 'do'? I'll show you."

She indicated that he follow her further into the building. There was a set of open double doors that led through to the training area he recognised from before, but instead, they took a left and went down another corridor to the end. There were no locks or coded panels or retinal scanners—not that that was warranted when the majority here lacked eyes to begin with—but the most surprising thing that he noticed was that there was no technology at all, no security other than to help them get into the building. It was all very basic and trusting.

That was until he walked into the next room, where all their technology was situated in one location.

"Gil, welcome to the Axeon City Hub."

She opened the doors to what looked like, at best, a fully operational recruitment centre, or at worst, a war room. He had to assume that the Sense Shifters were the good team in all of this and that he was on the correct side.

The room was split. On the ground level, the

walls were covered in notice boards full of papers with details on. There were pictures and printed words with a range of dots underneath. The floor was laden with desks and old-fashioned monitors, on which the viewpoint seemed to switch between different cameras. Then there was a mezzanine area above, which housed more desks and monitors. He was too low down to see what was on those.

"This is where we keep track of people who we believe to have syght or have lost their sight completely. We have installed our own cameras over the city that the government can't trace. Hence, why the technology is older here. Nobody cares for anything that isn't the newly upgraded high-tech version, let alone something that is obsolete. We run all our equipment on lower frequencies so that it's untraceable. Up there—" she pointed to the mezzanine area "—is where we can communicate to other cities that have Sense Shifters, in case the people we're tracking move, and of course, where we try to figure out when the next geological time shift pattern will happen exactly."

"What does that mean?" It sounded technical, and if the Sense Shifters were monitoring it, it had to be worth asking about.

"Every thirty-three years there is what is known as the geological time shift pattern, which means that, for a margin of time, gravity stops on this planet and resets itself, while the other reality continues on. This creates a particular style of a déjà vu moment. If a child is born on that precise moment, when this reality stops and the other continues, then they have what we call the Déjà Vu gene, which translates to the ability of syght."

"And I was born on that moment?"

"Possibly. We believe you might have been. It's difficult to track the exact point it happens. Your age matches up but there is a window of about five days where it happens and then to fine tune it down to the exact time is almost impossible. You'd be surprised how many babies are born in those five days, if we accurately guess the time shift that is. To know if one was born within one of these moments, you would need to ask your mother, to see if she experienced a sense of déjà vu. Then we will know for sure. If you are, you are one unique human being. You have the signs already there, but this is one crucial criterion you would need to meet to know that you have syght in its purest form."

All this time, all he had to do was ask his mother one simple question. That was going to be a strange one but at least he would get his answer. He might have to think how he approached that question.

Freer continued: "We can also monitor any potential births that might occur on that date and time too, rather than looking back at births that have already happened. We'd need to be able to intercept before any potential threat does as we might not be the only ones also looking for this child."

Gil was overwhelmed. He had not expected this secret society to be so expansive or invasive.

"You monitor people here?" he said.

The government were bad enough, watching every move you tried to make. But the Sense Shifters too? He felt uneasy about that information.

"It looks worse than it is. We aren't like the government who track you in everything you do. We only monitor the people we have been told about."

That meant they must have been monitoring him, which made sense, considering how she had approached him that day in the pit. But in which ways? And how far had they gone with it? There was obviously Terry, which he now knew about. But Terry owned his apartment. Were there secret cameras hidden around his place so they could watch everything he did? Gil was concerned by that thought—a lot.

"And no, we only use outside cameras. There are no secret ones in your home. If you were going to be followed or caught, we would want to know before they entered your apartment."

Maybe she was psychic. There was no chance she would have known his concerns about spyware inside his apartment.

"Your pulse quickened slightly when I mentioned about monitoring people. I assumed you were wondering if you had been. Yes, of course you were, but we have our boundaries."

There was some relief there.

"Each city has a variety of scouts who help us—Terry, for example—who might guide us towards someone they believe to be showing signs of certain syght qualities. This is a record of people over the years, not everyone we are currently monitoring."

She pointed over to a wall that was covered in clipboards, which each held reams of paper. Gil was too far away to read the details but there were screenshots and photos, with what he guessed were notes about who they were and what qualities they were showing.

"Once they are past the age bracket, we strike them from the list. Remember, they have to meet certain criteria. We also monitor the hospitals, mainly the psychiatric wards; people who have lost their sight usually end up there, a place that many forget about. Other than Anders Hilgaard, of course." She said this last part under her breath.

Gil wanted no part of a cult or a system like this, or anything that could get him into trouble. So far, the government was naïve to the Sense Shifters, but if they were alerted, they would soon shut this operation down. Then, Gil would be on his own— no one to train or protect him. What would he do? Forget all about syght and see out the next two years as a fugitive? Wait until he was inevitably caught, used and tortured until the 55 had what they wanted? He hadn't truly felt endangered yet, other than when Freer chased him down, but if he was to believe what she said, then he should be scared.

"How do I know I can trust you, though? I don't know you and this all looks eerily similar to what the government does…"

"We aren't keeping you here. You can leave whenever. I wanted to be honest with you in what we do so you can make that choice—an ability which you still have. We require nothing from you, Gil. Only the chance to protect you."

"You live in secret because you know the government would stop all of this. How are you any better than the 55 and their business?"

"We live in secret so the 55 stay unaware about us. We wanted the rumours and the history to die when the government shut down the first ever group. And they did. We had a duty to those who had this skill to find out what it could do before it ended up in the hands of those that wanted to exploit it. Without us, someone else would have found it and that bears no thinking to what could have happened."

"If you want to be secret, then why not live in the country, away from the troubles of the city?"

"The people out there are already protected. No 55 member is going to be looking for someone in the country. They already have that protection. It's a dying culture. Many think there aren't any people who live out there anymore."

"My family do," Gil said abruptly.

"Good. Keep them there. But we have to be here. This is not a choice for us. The people in the cities are exposed; they need our help and protection. With every birth within that time shift, one of them will be born on a déjà vu moment, that is another potential person who might have syght. And each day, more people are losing their sight. We want to help those that don't—or can't—get the Spacial lens."

"Exactly. Let Syngetical help those people. That's what they are there for!" Gil was finding himself becoming a spokesperson for the company again, but now he had reason to be. They were his employer. He was still not certain that the Sense Shifters were the right side to be on. Yes, Terry supported what they did, but it was the monitoring potential syght members that wasn't sitting well with Gil. It sounded as though it was another branch of the government in disguise. To track what the poorer classes did, the people that couldn't afford to live. It was evasive—where was the freedom? The privacy? They were another group of people being shepherds trying to control their sheep.

"They can't help everyone," Freer replied.

This was not what Gil thought it would be. He thought it was a group of kind strangers, but this was an organisation. There had to be something wrong in what they were doing. He felt as something was crawling over his skin. That they knew everything he had done. He had no concrete evidence that what they were doing was with bad intentions, but it all sounded too good to be true. They wanted to help; he could see that. But there was something that made him feel like it had to be wrong. But when he thought about it, was Syngetical any different? Their ethos as a company was also to help…

This had all happened too fast, the news of him having syght, then the Sense Shifters, and now his new job. He hadn't had time to process it all. As he usually did, he went into defence mode, for survival.

"I think I better go," he said.

"If that's what you choose, then I won't stop you. Gil, we only want to show you how to protect yourself by using your potential syght. There may be a time that you're going to need it."

"I also might not. Nobody has ever come after me. I've never been in trouble and I keep off the radar. If anyone was after me, they would have caught me by now. The only people that have are you."

He had to be sure that the Sense Shifters were honourable. They could be luring him in on false pretences—not that he wanted to be caught by the other people that were supposedly after him just to prove that Freer was correct.

"Before, you knew nothing about the true meaning of syght or even if you had it. Now, you know and others know you have it too. It's your choice."

On one hand, he agreed with what Terry had said, that he should take what the Sense Shifters were offering, learning a new skill that might come to some good use. He did trust Terry and he had always looked after him. There was no reason for Terry to put him in harm's way. However, on the other hand, he had to feel safe, secure that he was doing the right thing. He had conflicting emotions: wariness and eagerness to get started. If he opened up this box, there was a chance he might not be able to close it again. His life would change forever: dealing with, coping with, managing syght on a daily basis. Or he could ignore it and carry on the life he already led.

If syght was about choice, then he could do with it presenting itself now. He needed help to know the right decision to make.

"My choice is I'm leaving."

Freer bowed her head and then ushered him to the exit.

"You know where we are, and we hope you honour our privacy, to not tell anyone else of our location."

"There is never any privacy, not in this city. Everyone and every action is watched, whether it's by you, the government, or probably the 55. I won't say anything about your HQ, but that doesn't mean someone else hasn't already located it. Everyone knows what we do and when, unless you're a salvager."

He chose not to mention that he was working at Syngetical. Freer seemed wary when she mentioned them earlier.

Freer had the nerve to talk about privacy and keeping the HQ a secret when they were monitoring everyone without people knowing. At least the government made it obvious. Gil hated hypocrites. This was his life, not hers. It didn't matter what she thought about the company.

He needed to talk to someone and he knew Terry wasn't the best person right now. He was part of the Sense Shifter's society, even if he classed himself as removed from it. His opinion was a biased one. He was still an informant for them. He knew he meant no harm, but whatever he said to Terry, it would naturally be fed back. He needed a neutral opinion, advice that was straight to the point. Rix was honest and would see the bullshit if there was any. She already knew where the Sense Shifters were based, so knowing a few more details about what they did wasn't going to make a difference. He also had Anders now, an older, more logical person who could help him decide.

He wasn't concerned with what Rix would say about what he had seen at the Sense Shifters HQ, but was more worried that she would go down and threaten to cut their throats, depending on what her opinion of them was. He could already tell what her response would be: 'Tell them to fuck off, spying bastards. You don't need syght anyway.'

"Excuse me, sir, do you have syght?" A voice came from behind him.

He was sure he heard correctly. He turned to see who the speaker was. The bass in their voice gave him the impression they were going to be much taller and broader than he was.

He turned around cautiously.

There was a man with a hunchback, preaching from a high stool, pointing to a sign that read, 'Do you have sight? Then allow your mind to breathe.'

"No. I mean, yes I do, obviously. But I'm fine, thank you," he muttered and then hurried off.

He did need some time for his 'mind to breathe', but not from him.

SIXTEEN

On the edge of Axeon City, Vivalda Xing stood under the awning of a crumbling townhouse. Bulltwine's Edge was not a place you wanted to be near in the day, let alone at night. It was the roughest part of Axeon City, named after an old family who governed the area before the government took control and 'shut it down', as was the phrase they used, but everyone knew the place was a bloodbath. Any mention of it was banned. Some of those who were taken there survived, but most naturally ended up dead. The area was supposedly abandoned and had been left as a ghost district, although there were rumours some still lived in the area. Others would visit for either prostitution, black market dealings or to relinquish unwanted people over the 'edge'—a deep gorge that, if you ever searched, you would probably find was filled with everything you could imagine. She had to stay hidden. Someone of her accolade was not meant to be in a place like this. This was for the lowlifes, the part of the city not monitored by cameras, where prostitutes could still earn a living. It was the only place you could really go if you were into that kind of pleasure. They were tricky to find. But Vivalda was not looking for a companion for the night.

The wind whistled around the desolate street. She stiffened up her collar. Her eyes had adjusted to the blackness of the landscape, and in the distance, she could see the edge. The small barbed wire fence, which alerted anyone not to go beyond it, had been torn apart. There were a multitude of deep track marks and scoring leading up to it. She knew what events had taken place here; she wasn't naive to that. She could imagine someone who had crossed the path of the 55 being dragged along, their heels digging into the loose soil, attempting to stop the inevitable fate—that they were going to end up in the gorge below. She could imagine the struggle, the muffled screams through the drenched gag, the fading echoes of a human as they were pushed into the fate that had been chosen for them. Their final wish would have been that they'd cracked their head open before they reached the bottom. The fact that Vivalda chose to know so little about it only highlighted the truth of how corrupt this city was.

She checked her display. She had the ATT Systems BioMobX chip implanted in her forearm.

Sixteen unread messages, most of which were from the Supreme House about updates for sanctioned laws, many she could assume would not affect her. She liked to run things her way—not that the board would know that and nor could they complain as she did get the necessary results. Not every city could work on the exact same laws.

Rain was due within the next hour, but she would be gone by the time it started.

It was 8.32pm and Atalon Keel was late.

She swiped to her contacts page and pressed on the icon for him.

"Where are you?" she said with a stern voice.

"I'm running behind," he replied in his deep, well-spoken voice.

"I can tell that."

"Come to the office. I'll meet you there."

The connection disconnected.

She quickly made her way out of Bulltwine's Edge. It had never been her preferred location for business, but, naturally, it was for the 55. It was secret, out the way and with no monitoring. It was the way they did their business. She had wasted her time here, but if Atalon being late meant they could go to a location more to her suiting, she was happy.

Her car was waiting for her at the first street lamp.

On her approach, the door opened skywards and she got in.

"Take me to Plaza One, Entax Tower."

It was a short drive down to Plaza One. At this time of night, the area was deserted and, anyway, it would not be an absurd view for the High Chancellor to be seen communicating with one of the 55. There was the agreed partnership, after all.

The two 55'ers Vivalda had within her city held their corporations opposite each other across the river. Neither wanted to look at a landscape that was obsolete or derelict, so they decided to face each other and dwell in the other's worth. Entax Tower was on the north side of the river, where Atalon Keel was the head of Entax Energy Supply. His contribution to the world was that he crippled all the other energy companies world-wide. He was able to manufacture a renewable source of energy that had no harmful effects on the environment and without fluctuations. Atalon was a scientist at heart and his family had had money originally. They invested in his research when the United party took over so he could compete with the other energy companies. Naturally, they won. With the support and funding behind him, he became the face of the company and also part of the 55. Since then, he had been able to explore further into vacuum energy—kinetic energy created from all types of matter in space—and develop techniques so that energy could be sustained.

She exited the vehicle and made her way into the building, passing through the facial recognition software at the entrance easily. The building was unmanned by human guards as the security system did a better job, and anyway, High Chancellors had the honour of being able to enter restricted public or private buildings without question.

The lift door opened and the button she needed to press had the word 'Keel' inscribed on the gold-plated panel.

A voice recording announced:

"State your name."

"Vivalda Xing, High Chancellor."

"Accepted."

The lift doors closed and the lift made its accent.

As with all of the 55 or people of wealth, Atalon's office was on the last floor. These people were egotistical. They had to have everyone they employed below them, to prove a point that they were in charge. They were showing their feathers as a peacock would—only doing it for vanity.

The doors opened again and there was Atalon, standing in front of a glass-panelled wall, looking out over the city skyline. It was an open plan office. Atalon was not one for confined places and was into simplicity. His large desk sat in the centre of the room. It had a chrome frame and a black glass top. The black leather ribbed high-back static chair was perfectly placed in the centre of the desk. A glass display screen was suspended from the ceiling, aligned with it. Three silver styluses were laid horizontally underneath one other on the right-hand side, digital counterparts for a fountain, a ball point and a pencil.

Over to the right, there was another table, a wooden V-shaped frame that had a matching black glass top as the desk did. It housed a variety of decanters, crystal cut receptacles and a range of mini glass bowls full of garnishes for the drinks. A folded white towel was laid neatly, with a golden knife perched upon it.

She walked into the room. She had been here many times before.

"Aperitif?" Atalon said over his shoulder.

She contemplated the idea.

"Not right now."

She joined him at the window. The city lights shone bright below, creating a network of dots that built up the blueprint of Axeon City.

Atalon was a distinguished gentleman. Well dressed, with a more traditional style compared to the new generation of fashion, often sporting a waistcoat and tie ensemble. His tie was currently loosened and the top button of his shirt undone.

"Tough day?" she said, nodding toward his tie.

"Just the end of it." His bright green eyes flashed at her. The front of his salt and pepper hair was ruffled. It was the first time she had ever seen Atalon slightly off from perfection.

"We need to talk," she said, stepping away from him and over to the velvet green lounge chair, the only colourful piece of furniture in the room.

"I often stand here and look out over the city. It's peaceful at night. Up here. It's quiet. No noise, no wrongdoing, just me and my city. A world view would be better, to see the grand scale of my accomplishments. Maybe I need a taller tower? We could easily extend, but time is not something I have to offer. It would have to be now." Atalon paused.

"Have you looked out and marvelled at what we have achieved?"

Vivalda thought about it. Her opportunity to answer had passed.

"I'm sure the government has no interest in taking a step back and admiring what is right in front of them," he went on. "Thirty-seven years of this new generation, and we've achieved everything we thought unobtainable, owning everything we dreamt of—almost."

"Did you hear what I said? We need to talk!"

"NO! You need to listen." Atalon's attitude changed. "I don't answer to you or discuss anything with you. I tell and you listen; that's what I pay you for."

Vivalda stood tall. The 55 were not intimidating to her. She was stronger than that. Her opinion, though, was not always taken on board by both of the 55 in this city. She would make it difficult for them, even if she was right and benefited from both the 55 greatly.

Atalon continued.

"Do not forget, your money is a bribe so I can avoid having to deal with you or the Supreme House, so no trouble leads back to me or my business."

"I will remind you of our agreement that it's also to inform you, is it not?" she fought back.

"We don't 'need to talk'; you need to tell me something. Those are two very different things."

"So, it was a bad day," she said. "Here's a tip: keep your frustrations to yourself when you are told no or when a decision doesn't go your way. Composure is your ally. What people don't know will only protect you. We both despise the Supreme House; I am on your side. That is why you help me and I help you. That is the basics of business when it has to be secret."

Vivalda had worked herself up. Whenever she dealt with the 55, it was as though she was having to train a toddler. They wanted only what they saw and forgot about anyone else around them—until they were in trouble and needed you. She was in a position of power to 99% of Axeon city; she was a High Chancellor, after all. But when it came to the 55, she might as well have been a doormat. They didn't need her as much as she relied on them. Despite the money she and the other High Chancellors received, their influence over the government, regardless of how the Supreme House wanted to disregard it, most knew who was really in control. It was better to stay close and know what was going on than be on the outside, looking in through a clouded window. She would use them until she reached where she wanted to be—having a seat on the board of the Supreme House.

Atalon was hard work, especially if he was in a mood. She wanted to get in, say what she needed to and leave. She was never one for small talk. A drink, however, would soften the blow, make this interaction bearable, calm her rage at what should be a simple warning. She headed over to the decanters.

"Where are you going?" Atalon bellowed,

following her with his gaze.

"To get that drink. I agree, it has been a long day."

She picked up a crystal tumbler and put it down hard on the glass surface. Then she picked up a decanter, which contained a dark brown liquid, and poured herself a large measure. It splashed over the sides and onto the surface top. She knew that would annoy Atalon. She placed the tumbler on the Temp Square and double tapped the button on the front to chill the bottom of the crystal.

"You do realise that is four million credits a bottle?" Atalon watched on from the centre of the office.

"Then I shall enjoy it even more." She took a gulp, gave a short exhale after and bit the corner of her bottom lip. Although the liquid was chilled, it warmed her up inside as it trickled down her throat.

"Why are you here Vivalda?"

"Now you want me to talk."

He paused before speaking again. She could see he was now intrigued to why she was here, but at the same time trying to contain his rage.

"I'm listening," he replied.

"Yesterday, I had our monthly Supreme House meeting with the board and all the High Chancellors. They are trying to investigate the ongoings of the 55. They want to send two informants to your annual gala."

"Do they know where it is being held? The government know they will be denied at the door."

"They know it's in Axeon City."

She took another sip, her taste buds adapting to the strong flavour. She could get used to this feeling the drink brought. She may not be able to afford that bottle now, but she would in the near future. She was over being the 55's informant. Her progression and promotion couldn't come quicker. There was no guarantee she would be given it. That was something she had to make sure happened.

"They are intrigued to know what the 55 are auctioning off. The rumours state that it's going to be a very special surprise."

"Then the board know more than I do. The auction happens every year and we are never told what is being auctioned in advance. Only the host knows. This year it's not me; it's Harry Qwhale. As I have mentioned to you in the previous years, it's usually a new piece of technology, like that replica revolver I know you have hidden away."

"You know my standpoint on weapons, especially ones used within my city."

It had been a gift—one she had not used and most of the time had forgotten about.

"Don't treat me like a fool. That Colt Peacemaker, long-barrelled old west revolver with modified electro pulse cylinder, that bargaining chip from Harry you happened to merely forget about. That weapon has Harry written all over it. I would be surprised it worked."

She stayed quiet. Harry was a briber, and at the beginning of this partnership, between the three of them, he had been a generous man. It was sweet talking, favour building, though none of it worked on her. She did, however, keep the weapon—not for it to be used, but to feel part of the 55, to have ownership with technology and one that others would have wanted, bid on, fought over. Harry must have told Atalon as she had very much kept this her secret. Weapons of any type were banned—new, old or replicas—and the majority were destroyed when the Uniformed Act came into force.

"Two years ago, I sold the first handheld space particle weapon prototype. Its functionality was dubious at the time and yet it still sold."

"What did it do?"

"It harnessed electromagnetic radiation from space particles, and when fired upon human flesh, it basically melted the skin and vaporized it at the same time. If it were charged to contain enough energy, it could kill you, probably one of the most painful ways to die. If not, it would leave you with radiation poisoning that slowly ate away at your cells via electrified pulses that zapped individual cells."

"Why would you want to create something like that?" She was sickened at the thought the 55 could want something like that, let alone create it. She knew she was strict and sometimes was wayward with her choices, but not to the extreme of what the 55 went to.

"Why not? Greed thrives on having something no one else has. In a society where guns, artillery, anything that goes bang was ceased and destroyed, you can't blame us for wanting something. With enough money, you can create anything—banned or otherwise."

Vivalda was silent.

"You understand the 55 members have businesses of their own? They need methods of dealing with said business if things take a wrong turn. Anyway, the weapon took a while to charge and often misfired—not my greatest achievement. I did pre-warm them it was a prototype. As a goodwill gesture, I gave back a quarter of what they spent on it."

"Who won the bid?" Vivalda asked.

"That's 55 business. I'm afraid I cannot divulge that sensitive information."

Vivalda knew that Atalon wasn't going to reveal the identity. the 55ers always limited what they told her.

"Was that all? They heard a rumour and wanted to know if it was true?" Atalon sighed and walked back over to the window.

Vivalda topped herself up.

"I don't care what you are auctioning—as long it stays clear of me and my plans."

Vivalda was selfish and she admitted that. Why let someone else affect what she intended to do? This generation was hard on survival as it was. She was not going to be one of them who suffered, not without a fight.

"All I need is a product, a lie, a plausible reason to why this rumour is going around, so I can go back to the Supreme House with it. I'd rather come to ask you than to Qwhale. I had to break his finger last time I spoke with him. He seems not to understand boundaries."

She took another gulp of her drink, swashed it back with force. Her firm grip on the tumbler tightened.

"Tell the board that Juton Pollar is auctioning off the second version of her two-person space craft. They will believe that, as it hit the news the last time. To conquer space is many people's dream."

"That's what will be told. The government will hold no further investigations."

She had her answer. She would give the Supreme House the information they wanted. That gold star was now hers and she'd make a huge leap up the ladder when it came to choosing who was next in line. Easier than she thought.

"They better not hold any investigations. So, this matter will be resolved and the Supreme House will be none the wiser. I can trust you that this will be enforced?"

"As always," she replied and took another sip of her drink. That one hit her. In the short space of time, the effects of the strong liquor were starting to make themselves known.

"Good. Is that all?"

She finished off her drink. She shuddered after.

"It is for now," she said, referring to the situation, but maybe the drink also. This was business, not pleasure—far from that. She had to keep a level head.

She placed the tumbler back onto the glass table to make sure it would leave a ring mark. She gave him a smug look as she walked away.

"A parcel will arrive tomorrow to your office. Make sure only you open it," Atalon said as she approached the lift. "A bonus for the information given today."

She stood in the centre of the lift as the doors closed.

SEVENTEEN

The more Gil walked, the more the feeling of foolishness grew. He had been tricked to believe he had a skill that many had not been able to explore, only to find out the people he had trusted were just as invasive as the government. He found it hard to see what the Sense Shifters were doing was moral. Watching people, spying, until they were certain they had this syght. He still couldn't be sure that they weren't the villains in all of this. They said it was for the protection of others, but what could the 55—or whoever else—truly be able to do with this skill? And anyway, he still didn't know whether he would be able to get to the stage where he could fully use this ability.

The Sense Shifters were as much fraudsters as the fake ones were. If syght was as important as Freer made out, someone else would have figured how to use it by now—it was 2082, after all. This myth had been around for over forty years already. The only part he struggled to piece together was that surveillance room. There was no way they'd be able to operate all that without outside help, no matter how outdated the technology was. The more he thought about it, the more his mind led him to outlandish reasons to why he shouldn't trust them. Maybe it was either fake recordings from years ago, or they were secretly working for the government under the High Chancellors orders, hence, why they remained in secret. They could be monitoring people of particular interest: the 55, criminals, people they knew would cause trouble. Either way, he knew he was better off staying clear and not getting wrapped up into something only to be told it was all a big lie after all. But he still had that nagging feeling that he could be wrong. Were they trying to help him? There was a curiosity still there. It was whether he should make the leap first, before checking he was landing on the correct team.

He wanted to confront Terry about it but he was too frustrated. He knew his old boss was looking out for him but, for a moment, he had hoped that he would be different to everyone else.

But then he had a thought. Did Rix know about this? She was the one who had told him about the myth and the original stories, the first person who had been convinced he had syght. But then she had been angry when Freer mentioned she couldn't learn syght, which Gil still found odd. Again, he had built this notion up in his head. He knew Rix liked to play games with him, but if she was, this was going too far. The years of jibing had given him a complex. He had rumbled her plan, if there was one in place. Either way, he had to know whether Rix was in on something.

"Did you know? Was this all a big joke to you?" he said as he stormed into 'Jacking', the stall where he knew Rix would be. He was no fan of Jacks, the stall's owner.

"What the hell you talking about?" she replied. She was perching next to Jacks on the arm of the chair. Jacks had his arm round her.

"Making me believe about syght, the Sense Shifters… Was it to give me something to do? Something to laugh at when I started this bullshit training?"

"Making you believe what, Gil? What are you talking about?"

"Hey man, you can't come in here shouting your mouth off," Jacks said, looking over his shoulder towards him. "This is my sanctuary. I need my focus, yeah?"

"FUCK OFF, JACKS!" Gil shouted back.

Rix slipped off the arm of the chair, and Jacks stood up. Whenever Gil had seen him crowded over his monitors and his workstation, Jacks gave the illusion that he was small, but he was taller than Gil and intimidating too—not that he was muscular, but he oozed confidence, like most young cocky twenty-something men did.

"You want to say that again?" Jacks asked with

intent.

"This is between me and Rix, Jacks, so stay out," he said, keeping his composure. He was by the exit, after all. If he needed to run, he could.

"But you're in my establishment and I'm with a client."

"Rix ain't your client. She only comes to you to flirt so she can get the job she needs done quicker."

He knew he had crossed a line with that.

"What the fuck, Gil?" Rix stormed over and pushed him hard. He stumbled back. The pain rippled over both sides of his chest.

"Why you coming here being jealous? Jacks is finishing off my Holo palm chip hack. What's your problem?"

"Were you in on all this syght crap? Making me believe something that isn't true?"

"I've never heard of syght," Jacks added.

"Exactly my point!"

Rix shoved him out of the stall, away from listening ears, shouting out to Jacks as they left. "I'll be back in a moment. Amend that last bit of coding and piece the chip back together."

Jacks let out a half laugh, half expulsion of air.

"You finding this funny?" Gil asked.

"If I knew the joke, then yeah, maybe. What the fuck you coming here kicking off at me for? You best have a better explanation than you being jealous."

"What? I'm not jealous of anything. But I did notice you and Jacks were getting close—"

"GIL!" she screamed.

"Did you and Terry make up everything about syght and the Sense Shifters to give me something to do?"

"What?" she said, her voice full of anger and confusion.

"I've just got back from where we went the other day and saw more of their hideout. I guess you could call it that. It's one huge monitoring place, watching all the people in the city, ones with syght."

"Will you stop saying syght so loudly? You're going to get us into trouble."

"Drop the act, Rix. It isn't true. I'm not being the fool."

Even Gil felt like he was out of control of his thoughts on this one.

"Gil. I never made anything up and have no idea why you think me and Terry, of all people, would do something to wind you up. Yeah, maybe I would, but I work solo and Terry isn't exactly one for practical jokes, is he?"

Gil knew that statement was true. Terry was not the joker.

"You've made this up in your head. So, don't come at me."

"Alright, okay. I get it," he said. It was a line he often said to give himself some time for composure, his anger flurrying out of a simple thought. His school years had not been kind to him. He was wound up a lot, gullible and easy to manipulate, so now he was an adult and had escaped all of that, he deserved a bit of respect.

Though if it was all a wind up, it was a huge accomplishment. He had witnessed this syght; that he could not deny.

"Whatever you saw, I am clueless on it. If it looked dodge, then it probably is. Name something that isn't in this city. A secret cult hiding from the government? We do the same thing—well, you do. How is it any different, being a salvager? So, they are probably monitoring people to find others and protect them…"

"That's what they said! See, I knew you were in on it."

"Gil, enough! I've not made this up. Syght is serious. Did you not see how annoyed I was that I couldn't have it? This up here…" She pointed to her temple and then back at Jacks' stall. "Or that Holo palm chip in there. That's what's stopped me learning something that you can. I've been modified—not something I would have chosen if I'd known the consequences."

Her eyes began to well up, her forehead pulling taught—a desperate look of resentment, an emotion that she had never shared before. Gil was unsure if he had ever seen Rix cry.

"I wish I had that chance, the choice, Gil. So, you trying to kid yourself out of it and trying to find any reason not to explore it, it makes you more the fool."

It was a surprising response. He would never have imagined that Rix would be saying this about syght or the Sense Shifters.

She wiped at her face with her arm and expelled her frustration once more with a groan.

"Rix—"

"Unless that's an, 'I'm sorry', I don't want to hear anything else."

She shied away from him, her finger raised, pointed stiffly towards him.

He realised he had misread this situation.

He was wrong, horribly so. At times, Gil thought Rix must have been built rather than born. For once, he was seeing true emotion from her, something he knew machines couldn't portray, to his knowledge. She was his friend, a true friend, of a long time. All she wanted was the best for him. He had to soften the accusation he had just hurled at her. He needed her genuine, honest opinion. Whatever her answer, he had to trust her, like he had always done. He had been an idiot.

"Do you think I should do this training?"

"Gil, this is not a game. You have to. You heard what Freer said. This isn't a conspiracy and they aren't an elite government training facility. Whatever you saw was there because it had to be. Do what you want, Gil. That's your choice to make, whether you see it or not."

He knew he had upset her with his words. His straight-to-point approach had not been the tactic he should have led with. He had messed up.

She shook herself, and looked at him seriously.

"And nothing is happening between me and Jacks."

With that, she headed back towards the stall.

"Sorry," he called out, feeling the biggest relief that she had denied what he thought he had seen between them.

She looked back, nodded and waved her hand as if he should follow.

Gil walked towards her, but making the decision to still stay outside the stall, away from Jacks.

As she collected her Holo palm chip and paid Jacks, he heard him say, "Rix, that's too much."

"It's earned. You did more than you needed and, you know, for getting you involved with the other stuff."

"Chill, we're good. Not the worst thing that'll happen today." He laughed.

She nudged him in the shoulder lightly with her fist. Gil felt an uncomfortable feeling in the pit of his stomach: an ache, a flutter.

"Tell Terry he owes me, though. Threatening don't come for free."

Rix took her chip and joined Gil outside.

"You're in his bad books," she said, pointing at him.

"With Jacks?"

"No, with Terry."

When he got home, Gil stepped into the shower and let the water trickle down his back, taking the time to trace over what had happened over the last couple of days. A job, syght, Freer, the Sense Shifters—there was a lot for him to process. One element he was unsure of was what to do about syght. He did want to learn. If he had an ability like this, he'd need the guidance to be able to learn it correctly. The consequences played over in his head. There were more of them than positives.

He needed something to stop the snowballing emotions in his head and the uncertain future of what was going to happen to him. He needed something to remind him that it can be easy to step back into what he knew, where he was safe.

He finished scrubbing the filth from his body and wrapped a towel around his waist.

"Hello?" he said aloud to his Holo Display. "Mum?"

"Oh, hello, darling. Nice of you to call. Everything alright?"

His mother looked worried. If Gil was calling her, then she usually assumed that something had to be wrong. She thought he lived a hectic lifestyle, trying to make a success in the city. That was far from the truth. Being a salvager was a part-time job at best. He just never saw the point in calling so much when he had nothing to update his family on.

His mother had never been back to the city since they'd left as a family. It wasn't her style. She preferred the quiet, away from people and the technology she didn't understand how to use—it all moved at too much of a fast pace for her.

"Yeah, fine, Mum. I got Grandpa's parcel."

"Oh, good. He was excited to send them over to you. He knows how much you enjoy all that stuff."

"Yeah," he replied. "I got a new job at that company I wanted to work for, Syngetical. Still not quite sure what I am meant to be doing, but it involves what I know about, sort of."

"Oh, I'm happy for you. Well done. See? I told you it would all be possible. Just had to give it time. Bet Terry is proud too."

"I remember the first job we gave you out here. Well, a sort of job, to keep you busy and teach you what a job consisted of. Was quite funny seeing you bounce around the yard doing the chores we gave you. Until you were old enough, then we could get you on the actual workings of the farm side of things: picking, seeding, planting. Getting you up early was harder, the older you got…"

She trailed off as she normally did when she dipped in to one of her stories of the past. She liked to reminisce. Gil knew that parents had the same feelings about their kids as the kids did about the adults—they couldn't wait to get away from them when they were together, but missed them immensely when they were gone. Telling a story was his mother's way of dealing with the distance between them. Normally, he would zone out and not pay much attention. She had the tendency to repeat herself. But this time he was happy to listen and hear a familiar voice. It was comforting, the distraction he needed.

An hour passed without him even realising it. His hair was now completely dry.

"Well, your father had no idea what he was

doing. He tried to help, but the doctors told him to step away, so he did and then he paced around the room." She laughed. "It was very funny to watch. Although, I was slightly distracted with trying to give birth to you, so he was just annoying me. It must have been the drugs. Your father doesn't normally annoy me with his little panic routine."

Gil looked over at his techpack that was sitting on the side cabinet by the door—a reminder of where he was going before Rix called. He had left it filled, part of him still eager to go.

"It's strange what you remember when you have so many emotions running around your head, drugs in your body and a tiny little you coming out of me."

"Mum, that's gross."

"Well, it's true. That's what happened. There was a point I thought I had too much of the oxygen. I thought I had already given birth. I could see the doctor already showing me the baby when actually I had to give one more push. That's when I decided to put the oxygen mask down."

Gil snapped out of his lull.

"What did you just say?"

"I put down the oxygen mask. I know when enough is enough."

"No, the bit before it, Mum."

"Oh, it was the effects of the oxygen. I wouldn't worry. You often think things have happened when they haven't—not that giving birth is something you can forget. You turned out alright, dear."

"But you had a deja vu moment, right?" he

asked.

"Yes, everyone gets them, Gil. I was high on oxygen at the time, remember? It's no big deal."

"Mum, I've got to go. Sorry, I have to dash. I have a meeting to get to. I forgot the time."

His mother had confirmed it. It was exactly what Freer has been talking about. He was born on that geological time shift pattern, the very moment that gives the child the syght ability. He did have it. Rix was right all along.

This only confirmed what he needed to do.

"Oh, that's okay, my love. Lovely chatting to you. I know you are busy. Enjoy your meeting and call us again when you are free please. We miss you."

"Miss you too. Say hi to everyone for me."

"Okay, dear. Love you…"

He ended the call, picked up his techpack and left the apartment.

He knew where he needed to go. Now was his time to listen. Ignoring the Sense Shifters once had already proved pointless. There were too many signs leading him back to Freer. It was confirmed. It was in his DNA. If he left it dormant, this whole situation would only end up with him or others getting hurt. If the Sense Shifters led a life of secrecy, then so could he.

He arrived at the bottom of Lower Mile and headed towards the forecourt.

He banged on the door hard. His brow had small droplets of sweat, which ached to run down his forehead. He held a tight grip on his techpack.

The door opened. Freer was standing the other side.

"Teach me what you know," he said in one breath.

EIGHTEEN

"Again!" Freer shouted.

It had been three days and Gil was attempting to settle in to his training. The majority of it consisted of Freer throwing objects at him while she told him to either dodge or catch. Gil was starting to bruise.

"Dodge!" Freer swiped a wooden pole towards his legs. He landed on the mat and turned over his ankle.

"Ah, shit. That hurt. Stop…stop."

He hobbled over to the bench.

"You have to avoid thinking only in the moment of what is happening. You have to see slightly beyond to see the consequences of that action," she said as she joined him.

"How am I meant to do that?" He grabbed his ankle, just as a piercing pain shot up his shin.

"You keep the eye you closed shut for longer. As you would be in that reality, you mustn't automatically switch back straight away. Control your ability of choice and control the outcomes of your decisions. This is why you are valuable to the 55."

"It's a bit hard to remember all these things at once. I'm trying my best—not exactly an easy skill to pick up."

"I can see you are trying. Syght will not fall into your muscle memory overnight, Gil. It takes months, sometimes years. I have only trained people that have lost an eye already. I am learning as much as you are in this. You may pick it up quicker or it may be a stubborn skill to control. But if your limits aren't pushed, your body is not going to improve its speed and reaction times."

"You've never trained anyone with syght before who has both their eyes?" he asked, suddenly feeling as if any faith he had left remaining had gone.

"Normally, people with your genes, those who have syght, die young. The mind and the body can't deal with being in two realities at the same time."

"Oh, well. That's promising to hear."

"You are older, Gil, and we are training you at a rate that you can adapt to slowly, while you begin to understand how actions and reactions work. Throwing anything complicated at you is obviously going to overload the brain and have effects on the body. There is only one of you, but your mind thinks otherwise. And one heart cannot pump blood for two bodies when the brain is telling it to."

Gil nodded. "Should I write this all down?"

"No, you learn it practically. That's the way syght

works. Back up on your feet."

He put his foot on the ground tenderly and stood. It stung initially, but he walked the rest of the pain off.

"Let me show you something," she said.

She positioned Gil in the centre of the mat and stood directly in front of him, an inch or two away. She was slightly taller than he was, so he needed to look up to see her.

"The closer you are to the object, the clearer you see the two realities, your two options available. This is why we need to improve your blink speed and reaction time after you have seen your choices. The later you leave it, the better it is for you to choose your outcome."

"So, what are you going to do?"

"I'm going to hit you, hard. I want you to move out of the way."

"What? I'm not doing that!" He began to walk away.

She grabbed him and moved him back into centre. She held on and said, "Ready?"

"No, of course not."

"I have already told you what I'm going to do, so your prep is easier than it would be if it had come out of nowhere. You can't change what is going to happen as you are not the one initiating it. You can change the outcome as it happens, though. I'll count you in, one... two..."

He tried to wriggle loose, but Freer had a firm grip. On the count of three, she launched a punch towards his abdomen.

He blinked as fast as he could, but it hit him square in the stomach. He crumpled to the floor, coughing.

"You panicked."

"Argghh, of course…I did," he spluttered.

"You need to control that panic. Understand what is happening and accept what is in the moment. Try it again."

"I really don't want you to punch me again."

"Then move out the way."

She pulled him back up to his feet. He'd never been punched before, not properly. Rix play-fought him most of the time and that hurt enough. He was a weak, lanky-yet-small individual, the type that would run from a fight before there was even talks of one starting.

Freer held him again in the same position and counted to three.

He breathed in and tensed his abs in case he was hit again. From the force of that last punch, he could tell that Freer had no ambition of holding back.

He focused on her hand, where her fist was going to impact on his body.

"Three…" she said and he rapidly blinked between each eye.

Through his eyes, it seemed as if the punch took forever to land, and he tried to see if he could see a choice that meant he could evade being hurt again.

Freer was right. He could see the world split into two, like the screen of a multi-player video game he remembered from his childhood. Both the realities vibrated, causing his vision to become blurry. It was as though he couldn't lock one reality into place, but through the murkiness he knew there was an option.

He moved sideways on and Freer's punch missed him.

He took a huge sigh of relief.

"Impressive." She smiled.

"All that effort just to miss a punch?"

"It will become second nature after a while. Also, there is one detail I left out. If you cross your eyes before you blink, it opens out the realities further."

"What?!? Are you joking?"

It had taken this long to tell him a vital piece of information, which meant he wouldn't have been punched. He might have to explain to Freer how teaching worked.

"No, I don't joke. It would have made you sick and dizzy, therefore, losing your control and focus. Remember, we have to build the ability up in stages."

"There is too much to learn!" He was getting frustrated. Every time he completed a task, there was something new he had to remember. There was no end to it and there might never be. This was an organic skill that could develop and grow as he learnt but also as he grew older. It wasn't like circuit boards. Once you knew how they worked and how the parts were connected, that was it. It was simple.

"You've done three days of training and already you are learning how to avoid a punch, Gil. I never said this was going to be easy."

They continued to spar for the rest of the day. Freer set a variety of exercises that they must achieve before they move on to the next. For the moment, Gil was learning the foundation of syght—how to blink when dealing with different scenarios—which involved seeing the two realities when an object was coming towards him or falling away from him. Freer said this would help improve his blink time and knowing when to execute a move at the correct moment. She said he had to learn this on his own. She used her other senses for this, so it was difficult for her to know how it worked for him. And anyway, she couldn't show him how to blink when she had no eyes to demonstrate with.

During their breaks, she would give him advice or explain the larger complexities of this new world that was opening up to him, how certain elements of life had been covered up to make you believe one thing was something else.

"Déjà vu," she said between slurps from a bowl of hot broth, "is when one reality skips ahead of the other before it can correct itself. Everyone experiences it, though few know what the reason is behind it. The gravity in both realities can differ occasionally. I explained how a geological time shift pattern is unique to the Deja Vu gene, which we now know you have."

Gil nodded.

"Time itself cannot be sped up or slowed down; it is a constant. Gravity, however, is an unstable entity and not constant; it's a natural part of life like the wind is. Gravity can dilate or slow down, as such, which does affect time as a function. Hence, deja vu."

"So, not everyone sees a deja vu?" he said, then blew on his spoon to cool down the broth.

"They do. Most describe it as seeing the same image or scene twice. I have told you what actually happens. The gene occurs when someone is born on a particular déjà vu moment, where the world sees something repeated at the same time."

It was confusing for him to understand, these complexities of syght, how what he thought he knew about the world was completely different. Slowly, it was starting to make sense.

He nodded.

"Syght is a displacement of the two realities at opposite ends of the universe. If mastered, it would allow you to switch between the two, to potentially live in both if you were capable of getting to that level. The older generation thought it would allow you to time travel, as they thought you could switch between one end of the universe to the other. As we know now, these two realities are happening at the same time."

"Is there anyone else you are training at the moment?" he asked. He could feel the aches on his body.

"No, only you."

"Thank you again for letting me stay here." It was something he felt he needed to say.

All this training and Freer offering board must

have been an expense. He could have gone home—not that that was the safest option right now.

"I'm sorry it's not like your apartment: full of technology to entertain yourself with."

"I don't have much of that anyway. I brought some newspapers to read with me."

She looked at him blankly.

"Newspapers. Companies must have stopped making them before you were born. I only know about them because my grandpa collected them—hoarded them really."

"What did they do?"

"The clue is kind of in the title. They told you what was happening around the world. You read them rather than watching the news on a viewer."

"Neither of which I can do." Freer smiled.

"No, I guess not. I can read them to you if you wish? I got sent the ones leading up to the 2040 elections and after too. Was hoping to find something about syght in them."

"Thank you, but I am going to get some rest. We have a long way to go yet. I'll leave you to your newspapers."

She rose from the table and took her bowl to the washer. She placed it over a small spout that came out of the middle of a metal draining board attached to the side. A jet of water sprayed up into the bowl, cleaning it in a few seconds. She left the bowl and spoon on a rack next to the board.

Freer may have been very modern in the way she didn't know what a newspaper was, but he had to smile at the old-fashioned way she cleaned up after meals. There was something reassuring about not having technology control everything, all of the time.

"Goodnight," she said.

"Night," he replied.

He stirred the remains of his broth around in the bowl, thinking about all that had happened. Was he stupid for being here? Yes, he was safe, but truly, how safe could he be? The 55 would find him eventually; it was only a matter of when.

As he was pondering this, another Sense Shifter entered the eating quarters, walking up to the cauldron on the side where he poured himself a bowl of broth.

"How's your training going?" he asked.

"Who knows what to make of it all, if I'm honest."

The guy sat down in front of him.

"You won't at first or potentially after either—none of us did. I was going mad, literally, before I came here. Any decision I made felt like I had no hand in deciding it. It was predetermined for me—the feeling of someone writing the story for me. You know what I mean? Sorry, I'm Nicon."

He extended a hand and Gil shook it.

Nicon had lost one of his eyes and wore a contraption over his head with a lens over his left eye. It looked similar to what Midi wore down at the pit.

"You trying to work out what this is?" He tapped the half frame. "This is a modified Spacial

Lens. Allows me to see what both eyes would see, rather than just one eye like a normal Spacial Lens does. Pretty nifty device, once you get the hang of it. They had to get their hands on a lens in its basic form and programme in what a second eye would see—basically, what my left eye sees but two inches to the right. It isn't quick enough for me to use syght, as no tech can be, so I'm trying to learn how to use my other senses as well. But I feel a bit more normal with this on."

He took a spoonful of the broth and then wiped the excess drops from his beard.

This was the first time he had spoken to another of the Sense Shifters. He had only interacted with Freer until now. All of them were here because society in some way had kicked them out. Gil wasn't sold on the idea of living a life of secrecy to this extent, but he had wanted to learn more about them, how they all differed, and now he had his chance.

"How long have you been here?"

"Can't remember really—two or three years now?"

Gil took that reply to his chest. It was though he had received another blow. Two or three years for him to feel normal again? He couldn't wait that long.

Nicon picked up the bowl with two hands, evidently not noticing Gil's panic, and slurped the entire bowl down in one.

"But you'll get it faster, I'm sure. Harder with one eye, isn't it?"

He left the table, taking his bowl with him.

"See you later…" he said, extending the last word as he waited for Gil to say his name.

"Gil."

Nicon clicked his fingers and pointed his index finger at him, then walked off.

Gil realised that, if he were to succeed, he needed to be more determined to. Nobody was stopping him from leaving and returning home, but this place was his safest option, where he was off the radar. If syght was going to make him feel as normal as he could again, then he needed to master it.

Each day felt as though it was the last: going to work at Syngetical and then coming back to the Sense Shifters' headquarters in the evenings—the same routine, the same scenarios: repetitions of the rules of syght so he would never forget them. Freer made sure he understood the basics and could recite anything back to her. A couple of weeks passed and he was feeling drained. He had lost sight of his own improvement. They had moved on from the foundations like blinking and onto reaction times, improving how quickly he could blink.

"I'm tired, Freer. I can't see it anymore, the realities. It's a blur."

"Tiredness will be your weakness. You have to look beyond that. The quicker you can blink, the less effort you will need to put in. You wanted to learn this at a faster pace than the other Sense Shifters, so I'm doing what I can. You need to keep up."

"I know, I know." Gil sighed, picking himself up

from the mat.

"There is a speed know as Planck time, which is the fastest known calculable speed. If you can get your blinking to this rate, you will have no trouble seeing both realities."

"Is that possible?"

Weary at the mere thought of the question, he almost didn't want to hear the answer. His hope was slightly draining out of him. This ability was turning out to be more of an ordeal than a blessing.

"If you can blink quicker than the quantum of time then, yes."

"Is that a joke? I can't tell." He was puzzled by her statement. The quantum of time was not a phrase he knew. If this was her idea of a humorous line, then Gil missed the humour in it.

"No, it's a fact. Hence, why it is easier for Sense Shifters than people with syght to learn. We may not be able to see both realities, but we have the advantage of understanding both, using our other senses and working at a slower speed."

"So, you aren't even sure if it's possible for me to be able to?"

"As I said, we are all learning here."

He sighed.

Each time he thought of anything negative, the thought opened up a wave of questions about why he was doing this. Parts of his training felt like a long dream that this was so far from real—Gil being in this situation—that all he needed to do was wake up and then he'd be back to normal again. The bruises, however, made it very clear he wasn't imagining it.

"I just had an epiphany: I need a day off," he said after one particularly arduous training session. "That's what I need, Freer. I need time to not think about anything and just rest."

"If that's what you want, then you may do so. But that is not an epiphany—just so you know."

"Yeah, I know. I was making a joke."

"Oh." Freer paused. He assumed she was attempting to figure out the joke.

"Another lie told as a kid?" He continued, breaking the silence.

"Yes, very much so. Like déjà vu, true epiphanies are not what most think they are. They are quite important when it comes to syght. It's actually when you see both options of a decision played out in front of you and you have time to decide what happens, rather than choosing an option in the moment. They are rare and you need both gravities in both realities to dilate at the same time for it to happen."

"Well, if my epiphany shows me either falling asleep or getting hit a lot more, then I choose sleep."

"You had an actual epiphany?" Freer asked in surprise.

"No, of course not; that was another joke. That's how you make a joke."

"I did not find it funny. It made no sense."

There was no surprise that Freer was not laughing. Gil had noticed she did not understand a lot of his attempted jokes. While living as a Sense Shifter had clearly improved the speed of her reactions, it obviously not aided her to develop a quick wit. He wondered whether he could give her a lesson in how to tell one, although it might take a lot longer than him learning syght.

"Jokes aren't meant to make sense. They are jokes. See? We are learning something." He laughed, but Freer did not follow.

He made his way back to his room within the camp, and lay down on the mattress. Maybe if he eased off on pressuring himself to learn syght in a fixed amount of time, it would happen naturally.

He rested his eyes for a few hours, but his attempts to switch off, to ignore the voices in his head and the resulting spasms of pain jolting through his body whenever he had a memory of being hit, were unsuccessful. He was too submerged in his own thoughts to not think about them. What he really needed was fresh air, to see natural light. It had been so long. If there was one thing he had learnt how to do, it was to see in the darkness. His eyes had adapted to the insufficient light enough that he could see different shades of shadows and was able to pick out what was reflecting the light within darkness.

There was sparse light in the Sense Shifters' place; the only room that had it was the surveillance room and Gil never needed to go in there. He never wanted to go in there.

Some fresh air would clear his mind. The sunlight would replenish his energy, as if he were a solar panel needing a charge. Although it would now be dark outside, maybe stepping out into harsh sunlight might be a bit extreme for his eyes to adjust straight away.

It was a risk going outside, knowing he was a target. He didn't know who knew about his syght—if anyone else did—and who might want him for their own greed. But he knew how to be incognito; he was still a salvager, after all. He hid in the darkness for a living and had so far avoided being caught. Some risks were worth taking. He was starting to think like Rix.

NINETEEN

Two weeks had passed since Gil had taken on his new role, and Cyra had been there one week more than him, he had learned. He felt reassured that she was as new to this as he was. There was no real clarity on what his title was, other than the knowledge of the task in hand—to make the Inter-Dimensional lens work so one could travel through space using it. When Cyra did speak with him, he understood none of the scientific jargon. He assumed it was more that she was verbalising her thoughts than wanting a conversation. She had so many questions and the electronic notes were building up. She had already arranged them into folders and subcategories so she could access the right question to ask at the right time. He gathered these were for Anders to answer.

Most of the time, he either read or tinkered around with spare circuit boards, much to the frustration of Cyra. He was happy to be involved, although his contributions were minor. He was as much a spare part as the old wiring lying around.

Anders had been absent since the day he had started. He had watched and listened to how Cyra had understood how a standard Spacial lens worked, the mechanics of how it integrated AI with biotechnology and the infusion of electrical impulses sent from the brain to a man-made optical lens, how it also adjusted depending on the user's requirements and adapted within changing environments. For someone who trained in science and not hardware, Cyra had taught herself a lot. Gil was impressed. She had now started reading through the books on circuitry, microchips, wiring and how the lens and the components were put together. He was hoping he might be able to help in this department. This was the part she would struggle with as it was hands on: hardware being pieced together in the smallest format to be able to be inserted into the eye socket. Gil had watched Terry do this numerous times.

Cyra was more about theories and calculations, running scenarios through a computer, and he could see her frustrations building when she had to test something without running a simulation first. He was eager to speak up and help her, but she bit back every time.

"I can help solder those two chips together?" he said hesitantly from across the room.

"No, Gil, you can't as you don't know the science behind it: the why, the how, the reason why these two have to fit together."

"I've read up on how a Spacial Lens is put together and I have training in how to solder and fix microchips."

The few things that Cyra had given him to do, he had messed up. He was nervous. He wanted to impress. She put so much pressure on him, watching him like a hawk. One thing he had learnt from Terry was a steady hand, but it was hard to be accurate when you were only given one chance to prove your worth and that was it. He knew he could solder two circuit boards together, much better than she could, but if it was not done in her way then she snatched it from him and re-did it. Her work in this area was untidy. The surface and lines had to be clean.

She had asked for a Spacial lens in its complete form and also all of its individual components so she could learn how to build one from the manuals. Gil saw she could retain information well, however she always needed to see it in practice, in its material form. She had no computer to run simulations—not that that would have helped her anyway. Nothing in Anders' notes suggested he had run trials through a computer. His tests were a practical trial and error until he found the intended result. There were no equations, no code.

Gil was still confused to how a piece of hardware like a lens would help someone travel through space. Cyra had told him—or lectured at him—about how she had to utilise a practical piece of hardware to translate theoretical equations into the ID Lens.

Anders had not cracked the answer, but maybe Cyra could with her knowledge of advanced space mechanics and quantum entanglement. Anders had created the structure for the ID Lens; all she needed to do was solve the equation.

Gil helped with the circuitry when she let him, but he often felt he wasn't required, that his presence annoyed Cyra. They had limited conversation and he wanted to be involved more. He could help. Anders wouldn't have given him this position if he couldn't. If it wasn't for his training with Freer, these would have been long, boring days. Reading was fun to a certain extent and he loved to acquire information, but he wanted the practical experience too, like Cyra was doing.

'*BUZZ*'

The sound alerted that the door had unlocked, which evidently surprised Cyra as it caused her hand, which was holding the solder to the Spacial lens circuit board, to slip.

Anders Hilgaard and Felcion Trux entered the room—their first visitors since Gil had entered.

"How are we getting on?" Anders asked with a smile.

"Getting there. I'm ahead of the reading schedule so thought I would try to manage both the reading and practical at the same time, to understand it clearer."

"Good. Ahead is what we like. Gil, may I introduce to you my head scientist for the Spacial Lens? This is Felcion."

"Nice to meet you, Gil." Felcion nodded slightly but almost with resentment—another person that didn't want Gil here.

"I have read through most of your questions on the system," Anders went on, "most of which you will find out through your reading, so I feel it would be a waste of time me answering them now. However, I have brought Felcion along to help with the Spacial lens questions and demonstrations. He will spend time with you over the next couple of days, making sure you understand the parameters of this lens and aiding in any problematic areas of the construction."

"Good! That's what I need. Gil is not exactly the assistant I need right now. It does not help my research when I have people who don't know what they are doing. Myles would have been a better candidate. Despite his distractions at times, he is knowledgeable and knows how I work."

He felt the dagger being pushed right through his chest.

"Give him time, Cyra. Help him understand so he can help you!" Anders said—another sign of a great boss, supporting his staff.

"Hello again, Cyra," Felcion said. "Obviously my time here is limited and I will help you in any way I can. I understand that you want to know more about the Deja Vu gene and what your original job role was searching for."

Gil was suddenly alert. He knew about this. He knew all about the gene from Freer. He might even have it. Was that why he was here? Because he might have the gene? But there was no way Anders, or anyone, would know. He hadn't even told Rix about it. He was curious why Syngetical was looking for the Déjà vu gene. He kept quiet. Anders had said not to say anything about syght to anyone. Gil knew it was linked, but did Anders?

Felcion had turned and whispered something to Anders.

"Yes, Felcion. She does." Anders answered at a normal volume for both to hear. "It will aid with her work. She has agreed to her contract and understands the consequences of exchanging sensitive information to those outside of this corporation or within departments. Isn't that right, Ms Wolverton?"

She nodded.

"Then I shall leave you all to discuss." He left the workshop and closed the door, the loud sound of the buzz alerting him that the door was now locked again.

"Makes me jump every time," Cyra said, embarrassed.

There was a silence between the three of them. There was some awkward tension between Felcion and Cyra. Gil thought it safer to stay out of this.

Felcion walked around the room, peering at all the other inventions lying around. His inquisitive look upon every station made his eyebrow quiver.

"You've not been in here before, have you?" Cyra asked.

"Not as such, no," he responded.

Felcion wandered over to where Cyra was perched. She had made a clearing on one of the tables against the side wall for the Spacial Lens set up. She was slowly piecing together one of the lenses from scratch. The circuit board was tiny and she was using a microscopic display to fuse together the four mini-intelligence chips it needed.

"Hmmm," Felcion murmured.

"What have I done?"

"I think you have misaligned the responses chip, and the syntax and neuron chips are the wrong way round. So, no signal would be sent from the brain to the lens when you connect it to the retina. All it will do is send a message to the brain that the eye lid is closed and display a black image." He pointed to the part of the circuit board where she had made the mistake.

Not that Gil would have said anything, but he had also noticed that too. He was proud his research was already teaching him something.

"Have I?"

"Both the microchips are very similar. I wouldn't worry. I spent three weeks trying to work out what the problem was when I helped design this lens. All I had to do was switch them around."

"Thank you. Saved me some time. I already feel there is a lot to cram in, with the month deadline Anders set me."

She removed the synthetic skin cell that kept all the chips in place and switched the two chips around.

Gil peered over from his table.

Both Felcion and Cyra looked at him.

"Just seeing what you were doing," he said, feeling as though he needed to apologise for his actions.

"Easy when you know how," she simpered. "And what have I done with the responses chip?"

"It's misaligned. That chip there allows the person to blink how the other eye would. It controls the involuntary action of the blink, closing it when something is coming towards it or blinking when something is on or close to the lens as if it were a real iris. So, a blink is recorded—"

"At 0.1 seconds, otherwise known as a decisecond." She finished the sentence.

"Yes, correct. Which is quite slow when you think of the speeds that we know of, those that are quicker than a second, such as light travelling through space, for example. Of course you know that: you are the expert in that field."

Gil was not, though. He was the idiot in the room.

"So, can you tell me about the déjà vu gene?" she asked.

Felcion sighed.

"I'm not sure how it will help you, but the orders have been set. Actually, I have to ask: what are you doing? Other than making a mockery out of my hard work."

"Excuse me?" Cyra was obviously taken aback by the bluntness of his statement. "I didn't ask to learn about the Spacial Lens or how to put the damn thing together. All I wanted was to study and explore the field in which I studied in. I'm not here to be taking jobs or push people out. Anders thinks I am useful for something. Whatever that has to do with this lens or that one over there is anybody's guess." She pointed to the ID lens sitting on the stand on the main desk.

It wasn't just Gil she was frustrated at—Felcion too; maybe everyone. He was starting to think that was just who Cyra was: straight to the point and wanting to solve everything. When obstacles were in her way, she took it out on others.

"What's that?" Felcion asked.

"The new ID Lens," she said as if it was the most obvious thing in the room.

"You mean the Video Xerox lens? The VX? That's what it looks like?" Felcion made a snarl with his mouth, his distaste at the style of the lens clear on his face. "Not the original design I had for the upgrade to the Spacial Lens. I guess Mr Hilgaard must have changed it. Not sure how that is going to work recording what people see."

Gil spotted that Cyra had the same expression on her face as he did. Felcion was his head scientist and didn't know about the ID Lens. That was odd. Both Gil and Cyra knew what they were working on—more Cyra than Gil; he had to learn through the notes and the sporadic information she blurted out to the note-taking system.

If Felcion didn't know, it was not his place to tell him, and by the looks of it, Cyra wasn't going to either.

"Yeah, that's the one. Sorry, with all these books, I must have muddled something up from something I read. So, the Deja Vu gene…?"

"They had found a pattern where young people were dying in their mid-twenties due to a particular disease," Felcion said, mimicking Cyra by jumping straight to the answer, "…usually hitting them around the age of twenty-five, depended on a number of factors: usually the host's environment. It's as though the gene is switched at a certain age. It's what we call gene regulation within the RNA code—the body performs this automatically. RNA is often seen as a copy or a repeat of the DNA template, you may say, therefore, it is what we called the Deja Vu gene."

That was incorrect. Gil had been told something different by Freer. So, which version was the truth? If Felcion had already been lied to about the lens being created, then the Déjà vu gene had to be a lie too.

"I understand that now." Cyra looked relieved, her shoulders dropped, having finally had this explained to her. "All I had been told before was a pattern—similarities in humans' certain DNA coding—but never the actual reason. Microbiology is not my field in the slightest, but it is an area I can understand when it is explained."

"If it helps, I don't really know anything. Would be nice to be told," Gil said.

Felcion sighed.

"Cytosine is one of the four chemical bases that create both RNA and DNA code. We believe it is this particular base that may be the weak link when the copy of the same base in the RNA is a different length to that of the same base in the DNA sequence. The Deja Vu gene is the abnormality of the cytosine base that causes the disease—we think. It's hard to know for sure right now."

"Disease?" Gil shocked. This was the first time he had heard it classed as that.

"If something is irregular in your DNA, then yes, it is a disease—something we need to fix and therefore cure," Felcion responded.

"So, what is RNA?"

"Did you not pay any attention through your education?"

He assumed that was a rhetorical question.

"It is a vital molecule, similar to your DNA—an acronym for ribonucleic acid that is found in your cells and is necessary for life. Your body uses the RNA to construct proteins so that new cell growth can occur."

Gil understood a little more, but with Felcion's resentment at having to explain Biology 101, he avoided asking more questions on that topic.

"Why is Syngetical being so secret about it?" Gil asked instead. "Surely, they should be telling people about it if it is affecting them?"

"We want to avoid causing panic. We still need to finalise and verify our findings. The idea was to be able to build a lens that was able to see when the patient was going to die, to utilise our technology and save them before it was too late. Once that cytosine base becomes irregular, it is irreversible. It was based on an old myth about a group of people being able to 'see' when there were going to die or something, winking between each eye and the distance between the object... I don't know. Either way. the government shut that down and we can't be seen going against the government's ruling, hence why everything is kept so secret."

That information, Gil did understand. They knew about syght too—the debunked version, though, not the actual ability he had. Syngetical was searching for people with this gene, wanting to help save them from an early death. He knew syght didn't show you when someone was going to die, so the lens was not going to work—for that purpose, anyway.

"Even if it's for the greater good?" Cyra asked.

"Not the point. You've seen our High Chancellor. Could you imagine if she got wind of this? Mr Hilgaard and Syngetical would be shut down. There are too many people who rely on us to keep them alive through all Mr Hilgaard's ventures."

"Thank you for explaining that to me, Felcion. I feel it should be told to the others also. We would have a better understanding of what we are looking for."

She smiled—the first time Gil had seen her do that.

"We tell you—well, them—only what they need

to know. We wanted to find people to be able to test the prototype on. That is proving difficult as we are yet to find anyone, or if we have, it has been too late. It's a very rare thing to find, it seems, although the evidence is out there. We have to be faster at locating it."

"You—I mean, we—will," Cyra said.

One question remained, which still played on Gil's mind. And he could tell it did with Cyra too. If Felcion had no idea what the ID lens was, then why was he being lied to? Gil knew the Déjà vu gene information was inaccurate. From the way Felcion skulked around the room and his comments on the ID Lens design, Gil could tell that none of this had been revealed to him, that this workshop was as much a secret to him as it was to Gil, and most probably Cyra too. The only person who would know was Anders Hilgaard. Everyone else was working on a lie. Gil was certain to a degree that this was correct.

For once, he knew more than Cyra did. The secrecy behind the Déjà vu gene also didn't add up. Anders was hiding something—not just from him, or even Syngetical, but everyone, globally.

The next two days passed rather quickly for the three of them. Gil had watched on, seeing how the Spacial lens was pieced together. The added help and support meant Cyra finally had her unanswered questions explained. She had almost doubled her productivity by having someone there in the room who knew what they were talking about and she had now erased many of the questions from the file.

"There you are. The complete Spacial Lens, built entirely by your own hands, Cyra." Felcion said, marvelling at her handiwork.

He sat back in his chair and wiped his hands on the cliché laboratory jacket that all scientists had to be seen to be wearing.

"With a lot of help from you, might I add. I now understand how this lens works and how to put it together. Thank you, Felcion."

He paused, a heartfelt expression on his face.

"I'm sorry I started off with an attitude towards you. I thought Mr Hilgaard might be replacing me. One has to always worry in these current times. You do have experience and a skill set that I do not possess and that could improve how we make our products."

He placed his hand on her shoulder.

"I best get back to my office. I only popped in yesterday to check on things. Let me know, or Mr Hilgaard, if you have any remaining questions. I am confident you know what you need to, now you have seen it in practise. All you have to do now is try on the lens and see if it works. Obviously, you would need a surgical procedure to see if the lens functions properly, but the alternative is: you can hold up the circuit board to your temple with the lens over your eye. It'll work off your kinetic energy and pulse when you move around."

He rose from his chair and headed over to the

double doors.

"Thank you again," Cyra said as she stood.

'*BUZZ*'

The room fell quiet, the first time in two days there wasn't a voice or the sound of sparks.

"Was it me or did you have the feeling that Felcion was left in shadows about certain projects?" Cyra said.

The first actual conversation. She was finally asking Gil a question.

"Somebody is lying to him."

"That was my assessment too. Why do we know information that is different from every other employee? Is that not strange? Syngetical hiding information?"

Gil wanted to keep the belief that there was a reason as to why. As Felcion had mentioned, they didn't want to scare the nation, but this was within the company itself. Anders had chosen not to reveal key and maybe vital information.

"He didn't know about the lens or the Déjà vu gene," he said.

Cyra's expression changed.

"What do you mean? He explained it to us."

Gil was now in a predicament. He needed to win over Cyra's trust, but at the same time, if he told her what he knew, was it breaking his contract? It wasn't about syght, only the truth on what the Déjà vu gene was. If they were working together on groundbreaking technology, they had to share information. He might be able to help her, to provide the answer that she was missing.

"Déjà vu is a gene—Felcion was correct on that— but it's not about finding the people who have it to stop them from dying. If you have it, it's about seeing two realities, seeing how choices in a certain situation will play out so you can choose the correct option."

Cyra was confused. For a scientist, she didn't seem to comprehend what Gil was saying.

He was restricted on what he could tell her. Anders had said not to mention syght to anyone. Theoretically, he had not said the word. He had only described it by explaining what having the gene could do.

"It's about blinking and how quickly you can do it to see your choices—"

"In a blink of an eye," she whispered aloud, interrupting him. The cogs were turning. He had ignited something, a thought, an idea in her head.

"The blink, on the ID Lens—it has to be faster. Gil, that's it!" She was delighted, exploding with energy.

"What did I say?"

"The answer to how we can get this lens to work!"

TWENTY

Another week rolled by and Gil made it his priority to focus his full attention on learning syght. He could now see into two realities through choices that had to be made at the last moment, and he could extend this vision to see how both realities continued on after the decision, but there was only so much lengthening he could do before he lost syght. Once a decision had been made, Gil automatically switched back into his reality. It was though his brain had closed the book and moved on. He had to learn how to keep the pages turning, how to guide himself through the reality into another decision. That's how he could keep the realities open, as well as his options. He often asked Freer whether it was possible to live in both realities simultaneously, but she always answered no—nobody had so far. She explained that the prefrontal cortex of the brain, which has influence on decision, could only last in the chosen reality until the decision itself was fully made and the next one started, therefore starting the process again.

"Are there not multiple options to any one decision, though? Why are there not multiple realities to then pick between?" he asked as he ducked out of the way of a flying kick.

"How many eyes do you have, Gil?"

"Rhetorical, right?"

"The answer is two. There are only two outcomes to anything. Yes or no, hit or miss, left or right. You cannot process options you cannot see in front of you. One choice leads onto another, there is no scope beyond that. For example, you are standing in a position and you want to walk forward, backwards, left and right. You are unable to see behind you, which takes out that option. Time and your progression in life, remember, is linear, so you are theoretically always moving forward. If you ignore your choices, you stay moving forward, therefore it is not a choice as you are already doing it. The only options then left are left and right."

This confused Gil somewhat. He understood that syght was very black and white; something either is or it is not. You can't see multiple decisions when you only have two eyes.

"You're processing it, aren't you?" she asked.

He threw a weak-handed fist towards her, but she moved out of its way before he finished swinging.

"Surely, there are always multiple choices?"

"You have to break down choice to the simplest

form for it to work. You overthink it and you fail to see syght. Let your brain choose the two options that are available. The options that either benefit you or not. Syght is heightened in dangerous situations. You start to fall: you either continue to fall and hurt yourself or take the action you need to do to stop yourself. I go to punch you: you see the options of me hitting you or you avoiding it. If you start thinking about the multiples—what if you punched at same time or if you slipped over or if someone entered the room—syght would not work. It is cancelled out. This is why pessimistics cannot learn syght. They worry too much about the what if. You have to focus on only the two choices and then work through one decision at a time in sequence. Yes, you could punch me as a counter but you must finish the first choice first, avoiding my initial punch. That initial decision is to not get hit or be hit. Your next choice would be how to react to that initial punch. This is your next decision. One at a time, Gil. Trying to work out multiple realities and outcomes to the tiniest decisions is too complicated; the brain can't process it and therefore you won't see it. Oh what we know, there is this reality and the other. Let your brain deal with the two realities."

She swiped her legs through the air and caught Gil in the shin. He reacted with a counter kick, which she caught.

"This means I can assume what you are going to do and allow that choice to play out. Remember, I cannot see, so I use my other senses to heighten what is 'visible' to me. I might be wrong, but in this case, I was right, because of the way I have taught you."

As well as learning the parameters of syght, he was also learning how to defend himself physically.

"Good. You are improving a lot, Gil. Let's end it there for today."

"Do you think I am almost finished my training?"

He could feel himself improving. He knew it for the fact that he could spar with Freer and only get caught out a few times—and she was a trained expert. The 55 were not and no one else had this ability, pure syght. He knew the basics. That was surely enough.

He had his job at Syngetical and he wanted to start focusing on it more. From reading and watching Cyra, he had made some progress and his working relationship with her was improving too. She was trusting him to help on the practical side, and he was finally proving he had skills that she was not so strong at. He had to make Anders proud.

"Syght is not something you learn and then put in a box to use when you next need it. It requires constant improvement. Your abilities grows as much as you do in life, so you need to continually explore them. It's natural, it can vary, and it can change. I think your training would be best suited by having it not so intense."

"What do you mean? Like half days?"

He felt slightly disappointed. He had made a remark and maybe Freer thought he was giving up or becoming bored. He wasn't. He enjoyed this, learning about syght and exploring what was possible. He was just excited about his other prospects too. He was worried he sounded ungrateful.

"No, I mean by not living here, going back to your life. For the Sense Shifters here, this is their home. We are providing them with something they lost in their real life, until they are ready to return to it. You haven't lost anything. You have gained something and have been nurturing that. You can still live your life as normal and have this training as something you do around the other aspects of your life. You are trained enough to be able to protect yourself outside of your quarters here."

"What about you, though? Will you ever return to a normal life? Is it possible to go back to…"

Gil paused in his own sentence, realising he knew nothing about Freer's life before all of this.

"…whatever you were doing before?"

"Unless I have the Spacial lens, I cannot return to what you are calling 'real life'. I am becoming a master. I have chosen to help others learn, and if I have any technology put into my eye sockets or head, I'm going to lose what I have spent too long developing. This is my real life."

Sight was not everything to Freer; losing it gave her so much more than ever having it to begin with.

"We will continue to train in the evenings and drop down to four nights a week, starting from after tomorrow night. This will allow you time to rest and distract yourself enough to be ready for the next session. That afternoon and evening you had off, whatever you did, it worked. You came back mentally ready and you absorbed what I taught you."

"If you think that's the best choice for me."

"I think it's the only choice."

"Well, not really? I still have a choice to—"

"It was a joke, Gil. See? I can learn from you too." She smiled.

"Oh, a joke. Right. We'll work on it. But great start." He laughed.

He spent one final night at the Sense Shifters' dorms and went back to his apartment the next day. It was exactly how he had left it, apart from the fact that a set of brand-new tools were sitting on his kitchen side. Beside them was a note that said, 'Good luck at your new job'. The letter was signed with a 'T' at the bottom.

Someone must have informed Terry. He felt guilty. He hadn't had chance to talk to him about it— not that he would have stopped Gil from taking the chance of a lifetime. The tools, however, were a nice gesture, although they had come three weeks too late, and with the technology Gil was experimenting with, they might be a bit redundant.

Gil headed back over to Syngetical. It was later in the day than he wanted, but he knew Cyra would still be there. With his help, she had made a huge discovery. He knew she'd still be working on it.

'BUZZ'

Cyra was not startled by the alert this time. She was lost in her own world, walking up and down the centre concourse of the workshop, attempting to make the Spacial lens work.

"Gil, I've made a few tweaks. Something on the Spacial Lens isn't connecting, but I wanted to test it and get the right calculations before transferring them over to the ID Lens."

"What can I do?"

"Put this on. It's the modified Spacial Lens that we made with Felcion."

Gil was already a test dummy with Freer and syght so he may as well be one for Cyra. He thought that having syght wouldn't affect the results, as the lens wasn't working anyway.

He placed the circuit board against his temple and the lens over his eye. The view flickered on and off, a hazy view of the world through a blurred lens. His hand shifted how he held the circuit board over his temple as he attempted to find the right location for it. The shutter on the lens blinked every time the power surged through it.

He paused at the end of the room by the double doors.

"Are you having the same trouble as me? Something is showing, but it won't focus, right? I improved the blink speed but I think we have to go faster. Let me do some more calculations to the ID Lens."

Gil could see something through the lens but he was unsure what. It was showing something but not the workshop. A normal Spacial lens saw the world as everyone saw it. Cyra had tweaked this, though.

"GIL!" she shouted across the room from where she was now writing at her desk. He jumped in surprise, and for a brief moment, forgot what he was holding on to. He dropped the lens onto the floor. It cracked—all that hard work, the two days they had spent with Felcion, lost, the Spacial Lens, in all its glory, now ruined thanks to a momentary lapse in Gil's thought process. He had broken Cyra's creation.

"Shit!"

"It doesn't matter. We have the ID lens. Treat that as the prototype. It couldn't do what we needed it to, anyway, but maybe stay clear of this one."

He picked up the broken Spacial Lens and placed it on the table next to the ID lens.

"I'm sorry, I just—"

"It wasn't working, anyway. The drives, the boards—they are too old for what we need it to do. But we are seeing the same image so I think I know what I need to do for the ID Lens to work."

Gil knew they probably didn't see the same image. Unless he was imagining it…

There was no way they were building a lens…

The door buzzed, breaking his train of thought and Anders walked in.

"Evening, Ms Wolverton, Gil. How are we getting on today?"

"The reason why the ID lens has failed up to now was it was too slow," Cyra said, tracing her finger over some words on her paper. She picked up a pen and circled a number. "You wanted a lens to travel through space time, if that was possible. Now, time as we know it neither slows down or speeds up. It's constant. We measure it in change or progression; that's our perception of time. We move through time doing one thing after another, so we need to find a way of beating it—being ahead of it before the action happens. Blinks are measured as 1/10th of a second and that's what we calibrate the Spacial lens to. But what if we sped up the blink to Planck Time, the quantum of time, the quickest known speed of light travelling through a vacuum? Because what is space? A giant vacuum!"

Gil followed most of what Cyra was talking about. He had never heard of Planck Time but guessed it was a unit of measure.

Cyra was full into a breakdown of what she had figured out, explaining all her analysis so far. Anders stood there, silent, listening, with a somewhat intrigued looked on his face. He couldn't tell if Anders believed what she was saying or if this was all information he already knew. It seemed as if Cyra also had this thought, as she was beginning to ramble on, trying to throw something more impressive at him that he might seem more delighted about.

"If I can work out the sum to electromagnetism plus quantum mechanics plus gravity, it will equal the Planck scale of length, time, mass and energy needed. Then I'd just need to figure out how to quicken the blink to that level. Including the laws of relativity, it could highlight and or create a virtual black hole. Time would then be kept as the constant as all you would be doing is skipping through space rather than time."

She turned to Gil.

"Sorry, I know that may not make sense to you. But in short: it means I need to find the correct equation and make the right adjustments and the lens should work. All in theory, of course." She turned back to Anders. "Gil gave me the idea."

Cyra had given him praise. At last, he had made an impact. Anders turned and nodded at him with a smile.

"The calculation would have to be specific on the individual, but it would mean 'said' person could travel or at least see through space if the conditions were met!" Once again, she had gone off on her own train of thought, verbalizing what her brain was trying to process. After her expulsion of words, all the workings in her head having tumbled out, she breathed heavily.

"You've been busier than I thought you would be." Anders sounded impressed. There was nothing practical they could show him yet, other than a broken Spacial Lens, but she had explained her theory.

Cyra slowly eased herself down into the chair, looking light-headed.

"It's all…speculation. The first thing…we need to do is quicken the blink," she said in between breaths. "That will give us the ability to work with the other parameters."

"I assume that Felcion has caught you up with what you needed to know," Anders said. "From your revelation, I can see he has done a grand job. The two of you are working nicely together."

Gil wanted to ask Anders about Felcion and his knowledge—or lack thereof—on the ID lens, why was he being kept in the dark. His speculation was also starting to grow that what they were building wasn't what Cyra had been told. If Anders could lie to Felcion, there was a chance he had lied to both Cyra and Gil too. He needed to be sure before he enlightened her. She may not get to the stage where she achieved her supposed goal, but he couldn't put her in danger.

He could see formulas flying around her head. The idea was still fresh. He would let her work and he could explain further down the line, when it was only the two of them.

"Already using your knowledge. You might be my most valuable employee yet. Other than yourself, Gil."

He knew Anders was making a joke. This was all Cyra's doing.

"Thank you for speaking out before, telling us of your skill set. If you had kept quiet, we might not have reached this point."

A compliment from the CEO. She blushed slightly.

And it was an achievement. Cyra had worked out what Anders had been testing for years now. Gil could tell she wanted to enjoy this revelation. This was why she had trained in what she had. It all came down to this moment, and no doubt, there would be more in the weeks to come. Though, he was more concerned to what the calculations might reveal.

"Well, it's all still theory for the moment—"

"A theory soon becomes practicality. Well done, Ms Wolverton."

It felt like a big red warning to why Anders wanted this lens to work so much. Gil's thoughts were snowballing again. He had to be wrong.

"I'm going to start working on the ID lens and reading the material you have noted on your process so far."

"Ahead of schedule too. Very impressive. I shall leave you to it."

"And Gil has been a great help. The next few stages should progress much faster now I have someone who knows how to piece circuitry together."

"And there was you, thinking you were a bad investment, Gil," Anders said.

"I'm sure Cyra could have done it without me," he said. "She's not too bad with electronics."

"But now I do need you. This is where the theory becomes practical. Before, you were useless to me. Now is where you get to shine. This is where I have to trust your skills." She looked at him and smiled.

It was a relief that Cyra needed him. He knew she had been stressed trying to work out the theory, a part of this lens he had no knowledge on. From what he had seen, with her practical lens she was testing, she was tumbling towards a conclusion that she would soon wish she had avoided. It was adding up to one outcome and Gil could see it. He had to let Cyra have this moment before he intervened. They were a team now and he had to get Cyra to trust him, so he could show her what mistake she was about to make. Words would be no good if she couldn't see it for herself. She could also tell Anders of his suspicions, she could be dedicated to his work and throw Gil into the fire—he couldn't risk that yet.

"I'll leave you two to your revelation. Well done, both or you—very impressive."

Anders walked out the workshop confidently.

'BUZZ'

They were on the brink of discovery. Cyra had figured out how to create a revolutionary lens, of which its purpose and power, she genuinely knew nothing. Gil didn't want to lie to her as Anders had —or at least as he thought Anders had. There had to be a reason to why. Freer was trying to protect Gil, and Gil knew he had to try to protect Cyra. If she succeeded, then he could tell her. He had to gain her trust before he could be honest with her. Be part of the trials on this lens and show her what revolutionary disaster she was bringing upon this reality and the other. Apart from the bluntness and the stress she was going through, Cyra was a nice person. She wanted to help people. Otherwise, she wouldn't be working at Syngetical. She was like Gil—

she wanted to help prolong humankind on this planet.

The time was not now. Soon. It was something he might have to warn Freer about. He had already explored syght too much. He had been trained to a certain degree for if anything happened. There was still time that he could keep Cyra safe.

Gil had to be sure his suspicions were right.

And he needed for Anders not to find out.

TWENTY ONE

Gil had to escape for a few hours, break the mould of the routine he had become accustomed to. He met up with Rix the next morning before he started work. Cyra had also taken the same time off after the breakthrough—a treat she deserved.

He was finding it hard to know who he could speak to about everything. There was too much secrecy. But the one person he had always trusted was Rix. There was never any doubt to her loyalty. She may have been Anders' daughter, but she stayed clear of his work. He had to tell someone of his suspicions.

As they made their way toward Bulltwine's Edge, out of the way of city surveillance, he updated her on what had happened.

"Training is going well."

"A master of syght now, are we?" She chuckled.

"Far from it. It's developing. I'm starting to see more and controlling it, which is good."

"And there was you thinking you didn't have it. I knew it all along!"

She punched him in the arm. That never not hurt.

"And work—"

"You don't need to thank me; you've done that enough already. And I also really don't want to hear about how great my dad is and how you are changing the world, blah blah blah..." She trailed off.

"No, Rix. I wasn't going to say that. I know you despise talking about Syngetical, but I have to tell you something."

"Oooooh, workshop gossip. Pray, tell. Anyone caught your eye?"

"Rix! No! This is serious. The project me and this scientist, Cyra—"

"You like her, don't you?"

"Quit it. No. We have been working on a project for your dad and I'm not sure, not yet, but I think he is building a syght lens."

Rix went blank, mute, as though she powered down.

"Rix? Did you hear me?"

"Yeah, I heard," she said, with no emotion behind her words.

"If he—or I guess, we; or at least, Cyra—works out how to do it, then having syght doesn't matter. I think she will. We are so close to working it out but if she does, she'll be in danger too. She won't be able to defend herself like I'm learning to."

He awaited a response. Rix looked lost, as if he had said something so devastating, she was unable to process it.

"Rix! I think Syngetical and what they do is a cover-up for whatever Anders is trying to do."

She switched back on to respond.

"You're worrying again, Gil. Dad knew nothing about syght or the Sense Shifters until you told him. Why would he? Syght is organic. Freer said I can't have it because of the tech, so how would you be able to build a synthetic version?"

She had a point. Cyra didn't see what he saw through the Spacial Lens: a blurred view of two very different realities. She thought it was broken, but he knew differently.

"I saw it, Rix. We are so close. And I'm worried if she discovers it and I don't warn her, then whatever happens is my fault."

He chose not to insult Rix's father by accusing him of lying to his face. Regardless how much they were friends, that was crossing the line, even if it was true.

"How would he be working on a lens if he only just found out about syght? He's even helping you get the training you need! Did he not tell you what the lens is for?"

"He told Cyra, lied to—" Gil changed his approach "—explained to her it was a lens related to space travel. Cyra knows no different and she is working hard to achieve it, busting out hours to fix the problems Anders had with it, only for it all to be a lie. She's going to open up a world, the ones the Sense Shifters are trying to protect, the one they're trying to stop the 55 from reaching. This is her breakthrough as a scientist, and it's going to turn out to be the biggest mistake of her life."

"That's deep," Rix said. "Gil, you have to relax. Have you stopped to think that maybe being in a room with no windows all day and then a training room with barely any lightening is probably causing some paranoia up there?"

She tapped the side of her head.

A vehicle suddenly screeched around the corner at the bottom of the road they were on. They both watched as the silver van hurtled towards them, the debris flying out from beneath the wheels.

Nothing was normal about them, two inquisitive adults, being at Bulltwine's Edge, a deserted wasteland—they were going to stand out.

The van drove straight past them and down another street. All went quiet again.

They shared a glance.

"Let's have this conversation elsewhere," he said with slight panic.

"What you worried about? It was your decision to come here. Thought your new job had made you all brave and spontaneous now," she said, grabbing him. "Right here! I got him! Easy as that." She laughed as she held him. He was surprised by her firm grip. She could be strong when she needed to be.

Then the silver van was back, screeching out in front of them. A side door opened.

"What the fuck!" Gil said. His heart wanted to stop.

Rix let go of him, also stunned.

Three burly men exited the vehicle and approached them.

The first went to grab him but he ducked out of the way. The second threw a punch. Gil saw it coming straight towards his face and began to blink profusely between each eye. Freer had taught him well. He managed to dodge the guy's fist. As the guy stumbled after throwing the missed punch, he gave Gil a confused look.

The exchange happened all too quickly for Gil to keep up with, but by using his syght, he had somehow managed to get through it unscathed.

"GIL!" Rix yelled as she booted the first guy in the knee cap. He heard it crack. Rix could fight dirty. She had no need for syght. The guy screamed in agony.

The second guy picked her up and threw her at the fence. She landed hard onto the ground.

"Rix!" He ran towards her, but the second guy launched out his arm. Remembering what Freer said—the closer you are to the object, the easier it is to see the two realities—he quickly dropped to the ground. That arm came out of nowhere and he was quick in responding.

He kicked the guy in the back of the knees—

took him straight out and planted his face onto the concrete.

He ran over to Rix.

Two men were down and he had forgotten about the third. He was distracted by Rix, wanting to see if she had been hurt, when it was his surroundings that he should have been more focused on.

Syght didn't work when the danger was coming from behind him. He was no Freer; his senses were nowhere near as finely tuned.

He felt a hard knock to the head and suddenly blacked out.

The last thing he saw through his blurred vision was the sight of Rix scrambling to right herself and the inside of the door on the van closing.

TWENTY TWO

K1 Spire was the most secure building in Axeon City and the host venue for the annual 55 gala.

The event was being housed on the eighty-second floor. To get to it, you had to pass the safeguarding measures that were in place. The 55 gala was exclusive, an annual ritual for the elite and their selected guests only.

Hector Bosh, whose company implemented the security system within the building, had sent out handwritten invitations, each with their own invisible digital code.

Atalon Keel pulled out his invitation from his pocket. All he wanted to do was get into the gala, but he had to conform to the rules. It annoyed him that he had to prove that the technology created by another 55 member worked. They all knew each other. It was too dramatic.

The main glass doors held facial recognition software, with which the system had been pre-loaded with each member's digital scan. Atalon looked into the camera. The light shone green.

Once through the initial check-in, he was asked three questions through an ear piece, which had come with the invitation. This tracked his answers via voice recognition. He answered in a dull, unenthusiastic tone. He then inserted the invitation into a small chrome machine, which was located at the lifts, for the digital print to be read. If confirmed, all six lifts would return to the ground level and the doors would open. He would be very surprised if they didn't return and he wondered at who might want to try to impersonate him. There would be serious consequences if anyone did—not that Atalon took joy in administering punishment, but one must be held accountable for their actions. It was a philosophy he lived by.

A laser grid emerged in front of each lift entrance, the type that would slice through skin. Between lift three and four, part of the wall revealed itself where another lift was hidden.

"Of course," he said with a sigh.

He walked into the lift and it automatically closed, taking him up to floor eighty-two. The hidden lift could not have been the only surprise. That alone could not have been the security detail. It was too simple. He was almost disappointed in it.

"You're letting down the side, Hector," he

voiced to himself.

However, the lift stopped and opened out to a generic office floor. No grand entrance, no welcome party, and more disappointingly, no drink.

Atalon stepped forward. Hesitant. He checked the lift buttons. The display read eighty-two.

He felt a draught, a wind that quickly passed up the back of his neck. He stepped back again. He watched the scene in front of him closely. He was not one to easily fool. The lift doors remained open. He noticed that all the windows were securely closed; up this high, no company would risk having them open. So why the draft?

His eyes started to water as he stared into the office space, looking for that flaw. Hector's work had improved. The attention detail was as though it were real. Impressed by the imagery, he patted his pocket and found his invitation again.

"Let's hope I don't need this anymore."

He threw the small metal invitation into the room. It pixelated the floor as it fell through it and continued to fall for some time, ricocheting off the vent and landing with resounding 'ting'.

He smirked. A valid lesson that Hector's software taught—don't rush in.

The doors closed again and the room lit up. A droning sound came in three cycles and an automated voice said the word 'complete'.

It was the full body scan to confirm for a third time who he was, identifying the hidden blemish that Atalon had previously disclosed to have on his body.

Hector wanted to prove that his scan could pick up the smallest of marks on the skin or underneath, no matter what it was; the 55 thought they were perfect but they all had their own flaws—not that Atalon saw anything of himself as imperfect.

At this point, the buttons 'eight' and then 'two' had to be pressed to take you up the extra five floors to floor eighty-two—one instruction he had to learn. He did wonder what would have happened if he hadn't, but this had already taken too long and he didn't care enough to find out.

When the lift doors finally opened, a verbal confirmation of name and company 'locked' Atalon into the building so anyone else disguised as him would be denied at the main doors.

He stepped out of the lift. The entrance foyer led into a large drawing room, where the decor was inspired by the eighteenth-hundred French royalty, Louis XVI. There were long white pillars that lined the room, each with a gold flower motif at the top that trailed down from the ceiling, which added to gold embossed crown mouldings as one complete continuous pattern. The painting on the ceiling depicted the gods of ancient Greece perched casually amongst the clouds at dusk. Long bay windows opened out onto a veranda, which overlooked the forest that surrounded the city. This was the grand entrance he expected. No expense spared. This room was designed for the 55 to feel at home with the gods, to stand beneath their presence and feel that they were luxurious themselves. The gala was to be just as extravagant as the 55 thought they were.

The gala started at 1pm, with the auction at 2pm, hosted by Harry Qwhale, the other 55 member in Axeon City. Atalon was glad he didn't have to host it. It took time that he did not have to spare. Although, with Qwhale at the helm, he and most of the 55 were worried about what he would be auctioning off.

Out of all the 55 members, Harry was the most unhinged. Atalon knew that more than any. His trade was in vehicles. He owned Proton—'owned', being very different to 'managed'. The directors had thought it wise to put Harry's name on the company, that his would be the fresh young face to keep the company moving forward. As his name was on the deed, he became one of the 55, although Proton realised it was a move they should have thought more about. Atalon could see the mistake happening before the deed was signed. If Atalon cared for motor vehicles, he would have acquired the company himself, just to deny Harry the opportunity to be a 55er. Harry had a known history for being dodgy. He liked to do trade deals outside of board rooms and away from the scrutiny of his managing team. With his access to wealth, he soon realised that most would not say no to any idea he had. He also had connections with many on the street level: stall traders, the poorer classes, anyone that would do his bidding... He became the thug of the 55—not that any of them would say it to his face, unsure they were of the consequences of such an accusation.

Atalon knew all the 55, including himself, had

their ways of dealing with business, their personal lives and anything else—the secrets. Harry made it obvious to everyone what he was up to, which gave the 55 a bad reputation. Atalon was not going to take the fall for any of Harry's decisions or mistakes. They may have been part of the same city but he was not his father.

But Harry was out of place in events of this nature. This year was the first time he had been given this privilege, and the other 55 were suspicious to what he might be presenting.

"Ah, Atalon, a bit of class. The part of this city that actually proves it isn't a complete waste of the government's time," Jula Tamil, the owner of the food conglomerate Tessa, said as he entered the drawing room.

About time someone had given him the compliment he deserved.

"I knew it wouldn't be long before you insulted something," Atalon smiled and gave her a kiss on each cheek.

"I'm very surprised it's not you hosting this year's gala. It would have been a relief for everyone if you were."

"It keeps it interesting for us all, does it not?"

Atalon shared the same concern as Jula. Harry had not given any details away of what he was auctioning. Most usually gave a glimpse, whet the appetites of those hungry for something new.

"Interesting is not what I want. What I want is something I don't have."

"Don't we all."

He was unsure he would want anything that Harry was offering. His interest was more a concerned curiosity. He looked over to the entrance to the drawing room where Harry was welcoming the other 55 members.

They both laughed gracefully.

"Any insight to what we are getting our hands on today?" a gruff voice said from behind Atalon, a large man who went by the name Carrington Hulse. He was a 55er due to his buying up of all the aviation companies, liquidising all their assets and preventing air travel for two years, thus, creating a higher demand for it. When he re-launched a new, faster form of air travel with Stealth, the seats on each aircraft sold out immediately for the next year and his stock index rose at an incredible rate. Production could not keep up with the demand and so the invention of a smaller personal aircraft was created. People had the option of either purchasing one or take one out on loan.

"You, my friend, are going to have to wait for that little treasure," Harry replied. "I'm telling you this is the best year yet. It will be remembered."

Harry ruffled his hands together. That alone was the trigger for Atalon to not want to remember today. If Harry was excited about something, it was usually a sign to avoid it completely. Atalon was certain that no 55 member had ever done business with the man.

Atalon mingled and said his pleasantries, eagerly

awaiting the auction time. He had a bad feeling about it. By quarter to two, every 55 member had arrived. Nothing was going to stop any of them getting their hands on something unique, something that everyone else wanted, regardless of whether they knew what it was. They all had to have something exclusive; that was their excitement: their need for more. When you had the money, the power, the passage to have anything you wanted, winning an auction at the 55 gala was the only prize left. Though, Atalon vowed not to take part in the bidding this year—not with Harry hosting. He was wise to keep his credits.

At one end of the room, there was a stage area with a podium, ready for the auction to begin. At the other end was a Steinway Alma grand piano playing by itself. Pure white with gold trim, it blended in with the rest of the decor.

Atalon raised his glass above his head to indicate he needed a refill. A serviceBot was signalled by the action and one wheeled itself over to him. He placed the glass on the tray the serviceBot had laid out. He said nothing, which indicated he wanted the same drink again. The serviceBot recognised the remnants of the drink in the glass and filled it with a chilled, smoky whiskey.

He took the drink off the tray and the serviceBot moved onto its next customer. No interaction, no small talk—just the drink. The way Atalon preferred.

This was a function where every member dressed to the highest calibre. Three-piece suit or ballgown attire was requested. Atalon always obliged. He naturally dressed suave. That was his style. He would wear nothing less. Every year though, he marvelled in Hinny Lacete, a fashion icon and designer to the elite. She had ground-breaking clothing technology, and he had gone to her on a few occasions to design a jacket or a pocket square or two. Though, Hinny's modern style was generally one he was not keen on.

Today, Hinny was showcasing her 'yet to be released' Holoatal dress, performing a catwalk to show off what her design could do. Atalon still had his ear piece from his entry and placed it back into his ear to listen to her describing it.

"A holographic virtual display that can adapt and change to whatever designs you programme in to it. Its quadratic layered code means the projection is not translucent through to the skin. The underwear provides the decency and also the base for the display to project from. It is connected to the BioMobX chip, providing you the ease of changing your dress throughout your day. It could be a figure-hugging cocktail number…"

Atalon watched as Hinny transformed her attire every few steps, the smooth transition of outfits switching without her removing a single garment. There was not one point where she was indecent or revealed too much. Magical.

"…It can even portray accessories and jewellery, which can refract light correctly, depending on the angle the light is coming from."

At the end of her demonstration, she spun, to a round of applause and changed to a three-piece suit for the rest of the event. A three-piece suit was something of class and she suited it well.

'*CLINK CLINK*'

At the ting of the glass, the serviceBots shut down and any devices that omitted a digital output outside of the drawing room were suspended and blocked—another of Hector's inventions. Atalon checked his BioMobX implant: 'no service'. This was his quiet time.

The room turned its attention to the podium and fell to silence. The wind gently blew the long white sash curtains delicately into the room.

Harry Qwhale made his way to the podium.

"Welcome, one and all, to the only event that any of us should be attending this year, the annual 55 gala. I know there was speculation and doubts as to whether I could provide something of worth, of value to you. I ask you this: in a world where we can have anything we desire, any dream we can make happen, where any problem we have can be made to disappear without a trace of it ever existing, what is the one thing that any of us do not own?"

There was not much Atalon wanted that he could not achieve. It could not have been only him who had this thought.

He paused and looked out to the other fifty-four members in front of him. There was no response.

"We control this earth, we are the government, we say what goes and when, and the Supreme House are a bunch of fucking cock suckers who think we will do anything at their beck and call."

There were a few gasps from the floor.

It was rare that Atalon saw dislike towards the host of a gala event. It sounded more of a revolution.

"WE have the wealth. WE have the power to execute what we need. WE don't need to listen to them. We made this new generation survive. We are the reason all of this works."

Harry's tone differed that of the rest of the room. This was their day to revel in their accomplishments, their time to do what they wanted—be children, be bold, win that exclusive prize. But Harry was angry. Atalon had a slight sickening feeling. This was going to be a very different auction. He had to stay, though. Regardless of his morals and thoughts towards the man, he was now intrigued.

"We are the reason why we are here. This is our world and we have conquered it...almost. But there is still one thing we do not yet own nor run, though it's something we do have power over."

The sea of confused faces was clear. Atalon had no idea either.

"Come on, Harry. What are you talking about?" Carrington bellowed from the back end of the room. "We already have everything."

"You don't have everything, Mr Hulse. You do not own human life!"

A large smile appeared on his face.

"I'm not talking about employees, and I'm not talking about slavery, though that is basically what employee stands for. I mean, buying humans, to own, to keep, to display, to do as you wish because you have bought them. When we all have the technology, what else is there to own other than the humans who invent it, make it, scrap it, remake it? We can control people to a new level. There are a lot of people on the planet to buy."

A wave of grumbling began to grow amongst the crowd. Atalon knew what they were thinking. Humans were not something they needed nor wanted. With the right number of credits, it was easy to bribe someone from any class. Humans were everywhere. Half the time, they were a hassle, the problem. What would they do with a slave? That's what Harry was insinuating—as promised, something that most of the 55 probably didn't have, even if none liked to admit it.

"I can tell what you are thinking, though. So, let me change your thoughts on this. You wanted tech—I can give you something better than that. How about a human who has the ability of syght? Now you can own anything, everything, in this reality and the next. I present to you Gil Taberthorn."

TWENTY THREE

Gil felt woozy, mainly due to the black cloth in front of his eyes. His head was spinning. He threw his body about in defence, but with his arms tied behind his back, he could do nothing. He was a fish out of water. His head hurt. It was throbbing. His breath against the mesh was warm and came in short bursts. He rolled around. He was still in the back of the van, the screeching of its tires sounding every time it turned sharply from one corner to the next.

Then the van stopped.

What was he going to do? If he couldn't see through the bag over his head, he couldn't use his syght. He attempted to shake the bag off, and a drawstring whipped him in the eye. It stung. He cried out.

The door swung open again and the light behind

the men created their shadows on the black cloth. Two of the men were coming towards him. He kicked out, catching one of them in the knee.

"Ah the fucker!" the guy called out.

"Deal with it. He's a scrawny lad—barely touched you."

Gil kicked the other. He regretted it soon after as he received a kick in the back in return. That hurt. He just had to accept fate here. His ability was useless if he couldn't see—unless, like Freer, he could use his senses?

It was worth a try.

He closed his eyes. They grabbed him by his shirt and dragged him out of the van and along a concrete path. He could feel the vibration of the other guy walking by the side of him. He stretched his leg out and tripped him, and the man fell into the one who was dragging Gil. He let go of his grip and Gil fell backwards.

It worked, or something had. He was free.

He pulled himself up to his feet, he opened his eyes, still with the bag over his head and ran, guessing where he was going as he had no idea. He slipped off the kerb, his ankle twisted and he fell to the ground.

"Fuck!" he screamed out. He tried to hobble to his feet again, drag himself someplace where other people could see what was happening.

"Nice try." Then, a kick to the back of his knees. Gil went straight to the floor again. His senses were not quite where Freer's were. She had years of mastery. Gil was panicking and still only at the beginning of his journey; he could only just about use his syght when he could see, let alone when he couldn't.

The two blokes picked him up and carried him. No matter how much he wiggled, he was not escaping. Thanks to their firm grip on his lanky body, handling him was an easy feat.

He was taken into a building and through countless doors and lifts. The two blokes mumbled something between them. They stood Gil on his feet.

"Walk!" one demanded. He put his foot on the ground. It was sore. The stabbing pain shot up his leg, but it was secondary to his panic. He had to be calm. What was he going to do? How was he going to get out of this?

He could see the outline of a door in front of him. He was pushed towards it, and he approached it, limping as he did. The door opened, and the cloth bag removed from his head, the light blinding as he had become accustomed to the darkness. His breath was finally able to escape, unlike him. The tie around his wrists was severed, but he was immediately grabbed by the two men and ushered thorough the door.

A raucous explosion of noise came from the floor.

Gil found himself stood on a podium, facing a collection of people. Freer was right. The 55. They knew who he was.

"You all thought it would be impossible to find

someone who had it," the man next to him announced. "Many of you gave up hope, believed it to be a myth, and yet here I stand before you today with someone who is proven to have the ability and is in the early stages of perfecting it. I present to you, my auction."

Gil had kept under the radar. Nobody knew he had syght apart from a few.

He resisted being brought further forward, pushing against the two men who were forcing him onto a black square on the centre of the podium. They were too strong for him.

The 55 had him. He knew this day might come, but not so soon, not now. He wasn't ready. His training was only just beginning. He tried blinking rapidly. Nothing presented itself. He was unable to focus. This was what he had been so afraid of, all the stress, the worry, the fear that he'd be taken by someone who wanted to use him. There was a pack of greedy dogs in front of him, all wanting that chance.

He was placed on a black square on the floor, which activated. A yellow glow emitted around the edge and Gil went rigid, rooted to the spot, as though all his muscles stopped working instantly. He froze in place. He could feel an electrical pulse running through his body. It didn't hurt until he tried to move. What were they going to do with him? There was no way out of this. Everyone in this room could take a good look at him. They knew what he looked like, who he was. There was no more hiding in plain sight. The panic was so much he wanted to cry, but his body wouldn't let him. This wasn't fair. He never asked for this. In that very moment, he wanted to forget about syght. It was the one ability he had, and it looked like it wasn't going to be able to aid him now.

"I must admit, he was a tricky bugger to find, but I was still able to acquire him, with a little help from a few companions—always good to know people down on the street levels; they hear a lot more than we do. Terry Florence, in case you don't know him, has done well for us. Very well indeed."

Gil tried to open his mouth. He had questions to ask. Terry? How could he? He was meant to be on his side, protecting him. Yet he had sold him out. His jaw was locked.

"I know what you are trying to say," the man said, looking Gil directly in the eye. "Keep your splutter to yourself. You have a crowd to entertain. No denying now you don't have this ability. We won't let you off that easily."

With that, he turned back to the crowd.

"In case you have no idea what syght is, allow me to explain it to you. With this boy, not only can you control this reality, but you have the chance to control the other side of reality, somewhere that makes what we see and do here possible. Still confused? Let me put it in simple terms for all of you: our earth is made up of two realities, yet we only see one: this one we are currently run, play in and enjoy. But with syght, you can see and open up both realities—jump from one to another. Win this lad and you have the chance to conquer more than any other 55er, ever."

"How do we know he has it and he's not any other regular lower-class scum?" Jula asked.

"Do you think I would be that stupid to be offering him up if he didn't? Why would I want to make myself look like a failure, claiming I have brought the greatest gift of them all when I haven't?

Gil knew of their greed. They would make him do anything they wanted and he didn't want to think what would happen if he said no. Could he really be able to jump between the realities? Could he use his syght to get to that depth? If so, it was far more a powerful skill than he could ever imagine.

The 55's faces lit up with delight. The sound of discussion began to fill the room.

"I propose to you an answer to your inevitable question: if he does have it, then why am I not using him for myself? The answer is that this boy is priceless. Money means more to me than does conquering another reality—and I know how much you lot can offer. I'm happy with what I am, who I know. I'm even happy with any killing I do for sport. That's what drives me. Now, where do we begin the bidding?"

The room was electrified with excitement at the potential for what this unknown ability could do for a 55 member.

Gil was being sold. This was unfair. It was not his choice. The world was a different place to how it used to be in his grandpa's time, but humans being treated as possessions? That was criminal.

With his movement still restricted, all he could do was exhale heavily. Nobody else knew he was here. Rix had seen him captured, but there was no way she'd know where to look. The image of her face played in his head, the memory of her reaching out, unable to grab him. There was no escape. His life was over. Even if he refused to use his ability, they would find a way to force him—or extract it themselves. They were the 55; they could do anything.

As the floor discussed the potential offering, Harry walked over to where he was on the podium.

"Your world is about to change, and what a trophy you will be," he whispered into his ear. Gil wriggled, but his feet stayed planted. Pain shifted over his body like a wave.

"Now you have all had time to discuss and think about it, let's say we start the bidding at one hundred million credits."

Atalon Keel shouted his bid first, before anyone else in the room could put their hand up.

"Five billion credits. Let's start from there and make this a serious bidding war."

"Just the way I like it!" Harry screamed. "You have changed your tune from earlier, I see."

A rousing cheer spurred everyone on.

Within minutes, the bids had reached ninety billion. The higher the bids rose, the less Harry could contain his excitement. He was conducting the bids as though he was orchestrating all the people in the room.

Gil found the only part of him that he could move were his eyes and eyelids. There might be a chance for an escape after all. He tried blinking between each eye, but there were still no options, no choices—not now. It was too late. The outcome was the same; the room was the same; there was no alternative picture to see.

"Look, he's doing it!" a voice shouted out.

"One-hundred-and-fifty billion!!!"

The room quietened slightly.

"Do I dare say it? Going once…"

This was it. The end of Gil's life. He had heard the rumours about the 55 and now he would truly see what they were capable of doing.

"Going twice…"

Harry was giddy with excitement. He wanted to reach over and hit him, the hardest he had ever hit someone, which wasn't hard as he had never hit anyone. This was his survival. He had been given no opportunity, no choice—this was his future made for him. The very next words from Harry's mouth would signal the end of the auction.

"Two-hundred-and-twenty billion!" another voice shouted.

The room was shocked. To Gil, all the amounts of money that had been shouted were extreme, but this was something else, an amount for which he would never even be able to quantify how much that actually was, what it could buy him. The silver lining was that it was reassuring to know he was worth that much, even if it was a bid for his own life.

"What an offer! WHAT AN OFFER!! This is exciting. Isn't it exciting?" Harry said, turning to ask some of the 55ers closest to him. "And who may I ask is the owner of this wonderful bid?" Harry began to scan the room.

No one answered. With the movement Gil could make with his eyes, he could see the whole room. The 55ers were looking around, muttering amongst themselves. He could see the jealousy creeping into their faces for not being able to match that bid. It had to be the wealthiest 55er, not that Gil knew many of them by name. They were all as corrupt as one another.

The sound of well-tailored brogues could be heard, clicking against the varnished parquet flooring. The room looked around, searching, eagle-eyed for the person that had made this astronomical bid.

He could see them already plotting their revenge. Would another 55er go so far as to re-capture him? That would cause a war between them all. This was too lucrative a prize to lose. But Gil knew he was not the prize everyone thought he was.

He could see a figure walking through the crowd, a well-dressed person, from what he could tell. Each 55 moved out of their way, until Gil could at last make out who it was.

He attempted to let out a gasp. It stayed lodged in his throat.

The figure made their way up to the front of the

podium. They were here to make their stance, make their power known to all.

Gil was in shock as much as the rest of the 55ers. He was speechless—not that he had the ability to speak anyway. Why was he here to bid on Gil? He once again had thought someone was trustworthy when it turned out they are only in it for themselves. He had perceived this all wrong.

Anders Hilgaard stood in front of him, smiling, proud that he had won this auction. Gil had hoped and not a suppression of anger having to lose this magnitude of money to save his daughters best friend.

"And what a shock this is! The one and only Anders Hilgaard, everybody! He finally attends the 55 gala."

"Well, it was said that this year was going to be like no other, so I had to find out what you were offering."

He looked directly at Gil.

"He can't come in here and bid on the auction like that!" Carrington Hulse exclaimed.

"He had an invitation, just like any of us did, Hulse. He has the right to a bid, and especially at a handsome figure of two-hundred-and-twenty billion," Harry said.

Gil knew that anything could happen to him in another's hands—a 55er, he could just about imagine, but with Anders? He didn't know what to think or feel. If the vile rumours about the 55 were all true, then what could Anders want with him? The shock to why Anders would be here, doing deals with the 55, was something he couldn't get his head around. Did Rix know? Was she safe?

Harry was still as giddy as a child, no doubt already spending the money before it had even been transferred.

"So, going once, twice—any advances on two-hundred-and-twenty billion?"

Anders held his gaze towards Gil.

"SOLD!!! To Mr Anders Hilgaard. You can do as you wish with your purchase."

Harry tapped the display on his forearm to release Gil from the pad. He fell to his knees. Saliva, built up in his mouth while he was unable to speak, poured out.

"I'm going to be saving him," Anders declared to the room. "Auctioning a kid is low, even for the 55."

Did he hear correctly? Anders was here to save him? The world's saviour had come to save Gil. His idol. It was true; he knew it had to be. The relief swamped his body. Syght may not have saved him from this situation, but it seemed that Rix had. How else would Anders have known he was here?

"But he is unique," Harry said. "You'll see."

"Your funds will be transferred later today. Gil, come with me." Anders helped him up from the floor and protected him as they made their way through the crowd. Gil knew he still had a target on his back, but felt safe with Anders.

At the far end of the room, he looked back over his should and saw Harry watching from the stage area. He was delighted with his credits—that was all that he wanted. Some of the other 55ers were not expressing the same emotion. Some looked upon him in awe, but the tension was building underneath, arguments were soon to develop, and there was no doubt: Gil knew that a plot was starting to happen.

TWENTY FOUR

Anders escorted Gil to his office in SeeTech Tower. As they rode over, not much conversation passed between them, nor as they ascended in the lift up to the one-hundred-and-eighty-sixth floor. 'Get in' and 'Don't say anything', were the only things Anders said, a good indication that he was unwilling to talk.

They reached his office door and Anders unlocked it.

The door buzzed and inside, Gil was pleased to see Rix, sitting there waiting.

"Gil!" She ran over and wrapped her arms around him. He stumbled back from the force.

"Jeez, you stink," she said and took a few steps back, but underneath her repulsed face, he could see the worried look in her eyes. She cared. He had thought she had abandoned and left him to fend for himself, but she must have gone to get help. The Sense Shifters made no appearance to protect him. She was the only witness.

"Gil, please sit." Anders indicated to a chair next to where Rix sat. "My apologies for not saying much to you on the way over here; I had to be sure that no one was listening or trying to follow us. It is safer here to talk, especially when it's involving the matters concerning the 55. Gil, do you know why you were there?"

"They were auctioning me off, right?" He trembled on his words, shaken by the events still.

"And you know why?" Anders asked.

"Because of syght?

"I have seen you use it," Rix said. "You used it when those dickheads tried to get you in the van. And when we were in the Mustang."

"Do you understand how much danger you are in now?" Anders asked.

"I do, very much so." He was still shaking. "Freer said that if people found out I had it, they would be after me. Now it's happened. They know who I am!"

He hasn't wanted to believe it. reassuring himself that nobody would actually find out about him, about syght. But now, the 55, Harry especially, knew everything.

"They were right all along, Gil," Rix whispered. "People are after you. But how did the 55 know?"

"It was Terry!!"

Of all people he trusted, it was him who had

given him up. All this time. He had already been having suspicions about Anders, so when Terry was mentioned as being an informant for Harry, he didn't know what to feel. Behind the fear, there was anger, frustration and betrayal lying in wait. He was thankful Anders had saved him, but he was another one he was losing his trust in. He had to get back to Cyra, and stop her achieving her scientific breakthrough.

"Terry? Your Terry from Salvagers Bazaar?"

He nodded.

"That dirty lying fuck. As if he gave you up to them. How does he know any of the 55?"

"It was a man called Harry Qwhale. He said he knew a lot of people on street level and that people would do anything for credits. Terry must have told him somehow. Throughout all those years I have known him and he looked after me…"

Gil was upset. Terry, who he classed as his family, had ratted him out for credits.

"If Terry told them about me, then he might have told the 55 about the Sense Shifters too. What do we do?"

"Gil, we need to keep you safe," Anders said. "If there are people wanting to find you, and if word spreads to others you have syght, we might be in trouble. The main thing is that you need protection."

Protection from Anders meant being watched more. It would have been safer with Freer, but after what happened, Anders was not going to allow him to go anywhere without him knowing. This situation had played right into Anders' palms. Had he planned this all along?

If the 55 knew what they were working on, Gil would no longer be a target. This lens, this contraption—if Cyra could make it work, it would be worth more than the entire 55's fortune. He had a gut feeling that Anders only wanted this for himself, to see whether he could achieve what the 55 had wanted to achieve with him. His gut instinct had to be wrong. This was all for an experiment, to see if the idea was possible. That had to be all.

He was probably looking at it from the wrong angle. That's why he'd been told not to say anything. Anders needed to trust Cyra before he revealed any information to her, but now Gil was there and he knew about syght—what was he supposed to do? Did he want him to guide her, somehow, to this scientific breakthrough?

Gil was thankful that Anders had saved him—there was no escaping that if he had not have shown up, he could be anywhere and be subjected to anything by now—but if he was right, and he was building a syght lens, then there was no doubt that Gil was going to be the test subject. Gil didn't need a lens, of course, but Anders would, though.

He nodded out of politeness.

"I can protect you for now by the laws stated in the auction guidelines, but knowing the 55, they'll find a way around it soon enough."

"But you spent so much to win. I feel bad you lost that money just to save me."

The amount was astronomical. Gil knew he must

be a worthy investment for Anders to save him. He couldn't help but question why. With Terry having lied to him and given him up at the first opportunity, what's to say that Anders wouldn't do the same? Did he have another bidder willing to pay more for him? The man was too calm. He spent two-hundred-and-twenty billion to acquire him and he hadn't even broken a sweat. That was a hefty number of credits for a life.

"You are my daughter's best friend. I couldn't allow an innocent life to be in the hands of the 55. We all make scarifies from time to time, and no doubt you will have to do the same in time to come."

Was that a threat? Anders expecting something in return because he had saved his life? Gil had no plans to have to sacrifice anything, but it felt like Anders owned him now. Was he going to ask him for a favour now?

"See it as an investment rather than a purchase. You work at Syngetical, and you and Cyra have made real progress. Without you helping her, she may not have reached the stage you are at now."

"Okay," Gil said, not wanting to give away what he was actually thinking. He was piecing together the events that had led to this point. He had to be wrong, but he couldn't help wondering whether this was all a part of Anders' master plan. Was his endgame a sacrifice that Gil might have to make one day? The fear and the shock of being kidnapped was affecting his emotions. He couldn't even trust his out-of-control thoughts at the moment.

"Can the Sense Shifters protect you? If you were to stay with them?" Anders said as he went over to a long free-standing mirror in the corner. "I can send a vehicle to pick you up and we can monitor you at their location if need be."

He pressed a button on the front of the white front facade and it opened out to reveal a cabinet inside. He picked up a chip gun and a chip.

"This under your skin will help me keep track of you, Gil. It won't hurt. If you are taken again, I will know exactly where you are."

He walked over, the gun in hand, but Gil moved away.

"No, thank you. It's okay. The Sense Shifters said without any tech in my body I have a stronger chance at mastering syght. Anyone with tech—it slows down their reactions."

Another sign: wanting to tracking him, finding out where the Sense Shifters HQ was. Obviously, Rix knew already but it seemed as if she hadn't told her father. That was the way it had to be kept: secret. Anders was pushing to find out more and he was not going to give in to it.

"Oh, I see," Anders said.

Gil could see that Rix was squeezing the arm of the chair, trying to suppress whatever she wanted to say on that matter.

"I'll take Rix with me; they have already met her and allowed her in. They want to keep their location secret to keep their community safe. She can help me if I need it. They need to be able to trust me too."

"I can have your apartment monitored instead."

"I think I'll stay with the Sense Shifters. They had lodgings there."

It would be the safest place for him. Rix was the only one who knew where it was and how to get in. The 55 knew Anders; he was at risk if he stayed here. Despite the fact the security measures to enter the workshop were high-tech, he would have to leave at some point. Anders could still send a vehicle to escort him to and from work. He had already decided that he would instruct it to pick him up and drop him off at a different location, so Anders couldn't monitor where the car went.

"I need to go home and maybe not think about anything for a while."

Anders returned the chip gun to the cabinet. Rix stayed silent.

"I think it might be wise for me to arrange a vehicle for you to take you home."

"I would like that, if that's alright, of course." He needed a clear head for his talk with Cyra, and he also had to deal with Terry.

"One of my assistants will meet you in the foyer on the ground level." Anders opened up his display and tapped on a few buttons. A moment later, he confirmed it. "They are waiting for you now."

"I'll see you soon?" he said to Rix.

"Yeah, I guess. Who knows? I'll be around," she said bluntly. He knew that that was all he was going to get out of her.

He got up and thanked Anders. He still had his

suspicions, but he couldn't be rude; he had saved his life, after all. Part of him knew that he owed Anders for that at least.

"Glad you are alright," Rix finally said with a smile as he left through the door.

The unmanned vehicle took Gil home. He was filthy, unarmed and as he opened the door to his apartment, he was fully expecting someone to be waiting there for him.

There was no sign of forced entry. The door was still the faded shitty green colour it had always been. No 55er was going to know where he lived, unless Terry had told them. His apartment was hidden away, in the slums of the city. It barely looked liveable from the outside.

"Shit," he said, suddenly having a realisation as he pushed the key into the lock. If there was someone on the other side of this door, then they already knew that he was home. He should have waited, not gone straight home. It was too late now. Anyone inside would have heard him, and if he ran, they would catch him. Still, he had to take the risk.

He turned the key and entered his apartment.

He stood at the door and peered around into the kitchen and then his bedroom. Everything was as he had left it—unfolded clothes everywhere, unwashed and grotty—but no one was here.

His life was changing faster than he could keep up with. He had to take control. He had a responsibility to stop whatever was happening from going too far. It felt like everyone around him was untrustworthy, and his mind flitted between the people in his life: his mixed feelings on Anders, his growing anger towards Terry and how he needed to tell Cyra. Poor Cyra.

He had to hope that she had not solved her calculations yet—or would never at all.

TWENTY FIVE

It was late in the day and the sun was setting on the edge of Axeon City, the sky illuminating with red streaks within the wisps of clouds that trailed across the dimming blue sky. There weren't many who would be seen out past dusk: crime was easier to commit in the dark, with fewer people around to witness it. Gil was used to it, though. His salvaging work made him comfortable with the clientele he met. They had no need for him and vice versa. Although now, maybe he should be a little more careful.

Gil needed the shade to see and kept his hood up and his hat as low as he could to cover his face—not that he looked distinctive, but with a city full of cameras, there was bound to be someone monitoring him. There was always someone watching.

He kept to the busier routes and only ducked down tight alleyways where necessary.

By the time he reached the Bazaar, most of the stalls had closed, but even if Terry's stall wasn't officially open, he knew he would still be in the workshop. Terry always gave it an extra half hour before closing up. There was always at least one person that would come rushing in for something. Even if it was a problem outside of microchips and circuitry, he could no doubt fix it.

Today, Gil was going to be his final customer.

The gates on the front of the stall were half closed and a light shone from within. He could see Terry at his workbench, a few sparks shooting up into the space around him and fizzling out. The old man was tinkering away on a microchip.

He had trusted him for all these years, only to have been groomed until the time was right to be shipped off to someone else. To Terry, he was a product of design. A weapon—no greater importance than the circuit board he was working on. But unlike the other things Terry worked on, there would be no replacement if he lost Gil.

"Look, this one is still open," a voice said, as two people came jogging up Salvagers Bazaar.

Gil put out an arm.

"They're closed," he said firmly.

"I can see the guy still in there. All I need is a wire reattaching," said the other.

"Not today. Go somewhere else."

Gil was not usually one for confrontation, but

this was his time with Terry. He needed answers. His frustrations were becoming too overwhelming to hold back. His brief time at home had allowed his mind to wander back to Terry. He had to prioritise his tasks. Cyra was important, but Terry meant more to him—or at least he thought he did until now.

"There isn't anywhere else. They've all closed."

"Then you should have gotten here earlier." He turned to face the two of them.

"Excuse me?"

"One of you; two of us—move aside," the first said as the pair squared up to him.

In any normal situation like this, he wouldn't have pursued this threatening line. He would have stepped aside and been nice about it, not wanting to cause any trouble. The wire on the induction pad the guy was holding was an easy fix. Gil knew it needed a quick solder and reattach. But today, he had no patience, though he should have thought about what he was saying before he opened his mouth.

"The place is closed," he said firmly.

One of them pushed him out of the way. He stumbled over and lost his balance.

Before the guy could call out to Terry, Gil had shoved him back hard with force, a move he had learnt from Rix.

The guy fell into his friend.

"Hold this!" he said, passing the broken induction pad to them. Gil prepped himself. This was going to be the first time he could put some of his training into use.

"GIL?!?!" Terry called out.

He twisted round and saw Terry standing at the gates. The next thing he felt was a punch to his stomach. He crouched over.

"You two, out of here. We are closed," Terry said, pushing open the gate.

"Yeah, we were told. Come on, we'll come back tomorrow."

"Gil, are you—" He tried to right him.

"Get off me." He took a few breaths. "It's no worse than what you did to me, Mr Florence."

He walked into the stall and waited for him to follow. Terry closed the gate behind him.

"I know why—" he started, but Gil wasn't going to let him speak.

"If you know why I'm here, then you can answer my fucking questions." He took a breath. He was not respecting any of Terry's morals today, especially how he felt about swearing.

"I put all my trust in you! In what you taught me, in what you said... And then I find out that you were a part of the original group who discovered what syght was and still now you are working with them. Then I find myself taken to be sold off at auction, all because of you, Mr Florence. YOU! You told them who I was and what I could potentially have. You warned me about them, told me how corrupt they were, how I shouldn't be involved with them or their business in any manner, and then I find out you handed me over. Why?"

Terry said nothing.

"Why did you do it?!"

Gil stood, chest out, ready to pounce. Terry cowered slightly. Gil stared him out until he gave an answer.

"I had no choice," Terry said quietly, into himself.

Gil could see that he knew he had done wrong but still, it didn't make it right. All this time he had trusted Terry. He needed to know now if he still could.

"Everyone has choice! That is something I have learnt. If you have your sight, which you do, you have a choice.

"Not with the 55, you don't, Gil."

There was a desperate switch in his tone. Terry was fearful, wide eyed, scared for his own life, just as much as Gil had been for the past few weeks. He had to find out if it was an act or he was being genuine.

"I've known Harry since his early days before he came to be a 55er. He was no different to you or me. He was a glorified dealer. He exchanged products—car parts from one salvager to another—and worked his way up. He dealt with many of us and he likes to keep it that way so he knows what's going on and what he can use to his advantage. I never handed you over to them, Gil."

"YES, YOU DID! Harry named you as his informant. You are a lying bastard, Mr Florence."

"Gil, I promise you, I didn't hand you over to them."

"Then why was I there?"

Gil's voice rose. He was angry. He knew Terry was lying—knew he sold him out. These questions had built up in his head on repeat. There was no holding back for him. He was not going to leave until he was convinced that he and Terry were on the same team—or the opposite. He was certain that the answer might not be the one he hoped for.

"Harry came to me with your name, Gil. He had heard this rumour that you had syght. Now, Harry isn't the brightest spark. He wouldn't have known what it truly was or how to use it, but he had been told what it could be used for. He knew it was valuable and that people would pay a high price for someone who had it. They already knew who you were, Gil."

"Then why did you say I had it? You could have lied."

He could see it plainly, how easily Terry could have played it. All that Harry had done was question him. He hadn't been kidnapped like he had; he hadn't been dangled in front of the 55 as a trophy that everyone wanted.

"Lie to the 55, Gil? How?"

There was a chance that Terry could be telling the truth—Gil had not interacted with the 55 on a level that involved a conversation—but if Terry had known Harry for as long as he claimed, then he knew what he could have said to keep Gil a secret.

"They knew about your family in the country and where they lived, your closets friends: Rix, Midi, Dana... Harry said all of them would die if I was unhelpful. I was trying to protect them, Gil. Regardless if they had you or not, all of your family were in danger. I had to give them some kind of information, but then I went to the Sense Shifters immediately and warned them."

"Then why say nothing to me?"

It sounded like an excuse. No Sense Shifter had saved him; it was Anders. If Terry had said something, the kidnapping would not have happened. Freer had said nothing to Gil about the 55 or of any warnings. And if she knew, they would have used their cameras to make sure he was safe. But it was only Rix who saw. She knew what happened and it was her that had helped him.

"What would you have wanted me to do? Tell you that everyone you knew was going to die? You would have panicked, Gil, and no doubt left the city to go home to your family, putting them in even more danger. What was I to do? Your family asked me to protect you. I had to do what I thought was best."

"Anders Hilgaard saved me, no thanks to you. If it weren't for him, who knows where I would be right now."

"You don't realise. That was down to me and Freer. The last time you left the Sense Shifters' place, we monitored you, through their surveillance room—you know which one I mean. I had to let Harry know where you were, so I made sure it was a time when you were with Rix. I informed him yes. I had to give him something. We took a risk, but it worked. Rix reported back to her father, the one person we knew we could potentially count on to get you out of this mess."

Gil didn't know what to believe.

It was plausible what Terry was saying, but why was nothing of this plan mentioned to him? If Terry had kept this many secrets, what else could he be hiding from him, from Freer? Up to this point, when this syght had started to change his life, Terry had protected him, looked out for him. Before he knew Gil had syght. Unless, he always knew and Gil had just been his nest egg. There were too many arguments for both sides.

"Gil, I would never hand you over to them," he continued, a pleading look on his face. "I can see why you thought that and especially because of what Harry said to you. I cannot deny that: yes, I had a hand in it, but for no gain. There were no credits exchanged. The 55 have the power to find out anything if they wish, and they did, about you. No one is allowed to stand up against them. I'm sorry I kept that to myself, Gil. It had to look as though the 55 had once again got what they wanted. You have seen what they are capable of now. A threat from the 55 was something I couldn't risk not taking seriously."

"So, how did they find out about me? Even I didn't know I had syght."

If it wasn't Terry, then who was it? Someone must have given the 55 this information.

"I don't know. Harry has connections with many

people that others 55ers don't. Someone could have overheard you or followed you."

Gil could see the impact this ordeal had had on Terry. He looked older than before, his face withdrawn, his cheek bones a little more on show than they previously were. He spotted a tremble in his left hand. Terry was no leader of war; he was just like Gil, but older and with more knowledge about the world. Maybe he was telling the truth. Terry was a good man, and of course, he wouldn't want everyone that he knew to be tortured for something they knew nothing about. It must have been a difficult decision for him to make.

"Do you have it then?" Terry asked. "Do you have syght?"

He raised an eyebrow, intrigued—a hint of a lost hope, in anticipation of what Gil would say next.

"I'm not sure I can trust you, Mr Florence. This has already put me in more trouble than I wanted."

"Better not to speak about it then. I was only curious. The fewer people that know, the safer it will be. Let Freer do what she needs to do so you can protect yourself." He gave him an understanding look. "Hopefully, now the 55 have lost you fairly to Anders, this might all be over."

This was far from over. Gil was teetering on the edge of a life as a fugitive or somehow using his ability to change the world forever and doing some good. The 55 was very much now an everyday presence in his life. He remembered leaving the auction and how annoyed some of them had looked by the fact he had been saved by Anders. That was going to be the start of a feud, one that Gil had no choice in whether he participated, and yet, one that he had already been signed up to.

"The new job is going well," he said light-heartedly. The only relief in this whole ordeal was that he had achieved something: his dream job—well, a job at the dream company he had wanted to work for. He needed Terry to know, despite all of this, that he was doing well.

Terry smiled.

"That's wonderful news. You can show them what I have taught you."

"We've made loads of progress, a huge development in a new project we are working on. Anders said he would provide me with protection too, in case the 55 come after me again."

He kept it simple. He knew that Terry would worry if he opened up about Cyra and what she was unknowingly creating. The less anyone knew right now, the better it was for them. Gil had to handle this one alone.

"Well, that's even better news too. I'm happy to see you, Gil. When I heard nothing from you for weeks, I felt guilty that I had put you in this position. Freer told me you were safe, at least, but I'm glad I got the chance to explain why I had to do it."

"I understand, Mr Florence."

Terry had to be innocent. He had admitted what he had done was wrong, although it was for the greater good, and Gil knew that. He would have hated to see anything happen to his family. He couldn't put them through something like this. The 55, however, were very much still in the picture and knew far more about his life than he thought. He had tried to stay off the radar before now, but in this world, in this new life, it was going to be impossible. Someone else knew about Gil, and they were the true informant. He needed to find out who.

Terry looked at his watch.

"I'll finish this up tomorrow. I guess I'll need start looking for your replacement."

Gil knew his future had changed quicker than he'd ever imagined it would. His salvager job had been perfect for him, but it was never going to last forever. The 55 hadn't finished their business with him and he knew they never would until they had what they wanted. If he continued to work for Terry, he would be at risk every night at the pit. This realisation opened him up to the fact that he would be in danger, constantly.

"Gil, promise me one thing."

He nodded in response, encouraging him to keep speaking.

"Continue your training with Freer and explore syght. Don't become like the 55. Use your abilities to stop people like them from searching for others like you. Don't see yourself as an army or a cult, but as a defence against those who have greed as a driving force. You are important, Gil. You are a key part of providing the balance within society in this reality and, who knows, maybe even the other."

Gil could definitely feel the pressure to succeed. It felt like, somehow, it was up to him to save the world. Before, when he was still unaware the world needed saving, he could stay hidden; he was an unknown. But now, others knew of his secret, which tipped the balance.

"I will try. Though, I'm not sure I'm any good at using it."

"You will, when you need to."

As he made his way back to the Sense Shifters' headquarters, he thought about what Terry had said to him. He had to believe he was telling the truth or he would never trust anyone. Rix was his ally and she had given him no reason to think otherwise. Terry had proved why he did what he did; he wasn't a malicious person, not like many who lived in Axeon City.

He still had to keep a watchful eye on his surroundings. There was a bounty on his head and many wanted to claim it. And there was someone out there who knew about him, who he was and what he was capable of. He had to be prepared, and at the same time, find out who was feeding the 55 information. If he stayed out of sight and in the two places he knew was safe, the 55's source would be cut.

He had more pressing matters, right now, though.

Terry had been dealt with. Time would play a factor to see if he could fully trust him again.

Gil now had to stop—or save—Cyra.

TWENTY SIX

"We got business to talk about. Meet me at my office down on High Lore—new establishment I acquired," Harry said through his Holo Vortex 2.0 device.

"High Lore? I'm not stepping foot in High Lore, Harry. No business matter is worth mixing with the street level scum."

"I would like to remind you, Atalon, it was those scum that helped us acquire someone with syght."

"Well, we don't have him now, do we?"

"Be here for eight pm. I have a plan."

Harry ended the call.

His new office was in the depths of the city, where those living on the survival line dwelled. His knowledge from the street had proved worthy of the 55 and he wanted more. Now, with the money in the company account, not only were the board at Proton extremely pleased—although, still oblivious to how he obtained the large sum—but he had found a new pasture that no other 55er would dare to invest in.

Now, he had other matters to address.

Most who knew him knew to stay clear. He preferred to take on business himself, unlike Atalon, who was afraid to get his hands dirty. Harry had grown up fending for himself and knew no different. The rumours from those speculating on how he dealt with business spurred him on even more. It scared people, and that is how he enjoyed working, exhibiting a presence that meant no one would betray you or dare question. Anyone who challenged him would inevitably lose. He was ruthless, and although not the tallest or broadest person there was, he knew how to win a physical fight: no technology—just his own bloodied fists and pure strength.

Dealings with Harry came with two outcomes: either you benefited financially—the phrases, 'sorry, it's not for sale' or 'I don't know' would never be something you said to him—or you simply did what he said without financial recompense as you knew there would be consequences if you did not. Either way, Harry would be victorious. If he could see the potential for future trade transactions, then you were protected. But when it came to information, Harry did not deem one-offs as worth paying for. It was hearsay; anyone could acquire the same information if they were listening at the right time. That said, if the information turned out useful, then he might bring trade to you in the future, if you dealt in something he or an associate needed. Harry was fair in that way. He was a tradesman, after all, despite his methods being unorthodox.

That was the silver lining that came with dealing with the 55: if you accepted the terms and followed through on the order given, it meant you survived another day, with the potential extra business coming to you. If there was an issue—well, no one lived to tell the tale.

Harry approached the top end of Salvagers Bazaar and made his way to a narrow passage.

He pulled on the rusty metal door handle and entered the stall. It opened up into a small stock room. A shelving rack lined either side, filled with metal and wooden storage boxes. He had no care for what was inside of them and went into the stall itself. A warm glow from the hanging bulb highlighted the small workbench.

"Hello Terry!" he said in a slow manner.

Terry was startled.

"Oh, Harry, I didn't hear you come in," he said nervously. "What are you here for? I did everything you wanted with Gil."

Harry knew Terry had completed his task. He'd provided everything he needed for the auction. Terry the informant, his reliable spy, gave him the intel in the first place. The deal had worked out smoothly, more so than Harry imagined it would. Everyone played their part. That was until Vivalda betrayed them, not keeping the government on a leash and using the 55's partnership with Anders as a scapegoat. Harry didn't know why Anders was in the pockets of the government, but Vivalda should have handled it. And now, Harry had to fix the problem and obtain the kid, again. He didn't care that he was breaking the 55 auction code. Anders was an honorary guest—they thought he was one of them, one who wanted to obtain everything he could desire. He had never once attended a gala previously and then suddenly, the same year that the government begin to pry, and the same year of the greatest auction that would go down in gala history, Anders shows up.

He was not a true 55er; he was a problem.

"You did, Terry. You really did. But what I need to know now is where he is currently."

"I… I… have no idea. I haven't seen him for weeks, not since I told you where he was going to be," he stuttered. "I last saw him that morning."

Harry nodded and smiled, a twinge of insanity in his eyes.

"Do you want to think about that answer again?"

Terry stared at him.

"No? I haven't seen him."

The warmth from his face slowly drained. Desperation was in his eyes, asking himself the question, 'what are you going to do to me?' Harry could read him. This is what he thrived on: the fear of others.

"There, right there, Terry. You said that word: no. That is a word I don't particularly like hearing. In this case, because you did hold up your end of the deal and helped me obtain the boy, I'm going to ask you again and I want you to think—really think about what you want to say to me, okay?"

Terry rested the heat pen on the workbench, but kept it gripped tightly in-between his fingers.

"I have not seen him. I don't know what you want me to say."

"Stop lying to me!" he screamed.

Terry stepped back.

"Our deal has finished. You told me to check if the boy had syght, which I believed he did, and I told you where he would be."

"Yes, Terry, our deal was finished and this is a new one. Now, I know you're lying. What you have seem to have forgotten is people round here will quite happily aid me in finding out what I need to know. They said Gil was spotted here talking to you a few hours ago. So, Terry—and I mean this sincerely—WHERE THE FUCK IS GIL?!!!"

He could see that the man's hands were shaking more than they usually did. He looked around his stall.

"The answer on the wall, is it, Terry?" he asked him sarcastically.

Terry picked up a crowbar that was propped up against a pile of wooden boxes next to him. One end had a sharp point, enough to inflict serious damage if used correctly. He held it out towards him.

"Going to hit me with it, are you? Be easier if you told me where Gil was."

"I told you what I know!" Terry's voice was

trembling as he spoke.

"Then you need to find out then, or Gil's family, everyone he knows, will be gone."

"If you lost him to Anders, that's not my fault. I did my bit. I didn't want to but I did."

Harry frowned, his forehead creasing, his rising anger subdued for a moment.

"I never said Anders had him—more reasons to point that Gil was here after all. Not doing so well on lying, are you, Terry?"

He watched as he eyed the gate at the front of his stall. It was still marginally open.

He made a run for it, his old wearily legs carrying him, stumbling as he did. A pathetic attempt of an escape, one that Harry would not have to try too hard to keep up with. Though he was no young whippersnapper, he was in shape for a man in his seventies.

As he ran, Terry knocked into cabinets and loose paperwork that had been piled up, crowbar still in hand. He was panicking, trying to get out of the stall, into the open, no doubt hoping someone would see, someone would help. With Harry in the background, there would be no one to help him. He was the games master here; only he moved the pawns.

Terry's foot knocked into a heavy piece of machinery. His old tool sharpener. As he hit it, he tripped.

He tried to use the crowbar as a support to stop him from falling; a walking stick, a crutch.

But the sleek metal pole had no grip to it and it

slid through the palm of his hand as he put weight onto it.

The criss-cross gate was closer to Terry than he thought it was, and his head landed against the gate, grazing down it, taking chucks of skin away, as though the gate were a grater—pieces of his head, jaw, remnants of his face left to hang there as a memento.

Terry couldn't stop himself, and his only aid, the crowbar he was trying to use as a fall breaker, decided to punish Terry, as though it were on Harry's side. The crowbar impaled him through the left side of his chest, missing his heart by inches, breaking the skin, ribcage, layers of muscle, piercing his lung and coming out the other side of his back.

"Fuck!" Harry called out.

This is not how he'd wanted this interaction to go. All he wanted was to give a simple threat, maybe inflict some pain and walk away. Now the game had a time limit. Terry had the information he needed. He was Gil's confidant. Harry had no time to be flitting over the city looking for clues and chasing rumours. That was a hard fall, one with serious consequences.

Terry fell onto his side. The crowbar stopped him rolling around further on his back. He was struggling to breathe as he watched the blood trickle out of the puncture wound.

Harry stood over him and grabbed him by his apron, lifting him off the ground. Terry's eyes were barely open. He was unable to focus on anything.

Harry could feel his body twitching for air.

"You ain't fucking dying until you tell me where the hell that boy is."

He dragged Terry through the stall and out the back door to the alleyway. His new office was close. If he threw him over his shoulder and walked at a fast pace, he could be back in less than five minutes. He had to get the answer he wanted. He had no need for Terry to survive, but if he could prolong his life, there would be more time for interrogation. And plus, if he survived, then he would owe Harry. He would be in debt to him, and that was always a great place to be.

He checked his forearm display. It was approaching eight. Atalon could help. He would know what to do.

Harry kicked open the door to his new, not-yet-furnished establishment. A set of windows on the left wall allowed light into the room. They were murky with green algae, blocking any visibility from passing voyeurs.

He set Terry down on the long table that lay askew to the centre of the room, left by the previous owner.

Terry was still alive, the crowbar still skewed through him as though he were a human olive on a toothpick. The blood around the puncture wound had dried slightly.

"Come on, Terry. There you are. Right here!" He slapped his face a few times on the side that was untarnished by the gate.

Terry was barely conscious.

He heard footsteps.

"I must admit this is by far the worst building I have stepped foot into, Harry. Can we make this meeting as short as it needs to be?" Atalon said as he entered.

"We have a problem," Harry said.

"I know we do, and how do you propose—" He stopped mid-sentence. Harry had stepped aside and revealed where Terry lay on the table, struggling to breathe.

"Who the fuck is that?!" he exclaimed, breaking his usual relaxed composure.

"My informant, Terry. This was his own doing."

"Nothing is ever your doing, is it, Harry?" He rushed over to the table, removing his jacket and waistcoat as he did.

"He knows where the boy is. I need to find the information so we can isolate Gil."

"So, you thought you would drive a crowbar through him to make him talk?"

"Like I said, that was all his mistake."

Atalon grunted.

"We need to remove the crowbar and then assess the damage. Do you have a laser knife with you?" he asked, taking on a calm manner, as though he were a doctor.

"No, I haven't got anything here. I told you: I just acquired the building."

"Then, we are going to have to remove it and

hope it doesn't kill him. Hold him down."

Harry kept Terry still on his side, pushing down on his shoulder, while Atalon grabbed the curved end of the crowbar and pulled it slightly.

A shot of pain awakened Terry and he screamed into the stale air.

"On three, I'm going to remove the crowbar. It feels loose enough to have only gone through the muscle. It should come out in one movement."

Harry had to hope Atalon knew what he was doing. He wasn't squeamish—far from it—but it was the concern that this would delay the 55 in acquiring Gil again. This was not about the large sum of credits he had received. He didn't need to be here, doing this. Harry wanted to avoid the wrath of the 55. This would forever go against him. Just one more job—hand over the boy—then he could walk away from the situation, a well-established 55er for the rest of time.

"Ready?" Atalon said, his grip tight on the crowbar.

Harry could feel Terry's heart working overtime.

"One, two, three!"

He pulled the crowbar with all his might. It slid out Terry's chest smoothly. Terry screamed throughout.

Atalon threw down the bar. It clanked on the concrete floor.

The pair of them stood in silence and watched as Terry grabbed at his chest. Then, as if coming to his senses, Atalon removed his tie and used it as a tourniquet around the wound.

Terry coughed, splattering blood over the both of them. They reacted instinctively and dropped him back onto the table. His head cracked against the wood.

"I... will never..." Terry coughed again, violently this time. The blood trickled out of his mouth. "...tell you, where..." He wheezed in-between words. "...where Gil is."

The blood pumped out of the entry hole to where the crowbar had impaled him.

Harry grabbed him by the ruff of his apron and shirt and lifted him towards his face.

"TELL ME NOW, TERRY, OR I CAN PROMISE YOU I WILL MAKE EVERYONE YOU KNOW SUFFER IN THE SAME PAIN AS YOU ARE RIGHT NOW!"

Terry's eyes rolled into the back of his head. Harry shook him.

"ANSWER ME!!" he yelled.

"He's dead, Harry. Leave it."

He dropped Terry to the table. Harry would now have to go to work. He felt no loss for the man, more an inconvenience that this mess was extending longer that he wanted it to. Terry had helped the process dramatically in locating the boy. He would now have to use his other source. Maybe they were more reliable. Maybe they would be less caring on who they protected.

Terry's body was still, no movement, no breath. The blood oozed out onto the table, filling in the cracks, score marks and indents that had been made over the years.

"Fucking answer me!!" He went for Terry once more, punching him in the chest.

"He's dead, Harry!" Atalon said sternly. "He's not going to give you the answer you want. It's over. I don't know how you like to deal with business, but in my experience, this is how not to do it. If they have what you need, ideally, they should be alive. Is that why you brought me down here? To interrogate him?"

"I told you, I had no hand in him injuring himself. I wanted to tell you how we were going to get the boy back, as I know that Terry would have eventually told me."

"Well, too late for that. He's dead and now you have a corpse lying in your establishment. How you get rid of it is none of my concern. I did not want to spend my evening covered in his blood. This is on you, Harry."

"Wait a minute, on me? You are the one who let Vivalda have more control than she deserves. She is government. She should have apprehended Anders, rather than letting him turn up to the gala. This is your fault." Atalon approached him, but he continued. "Don't think that I am going to be intimidated by you. You are in my domain here. If you had solved this problem with Vivalda, this discussion would be null and void, and I would be minus one dead old fucker on my table."

Atalon knew he was right. He could see it by his

clenched jaw and his lack of response.

"Terry was the one person I had who knew where Gil was precisely. Now he's gone—thanks to you."

"This is not my mistake!" said Atalon. "You brought me down here to discuss business, not to keep an ally of yours alive."

"Well, he was alive when I brought him in here. And you were the one that pulled the crowbar out of him, killing him."

Harry was good at passing the blame. It was always someone else's fault, shirking the responsibility, then nothing could fall to him. He was already in hot water with the 55; now he had his sacrifice: Atalon was the one who killed Terry, not him.

"If we want the boy back so we can find out what syght can do for us, you need to pay Vivalda a visit. She is now the only one who has access to him, through Anders."

Atalon wiped his face and hands with his waistcoat, which was as good as ruined. He unbuttoned the top of his shirt.

"If we get the boy away from Anders, he will have no way of finding Gil again. If you paid that amount for someone, you are going to come looking. Anders blindsided us before, but we are prepared now. We are the 55; you need to remember that, Atalon. I'll get rid of the body: throw it down the gorge and no one will be any the wiser. Nobody will question it and we carry on as normal. You threaten

Vivalda and she'll do whatever we tell her to do. That's the deal we have—the deal you have with her. We retrieve the boy and no one will question where Terry went. He's just a lonely old man, one who probably died in his sleep or got locked in his apartment somewhere—no one cares, Atalon."

Atalon stood, still, then turned away, his head cocked towards the floor. Harry knew he was thinking, contemplating what he had said.

"Vivalda, I will deal with. But, Harry, if you bring me down here again to talk business and I arrive to see something like this—" he pointed to the body "—then I'll be sending you somewhere where you can spend the rest of your time with Terry."

"Oh, a threat, Atalon? How malicious of you. I'm going to remind you who you are talking to. Don't treat me with the same manner you do everyone below you."

With that, he grabbed the body underneath his arms and dragged it off the table towards a door at the back of the room.

"Vivalda is the one who caused all of this. She is the one we trusted and who betrayed the 55. She took from us something we had searched so long to find. This is your problem now."

Harry smirked at Atalon before exiting through the door, dragging his problem behind him. The door swung shut, and the body of Terry vanished.

Atalon needed to know why Vivalda had switched sides. No one betrayed the 55, especially High

Chancellors. They controlled the government, not the other way round. The 55 only wanted to make the Supreme House council believe that so they could continue orchestrating their businesses, their lives, their dealings however they desired. Unlike Harry, Atalon knew what the capabilities of syght were. If he had access to someone with syght, he would be untouchable. He could create something beyond the 55, a world he could rule.

Syght was the key to unlocking the greatest gift mankind could own. He could decide the outcome of anything people chose. He could control anything that existed. He could play God.

TWENTY SEVEN

The government building had cleared out for the evening. Other than those in the surveillance room, situated six floors below her office, Vivalda was the only one left. Her business sometimes extended past the normal working hours due to whatever meetings or negotiations she had to attend to, neither of which tended to be government-related. She had no recollection of when she last had a normal working day.

Spirits were luxuries that were hard to come by, and on the odd occasion, when she felt a sense of achievement, usually at the end of the week, she would fill a small copper tumbler with two cubes of ice and a large serve helping of triple distilled vodka.

She watched as the translucent liquid sloshed around the cup, smashing against the ice, and then took that first sip, savouring the cooling feeling of the fiery burn as it made its way down her throat.

The quiet of her office was a sanctuary in which to enjoy the drink. Occasionally, she might peer in to the surveillance room and people watch. She relished the fact that she could hold a vodka in hand too, when she visited. The pleasure she felt as her employees salivated over the expensive elixir gave her the dominance she loved as a High Chancellor. It was rare that she used her status to make herself feel better, but there were times that everyone needed that boost to their self-esteem, to feel desirable, invincible, untouchable.

She closed her eyes as she sat back in the chair. She soaked up the calm of the room. There was a faint monotonous beat, quicker than a tick on an analogue clock, that began to grow in volume rather speedily. Someone was approaching her office, and from the noise of their footwear on the marbled floor, it sounded as if they had a rage to unleash.

The door to her office was thrown open.

"What was our agreement?!" Atalon Keel exploded with venom.

She set down the cup and looked him in the eye.

"Which one? We have made too many over the years that I tend not to keep count of them anymore," she replied sarcastically.

"YOU SET US UP! Don't play naive with me, Vivalda."

"I can assure you, I have no need to play naive as that is not a quality I condone in my establishment."

Atalon looked ruffled, as though he had not slept for about a week. His usual demure of the suave older gentleman was lost amongst the five o'clock shadow on his face that was about six hours late. The open waistcoat covered in splatters of blood was a concern.

His eyes were locked on her. She knew he was being serious.

"Anders Hilgaard attended the 55 gala. I told you specifically to keep the government away. He was the only one that nobody would have been suspicious about attending. I gave you the information you needed, yet the government still pushed for an answer. Since when has Anders been working for the government?"

"He hasn't been. They are looking to bring him down as much as they are you."

A sight of Anders losing his empire was a scene Vivalda thrived to see. She wasn't malicious; she was fair. She probably had the same dislike that the 55 had towards Anders.

"You failed, Vivalda. The 55 are disappointed in you and now I look like a fool who can't keep their High Chancellor in order."

She stood, facing him menacingly.

No one controlled her; no one owned her, especially a 55er questioning her methods in her city. She was not to blame for this, nor was she going to take the fall for it. She was nobody's lapdog.

"You do not own me, nor do I take orders from you. We work together, a partnership, to both achieve what we want. The 55 do not run this planet; we do, the government. We keep the likes of you in order. We control your purpose how we see fit. We do what we can to achieve our goal of a world that will prolong human life, to rid the earth of what made it rotten before the Uniformed Act was introduced."

"And you think I can't end everything you have power over and ruin all you have achieved?"

"Do not dare threaten me, Atalon," she said through gritted teeth, suppressing the urge inside her to rip into him. She had a letter opener as an ornament mounted on her desk. It would only take a few seconds, and Atalon would feel her wrath.

"Anders won the bid on the auction. He has… what we all deserved a chance to claim."

"What? A young child with syght?!"

He changed his expression.

"How did you know?"

"This is my city, Atalon. You should be more careful with how you obtain your assets. Anders' daughter announced it as I was leaving his office. You really believe Harry, of all the 55ers, is capable of finding a myth? Someone that has the ability of seeing when that person was scheduled to die? The government shut down that theory decades ago. You are more the fool than I anticipated, Atalon."

At this, he laughed gently to himself

"You clearly have no concept of syght do you, Vivalda? The myth that it predicted when you are going to die was a cover up. Syght helps you cross realities. It gives you the chance to conquer a reality that is untouched by any of us."

"That is not possible."

"Isn't it?"

"You had no proof that kid had it, anyway."

"Harry is stupid, fucking bone-idle if you ask me, but when there is an opportunity for him to make some money, he would never present an ineffective product. The 55 would have voted him out of the group. He knows the way we work. No one would lie to a 55er, especially not Harry Qwhale."

"And did you see the kid use this ability?"

"No."

"My point exactly."

She picked up the copper cup and gulped some vodka.

The prospect developed in her mind. She had no idea this syght existed, in this form. To cross realties was a concept that was far beyond her understanding. She was no scientist, but she understood that the power and control over something new, something that everybody wanted, was a promising venture—an untouched society ruled by her own government. She wouldn't need the Supreme House then.

"I was betrayed as much as you were, Atalon. Anders is not an animal who can be caged into his building and simply told not to leave."

"I thought you had exactly that power to use!"

"People like Anders need to be dealt with in a different manner—something you fail to understand as you treat all with the same method: bribe, threaten, prove your point, kill if you must."

"And it works for a reason."

"Not when you are Anders Hilgaard. He is as protected as much as you are, if not more, as the public seem to adore him for some reason."

Atalon ran his hand through his hair and slicked it back.

"You are going to get that kid back and bring him to me."

"Won't that be breaking your precious 55 auction code?" she mocked, and took another sip.

"Don't you fucking dare talk down to me!"

Before she had a chance to back away, he had grabbed her by the throat and slammed her up against the back wall of the office. He held her there, her feet slightly raised above the floor. Atalon's large hand wrapped around her windpipe, tightening. She gasped. Her chest constricted, her ribs threatening to close in on her lungs. She attempted a roar, a cry of dominance to state her ground, but the vodka spat out over Atalon's hand.

"You are going to get that kid, Gil Taberthorn, and bring him back to me. That is your order. Do you understand?" he said slowly and clearly.

She gasped again as she clawed at his hand.

He let go, and she slid down the wall until her feet touched the ground, then he pulled her away from the wall and threw her back against it hard. His hand released slightly. She took a gulp of air, able to breathe normally again, taking quick in-takes of breath, as though she was tasting it for the first time.

But he did not remove his hand from around her neck.

"Do you understand?" he repeated.

She took orders from no one, nor was she one to be threatened. It never worked out for the general public, not for her own aids, and especially not the 55. If Atalon thought she was going to accept this behaviour in her office, he was in for a shock.

She swung a left hook into his ribs, which buckled him.

His hand released fully from her throat.

The satisfaction of her disarming him had spurred her on to more combat.

She raised her leg and kicked him square in the chest. He stumbled back, catching the corner of her desk, and then returned a full hand slap that caught her in the face. It stung. She hadn't ingested enough vodka to not feel it. Thankfully, adrenaline was all she needed.

He approached again to grab her, but she took hold of his wrist and twisted it over. He released a low grunt.

She pushed him up against a large metal filling cabinet on the other side of the room, his face squashed against the cold metal draw. A line of drool traced its way down over the chrome handle as he grunted again. She held his twisted arm against his own back, pulling it up towards his head. She wanted to hear it crack. The pleasure of hearing it break his bone in two would give her a bigger rush than the vodka.

"Never threaten me again," she whispered into his ear.

He wanted to fight dirty? She was fine with that.

He kicked back his heel straight into her shin and she hobbled back, releasing him from the cabinet. Her shin was numb. She tried to throw a few punches, but she missed him. Balancing her weight onto one foot and swinging a punch was difficult to do. She caught the end of his chin, softer than she had intended.

As she made another lunge for him, Atalon held out his forearm and close-lined her. She ended up sprawled out across her desk.

He used both his hands to grab her throat once more.

She was pinned. The desk was deep and her feet were hovering above the floor. She kicked one foot, the thin spike of her heel scratching the front side of her desk. That constriction returned in her chest and windpipe, tighter this time, enough air allowed in to the lungs to keep the pain of the struggle real, the fight as her internal organs wanted more. A pressure formed in her head as her brain began to slowly be starved of oxygen.

"I'm going to tell you this again," he said. "Get Gil and bring him to me. I don't care how. This is your order. If you do not, I will have you shot. You are immediately to make your way over to SeeTech Tower. There are two men outside this building. They will execute you in the street if you refuse or make a detour."

Vivalda spat at him.

"I will threaten you to get what I want."

Her nails dug into his hands, drawing blood. Her arm shook with the force she was trying to give out, the tension of every muscle in her fingers fighting to survive.

"Do you understand now?"

She spluttered in response.

"That, I will take as confirmation. I was going to be lenient, but I have changed my mind."

He released his grip on her and she gasped loudly, her back arching off the table, her head swinging back, taking in as much oxygen as she could. She coughed violently.

He walked out of her office and wiped his blood-covered hands on his trousers as he stepped into the lift. She had left her mark, for now.

She floundered back on the desk. Her eyes were watering, her intercostal muscles pumping her chest rapidly to facilitate the use of her lungs again. But soon, her worry started to outweigh her anger. She had crossed a line, a line which Anders Hilgaard had drawn. This had been the first real sign of the 55's greed and how far they were willing to go. Loyalty meant nothing if she didn't complete what they had set out for her to do. She would never have the 55 in her pocket—she knew that. She had to play them as much as they did her.

If she managed to get this Gil, she knew they would kill her after anyway. Maybe there was a way of using this syght the kid had? This was her chance to manipulate the 55.

Atalon was not going to rest lightly, even though she knew she was just an innocent pawn in his bigger game. It was Anders who had gone wayward from the plan, yet Vivalda was the one to suffer. She had to stop Atalon ruining what she had already sacrificed for a seat on the Supreme House Council. She had to learn about syght—not for her own greed, but to aid her accomplishments, her plans for a better, greater future. A 55-less society.

She had to think. Two of Atalon's men were outside the building. They would make themselves known, to put the fear into her. But Vivalda lacked the compassion required for fear. She was made of stronger material than anything that would let her be intimidated by hooligans. She was angrier at herself for not snapping Atalon's arm when she had the opportunity. It may not have helped the situation, but it would have shown him that she was not one to be messed with.

She unlocked a draw to her desk and pulled out a leather box. She pressed her thumbprint on the square pad at the top and it illuminated the print, recognising it. The lid popped open and inside was a government-issued plasma gun. Back in 2045, all weapons had to be destroyed, or you risked the death penalty for using or owning one. She had not needed to use her assigned weapon. It was for emergency cases. And in her mind, this still did not constitute one of those times, but she did want to use it for all the reasons she was not meant to. She usually set the example by abiding by the rules, but Atalon had gone too far. He had provoked this, not her. She knew this weapon was going to evoke a sanction of her own demise, but it would also gain her power.

Her gaze focused down onto the sleek, black weapon. She knew it was monitored. As soon as she fired it, an alert would be sent to the Supreme House council. She would have to explain why she had used it, unlike the 55, the only other people she knew who had weapons, though they denied every investigation into one of them firing one.

She activated the gun. It made a whirring sound.

She held it in her hands. It was weighted heavily. Even without shooting the men, it would do as much damage if she hit them with it.

Her conscious stepped in and questioned whether she should be doing this. If she stormed into SeeTech Tower and held a gun to Gil's head, she was no better than the 55. She'd be using the weapon for her own gain, even if it was for protection. The primary use of any weapon issued to High Chancellor's should be to gain power over an individual to make them do what you wanted them to. This was revenge. In the eyes of the Supreme House this would look like an unprovoked attack, in 55 territory. The council would not believe her story. She was no rule breaker—bend the rules, yes—but she needed a clean slate to be on the council.

She switched it off and sealed it back into its box.

Then another idea came to her.

She exited the government building, and as expected, directly in front of her were the two burly men, standing in front of a black vehicle, dressed as though they were a prototype Atalon, living as his shadow.

She pulled out the gift that Harry had given her—the Colt Peacemaker. Her secret had come to some use. Direct hits. Both the men instantly fell to the ground, dead before they had the chance to realise what was going on.

She needed protection, though. Atalon would soon find out two of his men had been killed.

Her conscious stepped up to the podium once again.

Who did she think she was trying to be?

This was 55 territory: getting involved with kidnapping, murder… The weapon she was currently holding in her hand was still hot from the expelled bullet.

This was not Vivalda's way. She had to forcefully stop herself from becoming this person before it was too late. She was not going to be corrupt like the 55, or no doubt, some of the other High Chancellors. Yes, she was stern, and from time to time, left certain government sanctions to one side, if she felt they were not suitable for her city. She had her methods, because she wanted to move through the ranks. However, she was a woman who had high morals and standards, and Atalon abusing her integrity was something she would not stand for. Dealing with the 55 had its benefits, but she always kept those business matters far enough away to not become fully involved herself. But now, the smoking barrel of the gun said otherwise. If Atalon found out that she'd killed two of his men, which he would, Vivalda would end up with the same fate.

She was not in control of this situation. She had to think. Her High Chancellor's authority was useless here. Any rash decisions or enforcement would start a war between the government and the 55. She was not going to be the one to initiate the fall of the new generation.

Her anger had passed and the looming threat of her inevitable death crept in to hold her, wrapping itself around her like a blanket. She had become privy to the feeling of regret, something she tended not to feel. This is how they suffered—anyone who befriended the 55. This is what they had to endure.

She needed a solution. Protection now was pointless, especially if she did not fulfil her assignment.

There was only one place she could go, one person who could prevent this all from falling apart.

TWENTY EIGHT

The lift moved slower than he needed it to. The anticipation was building as he watched the numbers turn over as he ascended to Anders' workshop. Gil wanted to be wrong, that Anders wasn't building a syght lens. His time with Freer had shown him the true power of syght within the wrong hands. Anders had done everything to help him, and other than this creation, this breakthrough that Cyra was working on, there was nothing he had seen that he thought suspicious.

    He had not chosen this and it was cliché to think that it had chosen him—it hadn't. It was just a fluke. If he'd been born a fraction of a second later, he would still be a salvager, working for Terry and no one would know who he was or care either. He wasn't going to allow others, innocent people, good hearted people, like him, to be destroyed. He didn't want Cyra to be mixed up in all of this.

All he could think about was how he was going to approach the conversation. He had a battle on his hands. On one hand, his employer was creating a lens that replicated syght for reasons that were unclear, but on the other, he couldn't be totally sure that Anders had evil intentions, and he risked ruining a career of a talented scientist he respected greatly.

'BUZZ'

He entered the workshop. Cyra was alone, once again working on the ID Lens. It had changed slightly since he last saw it. She had been working hard.

"Gil, perfect timing. Can you help me remove this fourth power chip for me and replace it with a gyrospace one instead?"

He had zero understanding to space mechanics and antimatter autonomy, and could barely say the words 'quantum entanglement', but he did know his way around a circuit board. How could he ignore her?

"Sure. Why are we doing that?"

"I think by having too much power running through the lens—" She looked up towards Gil. "Why are you sweating?"

Oh, because I had to run here and tell you, you are creating a machine that could aid the end of human life as we know it, was what Gil wanted to say, but it was too brash. He had to confirm first that what she was working on was what he thought it was.

He wanted to be wrong and put this down to another snowballing thought process. The world was already against him.

"I ran over to help as I knew I would be late. Sorry."

The first lie to Cyra. This was a habit he wanted to avoid. There were enough people lying already.

"Don't worry. I had enough calculations to perfect first. I've just started the adjustments. Come over and take a look."

He wiped his brow and headed over to the centre table.

"It's burning through the micro minichips here and shutting down all functions. Taking one away reduces the power, but the gyrospace chip improves the parameters of what we want the lens to focus on and draws on space particles that the human eye cannot see to use as its source of power instead."

Gil nodded, not really understanding what she was saying, other than the fact that it should work.

"Gil, can I ask you something?"

An inquisitive tone. He was worried about what that might mean. If she already had her own suspicions, maybe it would make it an easier way to explain everything.

"If you want," he said softly.

"I can talk to you about this as you know what I know about this ID lens, so theoretically, it's not breaking the contract... It's been playing on my mind, amongst all the scientific equations. Felcion was lied to about what we are working on, so neither of us said anything."

Gil nodded. He had more secrets than he could count.

"I can't help but think—and Anders has been more than helpful towards my career and I am grateful, very much so. I'm a scientist and calculations is kind of my thing…"

It was the first time he had seen her attempt a joke.

"…and all of it doesn't add up. I'm starting to think the reason why Anders couldn't get this lens to work is because it is designed to do something else, something we haven't thought about yet."

She had worked it out on her own.

Anders had played the both of them well, helping them where they needed so neither would be suspicious, providing a secure job—working on a unique discovery for technology and the world, yet for it all to be in secret. Keeping information secret could only benefit the one person who was asking for it to be kept secret in the first place.

This was the right time. He had to trust her. Whether she was spying for Anders or not, she had to know the truth about syght, what it was and why this lens could not fall into anyone else's hands. Hiding it from her made him guilty, guilty for the lying itself but also for putting her life in danger. To his knowledge and what he had seen, Cyra didn't have syght. She was an innocent bystander who was in the firing line.

"Cyra—" he started, but she cut him off.

"No matter what I do, the calculations keep changing. One thing works, yet the other part fails. This technology is impossible. There is no sense for it to work."

She pushed Anders' notepad away from her.

Anders must have kept the information from Cyra for a reason, in case she wanted to use it for herself or under orders by the 55 maybe—not that Gil received that vibe from her at all. Anders was protecting others. He knew it. He had been part of that protection.

"Gil? GIL?!!" Cyra called.

"Yep," he said, turning to her.

"I've been calling you for about a minute."

"Sorry, I was thinking about and processing what you were saying. It's all too technical for me to understand. I don't know much about space beyond the fact it's dark with a few billion scattered stars around it."

He was making himself sound like an idiot, but he needed time whilst he tried to figure out the best approach.

"I need to tell you—" He attempted again, but his urgency was overshadowed by Cyra's explosion.

"GIL! I've done it! I think. I've solved the equation in a practical sense!"

"Shit!" he said quietly, not loud enough for her to hear. The smile, the elation on her face—how could he ruin her moment of discovery? Every scientist's dream is a moment like this. It was eating him up inside, but he was also curious to see if Cyra had completed what she intended to do—create a working ID Lens.

She tinkered with a few more circuit boards, asking him to replace and reorder certain microchips. He did so begrudgingly, with Cyra breathing down his neck all the while to hurry him along.

"That's it. Leave it alone! That's what we need, right there. Gil, we have done it!" She hugged him.

The squeeze of that hug filled him with dread. He needed to tell her. He should have mentioned it when he had his first suspicions, when he first thought it might potentially be a syght lens. It had gone too far now.

"Cyra, I need to tell you something about this lens, about me… What Anders has made us build for him."

But it was as if his voice travelled in one ear and out the other. She was too eager to give it a try.

"We have to see if it works. Aren't you excited, Gil? All this time, and we have cracked it."

The constant reminder of Cyra using the term 'we' and not 'I', showed him that she saw them as a team, a team that trusted each other.

Cyra had nominated herself as the test subject.

"You sure you want to do this?" he asked.

"Why? Do you not?" she said flippantly.

She picked up the lens and placed the frame over her ears and in position on her face. As with the Spacial Lens, there was no switch or on button. It worked through photoplethysmography, which Gil had read about in the volumes of Spacial Lens books, a method that uses light and optical detectors to activate the lens, recognising when a human is attached to it.

She walked around the room, moving her head in all directions, hoping she would see something, a space leap as she had once called it.

As the minutes passed, he could see her expression fall, the joy of all their hard work turning into the frown of their failure, sinking in.

"That should have worked, Gil! It should have worked! This board, the exchange and reroute of the gyrospace chip into the wave regulator hybrid motherboard was the answer. I measured and set the parameters of that motherboard. Why why why doesn't it work?!"

She grabbed the lens frame, removed it from her face and held it between her hands. He could see the whites of her fingers as she squeezed it.

Gil could see her clear frustrations. Part of him wanted her to squeeze so tightly that the lens broke and it didn't exist anymore.

"ARRRRGGHH! That bloody hurt. Piece of shit!"

Cyra studied her finger. She squeezed it hard enough to inflict pain on the flesh, but not enough to damage the frame. Gil could see the blood come to the surface.

"The frame cut me."

An unfinished product with sharp edges, exposed circuitry and metal shutters wasn't exactly going to be friendly. Not that it had acted out in self defence.

She held her finger up towards him. There was blood. Maybe this was a sign that the lens wanted to survive; it wanted to work, so it was fighting back.

The test was over. Now, Gil needed to tell her. He was worried she might react angrily to him, that she wouldn't understand. He could show her how he used syght. He had proof now. He was starting to be able to control it, expand it, so he could show her what this could mean for people if this lens was finished—not for the people, the nation they were trying to help, but what it could mean for the ones who wanted everything, the ones who could create untold chaos with a device like this.

She sucked on her finger to heal the wound.

At that moment, the ID lens made a noise. The shutters blinked rapidly. From both their viewpoint, they could see through the lenses, see the orange hue shine brighter; they had been activated. The knowing tell that someone's lens was working was the faint orange screen they had in front of their eye.

"What did you do?" he asked.

"Nothing. I saw nothing. The lens wasn't working."

He could see the split screen view, still fuzzy: two lenses attempting to focus on different versions of the truth. He had seen this many times before. He had been right all along.

Cyra picked the frame back up and put it on. Gil stood and watched as her jaw dropped open.

"I can see," she said. "Something is there. It's

not focusing entirely, but there is an image or two—not what I was expecting, but we have made something happen."

She walked around the room again, attempting to refocus the images she could see. Gil knew what she was seeing—it was what he saw every day in training—however, the problem now was that it was constantly open, the two realities. No split-second decision.

As she was walking, Cyra caught her foot on the metal leg of a table. Gil had seen her make clumsy mistakes numerous times. She stumbled, unable to catch herself and hit the floor with her knee. Then she looked up at him with overwhelming delight in her eyes.

"I just saw it, Gil. I can't explain it. I saw it! I saw myself falling and I saw how to stop myself. The possibility of being able to do it but it was fuzzy, something not quite there but I saw what just happened!" Tears started to roll down her cheeks—the achievement of a long few months.

She took the frame off again and inspected the circuit board. It was covered in her blood.

"It's DNA," she said, aghast. "The lens can only work on the human's DNA. If we could adjust the vision, it might work fully."

It was a syght lens and now Cyra had seen it, for herself.

Anders was trying to build a syght lens and he failed. The answer was in Gil's DNA. That's what Cyra needed. That's why the lens would have never worked prior to this. Anyone without syght lacked the Déjà Vu gene, therefore the lens couldn't use their DNA code to open the two realities. The lens helped keep the realities open fully, for longer, constantly. Anders didn't need Gil anymore for syght; he just needed his DNA.

"A lens that can help you stop accidents occurring could lead us onto our original goal of what we want it to do. We now know how the ID lens needs to work. Go on. Give it a try."

"But it's covered in your blood," Gil said, not keen on the idea. He knew what the outcome would be.

"We have spares. Replace the board and try again with your blood. We need to test different subjects now, see how the lens is affected."

She hunted around for a circuit board of the same nature. She found one and handed it to him, who obliged and replaced the current circuit board with a fresh, unbloodied one.

"Here!"

She dragged him over to her desk and picked up a pin they'd been using to hold components in place before they were sealed.

"Hold out your finger," she said.

"Cyra, I think it's wise we don't do this. This is not an ID lens; it's for syght!" He couldn't contain it any longer.

"A what?"

"Syght is an ability to be able to see into two realities, to be able to decide which future action you make—like you did just now: fall or stop yourself from falling. You fell but you saw your possibilities, because of this lens. This is what it does, if not even more than we know. Giving it my DNA is going to give Anders and the 55 exactly what they need.

"What are you talking? We are giving Anders this lens, yes, it's his project he started. Come here!"

She pricked his finger.

"What the— That fucking hurt."

"Gil, I have to know if this works. After all the hard work we have put into it, we can't fail now.

"Think about it, Cyra: the lying, the secrecy... I can't keep this hidden any longer. I have syght; I have the DNA needed to make this work."

"Put your blood onto the circuit board."

Cyra was clouded by her invention, the fact that it was working. She wasn't listening to him. She couldn't see the danger that leered at them from outside this workshop—what Anders could do with this lens, what the 55 could do if they also managed to get hold of it. He was the tank to fuel its use.

"No, I'm good, thanks."

Why couldn't she see that he was trying to keep her safe?

"Well, we need to see how different DNA affects the lens. You might get a clearer picture than I did. And the blood is out already."

"Thanks to you." He sighed.

He needed a reason not to help her. The 55 were after him, and sooner or later, they would find a way into this building and recapture him. If they did, he was putting both of them at risk, and with the syght lens to hand, he may as well give up now. He had to find a way of hiding the lens—and himself—whilst protecting Cyra at the same time.

The part of the equation he couldn't quite figure out was where Anders fit in to all this. Anders had known all this time about syght. He knew Gil had it, yet he had still lied to him.

He wasn't safe here. He could destroy the lens now, but that wouldn't stop Cyra building a new one or keep Anders away. He had to protect Cyra and the Sense Shifters in this reality.

He had an idea.

He positioned his finger over the circuit board, letting the blood seep into the crevices.

"Okay, that's enough," she said with a smile.

When he put the frames on, the lens came alive and the shutters blinked rapidly, faster than what he had seen them do when Cyra wore it.

"Try and do something," she said, looking around the room for inspiration.

For the lens to work, he knew he needed an option, a choice.

Gil always found that the best environments to use syght were when he was falling, running towards something, or engaging in an activity that involved a narrow encounter with injury. In his mind, he formed a plan.

"Right, here goes."

He breathed. If his suspicions were right, then this was a syght lens that was capable of keeping the reality open for longer, so he'd be able to see further into a choice playing out, maybe even seeing more of the other reality, rather than split second glimpses. These were his expectations, and truly, he was scared to what might actually happen.

He walked towards the double doors at the other end of the room and waited.

"When I run towards you, I want you to try and hit me."

"What? I'm not doing that."

"If you believe it works, then I will be able to move out the way of your fist, right?"

"I guess so."

"So, hit me!"

It was a small room, so it would only be a few strides before he would be on top of her.

Cyra prepped, holding her fist up and ready. From her stance, he could tell that she had never needed to throw a punch before—but neither had he until he met Freer.

He ran towards her, feeling confident he would avoid the punch, completely forgetting this was Cyra's first experience with syght. She backed out at the last second and withdrew her arm timidly.

Gil panicked. Taking away the obstacle took away his choice. Without having been focused on what he was doing, he now had to quickly make a decision on how to avoid ploughing into Cyra.

The shutters began to flap at an incredible rate. The two realities made themselves known vividly, but in a way that he had never seen before. The options were clear, as though he could step right into the other.

He jumped out of Cyra's way, using his syght to make sure he landed without breaking something. Two options: crash into the table or barrel into the free space without any hurdles. He spun in the air and prepped his landing. The closer he got to the space, the more he could see how to land: right leg down first, with his right hand as backup, pushing his weight to the left.

He stumbled and executed his landing, free of any injury, crashes or unexecuted punches.

"So, it does work then," he said to Cyra, unsurprised that the invention had allowed him to do what it was made to do.

But Cyra was gone.

He looked around him. The workshop was different.

The clinical room was now a silkwort grey, and all the books, instruments and prototype inventions were missing.

Gil had no idea where he was.

He was in the other reality.

TWENTY NINE

In a blink of an eye—Gil's eye—he had stepped across the universe, billions of light years away. Without distorting time—to his knowledge—he had ended up in the reality of the choice that he had made. He was in an unexplored sector of the known universe, the first to have ever used syght to its full capabilities with the aid of the ID lens. He had become the only human to travel this far in space, and all without a craft or plasma engine, or having spent years seeing nothing more than a black sheet dotted with a plethora of stars.

He had no clue as to where he was, though. This was Earth 2.0—not that this was an improved world to the one he already knew, more an alternate earth where certain decisions have taken a different course. But how? He still couldn't get his head around how there are multiple outcomes to one decision and yet all ended up here—the place of discarded choice. Maybe Freer was wrong. She believed so heavily there were only two realities because no one had seen how to expand the mind further into seeing more. Was it capable for the mind to explore multiple choices, with only two eyes and be able to choose which reality from that vision?

He reminded himself of what Freer said: 'there are only two choices that can be made: two realities.' On that understanding, he knew he would have no reason to worry about where he was, as it was still Earth, just an alternative version of it. One that he hoped was like the world he knew, his accessible path of choice between two realities. He had chosen this reality over the millions that existed because it lined more with his choices in life. So there would only be two realities but it was dependant on the person who was using syght. No one had been in this situation before to know. Gil had to work out the answers to his own questions but also find the flaws in the Sense Shifters too, now he was experiencing it.

He wondered if what he had been told was true, then there should be no 55 after him, as they may not exist, no other syght lens, the immediate threat towards him, Cyra, the Sense Shifters gone. He had to hope, but there was no guarantee. No one had made this complete step into the other reality that he knew of, so there were no concrete answers to his worried thoughts. He was oddly calm—a feeling of safety with a hint of caution.

He stood in an unfamiliar room, which had a sense of familiarity about it. It was the workshop he had spent endless days with Cyra in, though it was decorated differently—darker in colour, less clinical and more organised, sleek as though the room had not been used. The layout was the same—the double doors that buzzed on every entry and exit situated in the same location—although, there was one large difference: the door was open, ajar. That door was never left unlocked.

The workbench that Gil normally sat at was still there, and it looked as if it was the same number of steps between it and the exit.

There was no sound or noise, no faint chatter of employees.

He opened the door further and saw a similar-looking corridor to the one in his reality. It led to another door opposite. Anders' office, he assumed. The wall to his right had the same window that opened out to Axeon City, but this was a slightly different perspective. It was rare that Anders left the two-way epidiascope glass in view for the outside world to peer in. He searched for a wall panel—nothing. He placed his hand onto the window, and as he pulled it away, left his print. There was no dashed white line around the frame, which projected the false display wall, like the windows in SeeTech Tower. This was as plain a window as they come—no hidden technology behind it.

He admired the view, the extension of the city into the forest. It was homely yet still full of nature.

He could see houses, the type he saw in the country, but no apartments stacked on top of one another, the ones he saw every day that leaked or had parts of them falling off—not that these details were clear from his view. The sun highlighted the clean, white, fresh facade of the housing and the lawns in front of them.

He had the urge to explore further yet, at the same time, was concerned to what he might find.

There was another door up on the left, next to Anders' office. In his reality, that room didn't exist.

Curious, he walked over to where he could see a plaque on the door.

'Rix Xing, Head of Advanced Biometrics and Artificial Technologies' it read.

'What?' If that was the same Rix he knew, the Rix he had grown up with and knew more than anyone, why was her surname not Hilgaard? He recognised the name, but could not remember where he knew it from. Even so, the idea of Rix working for Syngetical was more absurd than Gil using syght. Yet here it was: her name engraved on a door with a title.

He stared at the door handle. He wanted to open it, see if it was his Rix standing on the opposite side of the door, but if his choice to work for Anders had not replicated itself in this reality then he would be an intruder. And if that were the case, if he opened the door it would trigger a lockdown system.

He gripped hold of the handle.

There was no finger print scanner nor mouth

swab, no retinal confirmation nor any security devices attached on the door or the surrounding wall. He could see no technology at all. This version of Earth seemingly had nothing to hide. No secrets. Surely everyone had secrets? He had grown up in a world where keeping information disclosed aided one's fortune. This was odd.

He turned the handle delicately so as not to trigger any fail safes, though if a system could be foiled that easily, by slowly completely an action, then these security systems would be highly flawed. But still, the slow motion gave him confidence.

The door eased open smoothly and he could see an office behind it. From the brief glimpse he saw, the room held half-completed devices that he had no recollection of seeing before—Anders' workshop all over again. Tools were scattered next to these devices, and multiple panel display screens suspended from above a desk.

The lights changed to a harsh red glow. Red. The sign that he had done something wrong. From the ceiling, three steel caged walls began to lower—one within the office, one to his right in front of Anders' office door and one blocking the double doors to the workshop.

"Shit," he expressed out loud.

He paused for a moment, trying to decide what he could do.

The three walls started to close in on him, fast. He needed his choices. He was still wearing the ID lens, which was still activated. But the choice was already made for him: if he stayed where he was then he would be trapped at the entrance to Rix's office; if he moved, then he might avoid them.

He ran back along the hallway towards where the lift should be, the three walls a homing beacon locked on to him. They seemed to be able to move as freely as they wished to capture their intruder.

If outrunning them was not a choice, then perhaps standing still and avoiding them at the last second would allow him to use syght, so he could see the other reality and dive back into it.

He focused his mind, keeping alert as he bounced on the balls of his feet. The grinding sound of steel against the marble floor was distracting.

The thick cage glided through the office wall and emerged as a silhouette of itself, regaining its opaqueness when it passed through.

He blinked quickly.

He had done this before already. He had stepped into this reality, so there was no reason why he shouldn't find his way back.

The walls shifted in his vision as he switched between each eye. There was no option making itself apparent. The cage had to be closer. The closer the object, the clearer the choice. The ID lens hummed softly in his ear as the split of the two realities became clear. The shutters fired rapidly. He blinked faster, the steel gates grinding louder as they quickened. The lens opened up the realities for longer, without having to make a last second decision, it gave him time to think, assess, and see what he was leaping into. Could this lens, with his DNA now embedded onto it, be able to do more than just see what he classed as home and this alternate reality that had been drummed into him as all the other choices that weren't taken—were there other realities?

Gil saw his gap, the only opportunity to survive the approaching cage. He needed to jump between the two joining cage walls. The choice: stay put and become caught, or leap back to the reality that he now recognised as Syngetical. With his viewpoint split, he could see Cyra walking around, searching for where Gil had vanished too.

He dived, sideways, through the narrowing gap of the enclosing caged walls. He looked back at his trailing leg as he continued to wink between his eyes. His leg was about to get caught within the cage, cutting his foot clean at the ankle. He had misjudged the leap. He could hear his own scream, could witness the spray of blood against the marble floor. He took an inhale of breath and pulled his knee up towards his face. He would land on his back. It would hurt. There was no gymnastic landing he had perfected—but he'd rather keep his foot.

His knee shot towards his face and connected with his nose and the top line of teeth, knocking them hard. There was a crack. He didn't know if it was his nose or a tooth breaking off.

As expected, he landed on his back, onto the floor and slid straight into the corner of a pillar. His slide was stopped as his head hit the concrete, opening up a cut on the back of his head.

All of these injuries, he had caused to himself—his lack of control, allowing the panic to manipulate his actions. Freer had taught him to breathe, that he was in control of what he did and what he saw. That was a weakness of his, allowing other emotions to decide what he was to do. Hesitation, as he had been taught, left undecided choices. Syght had to be one or the other.

Thankfully, this time, he was lucky.

He reached out to the pillar and grasped it gingerly, pulling himself upright. He was back at Syngetical.

Cyra stood in front of him, her face filled with astonishment.

"Where... did you go? You vanished."

She was shocked. He imagined she had a thousand questions about what had happened to him and why.

"How long have I been gone for?" he asked, surprised that he had pulled it off. He had made it back. Relief was amongst his other concerns. His training had worked. This is what syght was. Although he had been aided, this was the ability Freer was talking about, how he had experienced what he had. He couldn't help but feel amazed by it. The lens was more powerful that he could ever be. It allowed him to fully immerse himself in the other reality. Without the lens, could syght allow him the same pleasure? He was far from that stage, and this lens had accelerated his training. He had achieved what the 55 wanted, what they believed he was able to do.

His suspicions were right. He and Cyra had created what was so long thought to be only a myth. They had brought it to life. But with them still being inside SeeTech Tower, this was now a dangerous contraption in the wrong hands. And the lens had his DNA in the circuitry. He wondered whether it could work with anybody.

He had to know what Anders wanted to do with the lens.

"Ten minutes or so," Cyra said. "I looked for you and waited in the workshop. Then I came out to the corridor. How did you end up out here?"

He felt reassured that what Freer knew about syght was correct. Time is a constant, no matter what reality he was in. Time was the link between the two.

"I should probably try and explain something to you," he said.

She nodded.

He guided her back into the workshop and closed the door.

'BUZZ'

The reassurance of the annoying sound confirmed he was back in his reality.

"Your lip! Your nose!" Cyra pointed, alarmed. Now that he was aware of the injuries again, he could feel the blood dripping down his chin.

"I hit myself," he said, wiping his face on his sleeve, leaving a streak of red.

"Does it hurt? You need to get that looked at."

He hunted for a reflective surface to see the damage, settling on the chrome pad on the hovering graviBall.

"Not too bad," he said as he examined himself. He wiped his nose again and checked his teeth. No cuts or breakages.

"Where did you go?" she asked.

He looked at her. Her expression was conflicted, as if she wanted to know, but there was an underlying fear that showed she did not quite want to find out.

"This lens you have been working on is not designed for space travel, as such. Like he did to Felcion, Anders lied to you, and for a reason. You have created something that allows you to switch between the two realities that make up the world as we know. Me avoiding the clash with you, when you decided not to throw a punch. I chose to miss you. I saw my options open up and I took the safest one."

"How—how is that possible? In all of my theories and studies that has not been mentioned. How can other realities make up ours?"

"This other reality, wherever it is in the universe, is far from here, like a mirror image of this one. It's different though, depending what choice we make in this one. Well that's what I have been told, there may be more, I don't know. Nobody has done that before. Does that make sense?"

"No, not really. That contradicts what I know and what I believe."

"But you saw it, right? When you put on the

frame and the lenses activated, you saw a split."

She nodded.

"That's the two realities opening up. All I did was move to the other for a brief moment."

"But how did you get back?"

"I made a choice."

"So, what does this mean? This lens? Why does Anders want us to build him one?"

Gil could see Cyra was beginning to believe him, fathoming the concept.

"The 55 want me because I have syght—not fully to this capability yet, but enough to be able to see that other reality to choose my decisions when they are presented. The 55 are evil and will do anything to get their hands on me again and this lens."

"Again? What? Are you in danger? Am I in danger?"

Cyra was panicking.

"Yes, sort of—more me than you. I need to know what Anders wants to do with this lens, why he needs syght and why he's kept it all a mystery. I'm starting to feel we can't trust him."

"Are you sure? Anders of all people?"

"I thought the same until today—until now. He knew I had syght from the minute I walked in, maybe even long before that. He needed me here for you to test this lens out on. This lens can't exist, Cyra. Syght… this lens… they are more powerful than we could ever know. It could destroy our world, this reality we all live in."

Cyra looked as though she had been hit by a truck, her small existence in this reality slowly crumbling around her.

"This was not your fault," he said. "You had no idea what you were creating. You did it. You made it happen. And at least now we can know what it is capable of doing."

He had to give Cyra some reassurance that her discovery wasn't inherently bad. It was a spectacle; he couldn't deny that.

"I have a plan. We can hide this lens, to protect us, to lie to Anders like he did to us. We need to get out of here now. There is a safe place I know… It may be tricky if I'm spotted, but it's the best place for us right now."

"Err…okay, yeah. Are you sure?" Cyra was fumbling her words.

"You have to trust me. We are a team. You have created the most advanced piece of technology in human history. We have to make sure nobody knows it exists, that nobody knows it's even possible to be created."

The Sense Shifters would know how to deal with Cyra better than he did. She was confused and scared, but she agreed to the plan.

'BUZZ'

Neither of them had unlocked the door.

THIRTY

The doors to the workshop swung open and Anders and Rix came rushing in. Why was Rix here?

"I called Anders. I had no clue what happened to you," Cyra said.

"Tell me everything that happened," Anders said slowly. Both he and Rix looked horrified, as though something terrible had happened.

"Me and Cyra made a version of a circuit board. We thought—"

"I don't care about how you made it! Tell me where you went!" he said sternly.

Gil looked at Cyra. She stayed silent and looked hesitant, as if she were a nervous animal being corned by poachers.

"To the other reality."

At this, Anders' expression changed, morphed into something sinister. He looked as though he were a shark ready to attack.

"It was the blood!" Cyra shouted out in fear.

"Explain!" Anders replied.

They both flinched at the sudden volume change. Anders' almost violent outburst validated his trust issues and he hoped that Cyra realised the same. He knew something was wrong. He could feel it. Anders had known what he'd been doing all along, what Gil and Cyra would finally achieve. He had to be careful. They were about to see a side of Anders they hadn't seen before, one that could go to extreme lengths to get what he wanted.

"I, errr, accidentally cut myself and my blood got into the circuitry. It... it activated it. But when we... when we tried it with Gil, he was gone. He went to this other reality place," Cyra said nervously.

"The Deja Vu gene!" Rix said with delight. "He does have it. I knew he did. I told you he would!"

Gil was confused. Rix hated her father's work. She never really wanted to talk about her relationship with him. Recently, he had begun to think that there was more than a dislike towards him, a resentment due to all the technology he'd had implanted in her body. But now, it looked like Rix was working with her father. He knew he might be jumping to conclusions, although, so far, all his hunches had turned out to be correct.

"Gil, hand me over the ID Lens," Anders said.

He felt a resistance within him. He had no desire to hand over this creation. Maybe it was because the training with Freer had unlocked his other senses, or maybe it was his subconscious telling him no.

"What's going on here?" Gil asked. "Rix?!" He needed to know something, anything. There were too many secrets at Syngetical and now Rix was yet another one. She was the one—and only—person he had fully trusted all this time. He wanted to be wrong. He wanted Rix to be the Rix he thought he knew. But what if it was all an act?

She sighed.

"You want to get into this now? Really? Fucking hell, Gil. You really are a whiny little shit, aren't you?"

Her face screwed up as she spoke, insulting him like a bully. He knew she was abrasive, but was this what she was really like? Just another ruthless, spoilt rich kid, no different to any other 55er? She seemed unrecognisable at that moment.

He was stunned.

"Tell him or we'll be here all day. The boy can't deal with you not being you. I don't have time to waste," Anders said, to the point.

"Fine," she said and turned to him, a blank expression on her face, no emotion or feeling behind the eyes. That warmth he usually felt from her when she insulted him was gone. "We planned this. That's the bottom line. Where do I start? You nearly killing that group of wasters in the Mustang—I told them to be there to see if you could avoid them, which would prove you had syght."

This was the biggest and most hurtful lie of them all. Terry had had a reason to lie, even Anders to some extent—not that he accepted that what he had done was right—but Rix was the dagger in the back. His stomach turned. He had shared everything with her. His worries, his achievements... But it turned out that nothing had been sacred as she had fed it all back to Anders. She was Anders' spy, prying information out of him, the boy with syght.

"How did we know?" Rix went on. "I know you want to ask so I'll save you the time. Dad always knew. You were one of many children he monitored who could potentially show signs of the ability in the future. You just so happened to live nearest to Axeon City before you moved to the country. Luckily for him you moved back."

"The Déjà vu gene," Cyra whispered. Gil turned and saw the realisation flood her face—her old job, what she had been trying to find all that time when she was looking through all those people.

"So, you would have let me kill those innocent people if I didn't have it?" He felt shocked that one of the most terrifying moments of his life, something he had only started to impress Rix, to show her he was daring, was just a test.

"A sacrifice for the greater cause. Lower class citizens aren't innocent, Gil," she said. "They would have deserved it somehow. They would have done something wrong. If anything, you would have been helping the planet if you had killed them all."

Cyra listened opened mouthed. Right now, she was the one person he could trust, the person he barely knew.

Rix continued her explanation, almost as if she

were taking pleasure in her deception. "The 55. I told them about you and about Terry. I was their true informant. Terry was just a middle man. It was easier to lure you in if we had his help."

"You??? Why, why would you do that?"

"We had to make it looked staged."

He had so many questions. Why would she bring Terry, of all people, into this? He was an easy target, a vulnerable older man who would want to help and protect anyone. He trusted Rix as much as Gil had.

She avoided his question, her rehearsed speech unveiling her scheming over all these years. She clearly took pride in it.

"I told the 55. They think I'm a nobody. Terry is the one they used to find you. Then we framed the High Chancellor. We all know she works for them. We then used her against the 55, creating conflict between them and the government to keep them both off our back."

Anders chuckled.

"I taught you well."

"The 55 all wanted you, Gil. Whether I instigated it or not, they would have found out who you are sooner or later. So, we hatched this plan. We legally obtain you through their gala with a simple bid, and you agree with it, thinking your hero, Anders Hilgaard, has saved the day. I knew you would trust him from the outset. You share too much, Gil—you really do."

A typical Rix insult—this one cut deep.

"Vivalda Xing looks guilty of betrayal as she

failed to stop Anders attending, ruining any 55's chance of gaining Gil."

Xing. There was that name again, the one he saw on the plaque in the other reality.

"We all win and we gain you legally under the 55 code, making dad the innocent one in all of this. Then we provide you with the blanket of safety and security, allowing you to train, while all that time you're actively helping us by working on the one lens that would help emphasise your syght."

Gil had nothing to say. His friend had betrayed him, his one true friend. His hopes that their relationship might one day become something more had now turned to ash. He remembered the odd flutter that would occur whenever he thought about it, the nonsensical emotions that happened at the smallest touch. It had always been a lie.

"And you—what was your part in all of this?" He had to hold it together. He was angry.

"To see if you had syght. Dad wanted to know, and in exchange, I got all the tech I could ever need or want."

"And us, being friends, that mean nothing to you?"

"Fuck's sake, Gil! Such a wet sap. Yeah, at first, I guess. But what six-year-old knows what they want? They just want to play and be friends with anyone, which we were. Dad says go be friends with him so you do. You're the one who moved away—not me. I grew up. I learnt the ways of the city. By the time you returned, I knew what I wanted, so I worked for it.

So, what if it meant I lost a friend? I already had anyway."

"It backfired, though. You couldn't learn syght!" A cheap shot, but it was worth it. He had to use what he knew would hurt her.

"Shut up, Gil! Fuck you!"

That hurt her. But at least her reaction was honest. She did want to learn syght.

Gil had to wonder: all this time, had the technology in her body been a way of Anders trying to provoke syght synthetically, as Gil and Cyra had done with the ID Lens? He had built Rix, manipulating her into what he wanted, rather than it being her decision. Anders was lying to his own daughter as well.

"Give me the lens, Gil," Anders demanded, stepping in.

"No!" he said defiantly.

"Gil, just give him the lens!" Cyra said, tapping him on the arm.

"I won't. I understand now. You aren't trying to save the world or help people out, are you? You want everyone to think you're the good guy in all of this. I respected you. I wanted to work here, in Syngetical, and be proud of where I worked, and all you have done is lie to me, to Cyra, to everyone. The whole world thought you were trying to help them when all it was was a cover-up for your real goal, this syght lens. Talk about hiding in plain sight."

As he said the words, it became clearer to him that Anders was just as greedy as the 55. He could now see his true intentions.

"You lied to Cyra," Anders said smugly.

Cyra turned to him.

"Did you?" she said softly.

"Gil knew about these two realities all along, Cyra. He has syght, the ability to switch between both realities. I put him here with you, knowing his ability would make itself known sooner or later. This is the raw material, the unique specimen we have been searching for. Gil was the one you needed to find in your old position. He was the key to making that lens work. I always knew an Inter-Dimensional lens wasn't possible. To travel through space without a form or propulsion? It's unheard of. You would be here a thousand years before you had a breakthrough. It's a bedtime story. You bought into the lie and went along with it, trying to achieve the impossible. And you did marvellously—the one part I couldn't work out, and you did: the integration of technology with natural selection, and it has worked out better than I imagined. A complete leap to the other reality, and all it took was a little blood. I've worked for years trying to create a synthetic syght lens. I even replaced both my eyes with my own technology to see if it was possible, but I couldn't make it work. It only slowed down my reflexes. I tried on Rix when it failed on me, rigging up her body with technology—"

"Stop, Dad. I know!!" Rix screamed out. "You fucked my life up, forcing me to want the same dream as you. I could have learnt syght, but no. You thought it was clever to keep putting this biometric AI shit into my body, all just to reach whatever your narcissistic dream was quicker. I had no choice. You took that away from me, a kid at the time, bribing me to do what you wanted, not me. What child wouldn't have said no to gifts and advanced toys? I WAS A CHILD! Children don't have choice; they are told what to do."

An argument between father and daughter was growing, Gil and Cyra remaining the outsiders. They were distracted.

Gil contemplated an escape. But how would he communicate this to Cyra? How far would they get?

"I would have said no," Rix continued. "Look at me! Restricted like you now. Limited. You chose for me and you got it wrong."

"I don't believe you have it so bad now, do you, Rix? You're hardly living in the slums and struggling on the survival line."

"I'd rather that now, looking back on how this all turned out. My choice was taken away, forced by you, my path decided by you."

"I sacrificed a lot to find syght, Rix. Don't challenge me now!"

"No, you sacrificed me for all of it. A kid. I WAS A KID! I knew no better. You said, 'do this.' I went, 'okay.' You ruined my body because of your own failings. I agreed to it because I knew no better. Now I do. I could see how your admiration for Gil had grown, your desire to have him here. You needed him, knowing he has the very thing you want and I don't. I could have had it, but you were too impatient: you wanted to get there first, to conquer it before anyone else could and yet all you did was basically throw me away—until you needed me again, until you found someone you thought might have it and then you used me again, used me to bring in Gil. So, I actually feel sorry for Gil. I do. I manipulated him like you did to me, Dad, using him to get you what you wanted. I'm a fucking idiot, just like you are."

She pointed at her father.

"The only difference is, I didn't ruin Gil's life quite like you did mine. He can come back from this. He already has. He doesn't need you. If Mum was here, I bet she would have stopped it."

"Don't speak of your mother—"

"I don't know who the fuck she is!"

Gil remembered the name on the plaque in the other reality. Was the High Chancellor her mother?

Gil and Cyra stood watching on, still at the other end of room where they had been when Anders and Rix stormed in.

He had been gullible, just like the rest of the world, thinking that Anders was achieving something great. It was a hurtful, stabbing betrayal to know that Rix had been in on it all too, that she had pretended to be his friend. However, to have her own father manipulate her for years, and for her not to realise, was far worse. Yes, he was angry but, but his anger was far from the rage Rix was expelling.

He realised he had to protect the world, be the

hero he had refused to be. Freer's voice began to float in his subconscious: 'Syght is a responsibility—you need to prevent others, those for whom greed is their priority, from achieving it. There is no requirement to save anyone—you are no superhero; you are no myth. You are someone who just needs to keep the secret and not allow your ability to fall into the wrong hands.'

The problem was that his DNA was on the circuitry now. Could Anders use the lens for himself and skip into the other reality?

"Sit down, Rix!" Anders ordered.

"NO! I'm done with this." She went to storm past him, but he shoved her back. She landed against a workbench.

Rix ignited a retaliation. She launched herself at her father. Gil could see the fire in her eyes, the intent to want to hurt, but Anders produced a photon energy gun from somewhere in the room, the presence of which stopped her attack.

He pressed the weapon hard against her forehead.

Cyra screamed.

Anders' finger was on the trigger. He was willing to use it.

Rix was not backing down.

THIRTY ONE

Gil had not seen a gun in his lifetime, nor did he want to see someone blown to pieces in front of him. Anders was breaking government law by owning one. But Rix's expression was not one of shock. She knew Anders owned this. This was 55 mentality: to threaten, maintaining one's authority in the room by forcing the desired outcomes with a weapon, regardless if it was illegal or not. From what Gil could gather, most of what the 55 did was illegal, just nobody knew about it as they protected each other. The elite hid behind what they owned.

"I will pull the trigger if I have to," Anders yelled. "You are a sacrifice I am willing to make if you stop me."

Rix stood there, her fists clenched by her sides. Gil knew she hated to admit defeat. Her father had pulled the wild card. She had no choice. If she did have an option, then it was only life or death. Rix didn't seem bothered. She pushed her head against the barrel, as if she wanted it to happen. Maybe she was pushing her father to do it so he might feel an essence of guilt for what he done to her. If he killed her, it would be on his hands. There were witnesses.

This had gone too far. He was out of his depth, and by the looks of her expression, Cyra was having a mild panic attack next to him. He held on to her, pulled her closer.

Gil was angry with Rix, hurt that she just saw him as a job that needed completing. However, he still wanted to protect her, he whispered, 'just sit down'.

At this point, Rix had given up caring about anything. He knew she was daring, but this was too far—unless this was her means of escape.

"I will not be asking again, Gil. Give me the lens."

Anders pointed the photon gun towards him. Cyra stepped back, out of the firing line. Her eyes had started to tear. He needed to hold his composure. He had used syght before in a one-on-one confrontation and was confident he could manage a victory, even against a gun, a weapon that was capable of firing much quicker than throwing a fist or a kick. He would need to hope the lens could show him the options fast enough. He would also have to factor in the time it took to put the lens on. He was currently still holding onto it, ready for his escape.

He stood, facing the gun. A light blue orb circulated down the barrel of the weapon, the photon energy prepping to fire.

Anders stepped forward and in the silence of the room, he could hear the gun emit a low metronomic bass pulse.

"If you kill me, you won't have access to syght."

"Your blood is fused in that lens. Cyra said. You are disposable now."

"I'm the only one who has used the lens successfully. There is no guarantee that if you use it you will have the same effect."

He was effectively stalling, but he knew he had made a valid point. He waited for a choice to make itself known, to tell him what he should do.

"I know where the Sense Shifters are based," Anders said coolly. "Rix has been there, if you recall. If I kill you, I have plenty more to use. Suddenly, the realisation of your ability is not so special anymore."

He turned a dial. The pitch of the sound leaped up a couple of octaves.

No matter what he said, Anders was always one answer ahead of him. It was his fault. He had divulged it all to Rix, who in turn had told her father. Gil may have syght, but Anders had started to acquire all he needed to know about it before he was even born.

But what he hadn't factored in was the element of surprise.

As Gil stood facing the gun as Rix had done

moments ago, Rix raised her finger to her lips and indicated a shush. Why was she acting like she was on his team again? Was this another lie to force him to help Anders again? He was not falling for it. He had no trust in Rix. There was no reason why she would help him now.

She stood and booted the gun out of Anders' hands. It fired a shot into the ceiling. She pushed her father out the way and attacked him with her fists, ending the attack with a kick to the chest. Anders stumbled back over a table, knocking his head on a shelf. He was out cold, for the moment.

Gil grabbed Cyra by the wrist.

"Go!" he shouted.

He guided her towards the double doors, where she manically tried to type in the access code to leave the workshop, her fingers shaking. But seeing she couldn't do it, he pushed her to one side and typed in the number himself.

Behind him, there was no movement or sound from Anders.

BUZZ

That sound, blissful this time—a sign of escape, freedom... One step towards the survival of their own lives, but also the world's.

"Get the lift. I'll meet you there."

Cyra nodded. She was beginning to hyperventilate.

Rix stood above her semi-conscious father.

"That lens belongs here!" she said to Gil, the anger rising within her.

Gil wished for the right words.

"That lens belongs to me, not him. Piece of shit." She booted him in the side. "Give me the chance to use it, to see what he has wanted for so long, what it was worth sacrificing me for. Gil, please!"

There was so much he wanted to express to her: 'come with us', 'get out of here', 'fuck you'—all of them viable options of what he could say. She had already chosen her side.

"Let me see it and I'll help you escape. I want to take from him everything he took from me. I deserve the right to do that, Gil—not you!"

Part of him believed her, the part who still saw the Rix he knew—the Rix he thought he knew, at least. Either way, there was innocence to her voice. He had seen the impact Anders had on her life and now she felt like she deserved something back: revenge, compensation, whatever she thought she was owed.

He couldn't hand over the lens and not know what would happen with it. His trust for her had gone. This scene she was playing out in front of him might still be part of the act, a risk he was not willing to make. He would take his chances in the outside world with the 55.

"What's going on here?"

A voice came from behind him. He followed his instinct to run. Salvagers training 102.

As he pushed past the slightly dishevelled woman, he spotted she had a revolver in her left hand. He recognised her voice, mainly, from the news. It was the High Chancellor, Vivalda Xing.

"COME BACK!!" Rix yelled in a pleading tone, rather than rage-induced. She chased after him down the corridor.

Gil heard three shots fired and looked back, just in time to see the darts rip through Vivalda's chest, killing her instantly. He saw her fall, lifeless, to the marbled floor, the blood exploding out of her body. Only now did he truly realise the extent that Anders was willing to go to. That was one innocent life taken. Cyra was not going to be the next.

He turned the corner towards the lift, where Cyra was waiting, holding the doors open for him.

"Come on, Gil!"

He stopped, suddenly feeling a sharp pain, but he was unable to locate it on his body—it was as if it were a memory of something previously suffered.

He turned and saw two shots land into Rix's back. She fell face first, her body skidding along the glass floor.

Rix was still.

The two wound holes on her back sizzled.

He lost all emotion, his body and his mind blank, unable to respond to what he was staring at.

He approached. Rix's face was frozen. The blue jagged tattoo had subdued in its glow.

His friend was dead.

He looked across the workshop and saw two bodies strewn across the floor. Then his gaze turned towards the perpetrator of these crimes. Anders was staggering towards him.

A hatred grew within him. This man who he had admired had taken away the one true thing he cared for: Rix. He knew she had betrayed him, he knew it had been a lie, but he knew that truly, deep down, there was part of her who cared. All those years could not have been all an act. She was a human who had emotions, especially after the events that had taken place between her and her father. She had aided their escape. To start with, she had been an innocent pawn in all of this. She had been betrayed as much as Gil had. Regardless of what Rix had done wrong, he cared for the woman he thought he knew. He couldn't just switch that off.

His life had been turned into an unwanted danger because of one man's greed to be more than he was.

He positioned the syght lens onto his face.

He exploded into a run towards Anders. He had no idea what he was going to do—hit him, kill him, torture him for answers.

He saw fire.

Anders had fired at him. Missed.

Gil screamed, wanting to hit him with whatever he had behind him.

Anders fired again. The lens activated, but the shot missed anyway.

In front of him, Anders stopped walking, braced himself in a steady position and fired again.

The shutters on the lens moved in a different way as to before. The speed with which they flashed over the orange lens was invisible this time. It was only the noise of the hinges that let him know something was happening.

He winked between each eye, instinctively. He managed to dodge a few of the shots but as he came closer to Anders, the tears that were filling his eyes affected him being able to see the photon darts. They grazed him, frazzling the skin on his shoulders and legs.

He prepped a dive towards Anders, who fired one last shot.

The reality split and to Gil, through the lens, both looked the same. There was no choice available.

This was not the way Gil was going to die.

He thought he saw the photon dart in both. And then it shimmered, as though he was seeing them coming from all angles. There were meant to be two options, yet he saw variations of the same scene multiplied.

A tear rolled down his right cheek. He realised he was witnessing the refracted vision of one eye. There was a choice.

He veered right. The photon dart glided past him, and his life was restored. He landed hard on top of someone. There was no time to perfect a landing when death had given you only one choice, theirs.

"You can get off me anytime. Cuddles aren't really my thing."

Gil looked up. He was face-to-face with a woman he recognised. He knew those features: the shape of her lips, the brightest blue of her eyes that highlighted the tattoo on the side of her face.

"RIX!" His voice broke in the shock of seeing her alive, in front of him as he lay on top of her.

THIRTY TWO

Gil scrambled off Rix's body. His eyes darted all over her face to check she was real. No injuries, no marks. The only noticeable difference was her hair. Her short black style was now a mottled grey colour, and the shaved sides were now grown out long, with part of her hair pinned up at the back.

"You should have worn the wig," a light-hearted voice came from behind him.

He panicked. What was going on? He knew he had used his syght, and Anders had disappeared, so he had to be in the other reality. But Rix was alive. He had just watched her die.

He felt all manner of emotions: relief, joy, even after the treachery that Rix had brought on him.

He moved away from her and turned. His surroundings were the same as they were the previous time he had entered this reality, although now there was light pouring in from the window. Before, it felt a dream—a grey wash over the environment, drudging through the thick air. This was now real.

"Allow me to introduce myself. I am Vivalda Xing, CEO of Syngetical."

"What?" he said with no initial intention to.

"And you already know me," Rix stated as she picked herself up off the floor.

"That's your mum?!?" he asked, pointing at Vivalda in shock.

The two women looked at each other.

"That's one hell of an assumption to make when you've just been introduced to someone," Vivalda said.

"I...errr, saw the plaque on the door, from before. You both have the same last name!" He fumbled his words.

"We apologise for the security measures before. They made for an entertaining watch when the drone cameras picked them up. If we had known you were going to join us, the first time, we would have been here to welcome you."

"You knew I was going to be here again?" He was confused.

"I think we should explain a little to him, mother," Rix said. "His brain is melting, bless him." Even in this reality, she still had her wit—not much had changed there.

"This conversation might be more comfortable

in my office," Vivalda said as she held out a hand. Gil took it and pulled himself up from the floor.

He had escaped Anders, but the danger was far from over. He knew Anders was still alive and he hoped that Cyra had escaped before he could catch up to her. Gil was no hero, but he felt a duty to stop Anders and the rest of the 55 somehow. To his knowledge, Anders had no back-up syght lens. Although, he had learnt by now that Anders could be hiding anything.

They walked along to where Anders' office was, though here, it was Vivalda's. She opened the door.

He had been in Anders' office once and remembered how slick, clean and minimalist it was and how he highlighted his new creations, placing them on the shelves and tables as though they were ornaments. Vivalda's office was homely, welcoming, and had more of an indication to a living area than an office. Colour ran throughout the space: a lime green sofa and matching armchairs sat pride of place, with a low gold-framed coffee table in the centre. There was a pale blue kitchenette area in the corner, merely consisting of a water dispenser, and a drinks trolley full of a variety of bottled liquids. The blue tiles led up the wall and across part of the ceiling to where the window opened out to the world below.

"Gil, you obviously know the parameters of syght. It's clear you have mastered them well enough to be able to open up both realities. Please, sit." Vivalda indicated to the sofa.

Gil removed the syght lens from his head and

placed it carefully on the table. His head still working through his moral dilemma of what he should do, the right thing to do.

"Something to drink?" Rix asked.

He shook his head. He wanted clarification, not a celebration. There was no evidence yet that he could trust these two. He had had his trust destroyed from Anders already. What was stopping them—Rix, especially—from doing that to him again? Both looked safe and welcoming, but he had been fooled once before. He was on edge.

"Let me explain to you what this reality is," Vivalda started. "The world is made up of two realities: one that you have lived in for your entire life and then this place, which is where impacting decisions that were not made continue on. This is what we know of the universe, of syght, of how decision making affects the other reality. This is not to say we are correct on this, we aren't that deluded. This is our research and knowledge into syght and its mechanics. Syght is relatively new and has taken this long for someone to make the exchange fully between the realities. Syght is complex, so are our minds and sometimes they don't play well together, hence why people can die from using syght as the brain can't handle it. We break it down so we can learn how to explore it. Who knows what syght is capable of? How we perceive it now is making a choice isn't about what flavour of drink you chose, as that is personal. I mean choices that affect people, companies, life on a bigger scale. Choice has to be broken down into its most simplest form. For example, yes or no. You have probably thought how there are many choices to any decision to be made. There are, in some ways, but those choices are made up in our minds. We create the multiple choices. The realities are a lot simpler than that, they don't work on those complexities. Strip it back and what's your outcome, this or that, right or left, wrong or correct. That's how the universe works using syght. Humans over complicate matters when it can always be drawn back. If you have more than one option in your mind, syght will not work. We have done a lot of research to work out how syght happens and when. That's not to say that your reality is the bad and this is the good—not at all. We have as much trouble here, I'm sure, as your reality does."

Gil highly doubted they had the same trouble.

"There is no good or bad place, just an alternative. A different view of the human life on Earth. A different choice made."

"So, where are we now?" Gil asked.

"A small solar system situated in the Andromeda Galaxy. It is almost a mirror image of the solar system you know within the Milky Way. We have fewer planets orbiting our sun, which is the main difference—not to get into the exact technicalities. We have also explored space further than anyone from Earth has too. We can't travel galaxies currently, but people with syght allow that for us."

Gil was having trouble comprehending.

"Everyone here knows about syght; it's not

hidden. People just accept that they don't have it and move on," Rix said. "We have taught them about syght and what can happen between the two realities. People here understand that what happens on Earth can affect people here. It can sometimes be a constant changing battle with big effects. We learn how to cope. Sometimes people don't see the changes, just like you wouldn't see in your reality when changes happen here. You accept it as that's what has happened. That is life, as many would say. You dropping a glass wouldn't affect anyone here as that was your glass to drop, but you can see how to prevent it. It only affects you personally. It's the bigger decisions that make an impact, where it can affect the environment or others. That's where we see the noticeable changes, the ones that matter. One person turning down a job in one reality might affect who gets it in the other and how that company is run. Although saying that if one person commits a murder in your reality they are not automatically guilty here, as that version of themselves didn't commit the murder. That person, although they are the same and linked within the universe, they are not the same person. They are both accountable for their own actions depending what predicament they are in and what choice they chose to make. Syght, as we understand it is about making a choice on decisions when in the moment, not predetermined actions or long game scenarios."

He felt as though he was listening to a science lecture. The details of syght, he didn't need to know right now. That could wait. His decision now was to go back and stop whatever Anders was doing or stay here and be safer until the threat had passed. It was a life-threatening situation to be in if he returned. Anders and his compatriots would hunt until they found either him or someone else who had syght. It was the 55, after all. There was also the fact he had Anders' technology, which he had stolen. But of he stayed, took the chance to hide, regroup, it might be too late for him to stop them.

"We knew you were coming here—or were going to make the leap, as such—we were just unable to pin-point when. Freer did help us with that, though."

"Freer is here?!" he asked, surprised.

"Well, a version of her—yes. She is a Sense Shifter in your reality as she is here. Remember though, she is blind and uses her senses to communicate to this reality. She will never truly be able to step foot here as she is unable to 'see' it. But her version of syght means she can exist in both realities."

"So, I don't exist here?"

"No," Rix said bluntly. He missed how honest she could be at times. "When someone has syght, when you are born on the geological time shift, only one version of you is born. For everyone else, the people who don't have syght, there are two versions of them, but they wouldn't know that. They see themselves as them, as one person, and that is it. The two versions of that one person make their decisions in the universe and work together as one. You have syght, so you have no other you. That means you have the chance to live in both realities and all your decisions only affect you. Syght gives you this option. Pretty cool, right?!"

"What? No, of course not. Everyone gets two versions of themselves and I get one? If I die, that's it!"

"It's not as though someone dies and they are transported to the other to continue their life. Don't be dumb, Gil."

"Rix!" Vivalda scolded her. "Apologies for her. It's the other version of Rix—it sometimes creeps through."

"But I saw you die. I watched you! So, that means you are going to die here too? And you too…" He glanced at Vivalda. "…Anders shot you!"

Gil could still see the bodies lying in the corridor. He was the reason why they were killed, all because Anders wanted him. He couldn't have any more deaths on his conscience.

"What did I just tell you?! Obviously not!" Rix said, insulting his intelligence once again.

"Anders killed us both? Well, that's almost unbelievable." Vivalda chuckled.

"I'm surprised we didn't feel it," Rix added.

"Feel it?"

"A pain in the body that occurred for no reason as though it was a warning," Vivalda explained. "When they die, you feel a cold shiver, as though something has left your body—that's the other reality version of you—I guess, part of your soul. Strangely, it can also cause blindness in one eye—because you lose your choice when the other option fails to exist anymore. Therefore, like your reality, people can become mad from the lack of choices or options. I made the decision to replace my vision with lenses, and Rix also did when she was old enough to decide, so neither of us had to experience that torment."

Rix tapped her eye, and it clicked like a crystal champagne flute. Gil took a closer look. The technology must have been better here. Without it being pointed out, he would never have seen the difference.

"We take pride in the aesthetics of our lenses so people are not self-conscious about having a synthetic eye," Vivalda said.

"I wonder if Anders knows he killed us both?" Rix chuckled.

"You know, he has made a syght lens," Gil said abruptly, his tone urgent. "This lens could be used by someone without syght: he wants to conquer both realities. He's dangerous!"

"As long as Anders is alive here and there at the same time, he will never make the leap here. No two versions of the same person can exist in the same reality. Gil, you're safe here. If this lens helped you leap and you have it here in this reality, then it's away from Anders and he can't use it"

"You don't understand! I don't know what else he has he could use. He might be replicating this lens or even have another one ready to go. He is not what weigh up the scenarios; take it as a philosophy of, you are the first to travel amongst the stars without having seen any of them."

Vivalda's words were sinking in. That urge to run was softening.

"You are an explorer, Gil," Rix added.

He had not seen it from that angle before. He had conquered no land nor planet, found any new artefacts that would change mankind, yet he had travelled from one galaxy to another, through millions of light years in a blink of an eye. He had explored the parameters of space further than any known human in history.

In another time that would feel incredible—and achievement in life that he had never set out to gain nor even contemplated.

An explorer of the stars had a nice ring to it, but the glorious imagery that was displaying in his mind was soon washed away by the echoing screams of his potentially tortured family.

Today was not for him to marvel in what he had conquered.

His heart was racing once again, the revs high on his internal engine, ready to propel him into his reality. He had become the Mustang.

Gil ran.

The lens rapidly moved its shutters and Gil leapt back into his reality, into an unknown situation that lay ahead.

THIRTY THREE

The curtain of stars fell between the two realities as Gil watched them dash past. The split in front of him closed.

The dishevelled room he landed in showed the evidence of the demise of something great, the failings of experiments beyond what was capable.

Anders' workshop was quiet. Gil had not returned to be in the midst of a battle. He peered out the double doors and saw only Vivalda's body lying there, motionless, as it was before. Rix had disappeared, as had Anders.

The workshop had been left in the same state as Rix and Anders' fight had caused it to look—instruments broken, papers lying askew and the workbenches toppled.

What was he to do now? He had prepped for a

confrontation, one that might not end in his favour.

He kept the syght lens on, constantly looking over his shoulder.

If he left Syngetical now, he knew he would be seen. Putting himself into a lift that was controlled by Anders' palm chip, he may as well turn himself over. He had to make use of his time here before he returned to the other reality. If he could get to Freer somehow, find Cyra, Terry… There was too much for him to do and all of it consisted being outside of this building. Syght wouldn't allow him to leap to another location in Axeon City; that would have been too convenient.

He noticed Anders' notebook and papers spread out over the main workbench. The mantel that housed the ID Lens was snapped in two. Someone had riffled through the contents of that table; Anders was after something.

He went over and looked at how it had been left. The notepad was open on a page of calculations, written in two different people's handwriting, one of which he recognised as Cyra's—the solution to how the Syght Lens worked, the parameters needed for it to work at the correct calibration when the syght DNA was added.

If Gil were to take Anders' notepad and hide it, destroy it, remove it from this reality, he would not be able to replicate the lens.

This was his plan. This is how he could help protect people, for now.

The notepad had been left open for a reason;

maybe Anders was still in the vicinity and intended on coming back? He could be retrieving a replicate lens from a locked storage room somewhere in the building. Rix's body was also gone. Anders must have taken her somewhere. He had to hurry. Anders could return at any point and he was taking no chances on getting caught.

He picked up the notebook and any relevant papers surrounding it. He knew that Anders liked to work in an old-fashioned manner with pen and paper, rather than storing information digitally. Gil took anything that highlighted how the circuit boards and microchips were connected, any calculations or instructions that would aid Anders in building another lens. The most important aspect was Gil's blood. He would never have that.

He held as much as could. He hoped that he could get all this out before Anders came back. Having it in his hands would be a disadvantage if he was cornered.

He searched the room for his techpack, retracing his steps where he had been when he last came into the room. He lifted one of the toppled tables from the floor and found it underneath. Now he had somewhere to store the documents. This was maybe something he could show Vivalda and Rix, when he knew they were trustworthy, but that would be a long time yet. He would need these documents if the ID lens in his possession broke. He needed to be able to switch between both realities—for his own safety, but maybe also for his family and friends. If this lens truly did work for anyone, he could take his family to the other reality. It had to be better—and safer—than the one they currently lived in. There would be no Anders, no 55. He could live as close to a normal life as he could without having to worry about who was after him.

He shoved more papers from the desk into his techpack until it was full. He assumed that the pieces that had been spread out on the table were the most important, as Anders would probably have been looking on these for an answer.

There was one more place he had to check: Anders' office. He had to make time to search it as once he left, he wasn't returning to SeeTech Tower.

Gil snuck out of the workshop and quietly ran along the corridor to the office. The syght lens twitched slightly as he picked up speed, toying with the idea that he might want to make a decision to leap, showing him the new reality: his freedom, his safety. Gil smiled. The thought of him ruining Anders' life-long dream of a syght lens was one that he wouldn't forget anytime soon.

This was his 'fuck you' to Anders.

"Found you!"

He stopped immediately in his motion, moments from the office door. A cold chill crept around his body, as if Anders was somehow in his very bones. This was not what he wanted, though at the same time, he had expected it. Rigid to the spot, he was afraid to turn to see what his final moments would be.

He could do this; he had to win this somehow. He had seen what Anders was willing to sacrifice to make sure he succeeded. Syght was his card to play, but he could feel the worry, the panic building inside. If he couldn't think straight and control his emotions, his thoughts about Cyra and his family having syght was pointless, it wouldn't work. Gil cared too much for others, unlike Anders or the 55. This was one hurdle he had to jump and he knew the odds were against him.

"I own you, Gil. You signed that contract and now I have you back. You're going to take me to that other reality."

Gil slowly faced Anders, his palms sweating at the thought of death. Freer had told him to be calm, to focus his energy on syght so the options became clearer. But when there was a proton energy gun pointed directly at his chest, it was difficult to maintain that relaxed stance.

He knew that, with the syght lens on, Anders had to be careful with his aim. One slight misfired shot and the lens could be damaged. One risk Anders was not willing to make.

"Even if I wanted to, I couldn't. You exist there already. No person who is alive in both realities can move from one to the other. Did you not learn anything over all those years you were looking into syght? Your life's work was all for nothing. You wasted that time. Now, I have somewhere to be."

He could see that Anders holding his side. He was injured, the cuts on his face still fresh from the fight with Rix. Without the weapon, he would be easier to take down, his victory to claim. It came down to how quick Gil could outrun or outdodge a proton charge when fired.

He ran back towards the open door to Anders' workshops and threw himself at it. He blinked, allowing the split to be shown before him.

But he hit his head against the side of the door and fell to the floor.

"Not learnt anything? Oh, I have—very much so, Gil. This whole building is now surrounded in a syght defence shield. You didn't think I'd done my work? Well, us scientists like to think ahead, plan for what might come our way. So, it's lucky I did, very much so. As soon as you fled, all I had to do was flick the switch. Your abilities are useless here. Your return was a foolish one. I knew you would work out what Cyra was building, so I had to have a failsafe in place, to protect what is mine."

Gil held his hand to his forehead. The cut from where he had hit the door had drawn blood.

What Anders was saying couldn't be true—a syght shield. How could he have developed such a specific program? But if it was true, he was stuck here. If he was unable to use his ability within SeeTech Tower, even wearing the lenses, he was back to square one. He had to get outside, away from the shield. But he was on the top floor of the building and he knew how Anders controlled the security.

He used the door to pull himself up.

"Where is Cyra?" he asked.

"Dead! And I'm glad of it."

Guilt riddled his mind. He saw her run. He thought she would have got away before Anders could do anything about it, but he must have caught her—unless he was bluffing, an attempt at distraction. He had to hope that Cyra was alive and this was another untruth. She couldn't be dead. He needed her.

Anders was heartless. She had nothing to do with this. She'd been roped into an ideology of something she believed would help science. If Cyra had escaped and the 55 knew about what she did for Anders, they would be after her too. He had to help her; that was his duty. She couldn't suffer at the hands of the 55 because of his mistakes.

"Now, I need you out of my equation so I can go back to what I was doing. That lens is mine. And now you have proved it works, all I need is your blood. That works for me better if you're dead. I don't need you or your services any longer, Gil. Your contract is terminated. Thank you for your involvement here at Syngetical."

He typed something onto a panel on the weapon.

A bright electrical charge ran throughout the barrel and into the handle.

He aimed it directly at Gil and fired, but Gil's instincts were sharp. He had already dived out of the way.

The green shot hit Anders' office door where it vaporised the entire entrance and the surrounding glass tiles where the initial shot landed, leaving an electrical trail behind it.

If Anders was to make a direct hit, he would be dead instantly and erased from society. With no presence in the second reality, there would be no existence of him left.

He ran towards Anders' office. He knew he would be a target if he got into the lift. He needed a place to hide and work out a counter attack.

Another shot fired from behind and he ducked to the floor. The energy from the shot burned along the back of his neck, and as he stood up into the electrical trail, forgetting there was one, he felt the shock run through him. His body tensed and sent his muscles into spasm. He was paralysed for a moment.

"A game of cat and mouse! This should be fun!" Anders shouted.

This was not a weapon Gil could outrun and it was near impossible to manoeuvre around without his syght.

The feeling returned to his legs and arms and he quickly got himself up from the floor and backed up against the window, watching the door, waiting for Anders to appear. He was cornered. He had chosen wrong. How was he going to escape? Anders was blocking the only exit to the building and he was out of options.

He felt a breeze on the back of his calf. He looked to the side and saw that the last shot had ripped a hole into the side of the tower. Without realising, Anders had not only damaged his building, but created a means of escape.

There was his choice, the answer that he needed. Anders thought Gil was the foolish one, but it was more the other way around. It was not the conventional means of how to exit a building, but he had no other choices—not while he was up here, at least; he would, however, regain his ability to choose when he was a few feet from the building. The challenge would be that those few feet he needed were one-hundred-and-eighty-six floors up.

"It has truly been a pleasure," Anders said sarcastically as he entered the office.

Gil backed up closer to the hole. He could feel the air rushing in from the outside. The blast must have created gaps in the shield too, as his syght was fluttering back into focus, as though it were a display with a loose connection—but not enough for him to be able to use.

Once again, he was face-to-face with Anders.

"This time, it ends how I choose, how I decide," Anders said.

Without any choices, and without his syght fully back, Gil thought that this time he might be right.

He had one option though, he realised—one choice left. The other was death.

"I hope to not see you again," Gil said.

"The feeling is mutual."

With that, he took his choice and ran towards the open window and leapt though it without hesitation, driven by his need to survive so he could protect others. He had to warn them. Saving them was now greater than the risk of what might happen when falling one-hundred-and-eighty-six floors.

Anders' cry of anger was all he needed to hear. He had bettered him once again.

Before Anders had the chance to fire a shot, Gil began to freefall. His syght came back fully and allowed him to skip into the other reality.

His options were still limited. The decision was not to live or to die; it was to choose where to die: in his old reality or his new one. There were no other choices. As he fell, he blinked constantly, switching between the realities, hoping that one of them provided an alternative or something that would at least slow him down.

It was the same view in both: freefalling at a rapid rate, the ground approaching faster than the shutters on the lens could flicker. The air filled his lungs forcefully, making him unable to breathe properly. He took gasps in but was unable to release them back out, the panic clouding his decision in which choice to make, which reality might give him the option to live.

When faced with certain death, Gil had his first epiphany. He saw into the small future that was rapidly shortening, a glimpse into what the realities had as an outcome. The epiphany marked the end. He saw nothing past the black. Both provided painful outcomes, yet one had something: a breath after. A dying exhale.

And so it did… it went black…

THIRTY FOUR

Inhale.

Exhale.

Gil could feel his ribs moving, as his lungs inflated. They were sore. A tight pain shattered across his chest.

He opened his eyes wearily and saw Vivalda and Rix standing at the end of the bed, looking relieved. Rix was more delighted than he expected. This was a sight that Gil expected not to see. Was it a display from his memory?

The last thought he could remember having was choosing the reality he'd rather die in. The memory came back to him and he looked up at them, confused.

"I assume it was not your choosing to launch yourself out of the tallest building in either reality,"

Vivalda said with a hint of sarcasm.

He swallowed heavily. His lips smacked open as he tried to muster together a sentence.

"It was. Anders… had me cornered. He wanted the lens, my blood for syght."

One sentence alone was a struggle. The tightness squeezed along his ribs once more.

"I couldn't… let him have it. There are others at risk. I have to help them."

He wheezed.

"You risked surviving that fall to protect syght?" Rix asked.

He nodded gently.

"There was no option of surviving; syght showed me the same choice."

"Well, that's because you passed out before you hit the ground. You can't see choices if your eyes are closed," Vivalda continued. "You are lucky, though. When you left, we knew it might not end well so we tasked a swarm of drones to monitor our Novogalatica Tower and certain other areas of the city. If you were going to use syght to return back to this reality, we assumed you would be somewhere in or around the tower—not necessarily freefalling from its top floor, I hasten to add."

"He, had a… a syght shield. It blocked me… from using syght inside the building," he said, struggling past his shortness of breath.

Rix came to his side.

"The last thing we imagined you'd be doing was jumping from the top of the building. The cameras on the drones recorded the footage. We could see you switching between the two realities and then your body went limp. The drones found it hard to target you when you kept vanishing repeatedly. We did finally get a lock on you though, and the drones could slow you down by hooking onto your clothes—not quite in time to stop you hitting the water in the fountain, but enough."

"So, I'm not dead?"

"A few broken bones and with some reconstructive surgery to piece you back together, but no, you aren't dead. We used synthetic and carbon-based material to rebuild you. You landed pretty hard on your chest, so a lot of that had to be removed. It had shattered into thousands of pieces."

"What? No, I can't. Why have you done that?! I won't be able to use syght." He grabbed at the bed rails, attempting to haul himself up. The risk he had chosen to make had serious consequences. He was stuck here now. Without syght, how could he return? The lens had been tested on someone with syght, not without.

"Gil, relax. It's okay. We avoided using technology in your body, so you are still free from anything circuitry- or chip-based, meaning you should be able to use syght again—once you're able to walk first." Rix squeezed his hand.

He breathed and lowered himself back onto his pillow. He would know if that was true once he was fixed again. That was going to be a concern until then.

"I would prefer it you kept your antics of jumping out of buildings to a minimum though, Gil," Vivalda added.

"I don't plan it to be a regular thing."

His initial fight was over. He escaped from Anders with everything he needed. He turned his head slowly to a chair in the corner. Propped up on the seat was his techpack. Damaged, sort of in one piece but he had it—out of the hands of Anders. He still felt the guilt of letting Cyra go, though. He had no idea whether she was still alive, and wouldn't for some time. He could have done more, and he vowed that he would, once he could walk again. He was safe here away from the threat and danger of the 55. Although his brain was spiralling about what could be happening back home, he had to rest. He had to switch off. There was planning he had to do—one victory at a time.

"Good, glad to hear. We will need to keep a close eye on Anders to see if he's going to try to open the two realities. He may have another syght lens, but as he's alive in this reality, he has no way of leaping here. We need to find a way of stopping him. This matter can be discussed later, though. You need to rest and recover."

Vivalda walked towards the door, while Rix lingered by his bed.

"You're the only person I know to have fallen from one-hundred and eighty-six floors and survive. You are adding to those history books, aren't you, Gil?" she whispered quietly.

"We have a meeting to attend, Rix," Vivalda said as she opened the door, and then turned to Gil. "Rest. And no using syght."

Rix winked at him and followed her mother out of the room.

He was left with the calming hum of the ventilator machine and the fuzzy image of a reality attempting to show him a choice to a question he had not yet made. Syght was in him, embedded. There was no on/off switch.

Regardless of what syght was trying to show him, he chose not to see it...for now.

The sealed chamber hissed and a cold blow of air escaped as the door slid open. Along the back of the clinical blue-lit room, a man hung, suspended from the wall, attached to a number of machines. Parts of his body and limbs were missing. A multitude of tubes containing electrical and fluid-based matter were connected to the back of his head. The skin and a section of skull had been removed.

There were screens monitoring his vitals; all were stable. He was not conscious, but he was still alive. He would not wake from his dream-like coma. In his mind, he was travelling through the stars to far distant systems or whatever the brain conjured during its paralysis. No one was sure if the brain was aware of its current status, that the body it was housed within was not exactly the definition of 'alive'. Those who controlled the machines were providing him with an alternative life, one he thought was real. His life was in the hands of others, but what he decided to dream was still his own choice. It was one gift the proprietors allowed him.

"He's becoming a problem."

"Then, we need to find a way of dealing with it."

"We have the syght lens. We could take a trip into their crumbing society, restore order and deal with the problem of Anders in one go," replied Rix.

"He did solve the problem of eliminating us. We don't exist in the other reality any more. There is no longer anything stopping us from doing what we always intended: Overpower Anders, take over Syngetical, and conquer their reality."

Vivalda faced the man attached to the wall.

"See you soon, Anders."

SPECIAL THANKS…

To my family and very supportive friends to help make this book happen. To Lucy for her critical and honest opinion, very much appreciated. To Adim for making some of my words sounds better. To Joff and Anaish, for when you need your mates the most.

For more information about Ben Murrell visit and follow the author at:

facebook.com/murrellben

Printed in Great Britain
by Amazon